The MIDNIGHT SPY

The MIDNIGHT SPY
Copyright 2020 © Karen Hamilton
All Rights Reserved.

Cover design by Kiki Hamilton
Map by Virginia Allyn

This book is a work of fiction. All of the characters,
organizations, and events portrayed in this novel are
either products of the author's imagination or are
used fictitiously. No part of this publication can be
reproduced or transmitted in any form or by any
means, electronic or mechanical, without permission in
writing from the author.

Gaslamp Books

New York   Seattle   London

Also by Kiki Hamilton:

The Faerie Ring Series:
The Faerie Ring
The Torn Wing
The Seven Year King
The Faerie Queen

The Midnight Spy

The Last Dance

Unwritten

THE MIDNIGHT SPY

KIKI HAMILTON

This story is inspired by the prophetic quatrains written by Michele Nostradamus in the sixteenth century as documented within the *Prophecies* and the *Centuries*

The MIDNIGHT SPY

Chapter One

Ravensfell
Berjerac, Sartis

he Berjerac town clock tolled midnight, the rich tones of the bells echoing as Nica balanced precariously on the stone ledge outside her father's study. Perched five stories above the cobblestone walkway, to fall would mean certain death. To be caught—perhaps the same end.

She crouched in the shadows and held her breath. Her face, even her eyelids, were covered with black soot from the ashes of the fireplace. Every strand of long, blond hair was tucked beneath a black silk scarf worn low on her forehead, much like the pirates off the coast of Sartis.

Before her, a lead-paned window had been thrust open, the metal hinges groaning in protest. Light from the room spilled out into the dark night like water seeping from a jug, creating a silhouette of the young man who stood at the opening. A shard of moonlight winked off the blade he held as he searched the darkness—for her.

"Shanks, what are you doing?" A deep voice called from inside the room.

Mediche, Nica swore. Of course it had to be Shanks who had spotted her. Most of the men in that room, including her father, wouldn't consider the possibility that someone might risk their life traversing the razor thin ledge to spy on them. But this young man, Jonn Shanks, was new to her father's assembly of soldiers. Nica suspected spying from the ledge was something he would think to do himself. Shanks was a mercenary—cut-throat, bloodthirsty and fearless—the type of soldier her father valued most. Which made him the type she valued least—and considered the biggest threat—for no one could know of her plan.

Nica's heart drummed in her throat as she watched him, every beat warning her of danger. She was too high to jump and the ledge was too narrow to move quickly in either direction. She stayed frozen as his gaze landed on her. The subtle shifting of his body, the repositioning of the dagger he clutched—told her she'd been found.

She exhaled slowly, poised to react. Would he reveal her presence?

"Shanks! Come here *now.*" Nica recognized her father's impatient voice. She shuddered as she considered what Mosaba would do if he caught her spying on his meeting. She would receive no more mercy than any traitor. An image of the body that still swung from the turret wall filled her head.

The clouds parted and the hazy glow of the moon illuminated the sharp angles of Jonn Shanks' face. His gaze shifted from where she crouched on the ledge in the darkness to the walkway far below, as if to measure the distance. Then his head swung back toward her and he gave a brief nod. Was it in disbelief or approval?

Shanks pulled the window closed as he turned back to the room. "Have you found the map then?"

Nica slumped in relief against the stone wall. Safe—for the moment. Poised to retreat, she cast a last, calculating look toward the window. Had he latched the pane? She took a deep breath to ease the pounding in her chest. Did she dare try to listen in on the meeting again? She and Toppen, the wine-maker's apprentice, had been planning for months—waiting for a time when her father would be traveling—to steal the maps they needed to escape from Sartis.

"King Mosaba is taking people in the dark of night now." Toppen's whispered words echoed in Nica's head. *"Peylo Sipher's brother was snatched two weeks ago. Not a word since they took him away."* His voice had been low and tense. *"I heard there's some secret project going on near the Great Divide that your father needs men to work on. It must be for this war with Jarisa. If you don't volunteer he takes you."* Toppen's usually smiling expression had been dark and furious. *"Ruling Sartis isn't enough for him. He wants to rule Jarisa too."*

Nica inched toward the window, before she lost her nerve. There'd been a marked shift of activity at the castle in the last few days—messengers and soldiers coming and going. Something had happened. She and Toppen had agreed now was the time to go.

She kept her fingers in firm contact with the stone and mortar of the rounded wall as she slid her boots along the uneven surface toward the window.

Her heart pounded against her ribs making it difficult to breathe. She peered through the darkness— the leaded glass pane was ajar. She knelt under the window and closed her eyes to better concentrate on the conversation drifting through the small gap. The ominous words of her father were easy to hear.

"The war has shifted in our favor. Amistad Jacoby has been captured." Mosaba's voice rang with triumph. "The King of Jarisa is now my prisoner. He's being brought to Sartis as we speak."

A murmur rippled through the crowd of men gathered. The country of Jarisa was substantially larger than Sartis, both in population and land mass, boasting an army who had successfully garnered and maintained their military dominance over the continent for decades. To have attacked the king of Jarisa was an undertaking not without substantial risk.

"We have severed the serpent's head from its body," Mosaba gloated. "Only one person of true power remains in Jarisa who could be any threat to us: Jacoby's daughter, Jaaniyah. She is now the prize I seek." He spoke with a frightening finality. "I want her captured and brought to me alive. If she dies, so does the man whose hand commits the deed."

Outside the window Nica shivered. Her father kept his word. She had the scars to prove it.

"We can accomplish that task for you." Nica recognized Shanks' lilting brogue. The smoothness of his voice was a sharp contrast to the nasal, clipped tones of her father. "For a price."

Everything about the newcomer had a foreign cast, from his voice to the sun-bleached hair that reached to his shoulders, and a face so handsome she'd stopped in her tracks the first time she'd seen him. Luckily, she'd been hidden behind a carved screen and her reaction had gone unnoticed.

"Anything for a price, isn't that right, Mr. Shanks?" Mosaba said in a sly tone.

"Usually."

A murmur rippled through the group. Shanks was bolder than most.

Unable to resist, Nica stood up to peer into the room. She could see Shanks clearly. The flickering candlelight winked off the silver earrings embedded in the young man's ears. He couldn't be more than a year or two past her age of seventeen, yet he stood among the warriors in her father's office addressing the king without fear.

"The usual fees will apply," he said, "with an additional charge due to the risk of kidnapping royalty, which, as you know, is punishable by death." Shanks flashed Mosaba a charming smile. "I'm sure you understand."

Her father considered the younger man for a moment then a pleased smile crossed his weathered face. "Excellent." Mosaba moved his large frame to the desk and began digging through a thick stack of maps. He pulled a page free and pinned it on the wall so all could see as he pointed to one spot. "We can set up camp here…"

Nica inched higher to get a better view through the window. She needed to see which map her father was using. She had to know where the men were headed to pursue this Jaaniyah person because this was the chance they'd been waiting for to escape. When the soldiers left to capture the young Jarisan royal, she and Toppen intended to go in the opposite direction. She couldn't stay in Sartis any longer. She was afraid to stay.

Her movement outside the pane caught another soldier's attention—a brute of a man named Ingnor. She'd seen him beating prisoners in the town center last winter. His heavy black brows pulled down over his meaty face as he strode toward the window.

"Who's out there?"

Nica gasped and ducked to the side but her sudden shift in weight caused her foot to slide dangerously off the ledge. She swallowed a scream as her momentum carried her forward. Desperate to stop her fall, she clutched at the wall for a handhold, but her fingers only scraped the unyielding stones. An eerie sense of weightlessness filled her as she became airborne.

Chapter Two

 scream gurgled in her throat as she fell, the wind cool against her cheeks. Instead of panic, disbelief filled her. She never slipped. Was a simple misstep to be the death of her?

Before she could think of how to stop her downward flight, her left shoulder slammed into the stone head of a snarling gargoyle, four feet below the ledge. She hit so hard she expected the frightening visage to be severed from its crouched body. The force of impact propelled her back toward the building, beneath the ledge, and out of view from the window above. She clung to the tail of the creature to retain her purchase, painful gasps for air whistling from her throat. Above her head, the window closed with a *thud.*

It was several long moments before Nica moved. Her legs trembled and she fought to control the quivers that wracked her body as she pushed herself to her feet. She gritted her teeth as she tried to breathe through the pain in her ribs. It wasn't like her to fall.

The cutting wind added to her shaken nerves, slowing her return as she inched to the nearby parapet. She shivered as she climbed back over the edge of the balcony to safety. Nica stood for a moment, willing her legs to stop shaking. She pulled her jacket tighter and wrapped her thin arms across her chest as she gazed over the town that stretched into the distance, measured by yellow orbs of muted candlelight burning behind shuttered windows. Was anywhere safe anymore? Certainly not in Sartis—not while her father ruled. His quest for power bordered on madness; He seemed willing to risk everything to achieve his goal of ruling both Sartis and Jarisa.

Nica took a deep painful breath. She needed to keep moving—to get back to the safety of her rooms so tomorrow she could let Toppen know of Jacoby's capture. She moved away from the balcony and ran her hand along the curved wall of the turret, fumbling for the stone that protruded from the rest. She reached between the blocks of rock where the mortar had been purposely eliminated to press a secret lever. Four of the large stones of the wall swung inward to reveal a small pass-through.

Nica stepped into impenetrable blackness. She pushed the makeshift door back into place until the lever clicked and held her breath as she was submerged into darkness. She counted to ten to let her eyes adjust, and her heart to resume something closer to a normal pace. The darkness was dense and she slid her hands along the curved wall for balance as she eased her feet over the rough surface of the descending steps.

The stairwell was narrow and crudely made, intended to be used as an escape route if departure through the main doors in the tower was not available.

The steps led down to an underground tunnel that opened up outside the castle gates.

The shadows were always deep within the round tower but seemed especially dark tonight. The arrow slits in the wall, which also allowed light into the stairwell, were useless with a moon shuttered by clouds. Nica's nerves were still ragged from her near fall and her knees wobbled like a cup of Cook's pudding. She took a deep breath and squinted toward her feet, wishing for the eyes of a carpidi, those vicious cats that roamed the forests at night, to better see the uneven steps in the dark.

A rush of air brushed her cheek.

She stopped, a prickle crawling up her spine.

Without warning, a hand wrapped in her hair and wrenched her head back. The cold edge of a blade pressed against her throat, strangling her scream to a gurgle.

"Who are you?" The guttural tone of a Sartisian guard was harsh in her ear. She clutched at her assailant's rock-hard wrist, but couldn't force his grip to waver. Instead, the pressure against her throat increased. "I'll release the blade enough for you to answer," he said in a low voice. "Scream and it'll be the last sound you ever make—do you understand me?"

Nica gave a cautious nod.

"Tell me your name." The pressure eased but the blade remained sharp at her throat.

"Madanica," she choked out. "Mosaba's daughter."

Utter silence filled the tower. Had he not heard her?

The grip on her hair released though she didn't dare straighten her head with the blade still pressed against her flesh. There was a *scritch* and a small flame flared, casting a flickering light across the curved stone wall in front of her. In one quick movement her assailant dropped the knife from her throat and yanked her around so the light illuminated her face. She could feel the sharp point of his knife now pressed against her jacket just below her heart.

Nica gasped in surprise when the flame revealed the sculpted features of Jonn Shanks staring back at her with an equally startled expression. The corner of his mouth lifted in a mocking grin.

"What have we here? A midnight spy?"

She lifted her chin and hoped he couldn't feel her knees shaking. "Release me."

Instead of releasing her, his eyes narrowed as he examined her features. "I didn't know Mosaba had a daughter," he said softly. "You wouldn't be a spy *and* a liar, would you?"

"It is a well-kept secret," she snapped. "So his enemies can't harm me. How did you come to speak Sartish so well?" When he'd questioned her, there'd been no trace of the lilting brogue she'd heard earlier.

Instead of answering her question he measured her up and down. "How old are you?"

Nica answered without thinking. "Seventeen."

He tilted his head to the side as he examined her face with a strangely intense scrutiny. "Why are you disguised? Who is it you're spying on?"

With a start, Nica remembered the ashes she'd spread so carefully across her face earlier and the black scarf covering her hair. Bless the Ancients, what must he think? She tried to yank her arm free. "Release me now and I won't report you to my father."

The orange light of the flame illuminated his handsome face as he leaned close. His blue eyes were fringed with black lashes so thick Nica couldn't look away.

"If you go quietly, *I* won't report *you* to your father," he said softly. The flame disappeared at the same moment he released her wrist.

Nica didn't hesitate. She turned and ran down the steps, praying her feet would find their way safely over the trip-stair. Two-thirds of the way down the stairwell she fumbled with the handle on a small door leading to the back of a linen closet. Blood pounded so loudly in her ears she couldn't hear if he was behind her or not. She crawled across the freshly laundered pile of linens and cracked the door open at the other end to peer into the dim passageway.

It was past midnight and the corridors were empty. She slid from the linen storage and stayed close to the shadow-shrouded walls as she wound her way back to the safety of her rooms. Once there, she pulled the black scarf from her head to release her blond hair and gazed at the reflection in the mirror. Frightened eyes surrounded by black soot and as grey as a storm on the Nephalon Sea stared back at her. Would Jonn Shanks keep her secret?

Chapter Three

veryone had left the dining area by the time Nica arrived downstairs for breakfast the next morning. She glanced into the large, round room as she passed into the servant's corridor on her way to the screened area where her father insisted she eat alone. She wasn't allowed to mingle with the soldiers or the servants, though she did like to watch from afar, and knew all of them by name, even if they didn't know her.

The soldiers were particularly interesting. On the outside they were strong and fierce—putting on a bravado that dropped away when they didn't know anyone was watching. Willie Parsons' wife had just had twins and he often came to the castle with baby food stains on his uniform looking like he hadn't slept in days. More than once he had sneaked into one of the small storage closets off the dining hall and taken a nap during the day.

Hesper Jenkins, one of the younger soldiers with black hair and a shadow of a moustache on his upper lip, liked to sing ballads under the light of the moon. Recently, he'd taken to helping the stable master break some of the young stallions. Nica wondered if he hoped the other men might think him more manly if he could break the wild horses. He'd been limping something awful the last week and Nica had heard several of the maids giggling about wanting to massage his backside, where apparently he'd landed more than once.

And then there was Prudence Bellamy, a chambermaid who wasn't much older than Nica. Attractive, with a full head of lush red curls and breasts to match, she caught many a man's eye and loved to flirt with them all—until Jonn Shanks had arrived. Then Prudence only had eyes for one man.

"Your porridge, Miss." A young servant girl wearing a brown shift and matching head scarf slid the bowl in front of Nica, her eyes downcast, waiting to be sent on her way.

"Thank you," Nica replied and the girl flitted off as if afraid to be seen with Mosaba's daughter. Which, Nica reflected, was probably the case. Mosaba ruled with absolute authority and anyone who dared disobey suffered the consequences.

Nica lifted her spoon and stirred the steaming bowl, staring blindly through the carved screen that hid her from the dining hall. Maybe the girl didn't know who she was—for the amount of attention her father paid her, one would think she was nothing more than a chambermaid herself.

She imagined Prudence Bellamy's life—flirting as she pleased and walking free from the castle at the end of each day to return home. Yes, the girl had to clean chamber pots and scrub floors but she also flirted with men and had a life—she didn't live in fear and isolation like Nica.

Not for much longer, Nica thought with a tentative surge of hope. Tonight she would sneak into Mosaba's office and steal that map, then she and Toppen would leave and find a life of their own.

As if conjured from her thoughts, a familiar giggle drifted in from the hallway.

"Why, Mr. Shanks—" Prudence's voice was high and girly— "imagine running into you in the middle of the day. I thought soldiers were always busy sneaking around spying on people."

"Hello, Miss Bellamy."

Shanks voice was also easily recognizable. His lilting accent was noticeable and Nica wondered at his ability to disguise his voice at will, remembering how perfect his Sartish had been in the darkness of the tower. She tried to place his inflection but it was as foreign as he and she wondered if the accent was fake and perhaps intentional—a means to lull one into believing he was a friend.

"Actually," his voice was deep and rich and *very* friendly, "we do our sneaking and spying at night, when everyone is asleep."

Nica could imagine the charming half-grin on his face as he surveyed the ample cleavage that Prudence liked to display at all times.

Prudence giggled as if his statement had included some sexual innuendo. "Well, why are you here, then?" she asked. "It's rare that a soldier comes into the servant's hall." Her voice took on a hopeful note. "Are you looking for someone?"

"Actually I am."

Nica paused with her spoon halfway to her mouth, curious at which servant Jonn Shanks might have business with. Had he come looking for Prudence?

"I'm looking for Mosaba's daughter."

Nica's spoon clattered back into her bowl and she scrambled to her feet, ready to run. He was going to reveal her secret. Or threaten her. Or worse.

"Oh. Her." It was as if someone had punctured Prudence's happiness like a balloon.

Shanks didn't sound like he he'd noticed. "I watched for her in the dining hall this morning but I don't believe she appeared. Does she eat somewhere else?"

Nica looked from one side of the little room to the other as panic coursed through her veins. There was only one exit from this area and it led straight to where Shanks was talking to Prudence.

"She doesn't eat with the others," Prudence said. "Too important, I suppose. She's like a ghost—hardly anyone sees her, but they say she's an early riser—probably already come and gone by now."

"And where does she eat?"

Nica imagined Prudence pointing in the direction of the room in which she was now trapped. Her head swiveled as she looked for a hiding place—but there was nothing. Only the small table where she sat. Booted footsteps sounded on the stone floor headed her direction.

Mediche! Nica flew to the corner where the carved screen joined the stone wall. She crouched down and threaded her fingers through the holes in the screen, and tugged—pulling the lower portion free below where it was affixed to the wall. The wood had some give and she had the strength of the desperate. Thankfully, she was thin and able to slip through the small gap into the dining hall.

On her hands and knees she crawled under a table toward a nearby exit. Once she was sure she couldn't be seen from the small room she got to her feet and raced for the door, hoping the dining room remained empty and no one watched her.

Once in the corridor, she smoothed her skirt and inhaled deeply, trying to calm her racing heart. Jonn Shanks was dangerous. She needed to stay far away from him.

THE BELLS ON the clock tower tolled twelve. As the last peal faded away Nica poked her head outside the door of her chambers to survey the hallway through the muted light. As she expected, the passageway was empty. She hurried out of her rooms and up the stairs, her slippers a quiet *shush* on the stone. Only the guards were about this time of night and she knew their rotation well. A familiar surge of adrenaline pulsed through her.

Nica tiptoed as she approached her father's office. From her window she had watched his departure earlier in the evening and knew he had not yet returned to Ravensfell.

When he was in his office he always hung his keys on a peg by the door so he wouldn't forget them when he left. For months she had carried a ball of wax in her pocket, waiting for her opportunity, but he was obsessive about locking his office and pocketing the keys.

Finally, during the heat of summer, he had left the turret windows open. In the dark of night Nica had crept along the ledge and pulled herself into the room through the window. Using the wax, she'd made a mold of the key to his office.

How she'd had the nerve, she didn't know. A moment of madness was the only explanation. She was timid by nature and even worse, her father had made her fearful. But she'd disguised herself as a servant and snuck into town and had a key made.

She glanced up and down the hallway as she approached the door, then hurriedly slid the iron key from her pocket and shoved it into the lock. She held her breath but the knob twisted easily in her hands and she pushed the door open a crack to peer inside.

Empty.

Her heart raced at the thought of being caught but she needed a map. She and Toppen were headed across the border into Jarisa to Pont d'Suree. It was there that the University was located and where Nica hoped to start over. She was desperate to get away. Mosaba's anger with her seemed to grow by the day.

Nica slipped into the office. The desk was strewn with maps from a meeting earlier in the night and her eyes raced across the top layer of scrolls. These were not what she sought. Her fingers fumbled with the large pages as she shuffled through them. She knew which map she wanted, having seen it before during her geography lessons.

There! A corner of the page's gold edges stuck out from under several other maps. She grasped the edge of the paper and pulled it out of the stack. Nica hesitated. She couldn't take the chance of being stopped in the corridor with the map in her possession. Not at this hour of the night.

"Focus," she whispered as she folded the thick, stiff paper into a rectangle, creasing it tightly in an attempt to make it lie flat. With hands that trembled, she slipped it down the front of her dress. Though scratchy, the map disappeared neatly below the ruffles of her bodice. She gave her dress a satisfied pat, then turned and stopped short with a gasp.

Jonn Shanks leaned against the door with his arms crossed, watching her. He wasn't dressed in the red tunic of the Sartish army. Instead, he wore a pair of dark breeches that clung to muscled legs and a crisp white shirt. Gold buttons glittered from the black jacket that hung casually from his shoulders and it was obvious he'd not yet retired for the night.

Nica dropped her hand from her throat. "Y..you startled me."

"M'lady Madanica, I presume?" There was something about the deceptively casual way he slouched there, so motionless, so intent, she felt as if she were being stalked.

"Nica." She straightened her back, trying to recover her composure. "Call me Nica. Only my father calls me Madanica." She smoothed her skirt and wished she could vanish into thin air. Anything to escape that piercing gaze.

"As you wish." He shrugged off the doorframe and walked up to her—too close for comfort. He blocked her pathway to the door. "M'lady Nica." He bowed slightly from the waist, in acknowledgement, she presumed, of her status as the King's daughter— yet Nica didn't get the sense he considered her to be of any greater stature than he. In fact, he seemed to find her amusing. "It is my privilege to meet you." His Sartish was impeccable.

Nica feigned ignorance. "And you are...?"

"Jonn Shanks." He gave a short bow but his eyes went past her to the table piled high with maps. "Can I help you find something?"

Had he seen her take the map? His face was like a mask, impossible to read.

"No." She spoke a little too quickly. "No, thank you," she said again, slower this time. She took a step back and glanced toward the door. "I'll wait until my father returns."

The young soldier's eyes narrowed when she turned her head and the angry purple bruise on her right cheek became visible. Nica brushed her hair forward to hide the mark where Mosaba had backhanded her for interrupting him.

"Are you looking for Mosaba?" she asked. Did she dare try to walk past him? He was a full head taller and appeared to be as wiry and strong as the hand she'd failed to pry from her neck last night.

"No. He's left the castle." Shanks gave her an appraising look. "I saw the light and thought perhaps there was some trouble."

Nica laid her hand flat against the front of her dress, the hidden map digging into her skin. "No cause for concern." She took a tiny step forward. "Now, if you'll excuse me—"

He didn't budge. "M'lady Nica, forgive my impertinence. Perhaps you like to live dangerously, but I must warn you that you are taking great risks."

Nica pressed her lips together. She was forbidden to speak to her father's soldiers but his arrogance was too much. "And what of you? Why are you in my father's office at midnight?" Her voice held a dare. "If I didn't know better, I'd say you were spying."

"Speaking of spies—" his lips twisted in a smile that was much too charming— "I've been admiring the lovely scent of your perfume." His gaze challenged her. "Reminds me of the tropical hills of Jarisa. Laurisnips, yes?"

Caught off guard by his flattery, Nica's cheeks grew warm. The rare perfume had been a gift from Toppen. One of his brothers had smuggled it over the border. She didn't think anyone in Sartis would recognize the fragrance.

"You know," Shanks continued, "that scent is especially charming on the evening breeze." He tapped his finger on his chin and pretended to think. "Probably best enjoyed while facing south with an easterly wind." He looked around in mock surprise. "Why, I'd bet if we opened that window right there—" he pointed across the room to the window through which Nica had been spying the night before— "we could smell laurisnips even now."

Nica took a step back. There was no easy way to explain her presence on the ledge.

He lowered his voice. "Perhaps the difference between you and I is that I don't get caught spying unless I *want* to be seen."

"Trust me," Nica snapped. "I've plenty of practice if the game is hide and seek. I can hide well when necessary."

His smile faded and shadows filled his eyes. "I'm sure you could." Then he gave her a surprisingly boyish grin. "But I could find you."

Nica glared at him. "That sounds like a threat."

Shanks shrugged, his jacket moving smoothly over his broad shoulders. "Or a promise." He was scarcely older than she, yet he was already a soldier and one who had gained Mosaba's respect. Perhaps that explained his self-assurance.

For once in her life, Nica said what she thought. "You, sir, are over-confident. Which is simply a polite way to say arrogant and rude." She crossed her arms. "Should I set my mind to it, I could disappear right from under your nose."

Shanks chuckled and took a step back, clearing a path to the door for her. "I hope you won't put me to a test any time soon." He offered his arm. "May I escort you to your rooms?"

"Thank you, no. I know the way on my own." Nica brushed by him and hurried toward the door, intent on escape. Though he let her go, she could feel the weight of his gaze on her shoulders as clearly as if his fingers touched her.

Chapter Four

HighGarden Palace
LaBrice, Jarisa

he King has been captured."

Jaaniyah Jacoby stood at the window of her study and stared blindly at the view of tropical forest and jagged mountains in the distance as Heathron's words echoed in her ears with a dreadful finality. Her minister of war had delivered the bad news an hour ago.

Of all times, why *now*? Just as she was to assume a position next to her father's throne—the beginning of a transition to her own rule. A knock sounded at the door interrupting her musings.

"Come."

A guard entered. "How can I be of service, M'lady?"

"I need you to fetch Becknah for me—as quickly as you can."

'Yes, M'lady." The sound of his running footsteps echoed through the open doorway as the guard pulled the thick wooden door closed. Jaaniyah threaded her fingers together to still their trembling. Perhaps their scholar could tell her what the stars had to say about her father's fate.

A LIGHT SEQUENCE of taps sounded at the door—a familiar knock.

"Ian Becknah." The guard announced her visitor then bowed and pulled the door closed as he exited the room.

"You've heard?" Jaaniyah paused. The pained frown that creased the elderly face spoke volumes. Becknah was her father's oldest and most trusted advisor. If anyone could save the king it would be this man.

"Yes, M'dear, I've heard." Becknah shook his head as he approached. The gold thread interwoven within the crimson of his overcoat reflected the afternoon light. "Tis more than the wolf at the door this time. Tis the devil, himself."

"Mosaba?"

"Who else?" The old man shrugged, causing his silver hair to fall forward and brush his shoulders. "He requested a meeting at Ry'dontt. Jacoby believed the ruler of Sartis sought détente. The King went with the intention of negotiating peace."

"Never!" Jaaniyah spat the word from her lips as though it were poison. "Jarisa will never agree to peace while that barbarian lives." She paced toward the towering stone fireplace, the long skirt of her forest green gown sweeping across the floor. "Would he consider a ransom?"

The older man held out his thin, gnarled hands. "Can we afford to give him what he wants?"

"No, of course not." Jaaniyah faced the windows as if searching for an answer in the distant vista. "The only thing that will satisfy that madman is the throne to Jarisa and he'll only gain that over my dead body." Her brows pulled down in a frown. "I think we should retaliate now, and destroy Sartis."

"And the only thing to be gained would be the sure death of your father along with many others." The old man braced his hands on the arms of a chair before the fire and lowered himself to the seat. "Your father saw the need for peace. We must somehow move beyond war as the answer to our differences or we will be forever caught in an endless cycle of strike and retaliation."

"He has *my father*." The words slipped through clenched teeth as Jaaniyah tried to calm her rage. "We need to steal something equally precious from Mosaba."

A weighted silence filled the room.

"Now, there's an idea," Becknah finally murmured. He tapped a finger against his chin as he gazed up to the dark timbers exposed above their heads. "Perhaps there is something."

Jaaniyah stopped pacing and focused on the older man. "What?"

He stroked his beard, the rings on his fingers sparkling as though imbued with magical powers. "There is one other thing I've heard that Mosaba greatly desires."

"What's that?" Jaaniyah stepped closer.

Becknah peered at her over glasses perched on the end of his nose, his eyes crinkling in the corners as he smiled. "The Getheas Stone."

Jaaniyah's face twisted with confusion. "But that's a myth. A legend. It's not real."

Becknah cocked his head at her. "So they say. But most legends grow from a seed of fact and the willingness to believe. From what I've heard, Mosaba believes." The reflection of the fire on the crescent sliver of his glasses made his eyes appear to dance with madness.

"But even if the legend is true, Mosaba doesn't have the stone. How would we steal it?"

"By finding it first."

"Do you mean to tell me you believe the Getheas Stone actually exists?"

The scholar lifted his palms— "There are antique texts, information about the life of Getheas that says it does. Documents that suggest the Ancients—Getheas, Juneedika and Celestica—were the greatest prophets— and perhaps, magicians—of all time."

Jaaniyah sank into a nearby chair as she mulled over his words. "We don't even know where to look. How would we negotiate with something we don't have?"

"Ah, child." The older man spoke with a familiarity borne from long association. "It's not true that we don't know where to look. There have been clues left behind that point the way."

"Obscure poems every schoolboy has learned by the time he reaches the age of eight?" Jaaniyah scoffed in disbelief. "The story of the stone has been told for centuries. If it's really out there, why hasn't someone deciphered the poems and found the thing?"

"Perhaps it hasn't been the right time." He dipped his head to measure her over his glasses. "How are we to know that the quatrains—or 'poems' as you call them—aren't waiting for one in particular to make sense of the rhymes?" He lifted thin shoulders in an eloquent shrug. "It's not for me to say."

Jaaniyah scooted her chair closer to the old man. "Why do you think they're prophecies?"

Becknah steepled his fingers. "Because some have come true."

Jaaniyah's eyebrows lowered in a frown. "Such as…?"

Becknah began to recite:

> *"Beware a battle provoked by rage*
> *Unprotected by the golden cage*
> *A single blow through the eye*
> *The serpent and bear both shall die.*

This prophecy tells of the deaths of Montemier, known as the wild bear because of his temper, and his nephew, Pontfial, who was called the viper for the method in which he used his sword."

"Montemier?" Jaaniyah said. "I remember him— he was in our history books. He was the ruler of

Singaty a hundred years ago. That prophecy is about him?"

"Yes, Montemier's nephew was involved in a dalliance with the ruler's young wife. Montemier was so angry when he found them out that rather than follow the typical protocol of a joust, where he would wear protective gear, including his famous gilded helmet, he attacked on the spot. The young Pontfial defended himself and stabbed Montemier through the eye, killing him instantly. The ruler's ministers were so outraged they hung Pontfial without a trial." Becknah held his hands up. "And thus, the serpent and the bear both died. The pages were written over five hundred years before the event."

Jaaniyah sat forward, her eyes bright with curiosity. "Are there others?"

"Yes, many. One predicted the great fire in Carpis one hundred and fifty years after Getheas' death. Another predicted the assassination attempt of the Cardinal of Asini, just a decade ago. Of course, those are the few we've been able to decipher. There are books and books of quatrains that remain a mystery."

Jaaniyah leaned back in her chair, a doubtful look on her face. "And what exactly does the Stone offer that Mosaba would want so desperately?"

"Ah." Becknah threaded his fingers together. "The Stone is said to be a key. The lost manuscript, if you will—the missing puzzle piece that will let us decipher Getheas' prophecies and reveal the secret meanings of his predictions." His eyes gleamed. "The Stone will give us the ability to see the future."

The princess frowned. "How's that, exactly?"

The prophecies are like a giant puzzle—pieces of information that tell us what is to come—great secrets that will lead us to a new world order." Becknah focused his gaze on Jaaniyah. "Mosaba desires to rule both Jarisa and Sartis. Being able to see the future is a most powerful ally." He stroked his beard. "Perhaps an undefeatable ally."

"But we don't have the Stone." Jaaniyah gripped the arms of her chair in frustration. "How is it we would battle Mosaba when we have nothing?"

The old man looked away to the ceiling, lost in thought. "Our opportunity would lie in making Mosaba *believe* we have the stone. We would need to deceive him into thinking we have something he wants enough to keep your father alive."

Jaaniyah narrowed her eyes. "What are you suggesting?" A flicker of hope shot through her. "That we *pretend* to have the Getheas Stone?"

"An idea to consider," Becknah said. "It's well documented that all of the texts attributed to Getheas are stored here in Jarisa. If anyone would know, it would be us. But first, we must take a defensive position at our borders." Becknah pushed himself up straighter in the chair. "Has Heathron contacted you yet about the details of the attack? Has he identified where our security failed the King?"

Jaaniyah nodded, her enthusiasm fading. "He said the attack was an ambush. That Mosaba's men knew which trail our brigade was traveling." Her voice tightened with anger. "They were lying in wait. Heathron said our men were surprised and outnumbered." She tried to shrug off a shiver as she remembered her minister of war's description of the bloody attack and his suggestion that someone from inside their own ranks had sold them out.

"As I feared," Becknah said with a grim expression. "There is a spy in our midst. Perhaps more than one." He gazed into the flickering flames for a moment. "I must consult the Xanfere cards as well as the stars to see what guidance they might provide."

He shook his head. "There's no time to lose if we are to set these wheels in motion. Word must be leaked that you have knowledge of the stone's location. Spread a rumour that your father's capture has forced you to recover the long-lost Getheas Stone so you may use its power to battle Sartis and win." Becknah smiled with satisfaction. "That should give Mosaba something to think about."

Jaaniyah hesitated. "But how do I do that?"

The scholar stood, his crimson robes cascading to the floor. "Whose loyalties do you question most within your father's court of advisors?"

"Tarantu," Jaaniyah said without hesitation. Her father had warned her of his suspicions about his finance minister. She fell into step with the older man as he clasped his hands behind his back and walked toward the door.

"Then we must allow him to overhear a conversation that suggests you are in pursuit of a power beyond the imagination." He paused and his silver brows furrowed. "You do know that this course of action will put you at considerable risk. You were potentially a target before this. But by tying your name to this quest, Mosaba and his minions will come directly for you."

"Dear Becknah." Jaaniyah put a hand on his arm. "You have cared well for my family all these years. I am at risk by any measure and I'll gladly attempt this if there is a chance to save my father." Her voice wavered. "He's all the family I have left."

Becknah patted the slim hand resting on his arm. "Your father is a strong and fierce warrior. I pray that he shall live to claim the day."

Chapter Five

ool air permeated the vast hallways of Ravensfell as winter crept closer with each day. Nica shivered as she peeked out through a narrow window in the corridor on the way to her father's office. Fog swirled beneath the trees and stretched long ethereal fingers through the fields, watery sunlight glinting off the mist. How she wished she could disappear into the opaque clouds.

She clenched and unclenched her fingers as she hurried up the last flight of steps, her slippers silent against the stone. She rounded the corner and tiptoed through the antechamber to her father's office.

"Sir, you wanted to see me?" Nica concentrated on keeping her words crisp. She couldn't show any hint of fear even though her heart thudded against her ribs. Her father enjoyed that too much.

The dark, over-sized furniture in Mosaba's office made her uncomfortable and she tried not to look at the razor-sharp swords suspended in rows by their ornate hilts on a large wooden stand. The antique swords, as well as the barbaric tools of old displayed on the walls, fascinated her father.

She slid cautiously onto the edge of a high-backed chair in front of Mosaba's desk and waited as he meticulously cleaned and oiled the braids of an ancient, nine-headed whip. The arms of the chair wrapped around the seat like wings and the back had two glaring eyes carved into each side. It was like sitting on the lap of a harpy hawk, those giant predatory birds that lived above the Cliffs of Seniesta.

Nica perched on the edge of the seat, primed to flee, for Mosaba's mood often turned violent. He raised his dark head and contemplated her, his black eyes guarded by heavy brows. She could tell he was irritated.

"I have heard a report." His voice was controlled. Too controlled. "That you were seen outside the gates, Madanica."

His fist crashed down on the desk.

Nica jumped.

"Is that true?" Now his voice was mild, coated in deceit.

"N…no sir, I wouldn't dare go outside the gates." She dug her fingernails into the palm of her hands. "W…where would I go?"

"Exactly. You will not go outside the gates. I will have to punish you if I find that you do." He gave her a cold smile. "For your own good, of course."

"Of course," she whispered. Mosaba liked to punish her. Who would have told him such a thing? Was it Shanks? But Jonn Shanks had never seen her outside the gates.

With measured movements Mosaba picked up a long, thin punk. He tamped its wooden tip in a nearby candle until it glowed orange.

"Let me see your arm."

Nica's grip on her seat tightened. "Why?"

"NOW!" Mosaba roared.

Nica cracked her elbow on the wood as she thrust her right arm out toward her father. She couldn't stop her hand from shaking.

Mosaba's thick fingers wrapped around Nica's thin wrist and turned her arm over to expose the delicate skin. With exacting precision he moved the burning ember toward her arm and placed it squarely in the fold of her elbow.

Nica sucked in her breath and clenched her teeth against the pain, but remained silent. She saw the malicious light in her father's eyes before she dropped her gaze and concentrated on her toes curling against the leather of her boots.

"You will not go outside the gates," Mosaba repeated. "Understood?"

"Yes sir," Nica whispered, as her father moved the punk back to the candle. She folded her arms tight against her waist.

"I suggest you return to your lessons before I change my mind about your punishment." Her father glared at her for a moment longer then stood up and strode through an open doorway at the back of his office.

Nica resisted the urge to pick something heavy off her father's desk and throw it at his empty chair. She had tried to please him for the longest time. But her efforts were to no avail. He was always angry with her about something.

"I hate this place," she whispered under her breath. "I hate *him*." Mosaba liked to frighten her—to inflict pain. She unfolded her arm to look at the burn. The raw flesh stung and a blister was forming. His temper was getting worse and she often felt his dark, brooding eyes upon her. Each day she grew more fearful of what he would do next.

She had grown up sequestered, at her father's insistence, within the grounds of their walled castle.

"It's for your own safety," Mosaba had repeated over the years. His bloody rise as self-proclaimed ruler of Sartis had given him many enemies. Nica knew Mosaba feared they would somehow use her to get revenge.

It wasn't until the last year that she'd gathered the nerve to venture beyond her prison walls. Toppen had given her the confidence to try. She'd met him during one of his frequent deliveries of wine to the castle and they'd struck up a friendship. With his encouragement she'd found a way to sneak into town.

Sick and dizzy with fear, she pushed herself up out of the chair. Her father's warning had scared her. She wouldn't allow herself to think of the punishment if Mosaba caught her outside the gates, because she needed to talk to Toppen now. To tell him the news.

NICA HURRIED DOWN the back stairs to the ground floor of the castle. She was dressed in the familiar clothes of a castle valote—dark trousers and a long white tunic with a wide sash of maroon tied loosely at her waist. She had tucked her braids inside the customary black cap. The common outfit helped her blend in with the servants as well as the crowds in town.

She popped a small piece of wax, molded while still warm to a smooth curve, inside her upper lip. The wax made her lip protrude and caused her to purse her mouth while she talked. She didn't dare take a chance on being recognized. A pair of black framed glasses completed the disguise. The few people who knew of her wouldn't recognize her dressed like this.

Nica kept her head down as she made her way along the corridor. Last year, she'd overheard Hosh, a young assistant to her father's magistrate, bragging about a secret gate in the outer curtain wall. It had taken her a week of looking to find the little used, overgrown exit on the far side of the orchard. It was from there that she escaped from the castle grounds unseen.

With a furtive glance around the empty hall Nica slipped out through a side entrance that led toward the stables. The wind was beginning to pick up as she skirted the outbuildings and ran through a small stand of withered fruit trees. It wouldn't be long before winter set her icy grip upon Sartis.

Toward the back of the copse stood an arbor overgrown with grapes, the leaves bright orange from the first frost of fall. Nica cast one last glance over her shoulder then disappeared under the archway. She ran, her footsteps muffled on the soft dirt, fighting the feeling of being chased.

She reached the end of the arbor and swept aside an armful of thick hanging vines to reveal a plank doorway. The weathered wood slats were reinforced with iron ribs top and bottom and the metal squeaked in protest as she lifted the rusted lever of the handle. She tugged the door open just enough to slip her slender body through the space. An old trail led through the underbrush and it was only minutes before she emerged onto the road that led into town.

Freedom!

How she loved the anonymity of being able to walk about the streets and enjoy the cacophony of activity without being watched. A street vendor played his panpipe while children laughed and danced before him. Another sold potatoes— *'So tasty you'll be beggin' for more!'* They had potatoes at every meal. How anyone could want more was a mystery to Nica.

Far in the distance, a clock tower tolled the time from LaBricé, the court city in the neighboring country of Jarisa. The town sat shimmering like a mirage directly across the Great Divide from Berjerac. Like an echo, the clock tower of Berjerac began to toll in the crisp morning air.

"Let me read your future with the mystical Xanfere cards."

The compelling call of a man's voice sliced through the morning air and grabbed Nica's attention. As though pulled by an unseen string she stepped toward the crowd gathering. The magician's black and red silk cape billowed behind him and the black hat perched on his head made him appear taller than normal. His nose was hooked, a cliff between eyes as black as midnight, matching the straight black hair that hung to his shoulders. His striking appearance added to the power of his theatrical voice.

"Come close and learn what the Fates have in store for your future." His hands produced a deck of Xanfere cards as though from thin air. In one seamless move, he spread the cards face up across the black velvet-covered stand in front of him.

Nica stepped forward, the brilliant colors and vivid images on the cards drawing her toward them against her will.

With a sweep of his left arm, the magician scooped the deck back together and shuffled with blinding speed. The gilded edges of the cards sparkled in the sunlight, making them look as though they were suspended in air. Nica took another step closer.

Without warning, the slender man snapped his cape, stepping from behind his stand and into the crowd. People fell back as though fearful of his touch. He bowed in front of Nica.

"If you would be so kind as to cut the cards." In one smooth movement he raised his hand, the stack of cards balanced on his palm. His gaze probed her face as he waited. The crowd turned toward her, curiosity written on every face, and her heart plunged into her stomach. This was too much attention. Would she be recognized? How could she get away?

"Well...I..."

The magician indicated the deck of cards with a nod of his head and gave her a small smile as his cape fluttered behind him like a bird revving up to take flight. "Just pick a portion of the deck and place it in my other hand," he said in a low tone. "The power of the Xanfere will do the rest."

With shaking fingers, Nica reached forward and cut the deck. She placed half the cards in his other hand as she debated whether staying or running would attract more attention. With a flourish, the magician returned to his spot behind the stand.

"And now let us see what the Fates have in store for you." His voice rang out like a bell in the afternoon air.

Curiosity made Nica stepped closer as the crowd made way for her. In quick, efficient movements, the magician laid out six cards face up in a cross pattern, placing a seventh card face down by itself.

The pictures on the cards were a kaleidoscope of colors and shapes that teased Nica's eyes. Wands and swords slashed across their well-worn surfaces. Stars and keys danced among lightning bolts and flames. Nica's eyes skipped from the cards to the man's face, looking for any tell-tale indication of their meaning. Her breath caught when his eyebrows pulled down and his forehead wrinkled in concentration. His gaze jerked to her face with an unmistakable look of shock.

"You are surrounded by danger." The magician pointed to the first card. "Tread carefully for I see the Fates have a test in store for you."

Nica's legs were frozen in place.

"You are leaving on a long journey... I see betrayal.....there will be death..." He lifted his eyes to hers. "The looking glass will reveal the truth..."

Nica turned and ran, shoving her way through the crowd around her.

"Wait! There's more..."

The magician's voice compelled her to look back. He lifted his hand as though to stop her escape. With her head turned Nica didn't see the young man's back before she charged into him and the sound of shattering glass filled the air.

Chapter Six

ica gasped as red wine, the color of the prized quiizenberry, splattered across the cobblestones. The pungent aroma filled the air and she looked up to see Toppen's wide green eyes staring back at her. His red hair capped a face accented with a prominent nose and splattered with freckles. Relief washed over her.

"Oh Top…".

"What is wrong with you?" he barked. "Are Lucede's hounds chasing you?" His nose curled in disgust. "You've broken two very valuable bottles of wine."

"S…sorry." Nica took a step back, prepared to run again. Though she knew Toppen was acting, his anger scared her. She had lived with Mosaba's rages for too long to be unaffected. "I didn't see you."

"Yes, I assumed that, unless you make it a habit of attacking men carrying bottles of wine. Here." He thrust two unbroken green bottles toward her. "Hold these, while I get a broom."

Nica took the bottles as Toppen slid a corkscrew into his back pocket. She cast a furtive glance over her shoulder toward the group surrounding the Magician but she no longer held their interest.

"Ahhhh!" The crowd cried as the magical man pulled a pure white docelyn from inside his tall black hat and launched the delicate bird into the sky. The magician's hungry gaze, however, was pointed in her direction. Nica hurried around the corner into the shadows cast by the wine emporium, out of view of the disturbing stranger.

"You're graceful today," Toppen said when he returned from sweeping up the broken glass. He leaned against the broom handle and contemplated her. "Too many people were watching you. I didn't think it would be a good idea to draw attention to our acquaintance."

Nica started to point out that she was disguised but Toppen interrupted.

"Why did you run?" he asked. "Was it something the magician said?"

"What he said, what he did." Nica lowered her voice. "It was like he was really magic, Toppen. He made those cards *float* in the air. I saw it myself." She shuddered. "There was something about him—about his eyes, the way he looked at me—" she glanced over her shoulder to make sure they were alone— "as if he recognized me."

"What did he say?" Around the corner a loud cheer went up.

"Something about betrayal—" Nica grabbed his arm to make him look at her— "and death."

Toppen quirked his brows then shrugged. "Sounds like a cheery fellow. He probably says the same thing to everybody." A couple strolled down the street in their direction and he made a show of sweeping around Nica's booted feet.

"Let me put the broom back and we can talk more." Toppen disappeared into the building and returned carrying two new bottles of wine. "Your punishment for breaking my wares it that you're going to help me make my delivery this morning." After several steps he looked back and shrugged his shoulder at her. "Come on then, we haven't got all day."

Nica hurried after him, her boots tapping a quick staccato down the dusty cobblestones. Toppen shortened his stride so they could walk side by side. "And by the way, nice disguise."

Nica tried to jab him with her elbow but he dodged away, laughing.

"Now, now, let's behave. You've done enough damage for one day. Besides, you know I think you're the most beautiful girl in all of Sartis. Your eyes remind me of the Sea of Nephalon..."

Nica groaned.

"And your lips...ah, yes, those lips...they're the color of a spilled bottle of quiizenberry wine." He grinned down at her. "Food for a starving man's soul."

"Oh, please..." Nica laughed, but the day lightened around her. Toppen's humor was infectious; his compliments, though outrageous, were always nice to hear. She enjoyed being around him. It was a rare day anyone else ever paid her a kind word.

Toppen swung his arms together over his heart and knocked the bottles together with an alarming *clink!* "Oops," he said, checking for breakage.

"Very smooth." Nica rolled her eyes. "Though your tongue may be descended from gypsies, your grace appears to be a direct result of some rather unfortunate in-breeding." She gave him a smile. "Lucky for you, I enjoy your fool's humor."

"You're a brave one to talk about grace today," he replied, unconcerned with her insult. "And better the humor of a fool then the lies of a nobleman."

Nica grimaced. "Have they cut the body down yet?" Mosaba had caught a traitor posing as a nobleman within his court. Unable to explain the documents found sewn into the man's jacket, Mosaba had declared him a Jarisan spy and hung him from the highest turret wall for all to see.

"I don't believe the vultures have had their fill for he hangs there even as we speak. Or what's left of him." Toppen steered them off the main thoroughfare to follow a lesser used street lined with shops. "So, tell me, is that all the magician had to say? A little betrayal, a little death?"

"It was enough, believe me. And what about the journey part?" Nica skipped ahead to better see his face. "We didn't even know until today."

Toppen stopped. "Know what?"

"The reason I came to town." She lowered her voice. "It's time."

His expression froze, as though he didn't want the moment to pass and find that he had misunderstood.

"What has occurred?"

"Mosaba has captured Jacoby."

"What?" His words came out in a gasp. "Where?"

"The Jarisan king was headed toward Ry'dontt."

"Has your father declared war?"

Nica nodded, shivering at the ominous implications. "Mosaba is sending men to capture Jacoby's only heir, his daughter Jaaniyah."

Toppen seemed to thrum with excitement as he began walking again. "And what of the king? Is Jacoby still alive?"

"I think so. Mosaba expects him to be delivered to the castle today."

"Where, no doubt, your father will torture the poor man to death." Toppen gazed into the distance, his lips pursed in thought. "Mosaba's hunger for power has warped his ability to reason. Jarisa could crush Sartis if she decides to attack. *But,* it will give us the perfect opportunity to leave," he mused. "We better hurry before they start watching the borders."

The bark of an approaching dog startled Nica. She turned to see an old brown and white mutt loping up to them, her paws kicking up little clouds of dust while her long pointed tail wagged happily.

"Hello, Hope." Toppen slowed to a stop, tucking a bottle under his arm as he reached down to pet the head of the old dog.

"Hope?" Nica questioned. "That's a peculiar name for a dog." She squatted down, setting her bottles on the ground to rub behind the dog's ears. "Where did you come from?"

"She lives over there, next to the healer's house." Toppen nodded toward a modest cottage as he stacked Nica's bottles of wine under his arm. "Hope always says hello when I make a delivery to Is'bella." Juggling all four bottles of wine, Toppen approached the small white hut and knocked on the door.

Nica stayed where she was, petting the soft fur of the dog. She took a deep breath, enjoying her heady sense of freedom. She could almost imagine what life could be like without Mosaba glowering at her all the time.

A flash of color caught her eye. The red uniform of Mosaba's court soldiers was easily identifiable. Two men were walking down the other side of the street headed her way. The metal of their long swords blinked with the reflected light of the morning sun.

She stood up in alarm. What were they doing here? "Toppen..." she turned to see if he had concluded his business and was surprised to find him standing right next to her. "Are you done?" Her voice came out in a whisper.

"Nic, remember, you're disguised."

His calm voice soothed her ragged nerves and she could feel the weight of his hand on her back as he steered her under the overhang of a nearby doorway. "Relax," he said as he stepped closer, blocking her from view. He bent his head and before she could move his lips were on hers.

Nica put her hands on his chest to push him away but the catcalls of the soldiers made her freeze in place. Toppen, on the other hand, was anything but frozen and his lips moved on hers in a shockingly intimate manner. His hands slid around to her back and pressed her close until she was sure he could feel every inch of her chest against his.

"Toppen," she gasped, before his lips covered hers again. This was not how she'd dreamed of her first kiss. She jerked her head back and hissed, "*stop*."

Toppen raised his head and grinned at her. "I'm only trying to protect you, Nic. The soldiers can't see your face this way."

The strength returned to Nica's hands and she gave him a hard shove. "Thanks, but no thanks." Over his shoulder she could see that the soldiers had disappeared into the entrance of a pub.

Toppen's laughter followed her as she stomped down the street. "Hey, wait for me..." he called as he jogged to catch up. He walked beside her in silence, his hands in his pockets, whistling a tune under his breath. Nica saw him cast a sideways glance her way but she raised her chin a notch and pretended not to notice.

"So," he said, "who is searching for Jacoby's daughter? Have they left already?"

"I don't know for sure. I think there are four or five." She quickened her steps. "Some left last night, I think the rest go tonight."

"And will Mosaba join them in their hunt?"

"Once he gathers the information he wants from Jacoby, I'm sure of it." She looked up at Toppen. His red hair glowed in the late morning sun. "This is it. This is the chance we've been waiting for." The burn on her arm throbbed with her movement and her voice dropped. "I can't delay. Mosaba is getting worse." She knew Toppen understood what she meant without having to actually say the words. "This may be the only chance I get."

A frown crossed his face then Toppen nodded at her. "Then we go tonight."

ica's two hours of freedom with Toppen flew by and before she was ready she had to retrace her steps back through the secret gate into the orchard. Once inside, she pulled the glasses from her face, spit the wax piece into her hand and hid both in the pocket of her voluminous trousers. She rounded the corner of the stables and stopped to stare as soldiers escorted a manacled prisoner.

As if sensing her presence the battered, grey-haired captive wearily lifted his head. Nica's mouth dropped open.

King Jacoby.

It had to be. Streaks of blood had dried down the side of the man's face as well as out of the corner of his mouth. His nose leaned unnaturally to one side and he limped so severely that a guard had to support him. Emotion contorted his face when he caught sight of Nica and his eyes suddenly burned with a maniacal intensity that frightened her.

"*Juneedika dio simpra e'sa mia ya moiré,*" he whispered hoarsely in Jarisan.

Unsettled, Nica hurried in the other direction, automatically translating in her head: '*Juneedika, by the blessing or the curse.*' She'd heard of Juneedika—one of Jarisa's revered deities. He'd been praying to a higher power for mercy. A strange feeling of guilt washed over her. Was this man—this king—doomed to die here? She glanced back over her shoulder to see the prisoner reaching out to her with his one good hand.

She slipped through the side door and ran to her chambers, nervous and unsettled.

THE DAY DRAGGED by like the steps of a tired ox. Nica didn't dare pack the few things she planned to take until most of the castle had retired for the night.

It was mid-afternoon when she left her rooms and ran upstairs. She pulled open one side of a majestic pair of tall carved doors to slip inside the Grand Library, her favorite room in Ravensfell. Mosaba had once told her that he'd built the library to honor his sister. Her mysterious aunt had lived in the Ortawn, a labyrinth of stone tunnels and chambers buried deep under a desert area known as the Scablands, until her death. Now, the Ortawn was a Sartish prison of unspeakable conditions.

Nica shuddered as the thought of her aunt brought back memories of the dark tunnels of the prison. Mosaba had taken her to the Ortawn more than once, seeming to delight in her aversion to the underground dungeon. Even now, as she remembered the tangled web of hallways and jail cells carved among the rocks, she could hear the cries of the desperate and the ranting of the demented.

Nica tucked a loose piece of hair behind her ear and pushed the unpleasant thoughts away, relieved to find herself alone in the library. Overhead, a massive dome made entirely of amber glass lit the room. She stopped in the center and gazed up. On impulse, she spread her arms wide and twirled, imagining herself flying away into the sky. She was so excited. After all this time—all the waiting and planning—they would go tonight.

Someone cleared their throat.

Nica snapped to attention with a gasp. Jonn Shanks leaned against the end of a bookcase, his arms crossed over his chest, one knee cocked, watching her.

"We meet again, M'lady Madanica." His expression was blank, his thoughts secret.

"*You,*" she said. "What are you doing in here?"

Shanks raised one eyebrow at her. "Looking for something to read, of course." He unfolded his hands and slid a book back on the shelf, but his smile made her think he was lying. "M'lady Madanica—" he began again as he sauntered toward her. His skin was bronzed by the sun making the blue of his eyes that much more startling.

"Nica. Please call me Nica." She put her hands behind her back and clutched her fingers together where he couldn't see her discomfort. "How odd that we keep running into each other, Mr. Shanks." She tried to give him a cool look like the haughty ladies she'd seen at court. "It's enough to make me wonder if I'm being followed."

Shanks tilted his head and grinned. "Or perhaps just another fortuitous circumstance." His smile faded. "Have you heard of Jacoby's capture?"

"Yes, Mosaba is ecstatic." Nica took a step back. Why, oh why couldn't she be brave instead of afraid all the time? Once again he was too close for comfort. Should she question his right to be in the library or should she focus on escaping from him? "I heard he was captured on his way to Ry'dontt."

"Ambushed is perhaps more accurate," Shanks said, "yet when one has a complete disregard for rules of engagement then I suppose it's all a matter of semantics."

Though Shanks' tone was light, Nica felt an uncomfortable chill creep up the back of her neck. His comment bordered on treason. She cocked her head, curiosity winning out over her fear. "Is there some reason Jacoby's capture was inappropriate?"

"Surely you must know that Ry'dontt is a neutral zone." His eyes narrowed. "Mosaba called for peace talks with the sole intent of attacking Jacoby en route."

Nica blinked, unsure of how to reply. She knew Mosaba was not a man to be trusted—he hated King Jacoby with a passion that bordered on obsession—but to admit that to someone else, especially a stranger and one of his soldiers—could have deadly consequences. She fumbled for something to say in return. "I didn't know there were rules to war."

"Rules don't exist unless all parties agree to abide by them." His tone held a bitter note. "One would be best served to keep their head down and their nose out of the court's business."

Nica stiffened. "And do you take the advice you so freely give, Mr. Shanks?"

Instead of answering, his eyes traced the contours of her face, lingering for a moment on her bruised cheek. His steady gaze made it difficult to draw an even breath.

"I'm sure you know what I mean better than most."

Nica's cheeks warmed at the accuracy of his insinuation and she cleared her throat. "W...will you be traveling with Mosaba in pursuit of Jacoby's daughter?"

"I'm leaving soon. Tomorrow, in fact." He smiled at her, though there was a sardonic twist to the corner of his mouth. "Can I count on you to fill me in on any news of the court—" he paused, then added with a wicked grin— "or any secrets of Ravensfell upon my return?"

"A tale for a tale," Nica replied flippantly. "You share your secrets and I'll share mine."

Shanks let out a low laugh. "Negotiating now, are we?" He inclined his head. "Spies and pirates must band together." His expression became steely. "I'll trust you, if you'll trust me."

Nica cocked her head at him. "One must earn trust."

"Very true." Eyes as blue as the summer sky measured her. "But you can trust me."

Something quirked in her chest. There was no one she could trust except Toppen.

His voice lowered to a whisper. "What are you planning, Nica?"

She blinked in surprise. "I...I have no idea what you're talking about."

"I'll tell you this—" he leaned forward. He was close enough Nica could smell the clean scent of soap. "The map which you so cleverly concealed last night does not reveal the danger of traveling outside of Sartis right now. Especially for you. There are things you don't know. Yet." He put an odd emphasis on the last word.

Panic flared through her like a match to kindling. He knew she was going to run. "I'm not planning anything," Nica lied.

His intensity never wavered. "Trust me when I say that it's too dangerous right now."

Nica raised her chin and worked to keep her voice steady. "Thank you for the ...advice, Mr. Shanks, but I have no plans to travel or..or set about some mysterious plot or whatever you're insinuating." She forced herself to smile as she took another step back. This was life or death. She *had* to leave Sartis with Toppen tonight. "Though I'm sure you must have greater responsibilities to concern yourself with now that you're my father's favorite new soldier."

Shanks expression darkened and he opened his mouth to retort when a sudden sharp rapping on the wooden door made them both jump. Before Nica could move, the door was thrust open and the face of her tutor, Lady Angeline, peered through the opening, her expression sharpening when she spotted them.

"There you are."

With masked innocence Nica faced her tutor. "Lady Angeline, uh, where have you been?"

The woman's large body flowed into the room, her floor-length skirt swaying like a ship cutting a wake.

Shanks spoke low enough that only Nica could hear him. "You need to wait for me." Her eyes darted to his unsmiling face. "One week. I'll be back. *Wait for me.*" He turned and with a nod to Lady Angeline disappeared through the door.

The tutor headed straight for Nica. "Don't you try that coy act with me," she said as she marched forward, one meaty hand clutching several books, the other planted on her ample hips. "You know perfectly well that you were scheduled for astrology this morning to be followed by languages. I've been waiting."

"I had, um... uh... an appointment this morning." Nica fled across the room with Lady Angeline following on her heels.

"What appointment?"

"With my, ah... father, of course." Nica tried to sound forceful and confident though she was sure she failed miserably. "Don't you remember?" She cast a sideways glance at her tutor.

"I'll verify with your father later, but for now— sit," Lady Angeline commanded. She pointed with her free hand at the two overstuffed chairs positioned in front of the massive fireplace. For all of Mosaba's cruelty over the years, he had also insisted she be educated, especially in languages.

Nica chewed on the corner of her lower lip as she waited for the lesson to begin. It concerned her that Shanks suspected she was going to run. How could he have known? This could be her only chance to escape from her father without being caught.

"We're going to start with conversational Jarisan this morning." Lady Angeline's precisely enunciated voice broke into her thoughts. Nica nodded in acquiescence and gave Lady Angeline a contrite smile. She was pleased, for she didn't need to think much about speaking in Jarisan—the words came easily to her.

Unbidden, the vision of the manacled prisoner came to mind. By now he was locked in the dungeon, probably being tortured. Nica shivered at the idea. He hadn't looked like a king in his tattered, blood-stained clothes. Yet, there had been a ferociousness in his eyes when he'd spotted her that spoke otherwise. For a second, she wished she could save him. Nica shook her head. What an impossible idea.

Lady Angeline began a conversation in Jarisan and Nica answered each question easily. Thoughts of the prisoner lingered and she shoved herself out of the chair and moved to the open window in an attempt to escape the images that haunted her. There was no way to save him. She needed to get away from here and save herself.

In response to Lady Angeline's questions, Nica rattled off the names of Jarisan historical figures as she gazed out onto the village just beyond the guarded walls of the castle. Small puffs of dust, like dirty grey clouds, came from behind the loaded carts of vendors as they made their way to and from the town center for market. Dogs barked and in the distance, laughter rang out. Somewhere closer, the cry of a baby cut through the air.

Lady Angeline switched languages in the middle of the conversation and began speaking in Narsgedian. Surprised, Nica glanced over her shoulder at the tutor, but the older woman continued so Nica followed her lead.

A surge of excitement welled inside her. She couldn't believe the day was finally here. That it was almost time for all of the planning she and Toppen had done to become reality. She pushed the heavy, diamond shaped panes of the window open enough to lean out on the stone sill. The cool fall air felt refreshing against her skin. It felt like freedom.

"Tell me what you see out the window," Lady Angeline said. "In Narsgedian."

Nica began to describe the village below: A church with a single towering steeple, the fountain in the town square, the market area where the vendors parked their wagons to sell their wares and of course, the clock tower. Her eyes soaked in the familiar sights, as though to store them in her memory forever.

"Excellent!"

Startled at the exclamation, Nica looked over her shoulder to find Lady Angeline beaming at her.

"Wherever did you learn the dicadian rhythms of the Narsgededon forest people?" The tutor sounded incredulous. "I don't believe I've heard five people in my lifetime who weren't natives be able to enunciate the ariatic structure of the harmonic contrast like that."

Nica's lips twisted in a grin. "Why, Lady Angeline, you shouldn't be so modest. You know you've taught me everything I know."

The tutor raised her eyebrows. "Is that so?"

"Well, I suppose the songs that Y'ong Toobu used to sing might have something to do with it, too," Nica said, turning away to hide her smile.

"Y'ong Toobu?" Lady Angeline questioned.

"She was a maid when I was young. My father captured her in the Narsgededon and brought her back to Ravensfell." Nica's voice dropped. "I suppose she amused him—like keeping a wild animal for a pet." She sighed. "At the time she seemed very big to me but I realize now she was not much more than a girl herself."

Nica's vision clouded with memories. "She must have been very scared. All alone, taken away from her family." She tried to shrug away the guilt she still carried at not being able to help the girl. "We were two lonely girls without their mothers. So Y'ong Toobu taught me songs of the forest."

Lady Angeline's voice was soft. "And what became of this young woman? I've never seen her."

The weight of her memories pressed down on her and Nica wished she didn't have to answer. "She fell from the turret wall and died." Nica whispered the lie. Y'ong Toobu had jumped. And it was her father's fault.

Lady Angeline drew her breath in with a soft hiss, then spoke in a firm tone. "That is a sad story, but I'm pleased you've retained so much of the language. You have a special gift. We will now go on to Ajertaukan."

Nica repeated the phrases after her tutor. Though she liked to tease the other woman, Nica had to admit she enjoyed the praise Lady Angeline lavished on her for her ability with languages. In all honesty, Nica didn't see how anyone could find the subject difficult.

Lady Angeline's voice interrupted Nica's thoughts. "That will conclude our languages lesson for today. Remember to work on the guttural emphasis when in the second conjugative. Next time we will stretch you a bit and start work on Corsosh."

Nica glanced at her teacher from beneath her lashes. She didn't want to give the woman the impression she cared about the topic, but Corsosh? A twinge of regret twisted her stomach. That might be interesting, but she would be gone before the lessons began.

The Isles of Corsock were a bit mysterious. They didn't share a trading relationship with Sartis as the islands were located far away in the southern part of the Sea of Nephalon and they did most of their trading with nearby Singaty. It was rumored however, that Mosaba had befriended the ruthless pirate Canja, who had claimed one of the islands as his own.

The pungent smell of a roasting pig drifted on the wind and caught Nica's attention, bringing her back to the present. She inhaled deeply to savor the aroma. From her viewpoint she could see servants walking the pathways within the gates, meeting with traders and vendors. The sun burnished skin of the farming Ajertauks from across the mountains was always easy to recognize when they came to negotiate the sale of their abundant crops.

Nica caught sight of dark-haired Philicia, her father's latest mistress, walking with a companion along the garden pathway below, their heads bent together in conversation. She watched as the woman stopped, her hand resting on the young man's sleeve, a coy smile on her face. As their heads moved apart Nica inhaled sharply. Philicia was talking with Jonn Shanks. As though feeling the weight of her gaze, Shanks looked up and locked eyes with her. Embarrassed she'd been caught spying on them, Nica pulled back from the window. But not before she saw his lips mouth the word 'wait'.

ica eased the door closed behind her, careful not to let the iron latch clang against the frame of the lock. The last thing she wanted to do was alert the guards. She carried a large canvas bag on her back and the uncomfortable pressure of the buckle dug into her spine as she moved on tiptoe down the hallway.

Her father and his men were heading north to cross over the Great Divide—the huge canyon that split the continent north and south between the lands of Sartis and Jarisa—and continue on toward HighGarden Palace in LaBricé.

Nica patted her pocket where she'd hidden the map, reassuring herself once again she hadn't forgotten it. She and Toppen planned to go the opposite direction of her father and his men and take the southern sliver across the Great Divide, then head along the coast of Jarisa to reach Pont d'Suree where the University was located. They were counting on Nica's ability with the Jarisan language to talk their way out of any sticky situations that might arise.

As she tiptoed down the hall, Shanks' warning not to leave Sartis echoed in her head. Nica quickened her pace as though to outrun his words. She'd heard nothing more of the prisoner. Had she not seen the battered man with her own eyes she wouldn't have known the king of Jarisa was in the castle, so efficient was his banishment to the dungeons. Once again she suppressed a guilty twinge. She couldn't shake the feeling that she should somehow stop the persecution being meted out by her father's orders.

The hallway lanterns were dimmed for the night but the three-quarter moon cast a wash of blue light through the windows. Nica moved quickly through the stone corridors, confident of which hallways to take this time of night to avoid running into the guards. Her booted feet were silent as she hurried down the stairs. She slipped out a side door and headed for the stable.

Dim shadows filled the barn, swallowing her whole as she entered, yet it wasn't enough to stop the erratic pounding of her heart. This would be the tricky part—to take a horse without the stable master hearing her. She hurried to the far end of the stables and entered a stall where a horse nickered in greeting. Nica's breath came in small hiccups as she saddled the animal with quick, efficient movements. If she were caught now it would be very difficult to explain why she was taking a horse out alone in the dead of night. She tried not to imagine Mosaba's reaction should she be caught. She really didn't want to think about what he would do.

Nica led the horse out of the stall, his hooves quiet against the hard-packed dirt floor. She pulled herself into the saddle, glad for the black valote pants that she had thought to wear.

"Let's go, boy," she said softly as she urged her mount toward the stable exit. As they passed a nearby stall an alarmed whinny filled the air. Several other whinnies and snorts answered. Nica urged her horse to a quicker pace and glanced over her shoulder toward the stable master's sleeping quarters. To her horror, candlelight flickered to life in his window.

She kicked the mare into a run.

"You there! Stop!"

Nica bent low over the horse's neck as they raced from the large barn. As if sensing her uneasiness the horse spooked at more than one shadow blown by the night wind, making it difficult to keep her seat. Behind her, shouts sounded in the night. By the light of the pale moon, Nica steered the horse though the small orchard toward the hidden gate, leaning low over his neck. When they reached the arbor the horse shied and refused to enter the shadowed walkway, prancing in an erratic rhythm. Desperate, Nica slid out of the saddle and grabbed the horse's reins in a tight grip under its chin.

"C'mon boy, there's nothing to be afraid of." She spoke in a low, soothing tone, fighting the urge to jerk the horse through the arched passageway to the vine-hidden door. She cooed and clucked and with the whites of his eyes showing, the horse slowing entered the covered walkway, his ears flat against his head.

Once they reached the end of the arbor it only took a moment to sweep the vines aside and push the door open. Sensing freedom the horse bolted through the small opening to the other side, almost jerking the reins free from Nica's grip.

Outside the gate, Nica clambered back into the saddle. She was far enough away from the sentries posted along the parapet to be seen. She kicked her horse into a gallop and raced away from the castle. She was free! The big hood of her dark cloak flew back as she rode south. Toppen was going to be waiting for her at the fork in the road that led toward the sea port of Galeron.

Her heart pounded in time with her horse's hooves against the hard-packed dirt road. It was a long twenty minute ride before Nica reached their meeting place. She pulled her horse to a stop, conscious that her own shortness of breath seemed to match his heaving sides as she peered into the dark shadows of the surrounding trees. She searched for any sign of Toppen—but there was nothing. A wave of worry flooded over her. Had she arrived first? Had Toppen run into trouble and been delayed?

Nearby bushes rattled with movement. With an uncomfortable twist of her stomach Nica reached for the dagger hidden in her belt as she wondered what beast lay hidden there.

"You've got the map?"

Nica jumped at the sound of Toppen's voice. His elongated shadow swathed her in darkness as he left the shelter of a Junbutgen tree.

"Yes," she choked.

He frowned. "Are you all right?"

"You surprised me, that's all."

Toppen smiled and urged his horse close enough to pull her hood back up. The backs of his fingers lingered on the skin of her cheek. "Let's check the route one more time."

Nica pulled the map from the pocket inside her cloak and unfolded the parchment, smoothing the stiff creases. The wind gusted around them and blew the corners, making it difficult to read. He reached over and held one corner, balancing it between the two of them.

"We're right here." She pointed. "If we follow this trail we can reach the southernmost sliver in about four hours." Her finger traced a path along the dark brown color of the Great Divide. "My father's group is headed north, toward Jorcardan. There's a bigger sliver there that stretches across the divide. One that shouldn't be guarded." She glanced at Toppen to gauge his reaction. "I think we need to stay as far away from LaBricé as we can, especially now that Jacoby has been captured. I'm sure there are soldiers everywhere looking for him."

"Yes." Toppen nodded. "We don't do dare go all the way down into Ry'dontt and risk being seen. We'd be trapped there." His finger followed a trail on the page. "Once we cross, let's head down here toward Mar'ligaan and then take the route along the Cliffs of Seniesta back around to Pont d'Suree."

"Five days, you think?" Nica said.

"If all goes well." Toppen grinned, his eyes glowing with excitement. "Five days to freedom." He leaned close and before she knew what he was planning his lips claimed hers. She pulled back in surprise, but Toppen never blinked. He smiled into her eyes. "Five days until we start our new life."

Nica forced a smile as she re-folded the map and slipped it back inside the fabric layers of her dark cloak. She wished she had the same confidence as Toppen. Once she was further away from her father she would feel better, she told herself. Safer.

"Let's go, then," Toppen said. "This storm is coming up fast. We need to get as far as we can tonight." He gave his horse a nudge and they took off at a gallop.

THEY'D BEEN RIDING through the dark in a drenching wind-blown rain for what felt like hours when Toppen signaled for Nica to stop. The wool of her cape had repelled the rain at first, but over time water had soaked through the material, chilling her. She was shivering as she pulled to a stop next to him.

To their right stretched the Great Divide, a gaping chasm of rock that split the continent, providing the border between Jarisa and Sartis. The wind howled with an eerie moan as it blew across the great canyon.

"The sliver where we need to cross is just ahead." Toppen pointed into the shadows.

Nica edged her mount closer to the edge of the canyon, peering through the darkness trying to judge the drop as well as locate the sliver. She had read that in some places the canyon was so vast that the other side shimmered like a distant mirage. But in a few spots the canyon narrowed to a stone's throw. It was here that thin 'slivers' or land bridges existed, allowing passage, albeit treacherous, to the other side. She could barely make out a crooked finger of land stretching into open space.

"This is the only sliver south of Berjerac." Toppen said. "We should be able to cross here unseen. Unless, of course," his voice tightened, "your father has scouts watching."

Nica's breath caught in her throat. They were at war—of course her father would have scouts out. Why hadn't she thought of that before? She searched the surrounding trees for any movement.

"Let's watch for a bit," she whispered. "If I'm caught and returned to my father as a runaway I'll never see the light of day again." She nudged her horse into the dark shadows under a tree and dropped her reins. She shivered against the chill of the night wind and rubbed her arms, trying to regain some warmth.

"Well...if we're going to stop....here, hold these." Toppen handed his reins up to Nica and slid off his horse.

She looked at him with a frown.

"Nature calls. I'll be right back."

"*Now?*"

Toppen shrugged and disappeared into the trees.

Wind-blown clouds suddenly eclipsed the moon and the night grew darker. Nica's teeth chattered as she waited for Toppen to return, her eyes searching the night for any kind of threat. In the distance, thunder rumbled.

A shadow moved in the trees to her right and Nica heaved a sigh of relief that Toppen had returned. It only took a split-second before she realized the shadow was on horseback. Someone else was approaching.

The silhouette of a horse and rider emerged from the shelter of the forest, headed in her direction. Alarmed, Nica twisted around in her saddle to look for Toppen but he was still hidden among the trees.

"Toppen," she called quietly. *"Toppen."*

No answer. She was alone.

The dark figure rode a black mount, making them blend with the night. He rode toward her at an alarming pace. As he came closer, Nica could discern there were two riders on the horse, though the person in back rode in an oddly limp fashion. They appeared to be headed for the land bridge.

A blast of wind cut through the trees making the branches sigh and sway. Charging forward, the rider pulled his mount up at the last possible second to view the sliver before he began his crossing.

Without warning a bolt of lightning split the night sky, the brilliant flash illuminating the area as if it were day. The stranger's horse reared with a wild cry and turned an anxious circle. In that instant Nica's gaze met that of the rider. She recognized Jonn Shanks as though she looked at him from across a well-lit room. Then the lightning abated and the night went black again.

Nica sat frozen as he approached.

His voice was harsh. "What are you doing out here?"

"I…"

"Whose horse is that?" Shanks tipped his head toward Toppen's mount. "Why didn't you wait?" His face was as angry as the thunderstorm that surrounded them. He was soaked through, his hair plastered to his head. She could see a bloody cut along his jaw.

Nica's stomach churned. Would Shanks try to return her to her father?

"What's going on here?" Toppen called in a low voice as he emerged from the forest.

Shanks looked him up and down with a murderous glare. "Who are you?"

Nica clutched her reins tighter.

"Who's asking?" Toppen stopped and returned his glare, his hands clenched at his side.

"Stop it," Nica snapped. She stared at Shanks. "What are *you* doing out here?"

The young soldier didn't hesitate. "I need your help."

"Sorry, mate, but you're on your own," Toppen said.

Nica pointed to the body behind Shanks. "Who have you got there?" The limp way his passenger rode suggested he was either injured or unconscious. The heavy shrouding told her that his identity was important. Only one prisoner of any value was being held within her father's dungeon.

Shanks' gaze held hers. "I think you already know."

Nica shivered. She didn't want to know what Shanks involved in. Nor did she want to be part of it.

"I'm being followed," he said. "I need to lay a false trail or we'll be caught."

"But why?" She asked. "Why would you risk your life for this?"

"I don't have time to explain." Shanks slid from his horse and grabbed Nica's hand. "All you have to do is take him across the sliver." He spoke in a low tone. "Others are waiting for him there." He grabbed the finger of his leather glove with his teeth and pulled his hand free. He slid a crested ring from his little finger and handed it up to Nica. "Take this." He closed her fingers around the ring, the metal still warm from his skin. "Ask for Sebande. Tell him I sent you. If there are any questions show him the ring. That should guarantee you safe passage."

"What exactly is going on here?" Toppen demanded.

Nica bit her lip, uncertain.

Shanks ignored Toppen. He moved so fast, Nica was caught unaware. He cupped her face with his hands and held her with gentle strength. For a moment she thought he was going to kiss her. Instead he looked into her eyes with a fierce intensity. "Nica, *trust me*, you are doing the right thing. Never question that."

"Stop that," Toppen roared, and jumped forward to pull at Shanks' arm.

Shanks moved with blinding speed. In one smooth flick of his wrist he had the point of his blade at Toppen's throat.

"Don't ever tell me what to do," Shanks growled in a low voice. "Now get on your horse." Toppen scrambled to obey.

Sheathing his sabre, Shanks reached up and untied the cloaked figure from the saddle. With a muffled groan the man slid limply off the horse into his arms. Shanks carried him to Toppen's horse and heaved the dead weight up behind the winemaker's apprentice.

"What are you doing?" Toppen cried, trying to move his horse away.

Shanks grunted against the weight sagging down on him and swore.

"Toppen, don't!" Nica pulled hard on the horse's reins she still held in her hand.

Toppen gaped at Nica. "What?"

"We have to help him."

"Who is he?" Toppen asked. "And who is this?" he asked, trying to lean away from the limp form settling against his back. "What is going on? We can't be delayed by this Nica!"

Shanks flicked a rope around Toppen with a snap, causing another stream of protests, while he tied the dark figure to the younger man. Satisfied the silent passenger was safely secured Shanks turned back to Nica. "Hide by the clock tower in LaBricé. Watch for me there. Remain unseen until I arrive." A play of emotions crossed his face that Nica couldn't identify. "*Trust me, Nica,*" he finished in a harsh whisper.

He didn't wait for her reply but vaulted on to his horse and wheeled around. "I've got to keep moving. Those that follow me won't give up easily. Go now," he barked, then disappeared into the darkness.

"What the...." Toppen watched Shanks' departure then swiveled around to glare at Nica.

"Follow me." She yanked her hood back over her head and put her heels hard into her horse's side. As they neared the edge of the chasm, Nica's horse balked at walking out onto the thin, jagged strip of land. Though it was difficult to see through the darkness Nica could sense the precipitous drop of the canyon on each side of the crooked sliver of rock. She was beginning to wonder if she needed to dismount and lead the animal across when the horse began a tentative crossing.

The trail was a nerve-wracking thread of rocky path that wound through open air to the other side of the Great Divide. Even in the cold wind and rain of the storm, Nica could feel her palms sweating within her leather gloves. She gripped the saddle so hard with her knees that the muscles in her legs ached as the wind buffeted her, whistling its way down the canyon toward the sea. What had Shanks gotten them into? For whatever they were involved in was, at best, surely treason.

Nica let out a sigh of relief as they reached the end of the narrow sliver. She glanced back over her shoulder to find Toppen on her heels.

"Now what?" he asked.

"This way, I think." Nica tried to speak with confidence but even to her ears her words sounded weak and unsure. She didn't want to say she had no idea. It had been at her insistence that they'd helped Shanks. The weight of his ring was heavy on her middle finger where she had slid the band. She steered her horse to the right, heading north toward LaBricé, trying to convince herself she was doing the right thing.

"Halt!"

Nica jerked to a stop as she searched the darkness. Men on horses surrounded them.

"Who goes there?" The words were spoken in guttural Jarisan.

Chills ran up her arms like live spiders.

"I must speak to Sebande." Without thinking Nica spoke in Sartish. She heard the deep grumble of voices in the darkness around her and realized her mistake. She quickly repeated herself in Jarisan, *"Eso wa'se' ena Sebande."* For the first time she was truly grateful for her knowledge of the Jarisan language. She heard Toppen swear under his breath behind her.

A Jarisan soldier on horseback approached them, his dark skin providing additional camouflage in the night. He drew close enough that Nica could see his sword pointed unwaveringly at her heart. "I am Sebande."

Over his shoulder other soldiers emerged from behind the dark trees. Several had razor sharp arrows mounted and cocked on small crossbows, aimed in their direction.

"*Era'a shi'na ma. Le shom'baaun poa bi la'* Shanks." Nica spoke in Jarisan, hoping they understood that the King was the package she spoke of delivering. The soldier's weapons never wavered.

"Shanks?" The soldier who had identified himself as Sebande tilted his head, trying to see Nica's face hidden within the hood of her cloak.

"Yes." Nica nodded.

"What package?' His eyes were suspicious as they flicked to Toppen and back.

"There." Nica pointed at the shadowy lump behind Toppen. She could see the alarm on Toppen's pale face. She turned back to the soldier who didn't look much older than Shanks. "We must not be delayed. It's a matter of life or death."

The Jarisan soldier motioned to another soldier to watch Nica then moved his horse forward and slid his sword against Toppen's chest. The man called a command over his shoulder to the waiting soldiers.

"Toppen, don't move or they'll shoot." Nica warned.

Eyeing Toppen carefully, the young man reached up with the tip of his blade and yanked the hood from the passenger's face. The soldier swore when the face of the Jarisan king was revealed. A loud murmur went through the waiting soldiers as they recognized him.

As the passenger's face was revealed, Toppen jerked his head around to look at Nica, his alarmed eyes wide with questions and fear. The soldier jumped forward to cut the older, injured man down.

"Watch his arm!" Nica called out. "And his leg is wounded also." Sebande gave her a suspicious look but slowed his movements to accommodate any injuries. He yelled at two of his comrades to assist in lifting the king down.

"He needs medical attention. You'll find a doctor?" Nica asked.

"Yes." Another man grunted an answer as they transported the wounded man. The king groaned as they moved him but did not regain consciousness. Relinquishing his hold on the sovereign, Sebande stepped toward Nica.

"Who did you say sent you?" Once again he peered curiously into the folds of her hooded cloak.

Nica took a deep breath and looked him straight in the eyes. "Jonn Shanks." She rubbed the ring on her finger through her glove, hoping it would be enough to keep them alive.

The young man's look turned to one of confused surprise. "Can we provide you with an escort?"

Nica shook her head, pulling her hood a little closer. "Thank you, but no. We have other business we must attend to yet this night." She pulled her reins to the left and urged her horse back onto the trail. The faster they could get out of here, the better.

"*Appen' dichi*," Sebande said with authority. Like a wall moving, the soldiers shifted their horses to each side, creating a passageway for them.

Nica urged her mount forward, relief bubbling inside like water from a well.

"No! Stop them! Don't let them go!"

Shanks' voice was easily recognizable. His Jarisan words slashed through the night with the sharpness of a knife. Prickly fingers of fear clawed at her stomach as a wave of suspicion washed over her. Something was wrong. She shouldn't be part of this.

Nica kicked her horse hard but before she could break past the wall of men, the soldiers shifted again and blocked her path. Sebande urged his horse directly at hers, his arms stretched out to grab her reins. Frightened by the aggressive approach of the other horses, Nica's mount gave a wild snort and reared. Nica squeezed hard with her knees and clawed at the saddle horn to retain her seat but the horse was too spooked to control.

With a cry, Nica lost her grip and fell backwards. She heard Toppen's shout of alarm before her head hit the ground with a sickening *crack* and everything went black.

ica's eyes fluttered open. Strong arms stretched past on each side and gripped the reins in front of her. She looked down to see her hands were bound at the wrists. Her head ached and she was disoriented. It took a moment to remember what had happened.

"Don't speak." The voice was low and deadly serious. "Especially Sartish."

The events of the night rushed back to her and an image of Shanks' face swam before her eyes. *Traitor.*

"We've been ordered to take you to LaBricé. If you value your life, become invisible."

Nica didn't reply. Shanks had betrayed her. After she had betrayed her own father to help him. She fought the tears that unexpectedly welled in her eyes. And what had become of Toppen? Nica jerked around, immediately regretting her movement as pain sliced through her head. She searched the shadows for the other soldiers to see if Toppen was among them, but instead of the troop of men she expected, there were only two others, one on each side, slightly behind them. Each cradled armed crossbows as they rode.

"Your friend is taking a different route."

Suddenly his name came to her. Sebande. That was who Shanks had told her to ask for. He was the one who had captured her. Nica faced forward, glad for the oversized hood that covered her face. She gripped the hard leather of the saddle to hold herself upright. She didn't want to touch her captor.

The storm that had raged in Sartis was just working its way to the Jarisan side of the Great Divide. The cold wind pierced her damp clothes and Nica shivered. She clenched her teeth—as much to stop their chattering as to stop the fear that bubbled in her stomach from exploding through her mouth. She could not be returned to face the cruelty of Mosaba. She needed to find a way to escape.

THE FAINT GLOW of dawn was on the horizon when they reached LaBricé. As they neared what had to be Jacoby's palace Nica could see great stone walls lined with torches to light the night. Rather than approach directly Sebande followed a path through the forest that led around the perimeter of the huge structure.

"Declare yourself!" A voice rang out.

"Sebande Vatier—on business for the king." Sebande spoke with authority.

The guard must have recognized the soldier for there was a scrambling at the gate and one of two great doors swung open for them to enter.

"Keep your head down and your mouth shut," he growled low in her ear. "Do not speak or show your face under *any* circumstances." Nica bowed her head in assent, making sure the hood of her cloak shadowed her features.

"Ho, Sebande, what have you caught in the forest tonight?" A jovial voice boomed towards them. "Only the forest sprites would be out on a night like this. Is it a wood wench?"

Nica dared a peek out from under the edge of her hood. A large pot-bellied man with a leather belt straining around his overflowing stomach was closing the tall door with one hand, a crossbow held easily in his other meaty hand. He wore a white shirt covered by a red vest. His legs, in brown breeches, bowed as though bending under the great weight of his stomach.

"Tis not mine," Sebande replied. "It's a sickly boy Shanks chanced upon. Promised the dying mother he'd give him to Becknah for a cure."

"Shanks is here?" The big man's tone turned hopeful.

"Not yet. He handed me the boy and said he'd be back."

"Sickly, you say?" The guard's voice turned cautious. "How sickly? Will it spread?"

"Can't say for sure. Wouldn't touch him though. I'm going to keep him wrapped up until Becknah has a look." Sebande urged his horse past the guard. "Keep it quiet for now. I don't want a panic."

Nica heard the man grumble some response but she couldn't understand him. Her head throbbed with pain, making it hard not only to think straight but to understand their Jarisan words. The horse stopped.

What now? She didn't have to wonder long. Sebande dismounted then reached up and put his large hands around her waist.

"Not a word," he said in a low voice. Before she could protest he pulled her from the saddle and threw her over his shoulder like a piece of meat. Even though she couldn't be seen, her face burned with embarrassment. She debated about kicking him to escape but there was no one here who would help her. She gritted her teeth as his shoulder dug into her stomach. Sebande would pay for this humiliation—as would Shanks. One way or the other, she would get even.

Nica could hear Sebande's boots tapping on stone steps as he lugged her down a flight of stairs. The night became darker as they moved into some sort of passageway. She heard the creak of a door swinging open and saw the man kick the wooden planks closed with his booted foot.

With a grunt, he swung her back over his shoulder and set her on her feet. The rush of blood to her head made Nica dizzy and she swayed. Sebande reached out a hand to steady her but Nica pulled away and took a few shaky steps toward the stone wall, where she put out a hand to support herself.

She looked from under her hood at the small room where they now stood. Light from the torches out in the hallway cast a weak ray of illumination through the bars in the upper part of the doorway.

The room looked like a prison cell. Alarmed, she turned to the young man who stood before her.

For the first time since her capture she could see him clearly. He was as tall as her father, his skin the warm color of cinnamon. The bulge of his shoulders could be seen through the soft leather of his jacket and his eyes were as black as the long hair tied behind his head. He did not look happy. Sebande held up his hand to stop her from speaking and took a step toward her.

Nica backed closer to the wall.

"I don't know why you're here and I don't care," he said in a low voice. "I told Shanks I would guard your door—" he peered at her through the shadows of her cloak— "and that's what I'm going to do." Without another word, Sebande exited and pulled the door closed. Nica heard an iron rod slide into place on the other side.

She was locked in.

Chapter Ten

itting alone at the huge head table within the Great Hall, Jaaniyah eyed her father's empty chair. She ached with worry. What were they doing to him? Mosaba was rumored to be especially vicious. Was her father still alive? Footsteps echoed on the stone floor behind her as someone approached.

"M'lady. Remain calm." Becknah's voice was low in her ear. "We have word that your father has somehow escaped from Sartis but is gravely wounded."

Jaaniyah swiveled around and gripped the older man's arm. She started to speak but he held his hand up to stop her.

"He is with our men. He is back in Jarisa. They've secured him in a small abandoned cottage, just this side of the southernmost sliver. He's too sick to be moved. I've sent Thistlewaite to tend to him."

Joy coursed through Jaaniyah. Her father lived! She started to open her mouth but Becknah stopped her.

"We cannot speak of this, M'lady. Your father's very life depends on our ability to keep his location secret until he is well enough to be brought back to HighGarden." His words held a clear warning. "Mosaba will be livid with rage at the king's escape. We must be prepared for any kind of attack. You will need to be especially careful."

"I can't go see him?"

"No." Becknah shook his head. "Neither of us can go. It's possible we're being watched." He glanced over his shoulder to make sure no one was within earshot. "We can't take the chance that the Devil of Sartis learns of his location, for if he captures your father again he will surely torture him to death."

Jaaniyah cringed at the man's words. "Why do you think he spared him?"

"Mosaba must believe your father has important information, or else he would have simply killed him. I'm sure he never dreamed that Jacoby could escape." Becknah covered Jaaniyah's slim hand with his own. "The healer will know how to improve the king's health enough so he can travel. It should only be a matter of weeks before we can bring him home."

Sweeping his long robe to the side, he slid into the chair next to Jaaniyah. "I've discussed the situation at length with Eisle Heathron. We are in agreement that we need to make Mosaba think the king is back safe within the fortifications of the palace. We don't want him looking for your father in a place where we can't defend him."

"But how will you do that?" Jaaniyah whispered.

"We're going to pretend to sneak one of Heathron's soldiers in tonight, masquerading as the wounded king. He'll be wrapped in bloody blankets and carried on a sling. We're hoping that word will leak out to Mosaba that the king has returned to the palace, though no one will actually be occupying the royal suite. We'll keep the doors guarded though, so people believe the king is in his chambers. Eventually, we'll announce his presence and the fact that he will remain in seclusion to heal."

Jaaniyah nodded. Her mind rushed ahead to the possibilities. Her father lived. Relief swept through her like a summer breeze.

"You'll be informed when the imposter has been delivered so you can be seen going in and out of your father's chambers. You, I and Heathron will be the only ones who are allowed access."

"What about Thistlewaite?" Jaaniyah asked. "Won't people be expecting the healer to be here if the king is really here?"

Becknah's brow creased in a frown. "Of course, Thistlewaite will need to be seen." He drummed his ringed fingers on the table. "I'll need to give it more thought." He rose from the chair.

"Becknah," Jaaniyah said. "Do you know how my father escaped from Mosaba?"

The old man looked down, his grey eyes steady on her. "He had help, you can be sure of that. We'll learn more of the details with the arrival of one of our spies."

Her voice lightened. "Is Jonn Shanks coming?"

"So I've been informed." The old man pulled his robes close. With a short bow, he strode away.

"JAANI."

The word was just a whisper but Jaaniyah's eyes flew open. She fought the clinging web of sleep, trying to sort through her confusion. The room was dark, with only a sliver of light from the moon casting a narrow path across the floor. A dark figure knelt beside her bed. She sat up with a jerk and pushed herself away from the shadowy form, letting out a shriek of terror.

"Jaaniyah, it's me," he whispered, reaching out a hand to calm her.

She drew a deep breath. "Jonn?"

"Yes."

"Jonn." She scrambled on her hands and knees closer to him. "How did you get in here? Have you seen my father? How bad is he?"

He put a finger to his lips. "Shhhh. He's alive. I won't lie to you—he's badly injured and has been mistreated, but Thistlewaite is with him. If we can keep him sheltered for a few weeks the healer says he'll have a good chance for recovery."

"Oh, thank the Ancients," she whispered. She squinted through the shadows, trying to see his face. "Was it you? Did you get him out?"

"I had help," Shanks said. "That's what I need to talk to you about."

"A reward? Do they want a reward for their bravery? I will gladly pay." Jaaniyah clutched at his arm. "How much?"

"It's not about a reward. It's something else. I need to show you… something." Shanks' voice sounded hesitant.

A wave of foreboding washed over her. "What is it?"

"I can't tell you. I have to show you. We need to go now, while the castle sleeps."

Jaaniyah hesitated. Could this be a trap? She clutched the blankets close to her chest and sat back. She couldn't think of any place that he could possibly need her to go to in the dead of night. She searched the shadowed angles of his face for an answer as she contemplated his request. She trusted Jonn Shanks, Jaaniyah reminded herself. More important, her father trusted Shanks. "Where?"

"It's not far. Get dressed. Cover your head so you'll be harder to recognize." Shanks pushed off the bed and stood up. "I'll wait outside the door."

Jaaniyah watched his dark silhouette slide out the door and took a deep breath to still her heart. She considered what her father would do in this moment. Making up her mind, she threw the bedcovers to the side and slid out of bed.

The stones were cold against her feet, hastening her dash to the armoire. She pulled a long, hooded cape from the depths of the closet and tugged the garment around her shoulders, grateful for its warmth against the chill night air. With the oversized hood covering her head she pushed her feet into a pair of soft leather shoes and hurried to the door.

"I'm ready," she whispered.

Shanks emerged from the shadows. "Follow me."

They wound through the corridors amid the dimmed torches, sticking close to the shadows. Shanks took her through back hallways and down stairwells she hadn't traveled since she was a child. She followed his broad back wondering how he'd come to know the castle so well.

As they moved lower within the building, they passed an occasional guard. Shanks identified himself in a low voice as they approached, before a warning could be called out. The guards all knew him and none stopped them to question his purpose.

Jaaniyah could feel their curious eyes on her shrouded figure as she moved through the hallways behind Shanks like a ghost and wondered who they thought she was.

It was a good ten minutes of walking before Shanks paused at a stalwart door with a big iron lock hanging loose at the handle.

"Where are we?" she whispered. They were in a part of the castle she didn't recognize. She fought the ribbon of fear that threaded its way up her throat threatening to choke her.

"We're in a little-used part of the prison," Shanks said as he pushed the plank door open with his shoulder.

"The prison?" Jaaniyah echoed. She took a deep breath of the damp, fetid air and immediately regretted it. A note of panic crept into her voice. "Why are we here?"

"The person that helped rescue your father is here. You need to thank them personally." The door swung inward with a low groan. Steps led down into a long hallway that stretched away, lit by torches hung upon the walls. Shanks moved forward through the door.

Jaaniyah balked.

"Why couldn't you bring this person to me?" she asked. "Why are you holding them in prison? Have they done something criminal?"

Jonn Shanks looked at her. "We're almost there, M'lady." He reached out his hand. "Jaani," he added softly, "trust me."

Even in the dim light Jaaniyah could see the beseeching look in his eyes. Her heart gave a thump for a different reason. Jonn Shanks was not like the others in her father's band of warriors. She often found herself watching him, his easy smile, the friendly camaraderie he had with the others. Though young, more than once she'd heard the chambermaids talking of the women he'd courted and it'd been with a jealous twinge that she'd realized she wasn't immune to his charms either.

Jaaniyah reached forward and slid her hand into his. She welcomed the warmth and security that his fingers offered. She gave a nod and followed him down the steps.

Their footsteps echoed with a hollow sound as he led her down the long hallway and around a turn in the passageway. Up ahead a guard stood before a cell. Warned by their footsteps he was looking their way, expecting them.

"Sebande." Shanks nodded at the guard. "Thank you." He peered through the bars in the door into the dark shadows of the cell. "All is well?"

The guard's eyes flitted from Shanks to Jaaniyah's shrouded face then back to Shanks again. Jaaniyah wondered at the look in his eyes. Curiosity? Caution? Fear?

"She's alive," Sebande said.

She? A woman had helped save her father? Jaaniyah peered into the cell. Who could this be, that would risk her life for another?

"Sebande," Shanks said, "I need you to guard the entrance. No one, I repeat, *no one* can be allowed down here. *De'preche?*"

Sebande nodded.

"Thank you, my friend. I know you're tired. We won't be long and then you'll get the rest you need." With a nod and a hesitant bow toward Jaaniyah, Sebande moved away, his boots tapping down the corridor the way they had just come.

"Jonn…"

Shanks held up his palm to stop her. "Wait for just a second." He reached forward, slid the bolt free and pulled the barred door open. Jaaniyah stepped back to allow him room to enter the cell.

"Nica," Shanks said softly. He reached up for a torch and took a tentative step into the room, holding the light high. "Nica, it's Shanks."

Jaaniyah peered curiously over his shoulder. So far the dark lump in the corner hadn't moved or given any indication that it was even alive. Unsure of what to expect, Jaaniyah stood poised to run.

Shanks placed the torch in a holder on the wall and moved to stand in the center of the cell. He held his hands out from his sides as if in surrender. "I need to explain."

Jaaniyah's brow etched down into a frown. There was a note in Shanks' voice that she had never heard before.

"Can you stand?" he said. "I want you to meet someone."

Jaaniyah took a step back in alarm. She was not going to walk into that jail cell under any condition. What game was Shanks playing at?

"We want to thank you for saving the king."

"THIS IS THE BLOODY THANKS I GET?" The shrouded figure flew out of the corner and launched itself at Shanks' head. "BEING LOCKED IN A FILTHY PRISON CELL?" Shanks dodged her fists and put his arms up to protect his head.

Jaaniyah stepped back, shocked at the Sartish words pouring out of the prisoner.

"I risked my life for you! And you're nothing more than a bloody *spy.*"

Fast as a cat, Shanks reached out and wrapped his arms around the prisoner's upper body, pinning her flailing arms to her side.

"Stop it...you're not going to..." she wriggled and strained, trying to break free. The heel of her boot connected hard with his shin.

Shanks released her with a grunt of pain and took a wary step back.

The prisoner jerked away and hurried to the wall, her chest heaving with anger and exertion. Her hood had flown back in their struggle and now lay flat against her back. The blond highlights in her hair shone in the light of the torch as she glared daggers at Shanks.

From the hallway, Jaaniyah moved forward, craning her neck to see where the wild creature had run after attacking Shanks. Jaaniyah sucked in her breath with a loud gasp as she laid eyes on the girl who stood in the corner with fists clenched and a snarl on her face, ready to attack again.

"*Asa Sabra*," Jaaniyah whispered. The world started spinning out of control. She staggered against the door and reached out blindly to catch herself.

The girl in the cell had Jaaniyah's face.

They were identical.

As Jaaniyah banged into the door, Nica jerked around.

Shanks relaxed his defensive position. He stepped toward Jaaniyah and slid an arm around her waist to support her, pulling her into the cell. With a gentle hand, he reached up and slid her hood back.

"Nica," he said, "I'd like you to meet your sister, Jaaniyah Jacoby."

Chapter Eleven

he silence that fell within the room was so brittle it seemed a sharp word would shatter the air around them into a million shards like pieces of glass. The fight drained out of Nica as she stared at the girl who stood next to Shanks. She had an eerie sensation of being outside her own body and looking back.

What had Shanks said? *Sister?*

The girl looked as though she, too, were having problems with her hearing. She stared at Nica with her mouth agape. It was like looking in a mirror. The same grey eyes. The same long, blond-brown hair. The same straight nose.

"Jonn," Jaaniyah finally choked out. "What is the meaning of this? My sister died as an infant."

Shanks removed his arm from Jaaniyah's waist and took a step closer to Nica centering himself between the two of them. "Was your sister a twin?"

"Yes." Her voice was faint.

"And how did she die?"

"I…I only know the stories I've been told," Jaaniyah stammered. "She drowned in the river when we were very young. It was during the Feast Day celebrations and we were under the care of a nanny."

"I'd say the nanny couldn't be trusted," Shanks said calmly. "Because the two of you are identical. You have to be sisters."

Jaaniyah narrowed her eyes at Nica. "Who are you?"

Nica forced herself to hold a level gaze even though the other girl exuded a haughty air that was intimidating. "Madanica Santos."

"Santos?" Jaaniyah repeated the name in disbelief. "Are you related to that barbarian, Mosaba Santos?"

Nica lifted her chin a notch. "He is my father."

Jaaniyah jerked her head toward Shanks. "You dare to bring Mosaba's *daughter* here?"

Shanks returned her angry gaze unperturbed. "Jaani, your father wouldn't be alive tonight if it weren't for Nica's help. It's that simple." He paused to let his words sink in. "And since Nica is clearly your sister, then you must realize that you have the *same* father. The only difference is that Nica has had the extreme misfortune to have been tortured by Mosaba all of these years."

Nica's eyes flicked to Shanks. How did he know about Mosaba?

Jaaniyah pointed at Nica. "Let me see your arm," she commanded. "Then we'll know for sure."

Nica blinked in surprise. How could this girl know of her mark?

"Show me!"

Though part of her wanted to refuse the order, Nica slid her left sleeve up and turned her wrist over to show a brown birthmark shaped like a star.

An expression of amazement crossed Jaaniyah's face. The other girl slid her own sleeve up and revealed an identical star shaped mark.

"This birthmark follows my father's lineage," Jaaniyah said in a low voice. "It's called the Star of Jarisa."

Shanks held his palms up. "I couldn't tell either of you. You'd never have believed me. The only way you would both accept the truth was to meet—face to face." He frowned at Nica. "I was going to talk to you about leaving Sartis when I returned, but apparently, you had plans that couldn't wait."

Nica struggled to absorb the shocking revelation. She was a twin—stolen and raised by Mosaba. The idea was incredible, yet at the same time, explained so much: Mosaba's dislike of her; the ever-present fear he wanted to hurt her; his insistence that she be sequestered within the walls of their castle. He hadn't kept her locked up for her own safety as he'd led her to believe. It was so she wouldn't be seen and recognized.

Another thought crashed over her. She was from Jarisa, not Sartis. She was a Jacoby. It had been her own father whom she had helped save tonight. She remembered Shanks' determined look as he had held her face between his hands. '*You are doing the right thing. Never doubt that.*' She bit her lip hard to stop the tears threatening to fall.

With unexpected suddenness, Nica's legs gave out and she sat down on the floor with a *thump*. She closed her eyes and took deep breaths, trying to regain her composure.

"Nica?" Shanks voice was gentle.

She held her hand up to stop him. It was all too much. She couldn't take anymore. Not another word. She remembered the strange the Jarisan guard had given her when they'd handed over the wounded king. The man had seen her face within the shadows of her cloak and his behavior toward her had changed. Now she understood. He had thought she was Jaaniyah.

The tension and exhaustion from the previous days were taking their toll and an odd shaking started in her legs and moved into her hands.

"Jaaniyah." Shanks seemed to understand what was happening. "We need to get Nica to your chambers and let her rest. We'll need to hide her there for a few days until we figure out what to do next."

There was a long moment of silence as Jaaniyah stared down at Nica.

"Do you trust her, Jonn?"

"Yes." He nodded. "Implicitly." His look hardened. "You can't even imagine what this girl has lived with all these years."

Jaaniyah took a step back. "Fine. How do we get her there?"

Shanks moved to Nica's side and put an arm around her back. "Can you walk?"

"Yes, of course I can walk." Nica pushed herself up from the floor and away from Shanks. But her legs continued to shake and she wondered if she really could walk out of this cell.

"I'll help you," Shanks said quietly.

"No thank you." Nica jerked away. "No doubt you'll sling me over your shoulder like a bag of flour, just like your oversized guard. My stomach still has bruises from his bony shoulder."

"Sebande carried you over his shoulder?" Shanks' voice sounded strangled as he escorted both girls out of the cell and into the hallway.

Nica glared at him. "You think that's funny, do you?" Suddenly she straightened and took a threatening step towards him. "Where's Toppen?"

Shanks expression became guarded. "He escaped."

"From twenty guards? You're lying, Shanks," she snarled. "He's dead, isn't he?"

The muscle in Shanks' jaw flexed as he contemplated her question. Finally he shrugged. "I don't know if he's dead or alive. When I sent you with Sebande, I let Toppen go. I didn't want him with the king and I have no need for a Sartish wine apprentice." Shanks' nose curled in derision. "So I gave him his horse and told him to ride as though Lucede's hounds were after him." Shanks raised his eyebrows and gave her an insolent look. "You should thank me for saving his worthless life."

Nica held his gaze for another minute, debating the truth of his answer. Finally, she nodded. "Thank you, for that, at least." She turned away and reached a hand out to the wall to steady herself as they walked down the hallway.

"Pull your hoods up," Shanks said. "We need to keep this secret to ourselves for now."

SHANKS SENT JAANIYAH with Sebande and took Nica along a back route through half-lit passages and unused stairways. They didn't speak as they walked and Nica kept her head down, afraid someone would ask her questions she couldn't answer.

She refused Shanks' arm, but her steps slowed and her chest heaved as they climbed one set of steep stairs after another.

Shanks stopped and turned to face her in the secluded stairwell, blocking the way. It reminded her of the moment he'd caught her on the turret stairs in Berjerac.

"Nica." He put a finger under her chin to raise her face. She jerked away, glaring at him. "This wasn't the way I'd planned to get you here. But when I saw you there at the edge of the sliver...' he hesitated. "I knew the soldiers were on the other side...there wasn't a lot of time... it was the only way I could think to save you."

"Save *me*?" Nica asked in surprise. "You mean you weren't being followed?"

"Well." He seemed to choose his words carefully. "The guards who held Jacoby were sleeping off a strong drink and were in no shape to follow me quite yet." He brushed his long hair out of his eyes. "It was the only way I could think to alert Sebande before you rode right into them."

His handsome face was familiar, yet the only things Nica knew about him for sure was that he was a spy. She couldn't trust anything he said. The only other thing she knew was that she was alone among the enemy, being held like a pawn in an intricate game of Masaa.

"There is much I don't understand," she finally said, "but I do know I'm away from Mosaba and still alive." It wasn't a thank you, but it wasn't a declaration of war between them either.

Shanks lifted his eyebrows. "I'll take that to mean we're friends."

Nica opened her mouth to retort but Shanks put a gentle finger to her lips. "Shhh, don't spoil it."

WHEN THEY REACHED the tall, ornate set of double doors that led into Jaaniyah's chambers they found Sebande standing there.

"How's the weather?" Shanks asked as he pushed one of the doors open.

"*Sesp'i va.*" Sebande said, his face expressionless.

Calm winds. Nica automatically translated the Jarisan words in her head. Why were they talking about the weather?

Shanks nodded and beckoned for Nica to follow him. She ignored Sebande but felt the weight of his dark eyes on her as she passed.

"There you are," Jaaniyah said in a waspish tone. "What took so long?"

"We took the back stairs," Shanks said lightly. "It's a longer route."

Nica scanned the room before her. Rich paintings hung from the walls: Snow-capped mountains, dazzling rivers, tropical jungles. It was almost as if jewels had been encrusted in the artwork to dazzle the viewer with their glittering beauty. Tall ornate vases stood on intricately designed pedestals, an eggshell quality to their perfection. The rich, dark brown hides of giant wildebeare were strewn over the stone floors, the translucent glow of the ivory-tipped hairs soft and beckoning.

"Yes, well, now what do we do?" Jaaniyah asked. She turned toward Shanks as though she didn't want Nica to hear what she said. "Have you talked to Becknah?"

"I have."

"Then you know about the delivery."

"Yes," Shanks replied. "But that's not going to happen until later. Closer to dawn, I believe." He looked around. "Until then, I think we all should get some rest. Jaaniyah, in the morning you'll need to tell your ladies and maids you don't want anyone entering your chambers for a while. We'll put a guard on your door for now."

"No maids? What in the world will I say is my reason?" Jaaniyah asked.

Nica didn't miss Shanks' smile and the easy familiarity between the two.

"You're the princess," he said. "Since when do you need a reason?" His lips twisted in a grin as he chuckled. "Just tell them you want some privacy for once."

He walked to another set of double doors and pushed them open. "Jaaniyah, your bed's as large as a ship, can you and Nica both sleep in it?"

Jaaniyah gasped and gave Shanks a horrified look. "Sleep together?"

Nica frowned. She wasn't going to sleep with this stranger. Even if she did look familiar. She glanced into Jaaniyah's bedchamber. A long, thin sofa sat against one wall, the diamond tucked upholstery and dark carved legs and frame as beautiful as a piece of art.

"One of you could sleep there—" Shanks pointed at the sofa— "and the other in the bed. You could take turns."

Jaaniyah crossed her arms and gave Shanks a cold look. "I am not sleeping on the sofa."

"It's fine." Nica interrupted. "I'm glad to sleep there." She was so tired. She couldn't remember the last time she'd slept. She really just wanted to close her eyes and stop thinking.

"It's settled then." Shanks looked over at Nica. "You'll have to remain hidden for a few days. The palace is in turmoil at the moment with the king being captured. We'll have to wait to announce your presence."

Nica jerked her head up. "Where is the king? Did he live?"

"He was too injured to travel all the way here," Shanks said. "We have him hidden within Jarisa at the moment and have sent the healer to him. However, we're going to pretend to bring him home so Mosaba thinks he's protected within the palace walls."

"Jonn, should you reveal so much?" Jaaniyah frowned at Shanks and spoke as if Nica wasn't in the room. "She's lived in Sartis her entire life. Are you so sure of her loyalties?"

"I understand your concern, Jaaniyah, but I feel certain Nica wouldn't do anything to help Mosaba. You might remember she risked her own life trying to escape from him."

Nica looked at the young soldier in surprise. He almost sounded proud of her.

Shanks rested his hand on the hilt of the sword tied to his side. "I'll be back later. In the meantime, there will be a guard at the door, but not Sebande, so don't let him know there's more than one of you in here." He looked from one to the other before his eyes settled on Nica. His face was expressionless, but she thought she saw some emotion flicker in his eyes as he waved an arm and bowed stiffly from the waist. "Welcome home."

Chapter Twelve

er newfound sister was gone by the time Nica awoke the next morning. She took the opportunity to relax in her makeshift bed on the couch, trying to gather the energy to rise. It had been difficult to fall asleep and when she finally had, her dreams had been dark and fitful.

She spied a dark blue dress draped across the end of the princess' rumbled bed that she assumed was meant for her. She slid from her covers and hurried toward the basin of water Jaaniyah had mentioned would be available. Oh, how she longed to wash the stench of the prison cell and her frantic night of traveling from her body. Plus, being busy kept her from questioning everything she believed about her life to be true. At this time, she didn't know what the truth was and it was easier to *not* think about it than have questions without answers going round and round in her mind.

Nica peeled off her borrowed nightdress and let it drop to the floor. Last night, she had tucked her own clothes, the black valote pants, dark shirt and cloak, in a lower drawer for safe keeping. No telling when she might need them again.

She washed quickly, shivering from the combination of cool water and chilly air. The soap was scented with the fragrance of honeysuckle and the smell brought back pleasant memories of sunny days alone in the orchard, safely hidden from Mosaba's ire.

Nica toweled her hair as dry as possible and finger combed the long tresses into wavy strands that hung down her back. Shivering, she reached for the dress and pulled it over her head.

The dress was more ornate than she was used to wearing, with gold embroidery stitched in a V down the bodice and an elaborate design of gold stitching down the front of the skirt. The bodice was quite tight, pressing her breasts up and over the square neckline, even without the laces being pulled tight. Nica glanced down and tugged on the material trying to pull it a bit higher.

A knock on the door interrupted her and she turned with a start.

"Anyone home?" Shanks called into the bedchamber.

Nica inhaled. Shanks had brought food. The tempting smell made her stomach growl in anticipation. She stepped around the corner and saw his eyes widen.

"Oh." His eyes swept her from head to toe, pausing briefly on her chest, then his face went completely blank. "You look different." Then as if realizing perhaps he hadn't been the most tactful, he added, "I mean, I'm glad to see you're up and dressed."

Heat rose in Nica's cheeks. "Jaaniyah was nice enough to let me borrow a gown." She motioned over her shoulder. "But I need someone to tie the back."

Shanks set the tray he was carrying on a nearby table and bowed with a flourish. "At your service, M'lady."

Nica spun in place and presented her back to him trying not to think about what it looked like to have a young man she barely knew help her dress. His warm fingers brushed the skin of her back and her cheeks burned hotter. She twisted her fingers together in an effort not to fidget. "Do you know how?"

"Not much different than putting a saddle on a horse, I would think." Shanks breath was suddenly warm on her ear. "Though you stand still much better than my horse does."

His horse? He thought of her in the same class as *his horse*?

Just as quickly as her nerves had appeared, they vanished. "Is that supposed to be a compliment?" she asked drily.

Shanks chuckled. "In my world, it is."

"Because I'd hate to make your horse jealous."

He laughed louder. "No need to worry. My horse is a stallion." He whispered into her ear again. "He doesn't get jealous—he takes what he wants." He gave one last tug on the laces and stepped back. "There, all trussed up."

Nica turned around to face him. He wore deep brown breeches and a crisp white shirt, the laces at his neck undone, revealing the top of his muscled chest. "Thank you."

He inclined his head, but a smirk tweaked his lips. "The least I can do."

"That's true," Nica replied. She turned away before he could see her smile. The familiar weight and drag of her skirt reminded her how much she enjoyed the freedom of breeches. She stepped over to the tray of food. "May I bring the tray over here by the window? The sun is just cresting the trees. I like the light." She spoke in Sartish out of habit.

"Allow me," Shanks said, taking the tray from her and proceeding to a small alcove with a window seat. Nica sat down next to where he had balanced he tray and nodded at the sword that hung from his side.

"Do you ever take that thing off?"

"No need to." He smiled. "She's feather light and blessed with Mercedes' kiss. Would you like to see her?" In an effortless movement Shanks whipped the blade out of his belt so fast all Nica saw was a blur of light accompanied by a *whooshing* sound.

Her stomach twisted in an unfamiliar way. Was Shanks involved with someone named Mercedes? Perhaps she had kissed the blade for luck. She couldn't stop the question from escaping her lips. "Who's Mercedes?"

Shanks held her gaze with his mesmerizing blue eyes. "Mercedes is Death's gatekeeper."

Nica wrinkled her nose. "How charming."

Shanks gave a soft laugh and held the thin blade up, turning it to catch the light. "She has saved my life more than once," he murmured.

For a second, Nica wondered exactly how many times the sword had saved Shanks, then she shook her head. She didn't want to know about his mercenary lifestyle. What she should be wondering is how many lives that sword had taken. And what she was going to do now that Toppen was missing and she was here?

"Are you hungry?" Shanks asked, sliding his sword back into his belt loop.

"Yes," Nica admitted. "I'm starving." She eyed the food eagerly.

Shanks pointed at the items on the tray. "We've got ham, sausage, eggs and biscuits."

"They look delicious." Without thinking, she added, "Have you eaten? Would you like to join me?"

Shanks lips turned up in a lazy smile. His expression made her feel as if she'd played into his hand, making her regret her impulsive offer. She needed to remember that Shanks was not her friend.

"I couldn't possibly eat this much food in a week," she added, as though in explanation for her generosity. "And I'd hate for it to go to waste." At home, she usually ate alone unless she could find a servant who would sit with her and even that was rare, for most of the servants knew that Mosaba would not allow them to mingle with his daughter. To her surprise, he agreed.

"I'd be honored." Shanks sat down across from her and reached for a biscuit.

Nica dug in, enjoying the light flaky layers of the biscuit and fluffy eggs, seasoned with the spice of the sausage. She ate until almost half the tray had been consumed. Finally sated, she looked up to find Shanks watching her with an amused expression. A blush warmed her cheeks. She recognized the familiar tilt to his lips and realized he was going to start teasing her, so she spoke first.

"So, are you from Jarisa, then? Your accent doesn't sound quite right."

Jonn Shanks took a bite of ham. "How do you feel about being from Jarisa? Now that you know the truth?"

Nica glanced up at him. "Honestly, if I think on it too long my head starts to hurt." She enjoyed looking at him; at the scar that disappeared into his eyebrow, white against the golden brown of his skin; how his strong, straight nose leaned slightly to the right; the three small silver hoops that hung from each ear that seemed to fit him so naturally. "But you didn't answer my question," she continued. "You pretended to be a soldier for Sartis, but you weren't. You act now as if you're a soldier for Jarisa, and in fact, risked your life for Jarisa, but your accent doesn't ring true to someone born here."

Her eyes probed his face, searching for the truth. He needed someone to properly trim his hair—the strands stood up in disarray as if he had run his hands through his hair repeatedly and the shaggy ends were long enough they brushed against his shoulders. For the first time she noticed the purple shadows that colored the skin under his eyes as if he hadn't slept well either. "Exactly who are you, Jonn Shanks?"

Shanks' expression wavered. Nica saw a flicker of *something* in his eyes, then it was gone, hidden behind his amused expression.

"Ah, beautiful Nica." He spoke in flawless Jarisan. "When you ask so sweetly it's all I can do not to tell you my secrets and then make up some more, just to keep you happy." He gave an exaggerated sigh. "But I fear your loyalty has not been sworn to me, so I don't dare lay my life in your hands." He gave her an innocent smile.

Nica raised her eyebrows. So he could speak like a native if he chose too. Just as he had spoken in perfect Sartish when it had suited his purposes.

She responded in Jarisan:

> *"The strongest tree must learn to bend,*
> *Only a restless soul hastens down the wind*
> *Fingers to flames will always get burned*
> *Trust must be given, before it is earned."*

She was pleased at the surprised look on Shanks' face. "It's an old Sartisian saying my tutor taught me."

"I see I'm not the only one with secrets. And a philosopher, as well." He nodded in approval as his gaze dropped to where her breasts swelled above the neckline of her low-cut gown. She wished she could tug the bodice of her dress up to her neck, exposed before his scrutiny in more ways than one. His gaze returned to her face. "You're an interesting girl, Nica Jacoby."

Nica froze. Jacoby? Was that who she was? "I simply meant to point out that anyone can speak with a proper accent," she said sharply. "It's not an indication of birthplace. And you don't always speak in perfect Jarisan. There are times when I can hear something else in your pronunciation."

A frown tweaked Shanks' brows but he spoke in a light voice. "You'll learn that not everyone in Jarisa speaks 'perfect Jarisan', as you call it." He waved his long fingers at her. "In fact, you sound more Jarisan than some who were born here." He pushed the tray away and stood up. "Which is a good thing, as you shouldn't speak Sartish under any circumstances right now. There is too much unrest, too much anger at what Mosaba has done."

Shanks gaze shifted out the window. "I'll be gone for a day or two. You need to stay hidden in these rooms in my absence. There's no telling what Mosaba is planning—but there will be something. And soon."

"You're leaving?" Nica was shocked at how wistful she sounded and promptly wished she could take the words back. But the truth was she didn't want Shanks to leave. He was the only familiar face in a place she'd been told her entire life was evil and wrong. Though she had escaped Mosaba, she was now the enemy among enemies.

He swung his head toward her, a familiar smile tweaking his lips. "Why? Will you miss me?"

"No." Nica spat the word out and shoved herself angrily out of her seat. She knew better than to let anyone think she cared. About anything.

His expression shifted at her anger and his tone became crisp. "I won't be gone long. If you're desperate, find Sebande. He'll help you until I can get back. You can trust Sebande."

"Where are you going?" Nica said in a softer tone. "Are you checking on Jacoby?"

Something that looked like truth flickered in his eyes, but he blinked and his face became a mask. "I can't say, but it is true I have to check on some things."

Nica clutched her hands together and inclined her head. "Then may you travel with the blessings of the Ancients."

A look of surprise crossed his face. Nica flinched as he reached a hand toward her, but she stood her ground. As if sensing her fear, he slowed his movement and used a finger to gently move a long strand of hair back behind her shoulder. *"Yani 'sa.* And may they smile upon you as well."

Nica nodded and took a deep breath to ease the sudden pressure in her chest.

"Here you are."

Nica jumped at the sound of Jaaniyah's voice. Shanks stepped away and grinned over his shoulder at the princess.

"There *you* are. Are you ready to meet with Heathron?"

An odd sinking twisted in the pit of Nica's stomach as she stood there in her borrowed gown and bare feet. She had an overwhelming urge to run and hide—not only from the cool appraisal of the haughty girl who Shanks had identified as her sister, but also from the realization that she'd allowed herself to imagine Jonn Shanks was someone she might trust. He worked for Jarisa, not Sartis. He swore his allegiance to Jaaniyah, not her. She was nothing but a pawn to him.

"Yes, I'm ready." Jaaniyah held out her arm for Shanks to take.

He gave Nica a short bow, then turned his back on her and led Jaaniyah from the room.

Chapter Thirteen

hree days had passed since Shanks' departure. One day folded into another until Nica thought she would burst from the sheer boredom of staying hidden in Jaaniyah's rooms. Though more comfortable, it wasn't much different than being locked in a jail cell and she longed to explore and understand this kingdom of Jarisa. Though her sister was cordial and curious, she was also restrained and clearly unwilling to trust her yet.

Nica stood at the window and stared through the diamond panes to the courtyard below, listening to the muted voices and the tapping of soldier's boots on the flagstones. Her own curiosity was mitigated by the tension in the air, as everyone feared an attack from Mosaba was imminent.

She shuddered to think what they would do if they knew she was hidden within the walls of the palace. The view out the window gave her an eerie sense of déjà vu, remembering the day not so long ago when she had stood at the window in the Grand Library and listened to the cacophony of noise from the street in Sartis. A pang filled her chest as she thought of the plans she and Toppen had made. Everything had gone so drastically wrong.

Though Jaaniyah brought food several times a day, she kept a wary distance. It was almost as though she suspected Nica of being a spy for Mosaba. She hadn't offered an alternative to their sleeping arrangements so Nica continued to sleep on the couch. She did, at least, have a blanket and a pillow.

Their longest conversations were usually at night when the torches were dimmed and they could barely see each other through the shadows in the room. It was easier to talk without being reminded of their surreal connection.

Their conversations during the day, however, were stilted and uncomfortable, unable to move past the long-held animosity between their countries. They had talked only a little of how they'd grown up but Nica's questions had dwindled after a while, as it became clear that Jaaniyah was unwilling to reveal much personal information. At the same time, Nica was unwilling to admit Mosaba's cruelty, unwilling to relive his torture even in her mind. It was like trying to balance on eggs when she was around Jaaniyah.

"HAVE YOU ANY word of your father? How is he doing?" Nica asked as the afternoon waned on the fourth day since Shanks' departure.

Jaaniyah sat on the bed, reading, seemly oblivious to Nica's presence. Her eyes narrowed as she responded to Nica's question. It was as though she held her sister personally responsible for Mosaba's attack upon her father.

"He's still alive," Jaaniyah said. "That's all I know."

"Well, that's good. One day closer to coming home, then." Nica smiled but Jaaniyah had already turned away. Nica bit back a sigh and sat down next to the window she couldn't even open for fear of being seen. "When do you suppose Shanks will return?"

"He didn't say. Why does it matter?" Jaaniyah's voice was cool as she peered at Nica over the edge of her book.

"I just wondered if he knew when I might get out of this room. I don't think I can stand being stuck in here for much longer."

Jaaniyah's grey eyes didn't waver as she stared at Nica. "And where would you go?"

Nica took a deep breath and tried to ignore her rising temper. "Wherever I please, I suppose. I'm free to go where I choose, you know."

"Not in Jarisa, you're not," Jaaniyah retorted. "If people knew who you were, they would string you up."

"Oh, is that so?" Nica got to her feet, her hands clenched at her sides. "I've heard tales about what barbarians the Jarisans are. You've just confirmed my suspicions."

"You eat *my* food, wear *my* clothes and sleep in *my* room and you dare to criticize my country?" Jaaniyah's voice rose to a shout as she slid off the bed and stormed toward Nica. "I could have you cast out and then that madman you call your father could hunt you down like he did my father and ….."

"WHAT IS THE MEANING OF THIS?" A deep voice thundered, interrupting Jaaniyah's tirade.

Startled, both girls jerked around to face Becknah, who stood in the doorway to Jaaniyah's bedchamber.

Nica's heart raced in fear. They were found out.

Her eyes skimmed over the old man who stood staring at them with his mouth open. His long crimson robe was rich and beautiful, sparkling with gold threads. Nica could see his eyes dart back and forth between the two of them, while his mouth opened and closed several times reminding Nica of a fish in need of water.

"Jaaniyah?" His gaze moved from one girl to the other and back again, unsure.

"Yes, Becknah, of course, *I'm* Jaaniyah." Jaaniyah stepped forward. "And this—" she turned and held her hand out— "is Nica." She hurried behind the older man and shut the door to her chambers then shut the door to the bedchamber for added protection.

"Nica?" The old man's eyes behind his crescent shaped glasses looked her up and down in one sweep. "Nica *who*?"

"Please, come sit by the window and we'll explain." Jaaniyah slid her hand under Becknah's elbow and pulled him away from Nica. "Jonn Shanks brought her."

The silence within the room was deafening.

"But it can't be," the old man whispered.

Nica stood rooted to the spot, unsure of what to do. Her instincts told her to run, but there was no place to run *to*. So instead, she balled her fists as she stared at Becknah in perverse fascination to await his reaction. She would fight if he tried to hurt her.

"Juneedika?" he whispered the name, swiveling his head from Nica to Jaaniyah.

Nica froze.

"Yes, well, it appears that it might be possible," Jaaniyah responded, tugging on the man's arm to get him to sit.

"What did you say?" Nica took a step closer.

"Are you Juneedika, lass?" The man shook off Jaaniyah's hand and moved toward Nica, his brow furrowed in thought.

A chill ran up Nica's arms. Juneedika was the name King Jacoby had uttered when he'd spied her the day they'd brought him as a prisoner to the castle. At the time she'd thought it was a prayer for mercy but now....

"Who is Juneedika?" Nica asked.

"My sister's name was Juneedika," Jaaniyah said in a low voice.

A jittery feeling pulled Nica's heart into her stomach. King Jacoby hadn't been praying that afternoon. He had *recognized* her—he had recognized his own daughter.

"You are Jaaniyah's twin," Becknah said. He reached out both hands as though to embrace her face, but didn't touch her. "You are Juneedika." His voice was filled with wonder as a smile lit his face. "This changes everything."

THEY SAT TOGETHER in the alcove, the last rays of afternoon light pouring through the windows. "Where have you been? You had no knowledge of your true heritage? What of your mother?" He asked all the same questions that Jaaniyah had asked. "Obviously you understand Jarisan?"

Nica nodded.

"And how have you come to be in Jarisa?" Becknah leaned forward to listen to her answer.

Nica began to explain how she and Toppen had left Sartis at night intending to head to Pont d'Suree. "We were stopped while still in Sartis and asked to carry..." she hesitated, "a... package over the border." She shrugged. "Then we were arrested and I was brought here."

"Stopped?" Becknah looked to Jaaniyah with a confused expression. "By whom?"

"It was Jonn," Jaaniyah said. "Apparently he met Nica while in Sartis and recognized her."

"Ah, young Jonn Shanks." Becknah nodded and sat back in his chair, gazing through the window. "Now, it's beginning to make more sense. And the 'package' you spoke of? Was that our King?" He peered at her over his glasses.

Nica nodded.

"Yes, of course it was. And you, my dear, are a hero. Saving your own father's life after all these years. It's the stuff of...." he paused. "Hmmm, I wonder." His fingers drummed the arm of the chair as he became lost in thought. "How very fascinating. Could it possibly make sense of..." his voice died off.

"Make sense of what?" Jaaniyah asked with a tinge of irritation. "What are you talking about?"

"The Avedla quatrains, of course." Becknah's eyes glowed with excitement. "I've studied the text of Getheas for most of my adult life. I've memorized many of the verses." He began to recite:

> *"The absent one shall reappear*
> *Amid a war that all have feared*
> *A devious plan, the tables are turned*
> *The gift of life given, shall be returned"*

"Don't you see?" A smile creased the wrinkles on his face. "'*The absent one shall reappear*—' the quatrain clearly speaks of Juneedika's return. '*Amid a war,*'" he turned from one to the other, "obviously the conflict between Jarisa and Sartis. '*A devious plan*—' there is no better description of Mosaba's ambush."

"You can't be seri—" Jaaniyah started.

Becknah raised a finger, "but '*the tables are turned,*' speaks of your father's escape and finally—" he spread his arms wide, the long sleeves of his robe, sweeping the air— "'*the gift of life given, shall be returned*'." He held his hands out to Nica. "Juneedika's part in saving her own father's life." Becknah clapped his hands together in delight. "Written over three hundred years before the events actually occurred. Quite amazing."

"Do you really think that has to do with *her*?" Jaaniyah asked.

Becknah rubbed his hands together, lost in thought. "It's brilliant—so obvious, now that we know Juneedika is alive." He pushed himself out of the chair and began to pace. His robes swept behind him, back and forth across the room. "Give me a moment, I've read something recently…" he held a gnarled finger up— "just need a moment to think."

Nica watched the old man pace back and forth, mumbling to himself. She was afraid to interrupt. What in the name of the Ancients was he talking about? At least he didn't seem to be angry with her.

"I have it!" he cried out, snapping his fingers.

> *"A war continues, destined to repeat*
> *Until two daughters royal born do meet*
> *The time has come to reveal the past*
> *That which is hidden, can be found at last"*

Becknah stopped in front of Nica, his excitement tangible. "'*Until two daughters royal born do meet.*' It has to be the two of you." He turned to Jaaniyah. "That lie we made up to trap Tarantu?"

"Yes?"

"It has become the truth. I believe now *is* the time to seek the Getheas Stone."

ay we read the quatrains?"
Jaaniyah's words were hesitant.

Becknah had resumed pacing.
"Of course, of course. We must all
re-examine the messages which
have been left." He glanced at
Nica. "And what of you, my dear,
how long have you been hiding here in Jaaniyah's
rooms?"

Nica shrugged, self-conscious at his renewed
perusal. "A day or two."

"We can't announce your presence until Jacoby
has returned, so you must remain hidden for a few
more days." Becknah moved from one side of the room
to the other but his gaze kept returning to Nica. "It's
amazing how much the two of you look alike," he
muttered. Finally he came to a stop in front of Nica.
"You must be curious to see the palace, the grounds—
your new home." He raised ringed fingers to his chin,
stroking his long grey beard. "Juneedika, certainly you
could feign a sore throat, yes? That would give you an
excuse for not speaking while I gave you a tour."

"Yes, I'd love too." Nica jumped to her feet before
Jaaniyah could discourage the idea.

The old man turned to the princess. "Jaaniyah, I'm
sure you would be gracious enough to remain hidden in

your rooms for a small bit of time to allow Juneedika a chance for some fresh air?"

Jaaniyah's lips pinched together as she grudgingly nodded.

Becknah clapped his hands together, a pleased expression creasing his face. "Shall we go now, then?"

Nica gave the older man a hesitant smile. "Yes, please." She followed him out the door without looking back.

BECKNAH LEANED CLOSE as they left Jaaniyah's chambers, so the guard still stationed outside the doors couldn't hear his words. "If others are near, I will appear to be discussing our military situation or other matters with you. Just look around and nod. You can ask me questions later. I want to take you by my study and show you the books. I'm quite curious to see if there are any symbols or languages there that you might recognize from your time in Sartis."

Nica took a deep breath, relieved to be out of that room. "What books are those?"

He crooked an eyebrow at her but his words were gentle. "Of course, you wouldn't know, given where you were raised, would you?"

They walked down an immense hallway. Huge wooden beams supported the vaulted ceiling overhead and the palace held a sense of opulence that was lacking at Ravensfell. The setting sun seeped through the stained glass windows that lined the upper wall casting a prism of rich colors along the corridor.

"They are known as the Avedla," Becknah continued, "the scripture and prophecies of Getheas, the greatest of the Ancients. The Avedla is a treasure which has been guarded within Jarisa for centuries." Becknah said. "A very sacred treasure. Most of the contents within the books are written as verse—as quatrains."

Nica frowned. "Quatrains?"

"Four line rhyming poems. Some of the text is said to tell the location of the Getheas Stone." He led her down a long flight of stone stairs. "You're familiar with the Getheas Stone?"

Nica nodded. She had learned the story of Getheas as a child. Mosaba was obsessed with the legendary Getheas Stone, a fervent believer that it was his destiny to control its magical power.

"Yes," she said softly, as she followed Becknah around the corner. "Wasn't it supposed to be inscribed with some secret?"

"The Stone is said to be a key—" Becknah said softly— "to the future."

They turned the corner and Nica stopped to stare in amazement at the room before her. Great wood corbels carved into fantastical shapes of mermaids and sea serpents held beams that arched three stories to support a carved panel ceiling. Two long tables stretched down the rectangular room with benches attached on each side. At the end of the hall, a raised platform stood with another long table stretched at right angles to the others in the room. Five huge fireplaces were built along each wall, blazing with light and warmth.

"The Great Hall," Becknah said in a low voice.

A smattering of groups sat at the tables. The men rose and bowed to Nica as she and Becknah passed by. Nica acknowledged their respect with a small tilt of her head but didn't allow her gaze to linger. One small man dressed in a black and white checkered vest stood and called Jaaniyah's name, but she pretended not to hear him, concentrating instead on her conversation.

Becknah led her out of a second set of large doors at the far end of the room into another hallway. "Come, my study is located near the top of Stargazer—HighGarden's tallest tower. The best view of the stars you'll find in Jarisa," he said with a smile. He pointed out items of interest as they walked and Nica tried to take it all in. She had lived in a castle in Sartis but this was truly a palace.

"Becknah!" A voice hailed them from behind. Nica turned to see a big bear of a man, half again as tall as she, hurrying toward them. "M'lady," he nodded at her and swept his arm in the direction of an open door. "If I may have a word." He took Becknah by the arm and pulled him into a nearby room.

"Eisle Heathron," Becknah replied as he winked at Nica, "since you are minister of war, you can certainly have a word."

Once they were through the portal, Heathron shut the door and began speaking in a low voice. "We've news that Mosaba is on the move. Troops have been seen gathering at both the north and south slivers. It's possible some have already infiltrated Jarisa." He looked from one to the other. "Becknah, what do your devices say? Have you read the Xanfere cards today? Are the stars still in agreement that the King should remain in his present location?"

Becknah frowned. "Eisle, you know we've been expecting Mosaba to retaliate in some way. His forces aren't strong enough to make a direct attack on the palace but we know he'll do something." He peered at Heathron over the top of his glasses. "There's something in the orb, but it's murky, unclear at this time. I've seen no signs that indicate we should move the King. For now, he's probably safest where he's at."

"Mosaba likes to create diversions." Nica spoke without thinking. "He'll make you look here—" Nica held one hand open— "when he's really doing something over there." She beckoned with her other hand. Both men gazed at her with startled expressions making her wish she could bite her tongue off.

The minister of war shot a quizzical glance at Becknah before he spoke. "Where did you learn this information, M'lady? Did one of the soldiers tell you?"

Nica hesitated. It was clear Heathron couldn't tell her apart from Jaaniyah and what she had to say was important—for her own good, as well as for the kingdom of Jarisa. She threw caution to the wind.

"I would suggest you keep a close eye on those places where you least expect an attack from Mosaba or his men. Because that is most likely where he will strike next."

Both men stared at her, appearing dumbstruck.

"Such as..." the minister of war finally asked.

"I'm sure you know who to watch and what to protect, Minister."

"Yes, of course, M'lady." He bowed his head.

"Is there anything further?" Nica mimicked Jaaniyah's haughty air.

"No," he shook his head, "No, M'lady. We'll keep a stout watch."

"Thank you." Nica nodded and turned to Becknah. "Shall we continue?" She thought she saw the hint of a smile as Becknah nodded in agreement.

"By all means."

NICA GLANCED AROUND the circular room Becknah referred to as his study. A cheery fire crackled heartily in the stone fireplace. Windows stretched up to the pointed peak of the roof, opening up to a breathtaking view of the sky shaded with orange and pink as the sun collided with the horizon.

Everywhere she looked, books were stacked, one on top of the other, in rickety piles. Three long tables were strewn with devices. Brass candlesticks stood two and three to a table, wax drippings puddled around their bases. Nearby an hourglass that had expired stood next to a three legged bowl and a cruet of oil.

Nica spied a sphere of the world, as well as tools to measure the position of the stars. On the far table, she could see what appeared to be a crystal gazing ball, a large book opened next to the orb.

"Over here." Becknah hurried to a messy bookcase toward the back of the room. Books of all sizes leaned against each other, stacked and double stacked in piles on the shelves.

"Hidden in plain sight," he chortled as he waved at the bookcase. "All of these, my dear Juneedika, are books of the Avedla. Getheas has written on many different topics—the stars, care of the dead, agriculture, politics, religion, mathematics. He wrote his thoughts on a myriad of subjects, yet the bulk of his writings remain a mystery. They are said to be visions of what is to come, encoded in verse, to be understood at some point in the future." Becknah ran his crooked fingers reverently over the spines of the books. "Over the years I've studied many of the quatrains, but most are yet to be deciphered."

He pulled a very thin black book from a lower shelf. Each corner was affixed with clamped silver along with four oddly shaped metal caps that held the leather cover to the pages. The old man pointed to a silver number stamped at the bottom of the spine. "The original texts are each marked with a number."

Becknah held the thin book up. "We've just discovered this text, shoved inside a bigger manuscript." He gave her a triumphant smile. "A once-in-a-lifetime find." He caressed the leather cover. "I've only had time to take a cursory glance at the verse contained within." He laid the book flat on the big desk and flipped through the pages of parchment until he found what he wanted. He pointed to the lines of verse on the page. "See what you can make of this."

Curious, Nica peered down at the page. There was only one quatrain listed on each page.   It was written in Sartish. She read the words easily.

> *"Between the cross and the crescent moon*
> *When the lion stands at high noon*
> *A secret of blood hidden by ancient lies*
> *At last revealed before one dies."*

Nica looked up. "Is that right?" she asked in Jarisan.

"Yes," Becknah nodded. "That is precisely how I translated it too, though Sartish is not an easy language to read." He peered at her over the rim of his glasses. "You also speak Jarisan beautifully. How is it that you are fluent in both languages?"

Nica shrugged, embarrassed at her ability. "I've been taught languages as long as I can remember. They seem to come easily to me."

"A wonderful gift. You will be most useful to your father." Becknah stopped abruptly and tilted his head to listen. "Someone approaches." He scooped the black book off the table and thrust it into Nica's arms.

"Take this and hide." He motioned toward the back of the room.

Nica didn't hesitate. Too many years of having to disappear in a split-second when Mosaba came near had trained her well. She grabbed the book and dashed into the shadows at the back of the room. She had already spotted a corner behind a tall plant where one side of a pair of emerald curtains hung, held back with a braided rope. She slipped the rope free, pulled the fabric away from the wall and slid into the space just as someone pounded on the door.

Nica clutched the thin book against her suddenly pounding heart and strained to hear what was happening.

The large door scraped open.

"Becknah." A man's voice.

"Tarantu. What a surprise to find you on my doorstep," the scholar replied. "Does our finance minister need his cards read today?"

"Though I appreciate your humor, Becknah, your presence is required downstairs immediately."

Nica listened from behind the curtain. Jaaniyah had mentioned the finance minister as being politically motivated.

"I am in the middle of some calculations, at the moment." Becknah's voice revealed no hint of discomfort. "Can I join you at, say, half past the hour?"

"No, you need to come now." Tarantu's voice held a demanding note.

"May I ask what matter holds such urgency?" Becknah's tone changed ever so slightly. "And the need for an escort?"

"The King has requested your presence."

"Really?" Surprise echoed in Becknah's voice. "I wasn't aware he was able to receive visitors yet."

Nica's eyes widened behind the curtain. *The king?* But that wasn't possible. The king wasn't even here. Heathron had faked his return—no one resided in the royal suite at this time. Questions exploded in her head as she realized that Tarantu could not be speaking the truth. Surely, Becknah must know the man was lying.

"He has demanded to see you at once." Tarantu's voice bordered on threatening. "Please accompany me."

Becknah cleared his throat. "Well, well, this is a serious matter. I shall come immediately and return to my rooms later to finish my work."

Nica heard a rustling of robes and the stout wooden door slammed closed as he exited the room. She counted to ten before she peeked around the corner of the curtain.

She was alone.

Chapter Fifteen

ica waited.

Becknah did not return.

A sick feeling of dread filled her. Tarantu's words didn't ring true—where had he taken the old scholar?

After twenty minutes, she pushed the curtain aside and stepped into the room, debating whether she should wait for his return or try to find her way back to Jaaniyah's chambers alone. Curiosity got the better of her and she moved to the table with the gazing crystal.

She ran her fingers over the smooth surface of the orb which was balanced on a golden tripod, leaning close to peer into the sphere. At the bottom, crystal facets sparkled, reflecting the light. But no faces, no images that she could discern appeared to reveal any information. She wondered what Becknah saw when he searched the depths of the ball.

Beside the crystal a large, thick book lay open with sketches of the planets and stars colored on the page. Nica peered closely at the constellations drawn there. She had learned about the order of the stars from her astronomy teacher. Out of habit she counted the constellations drawn on the paper. Twelve.

The configuration of Glandar, the mysterious thirteenth sign, was missing. Though centered precisely in the middle of the star signs, Glandar—known as the golden knight—had been deliberately left out of the astrology charts created by the Ancients, for reasons that seemed to have been lost over time.

Nica glanced over at the closed door. Still no Becknah. An uneasy knot began to twist in her stomach.

She looked down at the thin ledger she still held in her hands. The silver letters danced in old-fashioned shapes across the front of the black leather: *The Ages.* Engraved at the bottom was an odd symbol she didn't recognize. She fanned the paper, the pages whispering as they turned. What secrets were held within the rhyming verse? She thumbed through to the page which held the quatrain Becknah had pointed out earlier and re-read the Sartish words printed in a neat script:

> *"Between the cross and the crescent moon*
> *When the lion stands at high noon*
> *A secret of blood hidden by ancient lies*
> *At last revealed before one dies."*

Did these lines have meaning? Did they speak of an event that had already occurred—or one yet to arrive? Nica snapped the book shut. She had greater things to worry about than ancient poems. She debated again whether to continue to wait or try to find her way back to her rooms.

A deck of worn Xanfere cards were stacked neatly on one table. She stared at the silver stars winking against the black background and thought of the Magician from whom she'd run in Berjerac. He'd been right when he'd predicted she was going on a journey, that she would be betrayed. She wrinkled her brow in concentration. What was the last thing he'd said? *'The looking glass will reveal the truth.'* The looking glass. A mirror. Had he seen her twin?

She stared at the deck. Could these pictures tell her future? With trembling fingers Nica picked up the top card. The colorful images jumped out at her. A tall tower perched high on a cliff erupted in flames. A bolt of jagged lightening split the top, knocking off what appeared to be a crown. A man and woman plunged to certain death on each side as flames and smoke filled the air.

Nica dropped the card, sorry she'd looked. She could only guess at the meaning of those pictures and whatever the answer, it couldn't be good. Outside the palace, the clock tower tolled the hour of five and her anxiety at Becknah's departure grew. Something was wrong. She needed to warn Jaaniyah.

Nica hurried across the room and pulled the heavy door open. The circular steps that descended from the tower room were shadowed and dim, but empty. Without a backward glance Nica clattered down the stairs.

"WHERE HAVE YOU BEEN?" Jaaniyah snapped as Nica entered the bedchamber. "I don't know what—"

"Jaaniyah." Nica started to explain but the other girl talked over her.

"—could have possibly taken so long..."

Nica grabbed the other girl's wrist. "Listen to me."

Jaaniyah jerked her arm free. "Don't touch—"

"*Something is wrong*," Nica yelled. It was as though she glared at herself in the mirror, except the mirror was making its own face.

Jaaniyah's eyes narrowed in suspicion. "What do you mean?"

"Tarantu came and took Becknah from his study. He said the king had requested his presence—which we both know is impossible."

Jaaniyah's gaze searched Nica's face. "Did he see you?"

"No, Becknah told me to hide. But I..."

Her sister took a step closer. "Tell me exactly what happened."

Nica related the events leading up to Becknah's departure. "I waited, but he never returned. I didn't know how to get back to your chambers. I finally had to ask a guard to escort me. I told him I was feeling faint." Nica clutched the thin book Becknah had given her. "I think there's something wrong."

Jaaniyah gave her a cool look. "Such as?"

"I don't know for sure, but why would Tarantu say the king had requested Becknah's presence if the king isn't even here?"

"You must have misunderstood him. We speak a different language than you."

Nica eyed her sister, fighting the surge of anger in the pit of her stomach. There was no way she had become confused about Tarantu's demand that Becknah accompany him. "Or maybe—" Nica raised her eyebrows— "Mosaba has spies within this castle."

Jaaniyah blinked in disbelief. "Tarantu may be driven by greed but even he isn't that bold." She swished by Nica and headed for the door. "I'll go find him myself and demand an answer."

Nica followed in her sister's wake. "Jaaniyah, if you demand an answer from Tarantu you'll make him suspicious. Tell him you had an appointment with Becknah and he didn't show up. If he says he hasn't seen him, then we know he's lying. If he tells the truth, we'll know I'm wrong."

Jaaniyah sneered at Nica. "I know what to say to my own finance minister." She turned to leave but Nica's words stopped her.

"We saw Heathron on the way to the Becknah's study."

Jaaniyah glanced back over her shoulder. "And? Did he think you were me?"

Nica shrugged. "He didn't question me, but he was focused on other matters. He said Mosaba was moving troops for an attack of some kind."

"Where?"

"The north and south slivers." Nica hesitated. "But I think it's to distract us while he does something else—maybe something worse. If by some chance Mosaba does have men who infiltrated the palace, do you have any idea why he would be interested in an elderly scholar? Why would they take Becknah?"

Jaaniyah stood frozen, staring into the distance. "You must be wrong," she whispered. Then she ran out of the room, slamming the door to the bedchamber shut behind her.

Nica stared at the portal, fighting a sudden sense of being trapped. If Mosaba ever caught her she was dead. Especially if he caught her *here,* in Jarisa, among the enemy. Fear seethed through her body like the venom of a snake, making her feel sick. No one was safe if Mosaba's insidious web had infiltrated the walls of the palace. She shuddered at the idea, wishing Shanks would return.

Once again, she wondered why Mosaba had stolen and kept her alive all these years. It certainly wasn't because he enjoyed her company.

No, there was a bigger plan, but she couldn't see what it was. Yet.

Chapter Sixteen

 t had taken several queries and one or two interruptions requiring her opinion on other matters, before Jaaniyah was informed that Tarantu was in the stables. She hurried from the Great Hall in search of her finance minister.

The sky was streaked with orange and red turning to purple as the light faded into night. She crossed the dusty ward in the direction of the stables, hurrying passed a man who carried a torch and set the lanterns ablaze in anticipation of the coming nightfall.

Jaaniyah slowed as she neared the deep shadows of the large barns, the last rays of the sun highlighting the dusty motes in the entry but unable to penetrate to shadows deeper within the structure.

"Mr. Tarantu," she called, squinting to see through the dim shadows. On the far left side of the barn she spotted his familiar black and white checkered vest. "A word, please." She beckoned with her hand. "Now."

The petite man said a few words to the stable hand to whom he was speaking then walked with a quick step toward her.

"M'lady. Are you wishing to ride at this hour?"

Jaaniyah clenched her teeth at his overly sincere tone. "No, I'm looking for Becknah." She tried not to snap. "No one has been able to locate him." Remembering Nica's warning, she added, "We had an appointment and I was told he was last seen with you. Do you know where he's gone?"

Tarantu blinked. "No M'lady. I've not seen Mr. Becknah since noon—when he was with you." The finance minister blinked again, his brows pulled down in puzzled innocence.

"With me?" Jaaniyah sputtered, then remembered Becknah had been out with Nica. "Oh, that, yes, well—" she tilted her head. "Where did you see us, precisely?"

"When you walked through the Great Hall." Tarantu clutched his hands together and leaned forward from the waist as though in a perpetual bow. "I called out, but you appeared to be deep in conversation with the scholar."

"And you've not seen him since?"

"No, M'lady."

"Well, if you see him, please tell him we need to speak immediately."

"Most certainly, M'lady." Tarantu closed his eyes and dipped his head. "As you wish."

"Thank you. Please, carry on," Jaaniyah replied, fighting the urge to shoo him off with her hand. She watched as the little man hurried back into the deepening shadows of the stables. *Asa Sabra,* she swore silently. The only way to know if Tarantu was lying or if Nica was wrong was to find Becknah.

With a swirl of skirts Jaaniyah turned and hurried out the big stable doors. She cut the corner close as she exited, intent on her thoughts, and ran straight into someone walking a horse into the barn.

"Oh!" she cried as her chest slammed into theirs. The other person grunted in pain as she made contact. In reflex, she pressed her hands against the hard, leather-draped chest and pushed herself back. The heady scent of man and beast filled her nostrils as she glanced up in shocked surprise.

Jonn Shanks gazed down at her with a lazy grin. "Now this is a pleasant surprise. I had no idea you'd miss me so much, M'lady."

"Jonn," Jaaniyah breathed, a thrill racing through her. "You're back." She soaked in the pure manliness of him: his tousled hair, his startling blue eyes above a scrubby growth of beard. Rather than the finery of a Jarisan soldier, he was dressed for travel in leathers and boots, designed to blend in with the forest.

"Dirty, tired and hungry, but back—" Shanks agreed— "and mostly alive."

"Where have you been?" Jaaniyah cast a quick look behind her before she leaned close and whispered, "have you seen my father?"

A frown flitted across Shanks' face before he nodded. "Improving. How are things here?" He raised his eyebrows, making his meaning clear.

"I'm not sure at the moment." Jaaniyah said, vaguely irritated his first question was about Nica. "Becknah visited my chambers unannounced this morning. We had a most enlightened conversation."

Shanks eyes narrowed. "He met..."

"Yes, exactly." Jaaniyah nodded at his unspoken question. "And now, Becknah is missing. I've been searching for him."

"Missing?" Shanks frowned. "Becknah?"

"I can't find him," Jaaniyah said in a low voice. "*Someone* thinks he's been kidnapped—" she snorted out her derision— "however, *she* was the one with him at the time of the supposed disappearance." She pressed her lips together. "A strange coincidence, wouldn't you agree?"

Shanks searched Jaaniyah's face. "You're not suggesting she had something to do with this, are you?"

"I don't know what I'm suggesting," Jaaniyah whispered. "I'm just not convinced we should trust her, considering she was raised by—" Jaaniyah caught herself— "well, as she was and all. Don't you find it a bit odd, Jonn, the first time she leaves the room someone disappears?"

Lines of weariness were etched across his face and she wondered where his travels had taken him. "How do we know she doesn't have a spy here in the palace? Maybe she's working for her father even yet."

"She wasn't planning to come here to spy on you, Jaani." Shanks spat the words out. "She didn't know you existed until *I* brought her here. You forget who her true father is—" his tone held an underlying note of anger— "and you know *nothing* of the man she's been forced to call father."

Jaaniyah took a step back. She had pushed too far. Why did that girl matter so much to him?

Shanks took a deep breath. "Who is it you think could have taken him?"

"She says Becknah called him Tarantu, though she didn't see who it was." Jaaniyah hesitated, then whispered, "Becknah thought Nica's return somehow tied in with the Getheas quatrains. He thought it was time to search for the Getheas Stone."

Shanks cast a slow look around the area to see if they could be overheard. "I don't think we should speak of this here. I'll meet you in your chambers." His voice was solemn, matching the look in his eyes. "Is the guard still outside your door?"

At Jaaniyah's nod, he continued. "Go there directly and wait for me. I've got some business with Heathron and then I'll be up. Stay there."

Relieved, Jaaniyah nodded. If Becknah truly had been taken, she trusted Shanks to find him.

HEATHRON HAD JUST hailed Jaaniyah when a guard intercepted their path.

"M'lady." The guard bowed to Jaaniyah then nodded to the minister of war. "A man has arrived from the Isles of Corsock asking for admittance through the palace gates."

"Corsock?" Jaaniyah looked at Heathron. "Were you aware someone was coming? Did my father invite him?" Corsock was too far south in the Sea of Nephalon to make travel to Jarisa practical on a regular basis. It took almost the same amount of time from the new moon to the full to sail there. It was very odd someone would show up, unannounced.

Heathron shook his head. "No. This is news to me." A deep frown creased his forehead. "Most unusual."

"Please show him into the Great Hall." Jaaniyah instructed the guard. "I'll be there shortly."

"Yes, M'lady," The guard bobbed his head and hurried away.

"I'll accompany you," Heathron said. "This timing seems a bit suspicious to me. I don't know how, but if Corsock has heard your father's been captured this could be an attempt to gauge the situation."

"Do you think they're planning an attack?"

Heathron rested his large hand on the hilt of his sword. "I have no idea what they might be planning but I certainly don't want to take any chances given the current circumstances."

JAANIYAH ENTERED THE Great Hall flanked by Heathron. Guards, dressed in Jarisan colors of crimson and gold, stood at each end of the large hall. Next to one of them stood the stranger, his hands clasped behind his back, staring up at a mounted head of a huge wildebeare.

"Greetings," Jaaniyah said as she waited for him to turn and introduce himself.

He was dressed in a bleached white shirt and dark breeches, soft brown furs draped across his shoulders. His long white-blond hair was braided back with a leather thong, colorful glass beads strung through the plait. The man turned slowly and stared at her. His face was weathered as though he had spent much of his life outside and she could see curiosity in his pale blue eyes as he looked her up and down.

Jaaniyah raised her chin, and gave the man a cool gaze. "Welcome to Jarisa."

"M'lady Jacoby." The man gave her a sweeping bow. "Thank you for granting me entrance to your beautiful home. Allow me to introduce myself. I am Versonga Blacksmeer from the Isles of Corsock." He spoke with a thick accent, saying Isles so it sounded like 'ees lees' and rolling his r's with a trilling sound. "I bring you greetings and gifts from the southern seas."

"I'm pleased to meet you." Jaaniyah nodded. "Allow me to introduce one of our court ministers, Eisle Heathron." The men nodded to each other and murmured a perfunctory greeting.

"May we offer you food and wine?" She waved toward a platter which had been placed on a nearby table.

He inclined his head in acceptance. "How very kind of you."

Heathron eyed the man, his voice gruff when he spoke. "You are an envoy of Canja?"

Blacksmeer raised his palms as if in surrender. "Not in any official diplomatic capacity. But as I travel, I act as his representative and proffer his good wishes to the countries I visit." He bowed his head. "Today, I offer his good will to the country of Jarisa."

Jaaniyah motioned to the nearby seats. "Please sit, tell us how we might assist you." Heathron stepped closer to the visitor, openly sizing him up. "What brings you so far north from Corsock, sir?"

Blacksmeer smiled in response. "Exploring the continent, finding what's out there to be found." His posture relaxed. "I saw one of your spiny bears for the first time just a few days ago. The thing jumped out of a tree and almost landed on me." The tall man chuckled. "Thank the stars he missed me because I fear he would have punctured me with those quills."

"Ah, have you seen our brindy bucks yet?" Heathron's face brimmed with enthusiasm. "Now there's a sight to behold, to see a full grown male with a ten point rack on his head coming straight for you...."

They moved to the table where Blacksmeer and Heathron ate, drank and talked while Jaaniyah waited for them to finish their meal. She tried not to show her impatience as her thoughts drifted from her wounded father, to the missing scholar, from Jonn Shanks to her sister and this unexpected visitor.

"What do you do in Corsock?" Heathron's voice was loud in the quiet of the room.

Blacksmeer took a long drink of red wine, savoring the fluid before returning his glass to the table.

Letting out a satisfied sigh he replied, "As you know, we are ruled by Canja."

"The pirate, isn't he?" Jaaniyah interrupted. She had heard stories of the bloodthirsty ruler of the islands within the Corsocks.

"Yes." The visitor cleared his throat. "A bit wild, that man, but then, the Isles are wild country." He smoothed his white-blonde hair back with a rough hand. "I like to think of myself as an explorer."

"And you like to explore foreign countries?" Heathron watched Blacksmeer with a neutral expression.

The Corsock raised his wine glass and swirled the contents as he contemplated the question. "I do." He nodded. "I find the natural diversity of the continent fascinating and the hospitality surprisingly refreshing."

"So you're just passing through?" Heathron pressed.

Blacksmeer wiped his mouth on a cloth and scooted his stout wooden chair back with a low screech to cross his legs. "Yes, my plan was to stay in LaBricé for a fortnight or two. Make some day trips exploring before I head up over the mountains toward Ajeratauk." He tilted his head. "Is there a problem?"

"No." Jaaniyah said. "No problem at all. We would be pleased to have you stay in LaBricé during your visit."

"That is very kind of you, M'lady," Blacksmeer replied. "Have you had many visitors lately?"

Heathron boomed out an answer before Jaaniyah could speak. "Explorers, mostly—like yourself." The minister of war stood up. "You must be tired from your journey. Let me have the guard show you the way to your rooms." Jaaniyah rose, anxious for the visitor to leave so she could meet with Jonn.

Blacksmeer stood and bowed low before Jaaniyah. "My thanks again for your hospitality. I look forward to learning more about your beautiful country." His blue eyes seemed bright compared to his white hair. "I hope, M'lady, I'll have the opportunity to provide the same courtesy to you some day."

"Thank you." Jaaniyah nodded, both of them knowing full well she would never travel to the Corsocks. "I'll look forward to hearing more of your islands."

Heathron motioned for a guard to lead Blacksmeer away and put a hand on Jaaniyah's arm to hold her back. As the door closed behind their visitor Jaaniyah turned to the minister.

"What do you think?"

"We need to keep a close eye on him." Heathron's bushy red eyebrows were drawn down in a frown. "Versonga Blacksmeer is not just 'exploring'. He's here for a reason."

"And what do you think that is?"

Heathron's expression was grim as he stared at the door through which the explorer had departed. "I believe the man is a bounty hunter."

Chapter Seventeen

id you find him?" Nica jumped up from the sofa where she had been reading and stared at her sister with anticipation.

"I found Tarantu. He said he hadn't seen Becknah since the two of you walked through the Great Hall earlier."

Nica gasped. "He's lying, then." Her thoughts raced. "Did you look for Becknah? Had anyone else seen him?"

"I looked for both of them, but it's a big palace. Becknah could be in any number of rooms. He likes to squirrel himself away in the oddest places to read, or he could have left to visit someone." Jaaniyah took a breath and brushed her hair from her brow. "I found Tarantu in the stables but he was his ever-annoying self. Didn't act guilty in the least."

"You don't believe me, do you?" Nica sat back down with a thump. She was alone, even now.

"I didn't say that," Jaaniyah snapped. "After I talked to Tarantu I ran into Jonn and he said…"

"Shanks is back?" Nica looked up hopefully.

"Yes," Jaaniyah nodded. "He told me to come up here and wait for him. He said he'd be up shortly."

"Did you tell him about Becknah?" Nica clutched her hands together. Shanks would believe her. "About

Tarantu?" At Jaaniyah's nod, she queried further. "And what did he say?"

"He seemed surprised and concerned," she admitted. "But we'll know more when he comes up and he and I can discuss the situation. What have you got there?" Jaaniyah nodded at the thin black book Nica held in her hands.

Nica looked down. "Oh, it's one of the books of quatrains from the Avedla. It's called The Ages. Becknah gave it to me to look at and I forgot to set it down before I left his study."

Jaaniyah's eyes lit up. "Let me see it." She held out her hand.

Nica hesitated. Her sister was always so demanding. Did anyone ever tell her no?

"Well?" Jaaniyah snapped. "What are you waiting for?"

Nica handed the book over and began to pace around the room. Twenty minutes had passed before she asked, "When do you think Shanks is coming?"

Jaaniyah's head was still bent over the pages of the book. "Anytime. He said he had business with Heathron first."

Nica walked into the alcove and blew out the nearby candle. She peered through the diamond leaded panes out into the dark night. Where was Becknah? An uncomfortable chill spread through her at the thought Mosaba somehow knew of Becknah's plan to pursue the Getheas Stone. Mosaba was fascinated with the

Stone. He had been for years, believing it was his destiny to find the legendary artifact.

A movement below the window caught her eye. She leaned forward.

"Jaaniyah," she called urgently. "Come here, quickly."

Jaaniyah slid off the bed and hurried over to peer out the window over Nica's shoulder. "What?"

"Look down there. Along the wall with the torches." Nica pointed through the window. "Do you see that rider there with the long white hair? Headed toward the forest?"

Jaaniyah moved closer to the window, squinting to see. "What of it?"

"Do you know who that is?" Fear made Nica's voice tremble.

"Yes," Jaaniyah said. "I just met him. His name is Versonga Blacksmeer." She gave Nica a curious look. "Why? Do you know him?"

"I've seen him in Sartis before. He's friends with my... with Mosaba."

There was a long silence before Jaaniyah spoke again.

"Do you think he's a spy? He says he's just arrived from Corsock. Said he's an explorer, but Heathron thought he was a bounty hunter." She peered at Nica. "Do you think he's looking for you?"

Nica shivered at Jaaniyah's words. "I don't know," she replied. They watched as the rider disappeared into the forest. Nica took a deep breath and faced her sister.

"Do you think Becknah was serious when he said it was the time to seek the Getheas Stone?"

"I believe Becknah is serious," Jaaniyah said carefully, "though I can't say I believe the Stone exists. Becknah is a fervent believer in the texts of Getheas and has studied the Avedla for most of his adult life."

Nica nodded. "Mosaba, as well. He's always claimed to possess some of Getheas' original writings himself. Stolen from Jarisa, no doubt," she added quickly. She pushed away from the window. "I'm afraid Mosaba has something to do with Blacksmeer's arrival and Becknah's disappearance. Mosaba is a very superstitious man. He had the Xanfere cards and the stars read for him every day for a long time."

Jaaniyah turned to follow Nica. "And then what? Did he stop believing in the predictions?"

"No." Nica looked away. Her words were flat, emotionless. "Mosaba was drunk one day and killed the man for telling him a fortune he didn't like." She turned away from Jaaniyah's gasp of horror, closing her eyes against the memories that tried to push their way in; the vision of the man strung up in the courtyard, his eyes gouged out and his tongue cut from his mouth while he still lived.

"Your father is hidden and too ill to defend Jarisa," Nica whispered. "Your scholar is missing. You question the loyalty of your finance minister." She raised her head to look at Jaaniyah. "Your army no longer has the strength it once did."

Nica's voice trembled with emotion. "You don't understand about Mosaba. How vicious he can be. How obsessed he is. Right now he's outraged, not only at the escape of a prized prisoner, but he must know of my escape, as well. He won't stop until he gets what he wants or we're all dead. "

Nica continued, her words were low, urgent. "If the Getheas Stone does exist, and if it does have magical abilities or provide the capacity to see the future, then we are all doomed if Mosaba finds it first."

Jaaniyah's face was pale. "What are you suggesting?"

"It's simple. We need to find the Getheas Stone first."

"*We?*" Jaaniyah gasped. "Do you mean you and I?"

Nica nodded. "Remember that quatrain Becknah recited? About the two daughters royal born? Perhaps it's meant to be us."

Jaaniyah barked out a bitter laugh. "Are you *mad*? That's the most ridiculous thing I've ever heard. We're not even sure the thing *exists*. We wouldn't know where to *begin* to look."

Nica brushed by Jaaniyah and walked to the bed to pick up the thin book of quatrains that lay on the satin quilt. "What if the answer lies in the Avedla? In the texts of Getheas? Where else would it be?" She opened the book and fanned the pages. "There's got to be a pattern, a clue, something that makes sense."

"But the texts of the Avedla deal with a huge range of information," Jaaniyah protested. "How would we even know where to start?"

"Look what I've found." Nica pointed at the flowing silver letters on the cover that spelled 'The Ages'. "If you rearrange the letters of 'The Ages' you get 'Getheas.'"

"And what exactly does that tell us?" Jaaniyah's tone was not as sharp.

Nica let out a long breath. "There are twenty-six verses in the book. The same number as the letters in the alphabet." She brushed backwards through the pages. "There's one poem per page except on five pages. Each of those pages has two poems."

Jaaniyah moved closer to see the pages Nica indicated. "So?"

"I think the double entries are meant to be the vowels." At Jaaniyah's puzzled look Nica explained. "Each quatrain represents a letter of the alphabet. The vowels have double entries. What if we're meant to follow the order of the quatrains spelled out by either 'The Ages' or 'Getheas'?

"It couldn't possibly be that simple." Jaaniyah retorted. "Someone would have figured it out long ago."

"No," Nica said slowly. "Becknah told me they'd just discovered this book hidden inside a bigger text." She raised her eyes to her sister's. "Nobody but Becknah has studied these verses yet."

"I don't know…"

"There's a way to test the theory," Nica replied. She recited the alphabet as her finger counted through each page. "If it starts with 'T' for 'The Ages' the first quatrain would be this:

> *"When a witch's storm brews on high*
> *Serpent tongues fork the sky*
> *Upon the winter solstice return*
> *All of Carpis shall burn."*

"But that can't be it," Jaaniyah said. "That verse has already come true. Carpis burned from a lightning strike during a storm over a hundred and fifty years ago." Her eyes dropped to the book in Nica's hands. "See what verse lines up with G."

Nica flipped through the pages, counting under her breath. She scanned the seventh quatrain and a chill raced up her arms. "Listen," she whispered.

> *"A war continues, destined to repeat*
> *Until two daughters royal born do meet*
> *The time has come to heal the past*
> *Now what you seek can be found, at last."*

She looked up at Jaaniyah with wide eyes. "It's the quatrain Becknah recited when he discovered there were two of us."

"I don't believe it." Jaaniyah leaned closer and stared at the words for herself. "What does the quatrain for E say?"

Nica flipped back two pages. "Here it is." She pointed. "On a page with two entries." They read the first quatrain together:

> *"The power within a stone now lies*
> *For one to live, many will die*
> *An ancient promise marked with a seal*
> *A clue, long hidden, waits to be revealed."*

"That's where we need to start," Nica said. Her eyes glowed. "Where an ancient promise is marked with a seal. Any ideas?"

"Well, it's written in Jarisan, so I guess we need to start in Jarisa." Jaaniyah walked across the room, deep in thought. "The Ancients created a doctrine back when they divided the continent into countries. I've heard that referred to as the Ancient Promise."

"What did the doctrine say?"

"That empathy and friendship must be the common thread that governs each state."

"That didn't work out so well, did it?" Nica muttered.

Jaaniyah ignored her sister's comment. "They created a seal that represented the three Ancients: Getheas, Juneedika and Celestica and they stamped the seal on every official document as a reflection of this doctrine. They still do it today." She looked at Nica. "Don't you remember? Didn't you learn about this in history?"

Nica shrugged. "I remember something about it but I was never terribly interested in Jarisan history. Didn't they create a statue or something when they all agreed?"

"Yes." Jaaniyah's voice was faint, her eyes far away, seeing things not in the room. "They erected a statue to Getheas and the other Ancients but that's not where the seal is. The doctrine and the original seal are on display at the Museum d'History."

"Where's that?"

"It's in Our Lady of the Light," Jaaniyah said, a note of awe in her voice. At Nica's blank look, she added, "The cathedral. On the far side of the palace grounds."

Nica could hardly contain her excitement. "Then we need to go there tomorrow."

Chapter Eighteen

ica couldn't sleep. She stared through the dark shadows at the wavering light cast by a lone candle. The flame flickered and danced as if with a life of its own. She could hear Jaaniyah's heavy breathing from the bed. Her sister was asleep, yet thoughts of Toppen and Becknah, of the Getheas Stone and Mosaba kept Nica's mind from letting her rest.

Shanks had visited, though he had looked exhausted. Jaaniyah had pummeled him with questions which he had tried to answer patiently but he'd seemed worried and distracted to Nica. Jacoby was still too ill to travel. His wounds were no longer life-threatening, but he had developed a high fever and a hacking cough. Mosaba had men moving in many different directions, making it difficult to track his location. Their conversation had centered mostly on Becknah's strange disappearance to which there seemed no explanation. Shanks had departed after only a short visit.

Nica tossed and turned, trying to push unwanted memories from her mind's eye. Where was Toppen? Had her returned to Sartis? Was he delivering wine to Ravensfell again?

A soft noise from the outer chamber caused her to jerk upright on the sofa. Had that been the door opening? Was someone coming to check on Jaaniyah? The maids had not been happy they'd not been allowed to clean the room. The sound of muffled steps in the antechamber made Nica jump from the coach and race silently to the other room.

She couldn't be seen.

In a panic, she glanced around, looking for a place to hide. In a nearby wall, there was a small door that lead to the flues, the tunnels connected to the fires that heated the palace. Desperate, she yanked the door open and hoisted herself onto the jamb. Pulling her nightdress above her knees, Nica crawled into the space and pulled the door closed.

The space was cramped and tight. She braced her back against one wall and her feet against the other and slowly walked herself up the chute to where the tunnel ran along the ceiling of Jaaniyah's rooms. Nica flipped over onto her stomach, unmindful of the black soot that clung to her, and pulled herself into the tunnel. She pulled her skirt up around her waist and crawled on her hands and knees to a grate that looked down into her sister's bedchamber. Holding her breath, Nica peered through the shadows into the room below, praying she had imagined the noises.

A swath of moonlight cut through the room below and Nica covered her mouth with her hand as dark figures crept into view. Someone *was* in Jaaniyah's rooms. Nica leaned close to the grate, trying to make out who was below. She counted three shadows.

In a flurry of silent activity, the men moved as one. One man reached forward and yanked Jaaniyah's head back as he tied a black cloth in her mouth as a gag. At the same moment another yanked the covers off and trussed her ankles. A third spread what looked like a horse blanket on the floor. Nica barely had time to blink before a black hood was pulled over Jaaniyah's face. Her hands were tied in front of her and the two men picked her up by her shoulders and ankles and laid her roughly on top of the blanket. The third man rolled her up like she was a piece of dough. From above, Nica could barely hear her sister's muffled cries

One of the dark shadows kicked the end of the roll and there was an abrupt silence. He leaned forward and with a grunt, heaved the blanket containing Jaaniyah over his shoulder. Just as quickly as they had arrived the three shadows disappeared from Nica's view. The entire sequence had taken less than thirty seconds.

Nica sat back so fast she cracked her head with a meaty *thunk* against the stone ceiling of the small tunnel. With a muffled groan, she clutched her head and rolled on her side. A combination of pain and panic made it hard to breathe.

They had Jaaniyah. A thousand questions cartwheeled through her mind. Someone had kidnapped the princess of Jarisa. Like an eerie echo, Mosaba's warning she'd overheard from the window ledge that night she'd spied on his meeting reverbrated in her ears: *'Jacoby's daughter, Jaaniyah is now the prize I seek. I want her captured and brought to me alive.'*

Mosaba had captured Jaaniyah. Nica pushed herself to her knees. She needed help, but who could she trust?

Shanks.

She needed to find Shanks.

Nica crawled furiously back through the tunnel, barely conscious of the hard stone bruising her knees. She clamored down the chute and opened the door a crack, listening. Her heart pounded as though it might burst through her chest as she crept back into the room and ran for Jaaniyah's closet.

She jerked open the lower drawer and dug through the clothes to find the garments she had worn when she arrived in Jarisa. Breathing heavily, she slipped into the black breeches and tugged the sweater over her head. She ran to the mirror and tied the black scarf over her head – tucking her hair underneath. Instead of her own reflection, she saw Jaaniyah. She wasn't alone anymore. She had to save her sister. She wouldn't let Mosaba hurt her too.

Nica grabbed a thick black cloak with an oversized hood from Jaaniyah's closet and forced her arms into the sleeves. She yanked the hood up and hurried for the door.

She stopped. The book of quatrains was still by Jaaniyah's bed. She wasn't going to leave it unguarded. Nica retraced her steps and grabbed the book then raced for the door. She paused long enough to calm her breathing, slowly inhaling and exhaling. She needed to appear calm. With a deep breath, she pulled the portal open a crack and peered outside. Her eyes dropped to a dark crimson puddle on the stone floor where the guard usually stood. Blood.

She slipped out and pulled the door closed behind her. Nica ran silently down the hall, holding her hood in place over her head. She didn't know how to find Shanks. She didn't know where his rooms were located but she couldn't waste any time. She needed to alert someone before those men left the palace with Jaaniyah. She raced downstairs and headed for the Great Hall. Someone there would know how to find him.

The babble of voices could be heard through the two large doors that led to the Great Hall. Many of the soldiers stayed up all hours drinking and talking of war. As Nica neared she could see one of the large doors was ajar. Alone in the hallway, she peered through the crack into the Great Hall. Her eyes locked on a tall, thin man, his shoulders covered in furs. Versonga Blacksmeer. Nica recognized him in an instant. Mosaba's friend. The man Heathron suspected was a bounty hunter.

She backed away from the door. She didn't dare show her face for fear she would be mistaken for Jaaniyah—or worse—as herself.

Nica turned from the doors and rushed down the hall toward another exit. She yanked open the big door and slipped outside into the shadows of the courtyard. Torches burned along the perimeter wall, casting a soft glow against the night. Guards and soldiers moved about, unaware of the danger among them. Nica slowed to a hurried walk, pulling her cloak tight about her shoulders, careful to keep her head down, the hood covering her face. Maybe someone in the stables would know where to find Shanks, or perhaps she could ask one of the guards.

Suddenly a strong arm wrapped around her waist from the side.

"Hold, my friend." A voice spoke low in her ear. "I'd like to know who's working so hard to shield their identity. Who are you and where might you be headed?"

Nica was engulfed by the strong odor of whiskey on the man's breath and the smell brought back a primal fear. Mosaba had always been his cruelest when he drank. She jerked her head back to see her captor, ready to fight for her freedom when she caught her breath.

"Sebande, oh thank the Ancients, it's you," she cried.

The soldier's big arm dropped away as though burned. *"What?"*

Nica grabbed his arm and pulled him out of earshot of three men who stood nearby, waiting for him. "Sebande," Nica whispered hurriedly, "I need you to take me to Jonn Shanks right now. It's an emergency."

Sebande shook his head. "I can't do that." He hesitated, then leaned closer and said very low, "You're the other one?"

"Yes. Take me *now*," Nica said with unusual ferocity.

Sebande glanced over his shoulder at his comrades who stood watching them with bemused expressions before he turned back to Nica. "That's not a good idea."

"Now, Sebande." Nica gritted her teeth. "I command you."

Sebande hesitated.

"As you wish, M'lady," he said with a clumsy bow. "I've an errand." Sebande called to his friends with forced heartiness. "I'll meet you at the tavern in a bit."

Chortles and catcalls followed his pronouncement.

"Who's your friend, Sebande? Can't you share?"

"Aye, does she have a sister?" Drunken laughter followed but Sebande took Nica's arm and led her away, ignoring their comments.

"We need to hurry," Nica said. "It's a matter of life or death."

"M'Lady," Sebande started, then stopped. He took a deep breath and started again. "Shonn has been traveling extensively." He slurred Shanks and Jonn together and Nica wondered how much the man had had to drink. "I cannot account for his condition."

"I don't care," Nica said. "I need to talk to him *now*." She skip-walked next to Sebande's long legs as they wound through a maze of hallways in a side building. The tall young man finally stopped before a set of double doors.

He turned to face her. For the first time he looked her straight in the face. His gaze was intent. "It would be better if you could wait."

With a start, Nica realized that Sebande was much younger than she thought—even close to her age. His height and broad shoulders had made him appear older. And, she thought grimly, she'd never had a chance to look at him properly.

"This can't wait, Sebande." Nica motioned at the doors. "Are these his rooms? Is he in there?" A sudden thought occurred to her. Maybe Shanks wasn't alone. Maybe he was entertaining a woman friend. A sick feeling twisted in her stomach but she pushed her emotions away. There was no time to lose if they were to catch the trail of those who had taken Jaaniyah.

"It doesn't matter. Let me in there now."

With a sigh, Sebande knocked on the door. There was no answer. His eyes tested Nica one more time.

"Go on."

"Wait here." Sebande opened the door and walked in. Nica followed on his heels.

"Jonn?" he called softly. There was no answer.

They walked through a small sitting area. Nica could see the wavering flicker of light in the room ahead. She'd expected to hear the murmur of conversation but it was oddly quiet. Maybe Shanks wasn't in his rooms, after all.

They reached the open door to the bedchamber and Sebande stopped, putting his large arms on each side of the door jamb as though to block Nica from seeing what was on the other side. Her hear fluttered in her throat as she ducked under Sebande's arm and peered into the room with a mixture of curiosity and dread.

The room was warm from the heat of the fire that burned heartily in the grate. Something white caught her eye and she turned toward it. Jonn Shanks was shirtless, stretched across his mattress. A white cloth was wrapped tightly around his ribs. Fresh blood seeped from a wound underneath, a large red splotch staining the fabric. He was still wearing his dark breeches and boots, one foot on the floor, the other stretched out on the bed. His tousled head was turned to one side with an arm thrown over his eyes to block the light; his mouth slightly ajar as he snored.

"He's wounded," Nica whispered, looking up at Sebande in horror. "You knew. What happened?"

"He needs to rest."

For a moment, Nica had an unreasonable urge to cry. What else could go wrong? She shoved past Sebande, knocking her hood back and kneeled next to Shanks. His silver earrings glittered in the candlelight and she could see the lines of pain and weariness etched across his face. Afraid to touch him, she let her eyes trace his wounds. She was shocked by the number of scars marking his chest. Two especially large scars crisscrossed in the center to form a crooked V that disappeared under his wrapping. What had happened to him?

"We gave him something to help him sleep," Sebande said. "He needs to rest."

As though sensing their presence, Shanks dropped his arm from his face and turned his head toward Nica, but he didn't wake from his medicine-induced slumber. Nica tilted her face to stare into his.

An unfamiliar feeling flooded her as she gazed at the long eyelashes that shielded his eyes. Her gaze traced the prominent lines of his cheekbones, the strong cut of his jaw, covered with stubble. Little wisps of blond hair lay against his cheek and for a second she longed to brush them away.

It was a shock to see him so unguarded, so vulnerable. A strange, bittersweet ache filled her. Oblivious to Sebande's watchful gaze, she reached up with tentative fingers and smoothed Shanks' hair from his brow, wishing she could smooth away his pain as easily.

She bent forward and placed her hands gently on each side of Shanks' face then kissed him on the forehead as she would a child. "Be well," she breathed. His eyes opened and he looked at Nica with a glassy stare.

"Jaani?" His brow knotted in confusion before his eyes rolled back in his head and he slept again.

Her cheeks burning, Nica pushed off from the bed and stood up. Shanks was not her friend nor did she mean anything to him. Why couldn't she remember that? She hurried back toward Sebande, refusing to look at him. Without a word the young man led her back to the main entrance. He opened the door for her to exit and said, "I'll notify you, M'lady, when he's in better condition."

Nica nodded. "Thank you." She would have to take a chance. "Sebande, there's one more favor I need from you this night."

Chapter Nineteen

ica crouched, hidden among the dark shadows of the bushes and eyed the imposing structure of the cathedral. In the woods, twenty meters away, she'd tethered her horse. At first, Sebande hadn't believed her when she'd told him that Jaaniyah, and possibly Becknah, had been kidnapped. But the blood on the floor outside Jaaniyah's now unguarded rooms was enough to convince him. She'd told him of her suspicions about Blacksmeer and Tarantu and her fear they were taking her sister back to Sartis.

The young soldier had sworn to her that they would find and rescue Jaaniyah. When she'd made a request for a horse of her own, however, Sebande's willingness to help had vanished. It was only under threat of arrest, knowing he couldn't reveal her true identity, that the young man had acquiesced, and only after he'd given her a stern warning not to leave the palace grounds.

"I'm only going to the cathedral," Nica had lied.

"Then walk," Sebande had replied gruffly, but he'd met her as requested with a saddled mount.

NICA STARED UP at the majestic towers that rose on each side of the entrance to the cathedral.

Jaaniyah had mentioned that the Abbot lived in the back rooms and Nica prayed the man was asleep at this hour.

The church was an impressive structure. Shadows swayed across the magnificent arches and columns that decorated the front of the building almost as though other-worldly beings stood guard.

Nica pushed herself out of a crouch and ran on her toes toward the entrance, where she paused in the gloom of the arched doorway. The shadows were so deep she had to run her hands blindly over the ornately carved door to find the handle. The metal was cool to her touch as she tugged hard to pull the massive door open and slipped into the cathedral.

A vaulted ceiling stretched three stories above her head. Torches lit the passage down a long nave, huge arching columns supporting the painted panels above. Far down at the other end of the building she could see an altar with a wall of stained glass windows backlit by the light of the moon.

Her steps echoed against the floor as she took one tentative step after another toward the altar. Finding the seal of the ancient promise seemed like a far-fetched idea now that she was here.

A wave of lonely despair washed over her. Her only hope to help her sister was to believe Becknah was right—that now was the time for the power of the Getheas Stone to be found. If the quatrains in The Ages really pointed to the location of the stone, then she

needed to look for the ancient seal before she left
LaBricé.

Nica stopped. She stood in the center of a
convergence of eight separate hallways. She leaned
back and gazed in amazement up at the star shaped
window far above her head that glowed as though lit
from within.

"Do you like our lantern?" a gentle voice asked.

Nica jumped and whirled around to find a hunched
man in a long brown robe, holding a small torch aloft.
His grey hair was braided past his shoulders but his face
was clean-shaven and friendly.

"Oh, excuse me, sir," Nica said, taking a step back.
"I didn't mean to disturb you."

"Tis no trouble, child. You are always welcome in
the house of the Gods." He tilted his gaze up to where
Nica had been staring. "The lantern above lights The
Octagon—" he swept his hand out to encompass the
eight hallways— "which reminds us of how glory can
come out of ruin, hope overcome despair and death lead
to new life." He stared up at the magnificent star-
shaped window for a moment before he tilted his head
back down to peer at her through the shadows. "You
are visiting us late tonight, M'lady."

Nica's hood had fallen back as she'd gazed at the
cathedral ceiling and she suddenly felt exposed. It took
all of her willpower not to yank the fabric back over her
head and hide within its depths again.

"Yes. I'm here to see the ancient promise," she said. "Could you show me where to find the document and the seal?"

"I see," the old man said. His kind gaze took in her dark breeches and riding boots. "You wish to see the ancient doctrine?"

At Nica's assent, he inclined his head and said, "Certainly. This way, please."

His footsteps were a whisper on the stone floor. Nica followed, trying to soften the *tap tap* of her boots as she walked through the arched hallway. Near the end the passageway, the Abbot followed another hallway that led to a large glass and wood door.

He motioned with his hand. "This is the museum portion of the cathedral where we keep the historical documents." He pushed the door open and led Nica over to a glass case, the flame of his torch wavering as he walked. "Is this what you search for, M'lady?"

An ancient scroll covered with elegant script stretched before her in the glass case. The writing was oddly reminiscent of the quatrains and with a start, Nica realized Getheas must have written both documents. In one corner of the case an oval rock, about the size of her palm, rested. Three figures were carved into its flat surface.

"What's that?" Nica pointed to the rock.

The old man leaned forward to see where she pointed. "Ah, that is the seal of the Ancients you've asked about. The stone was carved and used as a stamp to mark any official documents the three Gods created. Would you like to see it?"

Nica turned in surprise to look at the Abbot. "May I?"

"Certainly." He held the torch out for Nica to take. "If you wouldn't mind." With both hands free he reached below the case and released a bolt that held the lid in place. Carefully, he swung the glass cover open and reached for the stone. "Here you are."

With a grateful smile, Nica returned the torch to him and took the seal in both hands. It was heavier than she expected. She ran her fingers over the carved figures and turned the stone over, finding it smooth on the other side. She closed her eyes, trying to remember the exact words of the quatrain.

> *The power within a stone now lies*
> *For one to live, many will die*
> *An ancient promise marked with a seal*
> *A clue, long hidden, waits to be revealed*

The power within a stone now lies…surely that line meant the Getheas Stone and not this simple carved rock? Nica turned the stone around in her hand, but could find no evidence of a higher purpose or hidden clue.

An ancient promise marked with a seal. Could that line of the quatrain mean the document before her? She eyed the page. She could see where a stamp of the rock seal had been impressed upon the paper. Nica returned

181

the rock to the case and ran a finger along the scroll. She looked over her shoulder at the Abbot. "May I?"

He hesitated. "Very gently, if you will, M'lady. Very, very gently."

Nica hands shook as she slid her fingers under the old parchment and lifted the document closer to her face. The writing stretched in neat rows along the page, promising equal and just rules for all. Nica traced the border with her eyes hoping to spot a clue waiting to be revealed, but the borders were clean. There was nothing out of the ordinary about the document. She started to return the doctrine to the case when a thought struck her. Maybe Getheas had hidden the clue on the *back* of the page—a place not obvious to the casual observer. Taking a deep breath, she turned the page over, the parchment crackling in her hands.

Nothing.

She held the paper up to the light.

The back of the page was blank.

With a sigh, she returned the scroll to the case and reached for the torch again so the Abbott could secure the lock.

"Thank you so much," she said, trying to hide her disappointment. Why had she thought she might be able to solve this ancient mystery? A bitter taste filled her mouth.

"Is there anything else you would like to see?" The old man asked. His kind eyes probed Nica's face.

"No, I thank you for your time." Nica smiled.

He turned and retraced his steps.

"The cathedral is awe-inspiring," Nica said as they walked among the arched columns and soaring spaces. "How old is it?"

The Abbott slowed and Nica caught the look of confusion on his face. Realizing her mistake, her cheeks flamed with embarrassment. "I just can't remember all the history," she stuttered.

"Built in the time of the Ancients, of course. It has stood here as the heart of HighGarden for many centuries now."

Nica stopped in the doorway to the nave and gazed up in fascination at the intricate carvings that lined the portal. "It's amazing they had the tools to create such detailed artwork so long ago."

"Yes." The old man nodded, holding the candle aloft. "Each of the carvings tells a story. Each of the stories has a name." He walked across the room. "Over here is one of my favorites."

Nica followed him as he stopped before an arched doorway lined with circles the size of her hand. Carved within each circle was a three dimensional figure. A smaller solid circle, the size of a coin, connected the carved circles. She gasped in delight as her eyes wandered over the intricate forms—some animal, some human. One circle held a picture of a goat, another was of a wildebeare, a third was of a man drinking from an overflowing cup. Above that was a carving of the cathedral.

Nica pointed. "What story do these carvings tell?"

The Abbot stood back and waved his torch along the arch of the circles. "This story tells of a bountiful life where the creatures and man coexist in peace and harmony." He was silent for a long moment. "They call this story 'The Promise of the Ancients.'"

Nica admired the detailed work of the figures, her gaze traveling from one to the next when his words sank in. The Promise of the Ancients—An Ancient Promise. With a gasp she jerked around to look at him.

"Is there a carving of a seal within these circles?"

"A seal, you say?" The Abbott spoke softly, as if being drawn back from another place. "Of course, right down here." He lowered his flame almost to the floor.

Nica dropped to her knees and peered at the carved circle in front of her. Three circles from the floor, the figure of a seal was clearly carved, his pointed nose tilted back, his easily identifiable tail resting along the bottom of the circle. Nica looked closer. There above the seal—on the small interconnecting circle between the carvings—something else was drawn.

"May I have the torch?" she asked. She held the flame close to the wall to examine the markings. Etched into the connecting circle above the figure of the seal, was the drawing of a crown.

Nica ran her fingers over the rough stone as a chill raised the hair on her neck. This was it. She was sure.

Holding the candle up, she worked her way along the column of spheres but no other connecting circle was marked.

She took a deep breath then pushed off the floor to face the Abbott. With a trembling hand, she held out the torch for him to take.

"Fascinating history, isn't it?" he said, with a gentle smile.

"Indeed."

"Shall we return to the entry now? It won't be long before dawn is ready to break and I must prepare for morning prayers."

Nica followed him, an image of the crown carved within the circle emblazoned on her mind's eye. The first clue. A crown. Somehow, it was surprisingly appropriate.

"Thank you again." Nica dipped her head to the Abbott.

"Bless you, my child," the old man said, as he placed his gnarled hand on Nica's head. "May you find peace."

Nica slipped outside. The moon shown down, illuminating the spires of the church in a bath of light. For the first time in a long time, a flicker of hope warmed her heart. With a lighter step she ran for the woods to retrieve her horse.

It was still dark among the giant trees of the forest. The bite of the air felt raw and cold after the protected warmth of the cathedral. Nica's breath came out in frosty gasps as she entered the clearing where she'd tied her horse and jerked to a stop.

The animal was nowhere in sight.

Chapter Twenty

ica turned in a full circle, looking for a trail that would suggest the tether had come loose and the horse still grazed nearby. But she knew the knot had not come undone on its own.

She was just ready to bolt through the trees when a whistle sounded nearby.

"Nic." A low voice called her name.

Nica froze. Only Toppen called her that. "Toppen?" she whispered, her heart thumping madly against her ribs.

"Nic." The whisper came again. "Over here."

Nica took a hesitant step in the direction of his voice, when suddenly Toppen broke through the brush and grabbed her arm. Nica swallowed her scream as she recognized her friend.

"Shhh, be quiet." He held his fingers to her lips. "There's a rider nearby."

He pulled her down in the undergrowth as she threw her arms around his neck.

"I didn't know what had happened to you," she whispered. "I was so afraid you'd been captured...or worse."

Toppen held her close for a minute, his arm protectively over her shoulders.

"That traitor let me ride free," Toppen said in a low voice. "I guess he thought I would run back to Sartis."

"You mean Shanks?"

"I don't know his name. It was the soldier who set us up to be captured." His eyes were dark with fury. "The one who forced us to help Jacoby escape. Now we're not safe in Jarisa or Sartis." His words resonated uncomfortably in her head for she knew they were true.

"Have you been hiding in the forest?" she asked.

"Yes. I've been trying to find you," he said. "But I can't speak this bloody language and I don't dare speak Sartish or I'll be arrested on the spot." He ran his dirty fingers along her brow. "Are you all right? What have they done to you? How is it that you can travel alone? Did you escape?"

"No." Nica hesitated. "It's more complicated than that."

Toppen gave her a quizzical look.

"Did you take my horse, Toppen?" Nica changed the subject before he could query her further. She wasn't sure Toppen would understand what she had discovered in Jarisa.

"I just moved her, so you couldn't ride off before I talked to you. You went by so fast I couldn't catch up. By the time I got here, you were already in the cathedral and I didn't dare risk the chance of being seen by someone associated with the church."

The sound of movement through the underbrush was clearly audible and Toppen abruptly stopped talking. He pulled Nica's hood up over her head and held a finger to his lips. They crouched frozen, listening, before Toppen nudged her with his hand and pointed through the forest.

Three shadows moved among the trees in the distance, the low murmur of their voices carrying across the still night air. The men seem unaware of their presence. Nica held her breath until they disappeared into the nighttime mist.

"Traders," Toppen whispered. They waited another five minutes before he cautiously stood up and checked their immediate area. "We should leave now before they know you've gotten away. We need to continue on to Pont d'Suree while we have the chance." He headed down the trail in the opposite direction of the palace.

Nica stared at his departing back in dismay. Pont d'Suree sounded like a distant dream. Part of her longed to follow him, but she couldn't leave and carry on with their original plan—not with the knowledge she now held.

Toppen glanced back over his shoulder to where she was still crouched beside a tree. "Nic!" he whispered harshly as he gave a sharp wave of his arm. The unmistakable sound of horse's hooves suddenly sounded through the night, headed in their direction. A look of panic crossed Toppen's face and he darted back toward Nica, motioning for her to get down.

Frightened, Nica pressed herself against the base of the tree, not sure which direction to run. Toppen dove into the brush beside her just as a horse and rider cantered into the opening. Without slowing, the rider steered the horse directly toward them. Nica heard the ringing *whoosh* as a sabre was pulled from its scabbard. In the next moment, the rider was on the ground, his sword at Toppen's throat.

Sebande's eyes flicked to Nica. "Are you all right?"

Nica's mouth flopped open in shock. "Sebande, stop," she cried. "That's Toppen, he's my friend."

"What are you doing here?" Sebande growled at the red-haired young man who was pinned to the ground by the point of the blade. Nica quickly translated Sebande's question for Toppen's benefit.

"He doesn't understand Jarisan," Nica said, tugging at Sebande's arm.

"Stop it," Sebande snapped, then added a belated, "M'lady. You cannot be heard speaking Sartish. It's not safe."

"Nica, tell him who I am," Toppen ground out.

"Toppen." Nica leaned forward and whispered. "Don't speak Sartish right now. Because of Jacoby's capture it's extremely dangerous—we risk being thrown into prison.

"Why is he here?" Sebande stared at Nica.

"He's been looking for me." Nica stood up. "He's going to Pont d'Suree. Just let him go and he'll be on his way."

Sebande gave her a hard look. "Convince him to go." There was a warning in his words.

"Toppen." Nica squatted down and whispered in Sartish. "I can't go with you to Pont d'Suree right now but Sebande will let you go if you promise to leave Jarisa." She gave him a pleading look. "Please. It's not safe for you to stay."

"What of you?" Toppen cried. Sebande growled and tightened his grip on his sabre, prodding Toppen's chest with the blade until he lowered his voice. "You don't mean to stay, do you?' "Why won't you come with me? Is he threatening you?"

Sebande glowered at both of them. "No, he's not threatening me. I have to stay. I can't explain it right now."

"Why?" Toppen almost pleaded. "Why can't you come? Let's stick to our plan Nica. Three or four days to freedom. We can still make it."

"Enough," Sebande said. He lifted his sabre from Toppen's throat and in one smooth vault, kicked his leg over his horse and pulled himself up. He held a hand out to Nica. "Get on my horse." It was an order.

Toppen scrambled to his feet as Nica stepped toward Sebande's horse.

"Nic, what are you doing?"

Nica wondered the same thing but she couldn't leave with Jaaniyah missing. She couldn't leave until she understood who she really was. She reached for the soldier's hand and he pulled her up to sit in front of him on the large saddle. Sebande held his blade loosely in one hand, pointed in Toppen's general direction.

"Tell him this is his only chance to leave Jarisa. If anyone sees him again, including me, he will be captured as a spy."

"Toppen, go, while you have the chance," Nica said in a low voice. "When I can leave I will come find you in Pont d'Suree."

Sebande didn't give Toppen a chance to answer. Instead, he jerked his horse's head around and kicked the beast into a canter. Nica tried to look back but Sebande's wide shoulders blocked her view.

They hadn't gone far before Nica asked, "Why aren't you following Jaaniyah?"

"Others are going after the princess." Sebande's tone was short. "My job is to stay with you."

"You mean you followed me?"

"You told me where you were going." Sebande's voice was tight.

"I didn't tell you so you could follow me." Nica tried to curb her anger. "I thought you were going to save my sister."

"She's not the only one who needs to be guarded," Sebande replied. He cast an eye at the sky. "We can't ride in like this. We'll have to find another way."

"My horse," Nica gasped. She twisted in the saddle. "My horse is still back there."

Sebande snorted with disgust. "If your friend has any sense, he'll steal your horse and get out of Jarisa while he's still alive."

Nica straightened in the saddle, gripping the saddle horn with both hands. "I'm not going back to the palace. No one knows the castle at Sartis, or Mosaba's moods, better than I do. Unless your soldiers can recover Jaaniyah before they get her to the border, then I'm her best chance of survival."

They rode for several minutes before Sebande spoke. "Aren't you afraid to return to Sartis?"

"Aren't you?" Nica retorted.

"Jonn's right," Sebande muttered. "You're not like other girls."

Nica blinked in surprise. "Shanks said that?"

"He also told me to guard you." Sebande's tone shifted. "You can argue with him about that, as well as about your return to Sartis."

The ride back to the stables didn't take long. Dawn was streaking the sky with swathes of pink light as they approached. Sebande pulled to a stop while they were still hidden in the trees.

"We can't ride in at this hour of the morning without exposing your face," he said. "If Tarantu is involved with Princess Jaaniyah's kidnapping, then we can't take a chance someone might report seeing you. There's only one way."

Nica glanced back over her shoulder and saw his lips press together as though trying to hold back a smile. Suddenly his intent became clear.

"Oh no." She pointed a finger at him. "You are not hauling me in there like a sack of potatoes again."

"It's the only way we can keep your face hidden. Do you have a better idea?" At Nica's silence he continued. "Slump forward and pull your hood over your face, like you're asleep. I'll go as quickly as I can."

Nica clenched her teeth in frustration. "Hold this." She handed him the book of quatrains she had pulled from the pocket of the cloak. "I want this wherever you're taking me." Nica glared at the soldier before she grudgingly covered her head and slumped forward in the saddle.

Sebande took the thin book and slid it inside his jacket. "Keep your head down—" he ordered as he urged the horse forward— "and stop talking."

He brought the horse into the stables at a brisk canter and slid from the saddle the instant the beast stopped, pulling Nica along with him. In one easy movement he slung her over his shoulder and headed toward the palace entry. Nica hung limp, letting her arms dangle, cursing Sebande silently with every step.

"Ho, Sebande, what about your horse?" one of the stable hands called.

"I'll be right back. My friend had too much to drink. I want to pour him into his room before he loses his liquor down my back."

"Aye, I see." The man chuckled, returning to his work.

Sebande exited the stables and hurried up the steps. Nica had no idea where he was taking her. More than once she wondered what she'd been thinking to agree to let him bring her back to the palace.

They traversed several hallways, without meeting anyone, for few people were up and about at this hour of the morning. Even the roosters hadn't begun crowing yet. Nica saw the bottom of a wooden door open and Sebande's booted feet cross the jamb before he bent down and stood her up.

"There," he said with satisfaction. He reached out an arm to steady her as the blood rushed to her head and she staggered to find her footing. "Safe and sound and no longer my problem."

Before Nica could reply a hoarse voice interrupted them.

"Sebande, what the hell did you do to me last night?"

As one, Nica and Sebande turned. Jonn Shanks stood leaning against the door frame that led into his bedchamber. He was still shirtless, the blood-stained bandage around his middle more red than white. His long hair looked damp and was swept back from his face as though he'd just washed.

"At least you got some sleep," Sebande replied. "Do your ribs feel better?"

"My head is pounding so bloody hard I can't think straight enough to know where else I hurt. Who the hell's with you? Are they part of your evil plot, too?" He took an uneven step in their direction, walking unsteadily as though the floor was heaving like the deck of a ship.

"It's me, Shanks," Nica replied, pushing her hood back from her hair, unsure of the reception she would receive. "Nica."

Shanks stopped. His expression sobered as his gaze went from Nica to Sebande.

"What's happened?"

"It's Jaaniyah." Nica moved closer to him. "She's been kidnapped." She wondered at the emotion she saw flicker across this face.

"When?"

She gave him the necessary details while he listened attentively, all signs of pain gone. She left out the part about visiting him while he slept.

Shanks jerked his head toward the other room. "Sebande, you can move faster than me at the moment. Would you please grab me a clean shirt?" Shanks took an uneven step toward Nica. "And light the torches out here," he muttered, "it's the least you can do." Shanks motioned to Nica. "Come sit over here. I want to hear what Sebande knows."

With a painful grimace he tried to hide, Shanks shrugged on the shirt Sebande dropped in his lap.

Nica nodded at his wound. "What happened?"

The young soldier smiled at her with a wry grin. "I met a sword that liked the taste of my flesh."

Nica eyed the bandages covering the seeping wound. "But I suspect the wielder of that sword was kissed by Mercedes before the fight was over." Out of the corner of her eye she saw Sebande turn to look at her.

"Ah, yes, I guess we had a conversation about that, didn't we?" Shanks gave her an easy smile. "I'll have to remember that you have a dangerous memory."

Nica noticed he didn't answer her question. "Not as dangerous as your lifestyle."

"Yes, well, hazards of the profession."

She nodded at his wound. "Have you had anyone look at that?"

Shanks gave a scoffing laugh then immediately winced. "Believe me, Sebande was enough. I don't think I could survive any more medicinal intervention." He looked at his friend, his expression serious again. "Sebande, tell me what you know."

Sebande told of Nica finding him and convincing him that Jaaniyah had indeed been kidnapped. "I told Heathron of the situation and he sent others to follow her trail. Then I brought *her*—" he jerked his head at Nica— "the horse she requested."

"Horse?" Shanks repeated, looking at Nica with a confused frown. "Why did you want a horse?"

Before Nica could answer, Sebande continued in a conversational tone. "She wanted to go to the cathedral. In the middle of the night. *Alone.* " He scowled in Nica's direction. "So I followed her and brought her back." Sebande put his hands on his hips. "And now she's your problem."

"I don't intend to be anyone's problem," Nica interrupted. "I can take care of myself just fine. You didn't need…."

"Now she wants to go to Sartis." Sebande ignored Nica. "On her own, of course. Because she thinks she can sweet talk Mosaba into returning her sister." The tall young man rolled his eyes in disgust.

Shanks' mouth hung open in a look of utter shock. "Bless the Ancients, girl, what have you done to Sebande? I haven't heard him talk that much since I nearly drowned in the river when I was five."

"It's because she's as hard-headed and stubborn as you," Sebande replied, clearly still irritated. "The two of you are enough to make a man drink and forget about stopping." He looked Shanks up and down. "You look well enough to care for yourself for a bit. I've got horses to tend." Unsmiling, he bowed his head. "M'lady."

Sebande was almost to the door when he stopped and whirled around. He retraced his steps, pulled the skinny volume of The Ages out of the folds in the back of his vest and thrust it at Nica. Without another word he stalked from the room.

Shanks looked at Nica. A grin twisted his lips. "Well, I'd say you've made an impression."

Nica lifted her nose. "I wonder if it's ever occurred to him that I don't enjoy his company any more than he enjoys mine." She placed the book on the table and opened the cover and brushed through the pages.

"T....T..." she muttered as she counted, running her finger ran down the page.

"What have you got there?" Shanks peered at the pages before Nica. "Is it a ransom note of some kind?"

"Here it is," she said, stabbing her finger on the page. "Listen:

A tower slowed watches and waits
An unwitting accomplice for the hand of fate
Now into a box what was once a row
The simple answer of where to go."

Nica looked up at Shanks, her eyes glowing with excitement. "A tower slowed... the clock in Berjerac runs several seconds slower than its twin in LaBricé because of the dry air in Sartis. Do you think that's what it means?"

Shanks shook his head. "Slow down, Nica. What are you talking about? What is that book?" He ran his hands through his hair, pulling the blonde strands away from his forehead. "Remember, I'm not at my best at the moment."

"Getheas," Nica said. "We think Mosaba is after the Getheas Stone."

"The legend?"

She held up the book for Shanks to see. "These quatrains might point the way."

"To where? Sartis?" Shanks' voice was edged with disbelief. "Are you mad?"

Nica glared at him. "I think Jaaniyah's kidnapping is tied up with Mosaba's quest for the Stone."

"So you're willing to risk your life to return to Sartis to chase a *myth*?"

She raised her chin. "There are some who believe. Mosaba is among them. It's possible the Stone exists and if it does, Becknah is right. We need to find it before Mosaba does."

She ran her fingers over the lines of the quatrain. "Based on this, it looks like we have more than one reason to go back to Sartis."

Chapter Twenty-One

heir departure from HighGarden went unnoticed with Shanks in charge. Though she wasn't sure she could trust him, she felt safer out in the open with Shanks than hidden alone in Jaaniyah's rooms.

They carried packs of food and water, along with the map she'd stolen from Mosaba. Nica had tucked a long dagger Shanks had given her inside the lining of her boot.

They didn't wait for nightfall to leave. Instead, they headed out in the early afternoon, Sebande riding ahead as scout. If Shanks was in pain, he didn't show it. Nica still wore her dark pants and riding boots, the oversized cloak hiding her figure. Shanks had insisted that they pack one of Jaaniyah's gowns, just in case.

In case of what, Nica didn't know. She couldn't imagine standing in Mosaba's castle again, in any kind of garb, but if she needed to, she would. She shuddered at the thought of Mosaba finding her identical twin. His rage over Nica's escape would know no limits and she feared Jaaniyah would bear the brunt of his anger.

THEY'D BEEN RIDING for several hours and the sun was an orange ball low on the horizon when Shanks signaled for Nica to pull her horse up beside him.

"How are you doing?" he asked.

"Fine," she said, shifting in the hard saddle. They were surrounded by unfamiliar forest. "How about you? How are your ribs feeling?"

"I assure you, I can feel every one of them," Shanks said.

Nica gestured toward his side. "Let me take a look and see what condition the wound is in."

Shanks shook his head. 'I'm fine." He pointed toward a rocky cliff in the distance. "I told Sebande we would meet him past the rocks over there. The horses need to rest and we can see what he says lies ahead. Follow me." His jaw muscles flexed as he clenched his teeth and kicked his horse into a canter.

Within thirty minutes, they had dismounted and Shanks had a small smokeless fire burning under an overhang of rock. He disappeared for a few minutes then came back and dropped a rabbit at her feet. Nica stared at the poor dead creature, then her eyes slid over to where Shanks was rubbing the horses down. Did he expect her to cook this?

She gritted her teeth and picked up the rabbit by its ears, noting the softness of the fur. She rested the blade of her dagger against its back and closed her eyes. She must have made a sound because the next thing she knew, Shanks had taken the creature from her hands with a strange expression, like he was trying not to laugh.

"Never skinned your dinner before, I take it?"

Nica shook her head, relieved to release her grip on the dead rabbit.

"Allow me," he said. He stepped to the edge of the campsite and within a few minutes he was back with the bundle of meat.

"There you go." He smiled at her. "We'll save that lesson for another day."

"Thank you," Nica murmured as she gingerly set what was left of the rabbit down on a rock. She found a stick and after a few tries, pierced the meat and propped it to hang over the fire and cook.

Shanks finished with the horses and turned them loose to graze in the underbrush near a small brook babbling through the rocky terrain.

"Will we be going back over a sliver?" Nica asked, eyeing the way Shanks was holding his left side. Did she dare ask to check his bandage again?

"It depends on what Sebande has to tell us." Shanks sucked in his breath as he eased down next to Nica where she sat near the fire. With the grimace, he adjusted his back against a rock. "He mentioned Toppen was in the forest outside of the palace."

"Yes."

"How did he find you?"

Nica shrugged. "I guess he'd stayed in the area hoping for word of what became of me." She glanced at Shanks from the corner of her eye. He seemed tense. "I told him to go on to Pont d'Suree without me."

Shanks leaned his head back against the rocks and stared straight ahead. "And what is in Pont d'Suree?"

"We were going to go to University there," Nica said. "It seemed like a good place to start over."

Shanks' face remained expressionless. "You must be relieved to know your friend is alive." He cocked his head to look at her. "Now tell me about these quatrains again." His lips curved in a smile. "I think my head is almost back to normal. Maybe I can make sense of what you're saying this time."

Nica pulled the book from an inside pocket in the back of her cloak and recited the poem telling of two daughters royal born.

"That was the first one; the quatrain that lines up in the 'G' position of the word Getheas. Becknah thought the lines referred to me and Jaaniyah." She bent her head and concentrated as she thumbed through the pages. "Here. This is the one for the first 'E'."

She began to read in a quiet voice:

> *"The power within a stone now lies*
> *For one to live, many will die*
> *An ancient promise marked with a seal*
> *A clue, long hidden, waits to be revealed."*

She raised her head. His blue eyes, fringed with dark lashes, were fixed on her with an intent expression. He was so close, she could see each whisker that shadowed his carved jaw. "Can you guess what it means?"

Shanks put a finger to his head, pretending to think before he threw his hands in the air. "I have no idea. Something to do with the cathedral?"

Nica blinked in surprise. "Well, yes, actually, you're right. That's why I went there last night."

He leaned close and whispered in a low, teasing voice, "Then tell me, fair maiden, did the clue reveal itself to you?"

"It did." Her voice came out in a whisper. It was as though she was being pulled toward him.

He reached up to brush away a strand of hair that had come loose from her braid. His rough fingers lingered on her brow before tracing her cheekbone. "And what secret did you find has been hidden all these centuries?"

Nica's breath caught in her throat at his touch. "It was a crown."

"Well, I'm glad to see you had enough sense to rest." Sebande's voice cut into their conversation. "But I wouldn't suggest getting too comfortable. We have a long ride ahead of us."

Nica reached for the sticks holding the meat above the fire with a guilty start. She hoped Sebande thought the color on her cheeks was from the heat of the small blaze.

A small sigh escaped from Shanks as he looked up at his friend. "What have you learned?"

"The princess and Becknah have not been seen at any of the slivers." Sebande hunkered down before the fire on the other side of Shanks. "Which means *if* they're heading back to Sartis they've either gone south to Mar'ligaan where they could sail for Galeron, or north through the Narsgededon forest, where they'll head for the Braaks'faa Valley and cut over through the Spires mountains."

Shanks frowned. "They wouldn't start a mountain crossing at this time of year."

Sebande picked up a stick and poked at the fire, causing a shower of embers to explode into the air. "Or, they're holed up somewhere waiting for us to leave the area before they cross a sliver."

"What's Heathron doing with his men?" Shanks asked.

""He's already sent Joneqy and Masiah down toward the port. But if Tarantu's men are ahead of them, they'll disappear with the princess like sea mist once they get into Mar'ligaan." Sebande cast an eye at Nica. "Are you cooking something?"

With a gasp, Nica jumped up and yanked the stick holding the meat out of the flame. Dark smoke rose from the blackened lump. There was a moment of silence as they stared at the remains of their charred dinner.

Sebande scowled and shook his head, then continued on as if there'd been no interruption. "He asked for volunteers to go into the Braaks'faa Valley but I heard there were no takers because the Valley is supposed to be haunted. So he sent Tanniers and Rushfont."

Shanks chuckled. "That should make a man out of Rushfont."

"The rest are strung out along the rim of the Divide."

Shanks raised his chin at Nica. "Since cooking doesn't seem to be one of your talents, perhaps strategic warfare is. What are your thoughts on where they might have taken Jaaniyah?"

Nica blushed at his sarcasm and wondered if he was irritated at her presence or just her incompetence. She glanced at Sebande to see his reaction, but his features were guarded and impossible to read.

She let out a slow breath. "Without knowing if the kidnappers are acting on Mosaba's instructions or maneuvering on their own, I hesitate to speak. But if they're following Mosaba, then they'll do what we least expect. In which case, their path back to Sartis would not be straight."

"Which route do you believe he would have them take?" Shanks asked.

"It depends on where they're holding Becknah."

"Why does that matter?" Sebande asked. "We don't even know if Becknah was kidnapped or not."

Nica hesitated. "Because I think Mosaba intends to go after the Getheas Stone. I think that's why they took Becknah. And now Jaaniyah." She took a deep breath. She had given this topic a lot of thought while she was locked in Jaaniyah's rooms. It was the only answer that made any sense. "I think that's why he stole me in the first place."

Shanks stared at her with a curious expression. "What part do you play in this?"

"I've always known of Mosaba's obsession with the Getheas Stone but I believed the stone was a legend—a myth." She brushed dirt from her pants. "But now that I've learned of the quatrains, I wonder. There's the verse that speaks of two royal born daughters reuniting. Becknah thought the poem referred to me and Jaaniyah."

"But if Becknah just found the book of prophecies, how could Mosaba know of the verse?" Shanks asked.

Nica shrugged. "Mosaba always claimed to have documents written by Getheas. Documents he kept secret and well-guarded." She wished now she'd paid more attention to his ramblings. "It's possible he had other information that tied Jaaniyah and I to finding the stone."

"Steal a child because of a poem?" Sebande snorted in disbelief. "You'd have to be insane." He turned away from Nica. "Shonn, what do you think?"

Nica peered at Sebande from under her eyelashes, trying to hide her hurt at his dismissive tone. Why had he slurred Shanks' name again? Had he been drinking? She would ask Shanks about that later.

"Mosaba's passion for war does have a sort of madness to it," Shanks said.

"Exactly," Nica agreed. "He desires control of both Jarisa and Sartis but his armies haven't been strong enough to battle Jacoby's. So he seeks any advantage he can find."

"Nica's right about that," Shanks said as he pushed himself up from the ground with a grunt of pain. "Mosaba is obsessively superstitious. He believes greatness is his destiny." Shanks eased upright against the rock, moving slowly. "If he has convinced himself that the Getheas Stone exists, what better way to claim a kingdom than by holding the key to seeing the future?"

"Do you think he has Becknah and Jaaniyah together?" Sebande asked.

"Yes," Nica nodded. "He'll hide them somewhere. Just pray it isn't the Ortawn."

Shanks and Sebande exchanged a look that Nica couldn't decipher.

"Why do you think he'd take them there?" Shanks asked.

"It's where he takes the prisoners he never intends to release," Nica said softly. "The Ortawn is his own personal torture chamber." She held her hands out to the warmth of the fire as she fought back a shudder. "Jaaniyah told me she and Becknah purposely let Tarantu overhear a conversation about going after the Stone so he'd pass the information on and Mosaba would be afraid to kill Jacoby. But it seems the trick has worked too well."

A series of loud cracks erupted from the fire as fiery motes sparked into the sky.

"Perhaps," Nica continued softly, "what Mosaba doesn't know is that the secret to finding the Stone is hidden within the texts of the Avedla. Maybe within one book in particular."

Sebande raised his eyebrows at her. "Don't tell me you think the Getheas Stone is real too?"

Nica gave the soldier a cool look. "I think you need to check Shanks' bandage."

Shanks scowled at Nica and pushed away from the rock. "I'm fine." He held up an arm to ward off Sebande as his friend took a step toward him. "Keep your bloody hands off me. You've done enough damage."

"Then let me look," Nica said. "If the skin around your wound turns red it will take twice as long to heal and will make you sick, besides. I spoke often with our healer in Sartis. He showed me a few of the healing arts."

"No," Shanks replied, brushing the dirt from the seat of his breeches. Sebande shrugged and turned his back to the fire. Shanks mimicked his movement and crossed his arms over his chest.

Nica put a hand on Shanks' arm. "Shonn, please."

Shanks stared at her, surprise etched across his face.

"You told her?" Sebande's voice echoed with disbelief.

Shanks ignored Sebande as he answered Nic. "You can look at my side but *I* make the decision about any 'healing arts' you want to try. Fair?" he said in a terse voice. At her nod, Shanks gave Sebande a piercing glare. "You stay over there."

"Come sit over here by the fire so you stay warm," Nica said. "I'll be as quick as I can." Shanks sat down on a rock and shrugged out of his coat. He frowned as he pulled his sweater up and leaned to the right so Nica could see the bandage.

Nica carefully unknotted the strands that held the bandage in place, noting he didn't have an inch of fat on him.

As the bandage came free, the odor of the wound rose from underneath the wrap. Nica's nose wrinkled at the smell. The blood on the last layer of fabric had dried and stuck to the wound. She had to work very slowly so she wouldn't cause any fresh bleeding as she removed the blood-encrusted wrap. When she'd pulled the last section free she fought to keep her face blank as she looked at the massive purple bruises that wrapped around his stomach. A four inch long, deep gash stretched across his ribs on one side.

"What happened, exactly?" she asked.

Shanks relaxed as he realized she wasn't going to cry or scream. He gave her an appreciative grin. "One man hit me with a broadsword before the other tried to run me through." He looked down at his side and added in a thoughtful tone, "I think it was the broadsword that cracked my ribs, but luckily, by then, there were only the two of them left."

"Luckily," Nica muttered. She bit her bottom lip as she put her fingers to the wound and gently probed the tissue to see how deep the damage went. Immediately, bright red blood began to flow. "*Mediche*." She swore and grabbed the wad of used bandage to press against the wound. A long shadow stretched over them and she looked up to find Sebande standing there.

"Clean cloth to re-wrap the wound." He held out a small bundle.

"Thank you." Nica reached up and took the cloth. "It needs to be stitched," she said, casting a worried glance at Shanks.

"Stitched?" Both men repeated the word in a tone of disbelief.

"Like a piece of cloth. To hold the flesh together so it can heal." She looked from one to the other. "Our healer taught me."

Shanks snorted in disgust "What was he, your tailor before he decided to be a healer?"

She ignored him and pulled back the pad of material to eye the torn flesh. "No black edges, yet. That's a good sign. It must have been a very sharp sword." She raised her eyebrows. "Luckily."

IT TOOK NICA almost twenty minutes to clean the wound. Shanks was shivering by the time she got done—whether from pain or cold, she wasn't sure. "We'll need to clean this again—" She placed the wad of cloth back against his side and motioned at Sebande— "but for now, press on this please."

Sebande did as she asked and with both hands free Nica took the new cloth and tore it into strips, then folded the strips into small rectangular bundles. Satisfied, she motioned for Sebande to pull back. Carefully lining up the edges of the wound, she placed

the clean cloth over the cut and pressed. "Hold again."
As Sebande took over she straightened the old cloth and
began to wind it around Shanks' ribs again.

"This may feel too tight, but it will hold your ribs
in place and relieve some of that pain. Hopefully the
pressure will stop the bleeding and press the skin
together to start mending. I'll need to check it again in
a few hours."

Sebande held one end of the cloth while Nica
wrapped it tightly around Shanks' ribs.

"Should I be able to breathe?" Shanks asked in a
strangled voice.

Nica didn't reply. Satisfied she had the bandage
tight enough she tied the knots to hold it in place.
"There. That should hold until I can get it stitched."

Shanks frowned. "Where in the name of the
Ancients do you think you're going to find materials to
sew up *my skin*?"

Nica gave him a sweet smile. "In Berjerac, of
course."

Chapter Twenty-Two

 ool air coursed over Jaaniyah, causing her to shiver, as the low mutter of voices roused her. She was no longer swaddled with the horse blanket, but covered by it instead. She gingerly moved her arms and legs. Her wrists and ankles were still tied. The gag pulled uncomfortably against the corners of her mouth, making it hard to breathe.

Pain lanced through her head as she tried to sit up against the weight of the blanket.

"South through … sliver… Galeron…..don't dmmmm.."

The Sartish voices faded to an indistinguishable murmur as she concentrated on breathing through her nose. Footsteps approached. The blanket was yanked to the side and a rough hand grabbed her arm. Fingers fumbled at the ropes that tied her ankles and the pressure holding her legs together released. Jaaniyah debated whether to kick wildly but decided to save her strength for a better opportunity when the bag was removed from her head and she could see.

With a grunt, two arms scooped her up. The smell of the man's sweat permeated the air.

"Get on," a voice said in rough Jarisan as he steered her leg over a horse's back. Jaaniyah settled into a saddle. Her captor yanked her bound wrists forward and tied them to the saddle horn. The weight of a blanket settled around her shoulders and hands fumbled under her chin as though tying the corners of the blanket in a knot.

"Do yer best to stay on," he growled at her.

Jaaniyah spread her fingers wide reaching for something to grip. Her wrists were tied to the saddle horn, so she slid her fingers under the front of the saddle and held on to the flat edge.

They started off at a bone jarring trot. Jaaniyah gripped hard with her knees and hands as her head bobbled back and forth and she prayed she could stay on the animal. Thankfully, after a few strides, the horse moved into an easy lope.

She shivered against the chill air. If she'd heard them correctly they were heading south toward Galeron. The town was a Sartisian stronghold overlooking the Sea of Nephalon. No one would even think to look for her there.

JAANIYAH WAS DIZZY with exhaustion by the time she was pulled her from her horse. She staggered when her feet hit the ground and only the rough hands under her arms kept her upright. She twisted her head, this way and that, trying to free herself from the black sack over her head.

"Ai right, ai right," a gruff voice grumbled.

The strings around her neck tightened as the man fumbled with the knot then mercifully the bag was pulled from her head. She inhaled the cool night air through her nose, thankful to be released from her dark prison.

"If you promise not to scream, I'll take your gag out too," a low voice said from behind her.

Jaaniyah jerked her head up and down.

"Not a word outa ye, or back in it goes," the man warned as he began to work the knot at the back of Jaaniyah's head. He pulled her hair as he struggled with the cloth but she tried not to wince for fear he'd change his mind. After what seemed like an eternity he pulled the gag roughly from her mouth.

"Thank you," Jaaniyah whispered hoarsely, lifting the top of her bound hands up to her face to rub the raw corners of her mouth. "I promise I won't scream. Please just don't put that back in. I can't breathe."

"Don't talk neither." The man pushed her forward toward a small cabin.

She took a deep breath of fresh air expecting to taste the salty tang of the sea. Instead, the sharp scent of pine filled her nostrils. Cautiously, she looked around. She couldn't see anything but forest surrounding them. She'd been wrong. They hadn't gone to Galeron. They weren't anywhere near the sea.

The man banged the door open and bent over to tie her ankles together again. Finished, he shoved her through the door. "You wait in there."

Jaaniyah stumbled forward and heard the door slam closed behind her. Before she could turn, a bolt shot closed. She was locked in. She turned to assess her situation. The room was very dark. If there were windows, they were boarded over. No light seeped in anywhere that she could see. The orange glow of a small fire burned in one corner, but a solid shield was in front of the flames, forcing the heat and what little light the fire produced, up toward the ceiling.

She shuffled a step toward the warmth, trying to breathe through her fear.

"From where do you come?" A voice whispered from the darkness.

Jaaniyah nearly screamed. She jerked toward the voice and lost her balance. She hit the floor with a painful grunt, slamming her teeth hard into her lip. Immediately her mouth filled with the bitter taste of blood.

"W..who are you?" Jaaniyah whispered, trying to keep her voice steady. She pushed herself into a sitting position, struggling to get on her knees to defend herself if need be.

"I am the King's scholar," whispered the voice. "They call me Becknah."

Jaaniyah gasped. "Becknah?"

"No." Becknah's hushed voice was laced with horror. "Jaaniyah, that's not you, is it?"

"Yes." She inched herself toward the old man on her hands and kness. "Where are you?"

"In the corner, to your right, I think."

Jaaniyah pulled herself toward his voice. "Are you injured?"

"No." Becknah said, "Just old. What about you, my dear? Did they hurt you?"

"Not yet," Jaaniyah said. She scooted next to Becknah and leaned against the wall. Her eyes were growing accustomed to the darkness and the glow from the fire added sufficient light for her to see through the shadows. The room appeared to be empty except for the two of them. "Are your hands tied?"

"Yes."

"Do you think I can untie the knots?" she whispered.

"You can try," Becknah, replied. "But maybe you should rest first."

Jaaniyah leaned her head back against the wall. "Why do you think they have both of us?"

Becknah sighed. "I'm afraid our plan has gone awry."

"What do you mean?"

"I fear they really believe we know the location of the Getheas Stone. I suspect Mosaba has taken the two of us so that we can lead him to the hiding spot."

Jaaniyah pressed her lips together. She feared the same thing. "But we don't know where the Stone is," she whispered. "What will he do to us when he realizes it was a lie?"

Becknah remained silent.

"They'll look for us. Heathron, Shanks, my sister. Nica knew you were kidnapped. She told me, but I didn't believe her. She told me it was Tarantu."

"Indeed, she was right."

"They'll come for us." Jaaniyah said again, as if repeating the words would make them true. "I know they will."

The door slammed open, banging against the wall. Jaaniyah sat back with a cry and stared at the shadowy figure holding a candle aloft. The small flame lit their captor's bearded face and long hair. He eyed them sitting together in the corner before he dropped some bread to the floor and set down a tall, metal mug.

"Here's your grub."

He disappeared back through the doorway, leaving the portal open.

"I'll get it," Jaaniyah said. She worked her way over to the food, trying to ignore the pain of the hard floor on her knees. The metal cup held a liquid she presumed to be water. She clutched the rolls in one hand and the cup in the other and pushed herself onto her feet then shuffled slowly toward Becknah, concentrating on taking little steps. After what felt like forever she had returned to the old man.

"Well done." Becknah steadied her with his bound hands as she sank to the floor beside him. He peered into the mug. "Bread and some water, it would seem." His shadowed face turned toward Jaaniyah. "What would you like, M'lady?"

Jaaniyah was struck by his odd formality given their primal circumstances. "Just some water for now," she replied. "Turn your back to me so I can work on loosening the ropes on your wrists."

"Certainly, certainly," Becknah mumbled as he bit into the bread.

"Did your devices warn you of this event, Becknah?" Jaaniyah asked as she fumbled at the knot.

"The Xanfere have been very mysterious lately, giving signs that are hard to divine."

"That doesn't sound helpful." Jaaniyah strained and felt the cord begin to give way. After another minute of prying, the knot released enough she could unwind the cords. "There, you should be able to move your arms a bit now."

Becknah's face grimaced with pain as he slowly brought his arms forward. "Thank you, M'lady." He nodded. "That is much better."

Jaaniyah reached for the cup and took a tentative sip to taste the water. Could the fluid be poisoned? But if their intent had been to assassinate her, she would never have left the palace in LaBricé.

She leaned her head back against the wall and closed her eyes. They would know she was missing by now. A vision of Jonn Shanks filled her closed eyes. He would come for her. She knew it.

"Ai right, it's time to go." The gruff voice spoke from the doorway again. Another large shadow stood behind him. "We'll take the old man first," their captor said. Jaaniyah shrunk back in fear as they approached. They went for Becknah first. One on each side, they slid their arms under his and lifted him up.

"Slowly, slowly," Becknah said. "These bones are old and fragile."

Their captor grunted but slowed his movements until the older man was upright.

"Grab his feet." Amid Becknah's protests they swung him into the air and bodily carried him out the door. They did not seem to notice his hands were free.

The larger of the two men returned and walked straight for Jaaniyah. She pressed back against the wall, biting her lip, trying not to cry out. He reached for her and pulled her over his shoulder. Without discernible effort he lifted her up and carried her out the door.

Outside, the air was noticeably cooler. The man dumped her into a wagon. Becknah was lying on his side, his hands tied again and the scholar had been gagged. Without warning, the first man stepped from behind and threaded a gag through her mouth again.

"Lay down and don't move." His words were short and clipped, spoken in rough Jarisan.

Jaaniyah did as he said, praying he wouldn't hurt her.

The man threw a large canvas over the wagon, pulling it taut above their heads. The gate of the wagon slammed shut, jarring the entire carriage.

"Unless you want to *be* dead, you better *act* dead," he snarled. His boots crunched over twigs as he walked around to the front of the wagon. One side of the cart pulled down as he stepped into the driver's seat.

"Move out," he called. The wagon jerked forward and they were underway.

EVERY BONE IN Jaaniyah's body ached from being rattled around in the wagon. She slipped in and out of consciousness, fighting to breathe through her nose. After several hours, the cart jerked to a stop and the low rumble of voices sifted through the air. Jaaniyah heard an occasional Jarisan word but she couldn't make out what was being said. It wasn't long before they started moving again, but at a much slower pace.

After what seemed like hours the cart came to another jerky stop and the tarp was pulled off. Trees towered above them, their branches creating an emerald canopy. Dawn was just breaking.

"Yer ride with me's over," the grizzled man said. His black eyebrows and beard were flecked with grey. He eyed Jaaniyah as if mentally measuring her value.

Another figure approached. This man was tall and dark, with a weathered face and cruel black eyes. Though well groomed, he looked like he had fought in many battles and enjoyed them. When his cold gaze fell on Jaaniyah a jittery feeling of dread filled her.

He snapped his fingers and pointed at her. He spoke so fast in Sartish she couldn't understand him but his guttural voice made Jaaniyah's skin crawl. Panicked, she looked at Becknah to see if he had understood what was said, but he was staring at the man with a strange look of fascination.

Another man jumped as though given an order and reached inside the wagon to grab Jaaniyah's bound arms. He jerked her sleeves up and turned her arms over so the bare skin between her wrist and her elbow was exposed.

The dark-haired man gazed at her arms for a long moment before his eyes flicked to hers, alight with a strange glow. Jaaniyah shuddered as chill bumps covered her skin. He spoke again but the only word she could understand was 'Ortawn'.

tower slowed watches and waits
An unwitting accomplice for the hand of fate
Now into a box what was once a row
The simple answer of where to go."

Nica finished reading and looked over at Shanks stretched out on his bedroll next to the fire. The reflection of the flames flickered off his hair making it appear to glow. She'd checked his side and was pleased to find no new bleeding had seeped through the wrap.

They'd ridden through the night for hours. Sebande had left them almost immediately to scout in other directions. It had taken Nica time to get used to the night sounds of the forest. Occasionally, she would catch a glimpse of glowing eyes in the brush and wondered what beast watched their passage.

"*'Now into a box what was once a row'*," she mused. They were camped in the forest awaiting Sebande's return. "What could that possibly mean?"

"Maybe it's a row of vegetables you put into a box," Shanks offered.

"Yes, and then....?" Nica waited. "How would that be a clue?"

Shanks yawned. "I don't know."

Nica was about to give a sarcastic reply when his eyes started closing. Of course, he needed to sleep, she chided herself. He was wounded and the Gods only knew what he'd been doing the last week besides battling multiple swordsmen at once. She stared at his unguarded face. His cheekbones protruded and his jaw was covered with stubble, darker than his blonde hair. He looked so young when he was relaxed. The sudden urge to protect him rose in her chest. She thought again of Sebande's sharp words: *'You told her?'* She was sure his comment had something to do with when she had slurred Jonn's name.

Nica returned her gaze to the book of quatrains, tracing the year etched at the bottom. So far she had read the quatrains for G, E and T. She flipped to the beginning and counted forward eight pages to correspond to the letter 'H'. She tilted the book toward the light of the fire and read the words neatly printed:

> *Above you'll find a glorified knight*
> *Near year's end he returns to fight*
> *His sword held high will be your guide*
> *Follow to where power divides*

She pictured the statue that stood outside Mosaba's castle. It was the figure of a knight, his sword arched behind his head as he swung in attack. The monument had been raised in memory of a significant battle fought in Sartis many centuries ago. Nica tried to remember if the sword pointed at anything that might be perceived as a clue, but nothing came to mind. She thumbed back to the fifth page for the letter E, where two poems were printed, and read the bottom quatrain.

Where tallest mountains and valleys collide
The ghosts of scattered bones reside
The tears of Gods this space created
It is here the answer has so long waited

The ghosts of scattered bones…a graveyard of some sort?

Intrigued, she turned to the opening page and read the first quatrain on the page for 'A':

What once had been exists no more
What is solid now was once a door
A veil of prisyms casts a brilliant light
But remains unseen in the dark of night

A sinking feeling filled her. How could they find something that didn't exist anymore? And what was a veil of prisyms? Nica fought a surge of panic as she considered the idea that they may not be able to figure out the clues. Could Mosaba be stopped without the help of the Getheas Stone?

The wood in the fire gave off a loud *pop!* as several logs gave way to ashes and Nica jumped at the sound.

Unsettled, she eyed the shadowy forest, but it was difficult to see past the glow cast by the flames. With one last wary glance, she turned back to the book and counted to the page that corresponded to the letter 'S'— the final clue.

Nica's stomach tightened as she gazed at the curlicues and loops that stretched across the page. The final quatrain was written in a language she couldn't read.

Behind her, a branch snapped.

Nica jerked around, searching the darkness. Someone was out there. Beside her, Shanks still slept, his sword released from his belt and lying near his hand. She set the book down and slid her dagger free from her boot. Shifting her weight to position herself between Shanks and whoever hid in the trees, Nica gripped the dagger tight in her right hand while she groped for a rock with her left. Was someone out there watching? Or was it simply an animal on its nightly trek? She took a deep breath, trying to calm her nerves.

Another branch cracked. Closer this time.

Nica stood, the dagger clutched in her right hand, the rock clenched in her left. She swiveled toward a rustling in the bushes. There was definitely something out there.

A shadow grew out of the underbrush.

Nica raised her knife and gritted her teeth. Bravery was not her strong suit. "Halt!" she called in what she hoped was a fierce voice.

For a moment there was silence.

"Sebande, *ocho sin quande*," Shanks muttered in disgust from behind her.

Nica whirled to find Shanks standing with his sword in his hand. She hadn't even heard him move.

Chuckling, Sebande stepped into the circle of light. "*Lo miant despue sinata, omacha*," he replied with a shrug. His dark eyes rested on Nica for a long moment. "*Ela cinquinta ay makata*." He raised his eyebrows at Shanks and grinned.

Nica had no idea what they were talking about but had a bad feeling it had to do with her.

"*Ci ma, ci ma*." Shanks lips turned up in a familiar smirk as he lifted his chin at her. "Preparing to gut someone, Nic?"

Nica still clutched the dagger poised as though ready to attack. "Only those who deserve it," she snapped as she let her arm drop to her side. She glared at Sebande. "What language were you two speaking?"

Shanks lowered himself to the ground with clenched teeth, the muscles in his jaw flexing. He let out a long sigh as he relaxed onto his bedroll again. "It's a secret."

Sebande joined them on the far side of the fire, chewing dried meat from his pack.

"Is that so?" Nica stared at him across the flames. "What does *makata* mean?" She was certain they had been talking about her when Sebande had used that word.

Sebande took another bite of meat. "It means brave." He chewed for a moment before he carefully said, "Nica."

A choking sound made her turn. Shanks was struggling to keep his laughter under control. "And now," he chortled, "we'll have to call Sebande *makata* because he used your real name instead of M'lady." He held his sides as he laughed, his face twisted with mirth and pain.

In response, Sebande threw the hunk of meat he was eating at Shanks' head. With a flick of his wrist, Shanks reached up and caught the missile, a twinkle in his eyes. "Thank you, I was getting hungry again."

Nica ignored their horseplay and gazed at Shanks with a dare in her eyes. "And are you the *omacha*?"

Now it was Sebande's turn to chuckle. His laughter was audible as he disappeared into the shadows and returned with another piece of meat.

"You're very good with languages, aren't you?" Shanks gave her an appraising look. "Some people might call me *omacha*." His lips stretched in a sly grin as he took her hand in his. "But there are others who I hope never want to call me *omacha*."

Sebande snickered again. Nica cheeks warmed, confused at Shanks' sudden show of affection. She regretted her impulsive question. Maybe *omacha* was a lewd word only men and soldiers used.

"What does it mean?" she asked again, debating whether to pull her hand free from Shanks' grasp.

He gave her hand a gentle squeeze. "*Omacha* means brother."

As his meaning became clear, Nica's chest suddenly felt too full to take a deep breath and she looked away. Shanks released her hand and turned to Sebande.

"What did you learn?"

"They caught someone in Mar'ligaan, but it was a decoy. Someone made to look like the princess." Sebande took a swig from a wineskin then continued. "Which means they know we're looking for her." He offered the bag to Shanks and took a bite of meat. "Still no sightings at the slivers and nobody has heard from Rushfont or Tanniers yet."

"So, Jaani could still be in Jarisa." Shanks held the leather wineskin as he stared at the fire, his brows furrowed in thought. "Maybe they're not going to try and take her into Sartis. Maybe they're going to keep her here to look for the Getheas Stone." He looked from Nica to Sebande. "I wonder if that means Mosaba is coming to her?"

NICA WAS THANKFUL her hood covered her features as they waited at the Jarisan side of the southern land sliver to cross the Great Divide into Sartis. Shanks had asked her to stay back from the group of men guarding the sliver while he talked to them, so she waited within the depths of the forest, hidden from view. Next to her, Sebande sat silent on his horse, ensuring no one came too close. Tired, dirty, anxious—she was feeling the strain of the last week. How could Shanks have traveled such distances wounded?

After more discussion about where to go, they'd agreed the Sartisian clock tower in Berjerac would not only let them look for the next clue, but would also allow them to find news of Mosaba's movements. Nica had convinced them she could dress as a peasant girl and blend in with the villagers. She'd so rarely been allowed to leave the palace, there was no one in town who would recognize her. Shanks, on the other hand, was at greater risk in returning to Sartis, but he'd been insistent.

After what seemed an interminable wait, Shanks rode back to them, pulling up close. "We can go over. They don't think there are guards on the Sartis side of the sliver. Mosaba must have his men engaged elsewhere." He nodded at Nica. "Can you follow me on your horse or do you want to ride with me?"

"I can ride myself, thank you," Nica replied, trying not to sound indignant. "Have the soldiers heard or seen anything?"

"No. Several men have just returned from the northern sliver. The only reported travelers there were some old Jarisans who were taking the body of a chambermaid with the pox over to dump her on the Sartis side of the Divide. No one else has crossed up there. Hopefully, we can get some idea when we're in Berjerac where Mosaba has headed and that will lead us to Jaaniyah."

Shanks spoke to Sebande for a moment about the route they were going to take.

"I'll go first, Nica in the middle, Sebande you follow, all right?" Shanks wheeled his horse around and headed back toward the crooked outcropping of land while the others followed. The orange and red rocks of the canyon glowed in the afternoon light. Nica was grateful the wind wasn't howling down the canyon as it had been on their last visit. Even so, it took all her nerve to force herself to look over the edge of the thin land bridge to the dizzying depths below.

She drew a shaky breath and tightened her grip on the reins. She had mixed feelings about returning to Sartis. The abject fear of her father—no, that wasn't right—of Mosaba—she corrected herself, was as intense as ever. Memories of her friendship with Toppen grew stronger and she worried anew what had become of him. Had he continued on to Pont d'Suree?

Her horse stumbled over a rock and she sucked her breath in with a hiss. Trying to steady her breathing, she focused on Shanks' broad back in front of her, his hair blowing back as he rode, relaxed in the saddle. She wondered at the life he'd led. There were so many layers to the young man—he seemed to have so many secrets. She hated to admit she was fascinated by him. His looks didn't help either. There was something about his face, his smile, even the scars that covered his body that were compelling in a rugged, dangerous way.

Nica gave herself a mental kick. Though Shanks was being kind to her now, she reminded herself that in the past he'd also lied to her and tricked her. She couldn't ignore his willingness to risk his life infiltrating Sartis for the benefit of Jarisa. Indeed, he was no friend of Sartis. She needed to keep her guard up around him.

Plus, there was his alliance with Jaaniyah to be considered. Their friendship had an uncommon ease and Jaaniyah's attraction to Shanks was plain for all to see. A twinge twisted Nica's stomach. Perhaps Shanks' only use for her was in her understanding of Mosaba.

"Stop it," she whispered under her breath. "Stop thinking." *'Into a box what was once a row'*. That was what she needed to think about—the key to the quatrain. She needed to figure out what it could possibly mean so they could find the Getheas Stone and stop Mosaba, once and for all.

THE SUN WAS setting as they arrived in Berjerac. Shanks led them to a busy inn not far from the town square. It was close to the main road and many travelers came and went through its doors, making it easy for them to blend in.

Nica kept her hood up as Shanks led her through the crowd. He seemed oddly aloof and Nica wondered if he was angry about something. Sebande followed close on her heels as they made their way through the noisy room. She'd never been in an inn before, and was amazed at the clamor. Voices blended together in a cacophony of sound with a few boisterous shouts and gales of laughter occasionally rising above the din. The sharp smell of ale hung ripe in the air and mingled with the wafting scent of cooking meat.

She found the large number of people crammed together unsettling, but aside from a few curious glances, no one paid any attention to them as they passed through.

Nica followed Shanks into their room and heaved a sigh of relief when the door closed behind them. Leaving the palace, riding for hours through the forest, crossing the sliver, and now navigating a town that was both familiar and strangely unfamiliar at the same time was exhausting. She sank down onto one of the two beds and looked around the small space in curiosity.

"How does your side feel?" she asked. Surrounded by voices all speaking the same familiar language she'd unconsciously slipped back into speaking Sartish. Sebande turned away with a grunt but Shanks sank down on the bed next to her and forced a smile.

"Fine. We must be careful not to attract attention." He slipped easily into Sartish too, making Nica wonder about his own ability with languages. "We have to focus on blending in with the crowd. Nica, your beauty will draw men's eyes, so you'll need to keep your hood up as much as possible or stay in the room. We'll only be here long enough to get a sense of what Mosaba has been doing and to figure out where we need to go next to find Jaaniyah."

Nica dropped her eyes, confused and pleased by his words. She cast a sideways glance at him but he was already in a discussion with Sebande about horses and soldiers. Did Shanks find her attractive? Or had he made his comment because she looked like Jaaniyah? She unplaited the long braid that had held her hair for the last two days and massaged her scalp, letting the long wavy tresses hang loose over her shoulders as she replayed his words in her mind, evaluating his meaning.

Shanks spoke to Sebande. *"Son mark'ra eso saben."*

His foreign words caught Nica's attention and on impulse, she put her hand on his knee and leaned forward, her long hair sliding off her back. "What language do you and Sebande speak?" She smiled hesitantly at him. "Is Shonn your name in that language?"

A brittle quiet fell over the room. Nica immediately regretted her impulsiveness. She pulled her hand back and glanced over at Sebande, but he was watching his friend with an unreadable expression. A familiar burn started eating at Nica's stomach. She shouldn't have asked.

Sebande turned abruptly. "I'm going to go get some food," he said in Jarisan. He disappeared through the door and slammed it closed as he exited. Nica started to push herself away when Shanks' hand reached out lightning fast and gripped her wrist. Nica froze, unsure of what to expect. When he looked up at her, she was startled at the raw emotion she saw in his eyes.

"Nica—" he started— "it's just…" He relaxed his grip and let his fingers slide down to hers. Nica didn't move, unsure of what was happening. Her heart pounded unevenly in her chest. Was he angry? She should never have been so forward.

"It's difficult to explain." He let out a heavy sigh as he pulled away and leaned his head back against the wall, pushing the heels of his hands into his eyes.

"It's all right." Nica carefully scooted backwards, trying not to wiggle the bed. Fear bubbled in her stomach like a noxious stew. "You don't have to tell me. I'm sorry I asked. " She inched backwards a little more. "I won't ask again. I promise." Could she stand and move away from him or would he try to stop her? Nica bit her lip and blinked hard several times to stop the tears welling in her eyes. She didn't want to cry in front of Shanks.

"Shaunismyrealname." He spoke so fast, she couldn't understand what he'd said.

"I understand, really." Nica pushed herself off the bed and stood up. "What did you say?"

Shanks took a deep breath, as though preparing to jump off a cliff. He reached for her hand and pulled her back down to sit next to him. "Come here. Don't be afraid," he said gently. "I won't hurt you." He smoothed her hair back from her face. "Shaun is my real name." This time his words were easily understood. "I haven't used it since I ran away when I was twelve. Sebande came with me. He's the only one who knows who I really am."

Nica tried to act unruffled at this shocking bit of news. If he wasn't Jonn Shanks, then who was he? "Will you tell me your real name?"

Shanks looked deep into her eyes. "Nic," he said softly, tracing her jaw with a gentle finger, "I've never trusted anyone other than Sebande to keep my secret."

The room faded away as she sank into his beautiful blue eyes. "You can trust me," she whispered.

He hesitated, his brows pulling down as if he was in pain. He took a deep breath. "My real name is Shaunte DeGran."

It took a moment for the words to sink in.

"DeGran?" Nica repeated. "DeGran as in the..."

"Yes." Shanks nodded. "Canja DeGran. The pirate king of Corsock." His voice sounded strained. "That bloodthirsty murderer is my father."

Nica covered her mouth with her hand at his shocking pronouncement. Words failed her at the magnitude of Shanks' admission. The snippets of information she'd heard about DeGran over the years raced through her mind. The man was brutal—that part was without question. Brilliant at the strategy of warfare. Uncommonly bold and brave. But a vicious man and without mercy. '*No traitor left alive*', was his motto. Canja DeGran was a man who Mosaba admired.

"I didn't know he had a son," she finally whispered. She tried to imagine what it must have been like to be a child in such a violent atmosphere. Not so unlike her own, she realized.

"So, you see," Shanks said, with a sad smile, "I recognized much more in you than your resemblance to Jaaniyah." He turned her arm over and traced the scars that lined the tender skin up and down her inner arm. "I had a father who liked to mark me, too."

Nica's heart sank. "The scars on your chest?"

Shanks nodded. "Carved into my skin because it pleased him to see me cry. He said he did it to toughen me up." Shanks sighed, his eyes distant with painful memories. "And then when I learned not to cry—" his lips twisted in a bitter grimace— "he said he did it to mark me as his property."

Nica reached for Shanks' hand and held his long fingers tight in her own. A tear escaped and ran down her cheek. Her heart ached. She understood only too clearly the reality he was describing.

"So when I was twelve, I ran away." Shanks spoke calmly, as though describing events that had happened to someone else. "Sebande's father had been killed in a drunken knife fight with another pirate. He never knew his mother. There was nothing left for him in Corsock and no one to care if he left. So he came with me." He shrugged. "And I became Jonn Shanks."

"I'm so sorry," Nica whispered, reaching up and cupping the side of his face with her hand.

His eyes were unfocused and distant as he remembered. "It was rough for a while. I knew my father would try to find me so we were always on the run. There were months where we didn't get enough to eat and more than one winter when I was sure we would freeze to death before we starved." He gave her a rueful smile.

"Sebande and I survived some terrible times. Then I met Amistad Jacoby and I found a purpose as a soldier. As a spy." He corrected himself. "Because I knew Mosaba was as evil as my father and I was determined to help Jacoby destroy him. But then I saw you."

Shanks traced her features, a strange longing on his face. "I saw how brave you were—spying on Mosaba yourself. I suspected how cruel he was to you. Yet you didn't break. You were strong. I was going to help you escape, but you didn't need me. You had your own plan."

"I didn't know..." Nica whispered, "I was afraid to trust anyone—"

Shanks' long fingers tangled in her hair and slid behind her neck, pulling her closer.

"I told you before, spies and pirates must stick together." His warm breath caressed her lips as he whispered, "I will do everything I can to keep you safe." His lips touched hers, gentle and soft. Nica could smell the sweet scent of his skin. She leaned into him, pulled by a desire she'd never felt before and his kiss deepened. Heat spread through her like the glow of sunlight, warming her from the inside out.

he town square was busy as they wound their way through the crowds the next morning. Nica wore a scarf over her head, her long blond hair braided down her back and tucked inside her jacket. Somewhere Shanks had found a peasant dress complete with a shade bonnet for her to wear. It felt strange to be in a dress again, but she blended in with the crowds that jammed the streets and became invisible.

She had molded warm wax and fitted a mouthpiece into her upper lip to distort her features and her speech. Ashes from the fire were used to shadow her eyes above and below giving her a gaunt, ill appearance. At a glance, she didn't look anything like Madanica Santos or Jaaniyah Jacoby.

Nica suspected Shanks and Sebande had acquiesced to her request and escorted her to the square so she would agree to stay in the room later while they sought news of Mosaba or Jaaniyah. She could tell they were anxious to be on their way, but Nica was unwilling to miss the opportunity to possibly find another clue about the Getheas Stone.

She had listened to Mosaba ramble on in his drunken rants for too many years to ignore how fervently he believed—not only in the Stone's existence—but also in the mysterious power the Stone held. Somehow, his quest for the Stone was tied to the kidnapping of Jaaniyah and Becknah. Of that Nica was sure.

Earlier, Nica had checked Shanks' wound again. The tightness of the wrap had helped slow the bleeding but as soon as she released the pressure a small trickle of blood began to flow again. She rewrapped his side with a clean bandage, using Sebande's help to get the wrap nice and tight.

"Doesn't look like you're going to need to do any sewing after all, does it?" Shanks gave her a pleased grin.

"Oh, yes it does," Nica retorted. "That cut still needs to be stitched. I just need to get a needle that's big enough and some catgut, then I'll fix you right up."

"*Catgut?*" Shanks repeated with a look of disgust. Even Sebande turned to look at her.

"*Se tigrynde blackmo,*" Sebande muttered to Shanks.

Nica frowned at Sebande. "What did he just say?"

Shanks bit back a laugh. "Something about an evil streak."

Nica's eyes narrowed and she glared at the tall young man. "Don't forget it, either." She turned away before they could see her smile.

IT WAS PAST ten in the morning when they stopped before the clock tower and gazed up at the impressive structure. The largest ring on the clock was lined with twenty-four numbers to indicate the hours of the day. Colored arcs on the interior indicated day and night as well as the seasons. A second, smaller ring sat on top of the first ring, marked with symbols for the constellations found in the zodiac. One arm of the clock was adorned with a sun while the other arm had a moon on the end, indicating their relative position during the day.

"What an amazing device," Shanks said, looking up at the towering clock. "I wish one of those clock hands could point us to where we need to go."

"Or at least point us toward the princess," Sebande replied in a low voice, speaking in Jarisan.

Nica glanced over at him in surprise. Sebande seemed to understand the local language just fine but apparently couldn't speak Sartish. Nica realized he must have been able to understand every word she and Toppen had said to each other, even though he had feigned ignorance.

"*Into a box what was once a row,*" Nica said. "Do you see anything that's a row?"

"No," Shanks replied. "Let's walk around it once then we'll go sit across the square and see if we spot anything." Nica scanned every inch of the building that was visible as they slowly walked around the large tower. There was nothing she could see that fit the quatrain. She tried to quell her sense of urgency. Now that she was back in Sartis, it was as if she could feel the threat of Mosaba more oppressively.

They walked across the cobblestone square and sat down on one of the stone benches. Shanks sat down next to her, leaning on arm on the bench behind her back. Sebande stood on the far side of him, his arms crossed, his expression distant as he searched the faces among the crowd in the square for any threat.

"Read the lines again," Shanks said.

Nica enjoyed the warmth of his body and the sense of security she felt when he was near. She fought the urge to lean against him as she recited the quatrain.

> *"A tower slowed watches and waits*
> *An unwitting accomplice for the hand of fate*
> *Now into a box what was once a row*
> *The simple answer of where to go.*

"It has to mean this tower," she said. "Because of the dry air, the Berjerac tower keeps time a few seconds behind the one in LaBricé." She looked around. "What else could it mean?"

"I agree," Shanks nodded. "But what's it waiting for? The arrival of something? Or someone?" He raised his eyebrows at Nica. "An unwitting accomplice for the hand of fate?"

She shook her head, staring at the words again. "I don't know."

THEY STAYED AT the tower for an hour before giving up and heading back to the inn. After they'd eaten, Shanks escorted Nica back to the room. "I'm going to scout around to see what I can find out about Mosaba. Sebande is going to stay with you." His face was serious. "He may not be in the room, but he'll be close enough to hear you if you need him." His lips twisted in a sweet smile. "While I'm gone why don't you figure out that poem?"

"Is that all I need to do?" she teased back. "Maybe I should capture Mosaba while I'm at it, too."

Shanks' smile faded. "No, you leave that part to me." His eyes were shielded again and Nica wondered what he was thinking. "I'll be back soon."

"Shaun," Nica said softly. He paused at the door and looked over his shoulder in surprise. "Please be careful."

THE DAY DRAGGED by as Nica waited for Shanks' return. Sebande didn't come to the room. Nica didn't know where he was, but she trusted Shanks had told her the truth and he was nearby. She thumbed through the book of quatrains but no hidden message became clear. She tried to sleep, but her rest was fitful, her nerves too ragged to really relax. Thoughts of what Shaunte DeGran's life must have been like growing up under the hand of Canja wouldn't leave her alone.

At the back of it all, like a melody that played over and over in her mind, was the memory of Shanks' kiss and the realization that he had trusted her enough to reveal his deepest secret. The knowledge gave her a feeling she'd never had before—as if a light had settled in her chest and warmed her heart. She was afraid to question too closely what that meant.

THE CLOCK TOWER tolled six and Sebande had brought her a tray of food, but he didn't eat with her. Nica lit a single candle and sat waiting on the bed, worry gnawing at her gut. It was dark when the door finally opened and she jerked upright, anxious to hear any news.

His tall figure filled the doorframe. His shoulders were hunched as though he were in pain and he blew on his hands trying to warm them. Sebande followed him into the room, a grim expression on his face. He cast a dark glance at Nica then looked away, making her wonder if he was angry.

"Did you learn anything?" she asked. Sebande brought over a tray of food that he had stored for Shanks and held it out to his friend. With a murmur of thanks, Shanks sat down on the edge of the bed and tore into the bread. Even several inches away Nica could feel cool air radiating off of him. He had to be freezing.

"Do you want a blanket?" she asked.

"No, a mug of something hot to drink would help though."

Sebande left the room without a word.

"Is he angry?" Nica whispered to Shanks.

"No," Shanks replied in between bites. "Sebande's father would beat him if he talked, so he doesn't talk much—even to me. I'm used to it by now. That's why I was so shocked at his outburst when he brought you to my rooms at the palace. That's probably the longest tirade I've ever heard from him." Shanks winked at her. "He must like you."

Nica snorted. "I hardly think *that's* the reason. More likely the opposite." She leaned a little closer to him. She loved how he smelled. "Did you find out anything about Mosaba?"

Sebande returned with two cups of warm cider and thrust one into Shanks' hand and offered the other to Nica.

"Oh, thank you," she said in surprise. She reached for the cup and smiled up at him. He returned her gaze without any expression, his dark eyes shadowed by the thatch of black hair across his forehead.

"Mosaba is at the Ortawn," Shanks said. "There doesn't seem to be any doubt about that information. Why—nobody would say." He shoved the last bit of bread into his mouth. "But, I suspect it means he's got a new prisoner."

"Oh no," Nica gasped. "Not the Ortawn." She would never forget the terror she'd felt inside that underground prison. "Do you think it's Jaaniyah?"

"I can't say for sure. I'm going to investigate a little further tomorrow."

Sebande stood a few feet away, his arms crossed over his chest. "I will go with you," he said firmly in Jarisan.

THE NIGHT FLEW by. Sebande offered to sleep on the floor so both Shanks and Nica could have a bed. In the morning, Nica stayed in the room while they left to fetch breakfast. She was afraid to think about what

Mosaba would do to Jaaniyah—or what he would do if he caught her again.

She pushed herself off the bed and paced around the room. Shaun, as she was starting to think of him, had clearly favored his left side this morning. The wound had started bleeding again in the middle of the night and the edges of the cut were red and becoming inflamed. He was moving too much, instead of letting his body heal, but there was no way she could make him stop and rest.

He needed a healer. Or she needed to get the necessary materials to stitch up his injury and keep it bound together to mend. Toppen had delivered wine to that old woman just outside the town square. He'd said she practiced the healing arts. Perhaps she would have what Nica needed.

When Shanks and Sebande returned, Shanks set out the food on the small wooden table while Sebande pulled out a stone to sharpen their swords. The fare was only sausage, gruel and some biscuits but the aroma permeated the room and smelled wonderful. Nica sat down at the table and eagerly dug into her platter. She glanced at Shanks from under her eyelashes several times before she got up the nerve to speak.

"You know, I'll be fine here by myself if you two want to go together this afternoon. I'll take a nap."

Shanks' head lifted, his silver earrings swinging with his movement. He gave her a shrewd look. "Where is it you want to go, Nica?"

"Go?" Nica echoed, surprised at his perceptiveness. "Nowhere… it's just that I know Sebande wants…"

He cut her off. "Where?"

Nica closed her mouth and looked at Sebande. He had a strained look on his face as though he was trying not to smile.

"Well, I did want to have another look at the clock tower." Nica pushed her food around on her plate. "And…well…" the rest came out in a rush, "there's a healer I want you to visit who doesn't live far from here."

"No."

"Shaun, please. You need to have someone tend to that wound."

Sebande made a disgusted noise in the back of his throat.

Shanks scowled at her. "I will not purposely reveal myself to anyone in this town who might be able to describe me later. Healer or no healer." His gaze was intent. "Is that clear?"

Nica took a deep breath. She wasn't used to standing up to other people. But this wasn't for her—it was for him. "Then I need to see her."

"Why?"

"Because she also specializes in—" Nica looked around the room in search of inspiration. Her eyes fell on a spill of lace from the gown Shanks had shoved into his bedroll before they left Jarisa— "womanly things."

Shanks raised his eyebrows. Nica's cheeks started to burn but she refused to look away.

"If we take you back to the clock tower and over to see this woman will you give me your word you'll stay in the room while we're gone?"

Nica relaxed, pleased he would help her rather than be angry. "Yes, I promise."

Shanks glanced at Sebande who sat on the edge of the bed with his sword across his lap, sharpening the blade. "All right with you?"

Sebande shrugged. "What's another hour?" He drew the stone down the length of the blade again with a quiet *whish.*

THE WEATHER HAD cooled and grey clouds scuttled across the even darker grey sky. They stood in front of the clock tower again and stared up at the figures and symbols. Nica shivered as a bitter wind cut across the town square. There was nothing different about the clock today. No rows to be found. No secret answers. She sighed and nodded when Shanks insisted they keep moving.

They followed Nica's directions through the cobblestone streets. As they passed the wine emporium, the vivid memory of Toppen's kiss made her lips tingle. That kiss seemed a lifetime ago. Unbidden, the memory of Shanks' lips pressed against her own replaced the other, like a flame engulfing a twig. She could remember the texture of his lips against hers, his smell, the touch of his fingers against her skin...

"Which house is it?" Shanks asked.

Nica jumped at his question. Luckily, the cold wind could explain the rosy color in her cheeks.

"That one at the end." Nica pointed. "The white one that looks like a beehive." As they approached, the friendly mutt who had greeted her before came loping across the street toward them. "The dog's name is Hope."

"Hello there." Shanks leaned down to pet the dog's soft head. At that moment, Sebande pulled on Nica's arm. She turned to find his tall frame right next to her. She started to step back, but before she could move, he pressed several coins into the palm of her hand. He leaned close to her ear and whispered, "for the gut string and needle." Then he stepped next to Shanks to pet the dog.

Nica stared down at the coins in her hand, then snapped her fingers closed. She glanced at Sebande but he had his back to her. She hurried toward the house.

"I'll be quick," she called over her shoulder, hoping they would have enough sense to stay outside. At her knock, the door creaked open and a frail, white haired woman, hunched with age, stood before her. Nica explained what she was looking for and held her breath as she waited for the woman's answer. After a careful perusal of Sebande and Shanks where they stood in the street talking, the old woman invited her in.

"Your friends are young and strong," she commented as she shuffled across the room to a rack of shelves against one wall. "They must care for you very much to escort you on this errand."

"Oh," Nica stuttered. "T..they're not escorting me, we're.. um... on our way to visit a friend."

"The blond one guards you," she said, "as though you are precious." She gave Nica a sly look over her shoulder.

Nica's jaw sagged. What had the woman seen to make her say such a thing? She turned to gaze out the window, studying the tall, strong silhouettes of Shanks and Sebande trying to see what the healer had seen. As she watched, Shanks laughed at something Sebande said, his white teeth flashing, and Nica's chest constricted with an emotion so powerful it took her breath away.

"How many hands do you want?" The old woman pulled several boxes from the shelf.

Nica jerked around. "Excuse me?"

"Hands. The gut string is measured in hands. How big is the area you want to stitch?" She held up her own hand. "Do you need one hand or more?"

"Oh, of course, hands," Nica said. She looked down at her hand and tried to imagine stitching Shanks' side. "I guess I better have five. The thinnest you've got. And a long, thin needle."

The woman pulled a knife from her apron pocket and after measuring the string, sliced it at the appropriate spot. She shuffled to another box on the shelf and pulled out a long needle. "Like this?" she asked.

"Yes." Nica gazed around the little room. Two rocking chairs sat before a cheery fire burning in one corner of the room. A long table stretched across the back of the room where an array of different herbs were laid out to dry. She wondered if the woman lived alone. "Do you have anything for pain?"

Nica was sure the healer had figured out her purpose for the materials. The old woman didn't ask though, and instead, moved slowly over to the table, reaching for a pile of green stems.

"Soak this and apply it to the wound, it should deaden the pain while you stitch." She reached for a different herb. "Keep this on the wound for the next few days until the redness is gone. Wrap it under the bandage and change the poultice twice a day."

"Yes, thank you." Nica held out several coins.

"I'll take one," the old woman said, holding out her gnarled hand. "You save the other." She wrapped her hands around Nica's, pushing her fingers closed around the remaining coin. "I suspect you might need it."

Nica gave the old woman a shaky smile, wondering what prompted her to say such a thing. She took the materials and slid them into the pocket of her dress. "Thank you again."

"Did you get what you wanted?" Shanks asked as she joined them outside.

"Yes, she had what I needed."

A sudden frown creased his brow. "Do you need to pay her? I forgot you probably don't have any money."

"It's all right." She glanced up to see Sebande's glare. She let her eyes slide away and smiled at Shanks. "I traded a scrap of lace with her."

"If you're sure." At Nica's nod, he said, "Let's head back to the inn. A storm is blowing in." He took her arm, as another blast of cold wind gusted down the street.

As they walked away, Nica glanced back at the little white cottage. In one window, the white curtain was pulled to the side and the old woman's face watched them through the pane. Nica raised her hand in farewell and suddenly the old woman's words echoed in her head: *'How many hands do you want?'* The words of the quatrain followed as though someone had spoken in her ear: *An unwitting accomplice for the hand of fate,* and then Shanks' comment about the clock: *'I wish one of those clock hands could point us to where we need to go.'*

"That's it," she whispered. "It's the hands."

"What did you say?" Shanks leaned close, but held his arm cocked to protect his side.

"The clock hands," Nica cried. "That's where the clue is."

Chapter Twenty-Five

ica practically ran back to the clock tower. Rain started to fall in big drops and the sky overhead turned as dark as the bottom of a soup pot. Impetuously, she grabbed both Shanks' and Sebande's hands as they reached the cobblestone square and pulled them over to stand in front of the tower.

"Look at the clock hands," Nica whispered. "That's where the clue is." She stared at the face of the multi-dimensional clockworks searching for what they'd missed before.

Shanks let out a slow whistle.

"What?" Nica looked from the clock to his face and back again. "What do you see?"

"The bloody hands point right to them, but they blend in so well you don't notice them."

"Ah," Sebande muttered. "You're right."

"Where?" Nica cried, straining to see what they both saw. "I don't see it."

"Look at the very outer rim." Shanks leaned his head close to hers and pointed. "Right where the hand with the sun is pointing? There are letters engraved between each of those carved animals. They stretch all around the outside of the circle." He looked down at Nica. "I'll bet that's it."

Nica squinted up at the clock. "I see them," she breathed. "They've been there all the time, waiting for someone who knew what they were." She looked around. "We need to mark them down."

Sebande rummaged around in his jacket and came up with a scrap of paper and a piece of lead and handed them to Nica.

"You read them out loud," she said to Shanks, "and I'll write them down."

"G...O...H...L...." Shanks began reading the letters and Nica carefully wrote them in a row on the page.

"S. That's the last one, "Shanks said. "And then it looks like there's a figure of an eye."

"An eye?" Nica glanced up to see for herself. At the very top of the circle between the first and the last letter was a clear drawing of an eye. "A crown and an eye. They must mean something." She looked down at the paper where she'd written the letters in order. "*Now into a box what was once a row*," she whispered to herself, eyeing the letters. At that moment a bolt of lightning cracked the sky and rain pounded down in a sheet of water.

"Come on. "Shanks tugged at her arm. "Let's go."

THEY WERE SOAKED by the time they entered the shelter of the inn. The common room was crowded as they made their way to their room. Unmindful of her wet clothes, Nica went straight to the table and smoothed the damp piece of paper out with her hands.

"G, O , H, L, I, O, U, E, O, S, T, G, V, F, Y, H, H, E, P, M, R, T, I, R, S," she read out loud. "They must mean something, but I have no idea what." She stared at the letters and tried to arrange them into words. An hour passed and she still hadn't made any headway. She looked over at Shanks and Sebande. "What do you think they mean?"

They both came and stood behind her, looking over her shoulder at the row of letters.

"*Into a box what was once a row,*" Nica repeated.

Shanks looked down at the paper and shrugged. "It must mean a cypher's box," he said, then went to dry and oil their swords.

"Ah, of course." Sebande nodded at his friend. "Like old man McTaggert used to do."

Nica looked from one to the other. "What's a cypher's box?"

"Count all the letters in the row," Shanks replied. "Then divide them into an equal number of rows and columns." At Nica's blank look he said, "It's easier to show you. Do you still have that piece of lead?" He held his hand out. "And something to write on?" Nica shoved the scrap of paper toward him. He counted the number of letters and began writing again:

G O H L I
O U E O S
T G V F Y
H H E P M
R T I R S

Nica peered anxiously over his shoulder while he wrote. When he finished, he looked sideways at Nica. "There you go—a cypher's box."

She stared blankly at the block of letters. "Does that mean something to you?"

Shanks pointed at the 'G' with this finger. "Start here and read vertically down each row." He scrunched his brow as he figured out where the breaks occurred between the words. "*Got hrough...*, no, that's not right, probably *Go through*," he mumbled to himself. "*Go through theveil*, no....*the veil...*" Finally he said, "That's it. *Go through the veil of prisyms.*"

"I don't believe it," Nica gasped. "How did you know how to do that?"

Shanks gave her a lopsided smile. "Nic, I can't reveal *all* my secrets."

From the corner where he sat oiling his sword, Sebande coughed.

Nica reached for the book of quatrains and flipped it open to the correct page. "*Now into a box what was once a row*," she read, "*the simple answer of where to go.* Go through the veil of prisyms." She lifted her head. "I guess that could make sense. But what's a veil of prisyms?"

Shanks stretched out on the bed, his face creased with pain. "I don't know."

Nica hesitated. He was getting worse. She needed to stitch up his side. If she could get some water she could tend to his wound right here in the room.

"Sebande." Nica smiled. "Is there any way to get some hot water?"

"What for?" Shanks asked in a wary tone.

"I'd like to have some tea. I'm a bit cold," Nica said. She shivered to convince him of her sincerity and went behind the blanket they had draped across one corner of the room to change in privacy. She slid into her black breeches and pulled on a dark sweater. She ran her fingers through her hair and tied the damp strands in a knot at the back of her head. Dry again, she began to warm up.

As Nica emerged from around the curtain Sebande disappeared out the door. Her stomach twisted at the idea of stitching Shanks' side, but she knew it had to be done.

"What's the next quatrain say?" Shanks asked with a yawn. His question startled her. His eyes had been closed and she'd thought he was sleeping.

Nica went to the table and pulled the book over. "We've found G, E, T so now we need the poem for H. She thumbed through the pages counting quatrains. "Here's what it says:

> *Above you'll find a glorified knight*
> *Near years end he returns to fight*
> *His sword held high will be your guide*
> *Follow to where power divides*

She looked over at him. "What do you think? There's a statue in front of Ravensfell that seems to fit this description. Do you remember it?"

Shanks nodded.

Sebande returned with the hot water and a bottle of some amber fluid.

"What's that?" Shanks asked suspiciously.

Sebande shrugged. "Something to take the chill off."

With a grunt, Shanks pushed himself off the bed. "You can get the chill off later, because we're leaving."

Nica looked at Sebande with wide eyes and pointed at her side but Sebande shook his head. He set the kettle down on the table and gathered his gear. It was only a short time later and they were ready to leave.

"You're not going to try and go into the Ortawn are you?" she asked.

Shanks grabbed his hat from the table. "We'll see what the wind blows in." He hesitated then stepped close to her. The door thudded closed as Sebande left the room. "Promise me you'll stay here," Shanks said, looking into her eyes as if he could see the truth there.

Nica nodded. Her emotions were in such a knot, she didn't think she could speak if she had to. Her fingers trembled as she reached up and brushed his blond hair from his forehead. "Come back safe."

"I will." Shanks lips hesitated as if he might kiss her, then he pulled back. As he opened the door Nica called softly, "May you both travel with the blessings of the Ancients."

DAY DRAGGED INTO evening and evening into night. Nica paced the room, read the book of quatrains, soaked the herbs and paced the room again. Where were Shanks and Sebande? She stared out the window and tried to settle her nerves, but something was wrong. She could feel it.

It was almost dawn when a thump came upon the door to her room. Lying awake in the dark, Nica sat up with a jerk.

"Nica," a voice called through the crack. "It's me, open up."

Nica lit a candle and ran to the door, her heart pounding. Her fingers fumbled with the bolt as she tried to throw it clear to open the door. As soon as she got the bolt released the door was pushed open.

"Get your things," Shanks said. "We have to go, *now.*" He limped into the room and picked up both his and Sebande's bed rolls. His eyes scanned the room.

A chill of alarm swept over her. She didn't stop to ask what had gone wrong. Too many years of fleeing at the sound or sight of Mosaba had trained her to react quickly. She jerked the privacy blanket down and pushed it into a tight roll. She threw a sweater on then grabbed her cloak. With no time to braid her loose hair, she tucked the long strands into a knot at the back of her neck.

"Come on," Shanks muttered.

She hurried to the table and shoved the book of quatrains into the inner pocket of her cloak, then picked up the crumpled paper covered with letters. She hesitated for a heartbeat then held it to the flame of the candle. Once the corner of the page caught fire she dropped it into a small brass tray. In seconds the clue was nothing more than a pile of ashes.

Her gaze stopped on the container of herbs she'd been soaking. She'd have to leave them. She turned away, then jerked back around as she realized they might be a hint someone was injured. Sweeping her hand out, she grabbed the container, intending to dispose of the contents outside.

"Pull your hood up," Shanks said, his voice hoarse. "Keep your face hidden." Loaded down with the bed rolls he led the way down the stairs, favoring one side. The great room was empty at this hour. Nica followed close behind, her heart pounding with every step as she wondered what had happened. Outside, the rain had abated but a chill wind still blew with frosty breath, causing her to shiver after the warmth of the inn.

From the shadows, Sebande emerged, holding three horses. His face was grim and emotionless as he held the horse for Nica to mount. Shanks climbed on his horse and looked back at Nica.

"Ready?" His tense expression frightened her.

Nica nodded. It wasn't a time for words.

Shanks kicked his horse into a gallop, steering his mount into the darkness of the forest. Nica followed, riding between him and Sebande. They rode past dawn, winding through the trees, walking the horses up streams, continually changing direction until Nica had no idea where they were. Occasionally, they'd pass through a clearing and she'd see the Spires Mountains far to the north, but beyond that, she was lost.

EVENING WAS SETTLING with black clouds when Shanks finally pulled up. Their horses were lathered, their sides heaving with exertion. He slid off his saddle and limped over to help Nica down. Shocked at his stiff movements, she kicked her leg over and slid down the side of her horse on her own.

"You're worse—what happened?" she cried, as she moved close to him and pulled open his leather jacket. There was a suspicious stain on one side. He tried to pull away but she held tight. "Let me look," she snapped. She lifted his sweater and gasped at the bright red blood that covered his middle and ran down one side. She whipped around to look at Sebande who watched her, his lips pressed in a thin line. "You should have told me," she said.

She turned back to face Shanks. "What happened? Were you attacked?"

"It was a trap." Shanks heaved a sigh. "I should have known better. I dropped my guard." He shook his head in disgust. "Jaaniyah is in the Ortawn. They knew we would come after her. They were waiting for us." He loosened the girth around his horse to remove the saddle, but Sebande stepped in and pulled the heavy load down for him. Shanks nodded his thanks and stepped back to give him room. He ran his hands through his blond hair pulling it back from his face, revealing black shadows of pain under his eyes.

"There's something else, too."

Nica tensed. "What?"

"Mosaba's men aren't the only ones looking for me. There's a man from Corsock who's also on my trail." Shanks almost looked guilty. "Our paths intersected tonight."

"Versonga Blacksmeer." Nica breathed the dreaded name. She should have known better, too. Mosaba wouldn't simply let her escape. He must have hired Blacksmeer to find her and in doing so, the bounty hunter had found his way to Shanks. So that's why Sebande was glaring at her.

Shanks lifted his head in surprise. "You know of him?"

Nica gave a hesitant nod. Sebande was watching her, too. "I think he works for Mosaba. I've seen him at the castle in Sartis before. I saw him in the distance at HighGarden and recognized him." She clutched her hands together. "I'm sorry," she whispered. "I should have warned you that my father—I mean, Mosaba— must have sent him after me." Did he blame her too?

Shanks' pained look softened and for a moment a bittersweet smile rested on his lips. "Nica, you have no need to be sorry." He reached out and caressed her cheek with the back of his fingers. "Versonga Blacksmeer is here because *my father* has sent him after me, as well. He has searched for me for years." He ran a thumb gently over her lower lip. "And now, it would seem, Versonga Blacksmeer is after both of us."

et me see it," Nica said again. She was standing next to Shanks, who was hunched over tending to the fire.

"No," he muttered.

Sebande came to stand beside her. He'd just returned from scouting the area and had confirmed no one had followed them. He held a horse brush in one hand.

"Shaun." His voice was low, but Nica heard an unusual undercurrent of emotion. "Your side needs to be stitched. Let her do it."

Nica looked at him askance, surprised at his support of her efforts. Even Shanks turned his head.

"What?" he asked.

"Unless you want to bleed to death before Blacksmeer or Mosaba runs you through, then get the wound stitched. Nica has the supplies." This time Sebande didn't hesitate as he said her name. "And take it like a man, would you? I can't stand cry-babies." He turned away and went back to brushing the horses.

"Traitor," Shanks muttered as he pushed himself upright, unable to stifle the groan of pain as he moved. He gave Nica a suspicious look. "What supplies?"

"Just some herbs."

Shanks raised his eyebrows.

"And a needle and thread," she added quickly. "I'll be as gentle and as fast as I can." She didn't tell him she'd never sewn skin before. Her heart thudded with nervousness as she hurried to pull the items she would need from her bedroll. She was thankful she'd ended up shoving the herbs into the pack rather than discarding them. The material around the herbs was damp and wouldn't be pleasant to sleep with, but it would dry eventually. The last item she retrieved was the dagger from her boot, which she positioned on a rock so the tip of the blade met the flames of the fire.

Sebande returned with a thin flask. "Drink this." He held it out to Shanks.

"Oh no, not that again," Shanks replied.

"Just one or two gulps. To take the edge off." Sebande thrust the flask into his hand then turned to Nica. "Where are you going to do this?"

Nica looked around and pointed to a flat rock not far from the fire. "If Shaun can lie on his side next to the rock, I can sit there and be at the right angle, I think."

Sebande nodded and grabbed Shanks' bedroll which he spread out next to the rock. Nica hurried over with her supplies and laid out the needle, the gut string, the herbs and a fresh bandage and wrap. She found a piece of wood to balance the needle on, and slowly eased it into the flames. Once the silver of the needle had turned black, she pulled it back toward her work area to cool, along with the knife.

Shanks stood rooted in one spot, his head swiveling back and forth between the two of them as though he couldn't make up his mind which one to yell at first.

"Drink now." Sebande motioned for Shanks to tip the flask up. "Or it won't do you any good." With a growl of defeat, Shanks raised the flask and took a deep drink.

Nica's hands trembled as she sat on the stone and tried to thread the catgut through the cooled needle. She let out a long slow breath to calm her nerves. This would be no different than stitching a piece of fabric.

With a scowl, Shanks laid down on his side at her feet. His head rested on the bedroll and he clutched a bunched sweater in his hands. It was too cold to take his coat entirely off so he had draped it to one side and unbuttoned his shirt to expose his wound. Nica cringed at the inflamed skin extending far beyond the reach of the blood-stained bandage, surrounded by bruises that were turning an ugly shade of purple and green. She could count every one of his ribs.

With gentle hands, she untied and lifted the bandage to expose the wound. A trickle of blood ran down Shanks' side. She grabbed a shirt she had laid out for this purpose and positioned it around Shanks' middle to catch the blood. "Sebande, I'm going to need you to hold this in place."

"Here." Sebande handed a smooth piece of wood to Shanks.

Shanks raised his head to look up at the other young man. "What's that for?"

"To bite on."

Shanks grunted in reply and clutched the wood in his hand as he laid his head back down. Sebande moved his big frame around to the other side and squatted down to hold the fabric as Nica had asked.

"I'll try not to cry," Shanks said, "and I'll try not to move." With a more serious expression he took her cold, shaking fingers in his warm hand. "You'll do fine, Nic. Don't worry about me."

Nica squeezed his fingers and nodded, afraid to speak for fear she'd cry. She looked at the deep incision and exhaled.

"Give me the flask," she said, holding out her hand.

Shanks and Sebande exchanged a surprised look.

"No, I'm not going to drink it, if that's what you're thinking," she said, positioning the flask above Shanks' side. "This is going to sting a little." Nica poured a small portion of alcohol directly over the cut. Shanks sucked his breath in with a violent hiss, and closed his eyes without speaking. Sebande leaned closer, his wide shoulders next to Nica's as he pressed down with the shirt to absorb the fluid and blood that ran off. Nica pressed the poultice to deaden the pain against his skin, keeping a piece of cloth between her hands and the herbs so her own fingers wouldn't feel the effects.

She held her hands there, letting the power of the herbs soak into Shanks' skin. After ten minutes, she removed the poultice and put her hands on Shanks' side, gently prying the skin of the wound apart. Like frayed ends of fabric she needed to see where the healthy tissue started so she could draw her needle there and make a lasting stitch. She eyed the edges of the wound carefully. There was only one small section where dead skin needed to be removed.

Nica picked up the knife and readjusted her grip. A dark hand reached across and covered hers.

"What are you doing?" Sebande's voice was low, but held a note of warning.

Nica paused and looked at him. His black eyes watched her and she had no doubt he would hurt her if he thought she intended to do Shaun harm.

"Sebande," Shanks interrupted them. "*Esa trinsa me.*" He twisted his head to see her face. "I trust you, Nic," he whispered, then closed his eyes again.

"I just have to trim off the dead skin," Nica said to Sebande. "So the skin can grow back together where I bind it."

Something flickered in Sebande's eyes and he removed his hand.

With a nod, Nica turned back to Shanks. She bit the corner of her lip in concentration as she pulled the skin taut and positioned her knife at one end. Holding her breath, she pulled the blade through the dead skin and was shocked at how effortlessly it sliced the tissue away. Shaun's eyes remained closed and aside from the tensed muscles in his jaw, his face remained expressionless. Nica slowly exhaled and set the incised skin to the side. She dabbed the blood away to assess the wound again.

Nica clenched her teeth. She held the two pieces of skin tight together with one hand and pushed the needle through Shanks' skin with the other. Shanks' let out a deep breath, but he didn't flinch. She didn't allow herself to look at his face for fear she wouldn't be able to finish.

Though the gut string resisted at first, Nica gave a little tug and after that was able to pull the thin membrane through his skin with ease. She threaded the needle back and forth, making a neat, tight seam as Sebande's dark eyes watched her every move. After the first few times of pushing it through his skin, Nica found it really wasn't so different from sewing a dress. She let out a sigh of relief as she finished the last stitch. With a smooth move, she picked up the dagger and sliced the excess string free without pulling on the incision, then knotted the loose ends.

"Done with the stitching." She dared a glance at Shanks. A thin film of perspiration lined his brow, but other than that, his face remained impassive. If she didn't know better, he could have been asleep. "Jonn?"

He didn't move.

A wave of panic went through her. "Jonn?" She grabbed his arm and gave him a shake.

"Ow – careful." He cracked one eye open at her.

"Jonn Shanks," Nica whispered, "you are rotten to the core."

"Sorry, must have dropped off while you were stabbing me over and over." His lips twisted in a half-grin. "I think Sebande was right about the evil streak."

Sebande coughed and turned away.

"Yes, well, not so evil you won't live," Nica replied. She took the blood-stained shirt from Sebande and poured more alcohol on one end to gently clean the area around the wound. When she was done she was pleased to see only a bit of blood oozed through the stitches and she knew that would soon clot and stop.

Nica arranged the second set of herbs on top of the wound. As she reached around, trying to feed the wrap under Shanks' body, he cupped her face with his hand and pressed his lips to hers.

"Thank you for taking care of me." His words were simple, with no hint of sarcasm. Warmth spread in Nica's chest as she nodded, focusing on tying the wrap in place, afraid if she looked at him he would see the love she felt for him.

"Just try and move slowly until those ends knit together. I don't want you to rip out all my hard work." She stood and stretched her back, heaving a sigh of relief.

Sebande appeared from the shadows and held out a small pot.

"To wash," he said.

Grateful, Nica plunged her hands into the water and cleaned the blood from her fingers. She rinsed the needle and the string too, then walked over to store them in her saddlebag. Sebande followed her.

"Nica." He stood unusually close to her, his voice low enough that Shanks couldn't hear him.

Startled, Nica turned to look up at him.

He stared at her mutely, as if searching for words that were difficult to find. "Shaun doesn't give his trust easily," he finally said. "Or his love." He gave her one slow nod. "You deserve both."

"VERSONGA TRAVELS ALONE. He's a tracker," Shanks said, as they sat around the morning fire. Nica had removed the herbs and put on a dry bandage, pleased to see the wound had not bled during the night.

"Does he know what you look like?" Nica asked.

"He does now." Shanks took a bite of bread as he stared into the flames. "He knew me as a child, last as a boy of twelve. He was probably guessing what I looked like now. Somehow, he figured out I was in Jarisa—that I was in the employ of Jacoby. Once the word was out that Jaaniyah had been kidnapped, as it must be by now, I suspect he knew I would come looking for her."

Nica gritted her teeth in annoyance. Was Shanks' relationship with Jaaniyah so well known that a stranger would become aware of his dedication to her so quickly? "How did he find you last night?"

"By rotten luck and bad kismet combined. He was smart enough to know Mosaba would take Jaaniyah to the Ortawn. It was by chance we approached the Ortawn at the same time on the same path.

Nica paused with a bite halfway to her mouth. "Did he attack you?"

"No. He snuck up from behind and pulled me from my horse. That's how my side started bleeding again." He shook his head in disgust. "It was my own stupid fault. I was thinking of other things."

Nica couldn't stop the thought that crept into her head. Had he been thinking of Jaaniyah?

"Blacksmeer doesn't want me dead. I have to be alive when he returns me to my father or he won't get paid. When Sebande approached he ran. But he'll be back. He knows we're here now."

Shanks poked the fire with a stick, causing a cascade of sparks to fly up. "On top of that, Mosaba has more guards at the Ortawn than ever before. It probably explains why none are at the slivers. A few came to see what the commotion in the woods was about. That's why we were in such a hurry last night. I didn't want Blacksmeer or Mosaba's men to follow us back to you or start asking in town and find there are three of us traveling together. We needed to be gone right then."

Nica sipped the warm drink Sebande had made for them. Not only was Mosaba after them, but this Corsockian bounty hunter was chasing Shanks, and possibly her, too.

"How will you hide from Blacksmeer now that he knows what you look like?"

"He can't," Sebande said flatly.

"So what will you...." Nica's words died in her throat at their expressions. "Oh. I see. You have to kill him?" A chill ran across her arms at their stony silence. "You know for a fact Jaaniyah is in the Ortawn?"

"That's what I've been told," Shanks replied. "And unless the increased guard presence was a decoy, that's what it looks like too."

"What of Becknah?" Nica asked. Even though her sister had not been the kindest to her, the idea of Jaaniyah in Mosaba's clutches within the Ortawn made her stomach roil.

"What I was told," Shanks replied, "was that two prisoners were brought in, one right after the other."

"How did they get across the Great Divide do you think?" Nica asked. "There's only the two slivers and the southern sliver is barely wide enough for a horse to cross."

"I'm not sure," Shanks said. "Maybe there's a sliver we don't know about. Mosaba has some secret project that he's been working on."

"The wagon with the chambermaid." Sebande took another sip of coffee and looked at both of them from over the rim of his cup.

Nica looked over at him. "What are you talking about?"

"Ah, of course. You're right," Shanks nodded. "Saying she had the pox insured that no one would look too close." He explained to Nica. "There was no dead body in that wagon they said carried the chambermaid with the pox, but rather two live bodies: Jaaniyah and Becknah. They must have handed them off to someone on the other side of the northern sliver and then brought back the empty cart."

"But you think Jaaniyah's still alive?" Nica almost whispered the words because she feared the answer.

Shanks' mouth pressed into a grim line. "For now. Possibly until Mosaba finds the Stone." He raised his eyebrows at her. "He kept you alive all this time. But Mosaba is unstable and unpredictable. We need to get Jaaniyah and Becknah back before Mosaba realizes they won't be able to direct him to the Getheas Stone."

Nica clutched her fingers together. "But how will we get in to help her? How will we get around all the guards?"

Shanks looked at Sebande then shifted his eyes to Nica. "We know another way into the Ortawn."

he last thing Jaaniyah remembered was a sharp rap along the side of her head. She opened her eyes to darkness, fighting the nausea that rose in her throat. She moved and pain lanced behind her eyes. Slowly, without moving her head, she took in her surroundings. She was alone in a cell carved from stone—as if carved from the very bowels of the earth. She frowned in confusion. Where could she be? When the answer hit her, it was like a physical blow: she was in the Ortawn.

The rope that had bound her hands and feet was gone, yet Jaaniyah couldn't bring herself to move. She had no idea how many days had passed since she'd been dragged from her rooms in HighGarden. She rolled onto her side and stared through the dim light to the barred entry. In the distance she could hear voices and noise but couldn't muster the effort to try to discern what they were saying. She was a prisoner.

She tried to sort through what she knew for sure. Her father was severely injured and possibly dead. Becknah was gone. Her finance minister had betrayed her and now Mosaba, the devil of Sartis, was going to kill her. Questions echoed so loudly in her head that she pressed her hands against her eyes trying to drown out the noise. "This can't be happening," she whispered.

"I want to see her and I want to see her now!"

Jaaniyah jerked at the loud roar of rage. Instinct made her sit up and crawl to the back of the cell to hide, the better to protect herself. She pressed her back against the stone wall and wrapped her arms around her knees. Fear ran down her spine on icy fingers and clutched at her throat, her heart, her stomach.

Approaching footsteps echoed outside her cell. A dark figure stopped and peered between the bars, keys jangling in his hands. The man fumbled to fit the right key into the lock. With a click the lock sprang open and the man pushed the metal door into the small cubicle.

Jaaniyah could see him squint in the darkness trying to locate her. As she watched, he crouched down, sweeping his hands before him along the floor, as if blind.

"Where are you?" he called in a harsh voice.

She could understand just enough Sartish to recognize his words. She sat silent as stone as she debated whether to try and kick him and make a run for the door or to stay hidden against the wall. But even if she made it out the door, she knew she could never find her way out of this labyrinth on her own.

The man went back to the entrance of the cell and disappeared out the door but reappeared within seconds carrying a lit torch. He held the light high above his head, waving it back and forth, as he walked cautiously into the small room.

The light fell upon Jaaniyah huddled in the corner. "Ah, there you are."

He walked over and stared down at her, his lip curled in a sneer.

"Don't look so high and mighty now, do yer?" He nudged her leg roughly with his boot. "Gittup."

Using the wall behind her for support, Jaaniyah pushed herself into a standing position. She wobbled for a moment, as the pain behind her eyes shifted to the back of her head, but at least this time she didn't feel like she was going to throw up. She eyed her captor with a blank expression.

He squinted at her. "Too stupid to be scared? Or scared stupid? No matter." He slipped a noose around her neck and yanked it tight. "Follow me," he said and pulled her along behind him.

As they emerged into the hallway Jaaniyah heard low moans and cries drifting through the shadows from other prisoners being held there. Their mournful cries made her skin crawl. She was led toward the end of the corridor where a red glow ebbed and flowed. The air got warmer as they approached the end of the passageway and Jaaniyah could hear the crackling and snapping of a fire. The path divided into the shape of a T and as they neared the end of the corridor, Jaaniyah gazed down over the edge of the path into a chasm with a roaring fire burning far down below. The man pulled her abruptly to the left to follow along a narrow corridor.

"The pit." The man grunted as he saw Jaaniyah's face. "Probably where yer gonna end up." He seemed oddly satisfied with that idea.

A thin trail wound round and round the perimeter of the cavern descending to reach the fire below. The raging inferno explained the warmth that permeated the underground tunnels.

She was led through a number of nondescript hallways carved from the porous rock, each one similar to the last. Finally they climbed a set of stairs to a plank door where a guard waited. At the jailor's hushed explanation, the guard pounded heavily upon the door.

The wooden portal was yanked open and a large man stood before her. His eyes glittered with black malice as he examined Jaaniyah from head to toe.

"Bring her in," he commanded.

His voice sent chills down Jaaniyah's arms and she fought a primal urge to run. This had to be Mosaba.

With lightening quick speed, Mosaba reached for the noose hanging from Jaaniyah's neck and drew it taut, jerking her into the room. Jaaniyah grabbed the rope with both hands in an attempt to lessen the tension on her neck. Mosaba laughed when he saw her grimace in pain.

He tugged her across the room and shoved her onto a small wooden stool next to a fire before he sat in a large, carved chair, keeping a loose grip on her tether. Jaaniyah kept her eyes down, afraid to look at him.

There was a long silence as Mosaba watched her. Jaaniyah dared one quick glance at the man and was shocked at the hate she saw burning in his eyes. Evil seemed to emanate from him.

"Do you know who I am?" His tone was dark and bitter—like the dregs of a jug of unseasoned ale.

Jaaniyah stared at the floor in front of his black boots and nodded.

"Your father left my hospitality before he told me what I needed to know," Mosaba said, his words measured. "I don't intend for you to do the same."

Her breath stopped in her throat.

"Do you know what I want?" His words were almost gentle as he stroked his short black beard with his thumb and forefinger. She shook her head. He leaned forward and pulled a glowing stick from the fire.

"I think you do." Somehow his soft words sounded more menacing than if he'd yelled. He reached over the side of his chair and lifted a jug, amber fluid trickling down one side of his mouth. "Hold your arm out," he commanded.

Jaaniyah tensed.

He set the jug down and wiped his mouth with the back of his hand. He stood from his chair and stepped toward her.

"I don't like Jacoby's, did you know that?" He stood inches from her now. She could smell the acrid fumes as the flames turned to red embers. "I had a dirty little Jacoby under my feet for years."

Jaaniyah didn't answer.

"Look at me!" he thundered.

Jaaniyah jumped, her gaze jumping to his.

"Hold your arm out, NOW."

Jaaniyah lifted her shaking arms up, the soft skin exposed. Faster than she expected he reached out and grabbed tight onto her wrist.

"Where is she?" His black eyes bulged with rage as he lowered the burning piece of wood toward her arm. "Where is Madanica?"

She shook her head, too afraid to speak. Mosaba slammed the red hot ember onto her arm and held it there. Jaaniyah let out a scream of pain and tried to jerk away but Mosaba's grip tightened until she thought he would crush her wrist. After what felt like eternity, he removed the burning piece of wood from her arm.

"Tell me."

"I don't know," she whispered, tears falling from her eyes. Nica couldn't possibly be aligned with this mad barbarian.

"MADANICA!"

Jaaniyah flinched as he screamed. Spittle flew from the corners of his mouth striking her in the face. He shouted the name so loud, she wondered that the stone walls didn't shake.

"You know where she is, don't you? And the Getheas Stone." He was shaking now, his hand clenching and unclenching reflexively. "You will tell me," he threatened, his voice soft again. "You will tell me everything I want to know."

"I don't know what you're talking about," Jaaniyah cried. She was going to die at the hands of this madman. What a cruel twist of fate that her twin should spend years with Mosaba and survive and she was doomed to die by his hand in a matter of hours.

"You two thought you had it all figured out, didn't you? Thought you were so much smarter than me. So much *better* than me. But I know more than you think. You don't know ANYTHING!" His words ended in a scream. He struck before Jaaniyah saw his hand coming. Her head snapped back and her teeth smashed together with an alarming crunch as the back of his hand collided hard with her face. Tears involuntarily sprang from her eyes as her brain registered the pain. She could feel blood gushing from her nose.

Instinctively, she raised her arms to cover her face to protect herself from further blows.

But the blows that Jaaniyah expected didn't come. Mosaba seemed to gain some measure of control. He yanked her back to the door by the noose around her neck and barked a series of harsh orders. Jaaniyah put her hands to her nose, trying to staunch the flow of blood, the fluid warm and sticky on her skin. The door opened and she was handed off to the same guard who had delivered her earlier.

The stones were rough on her bare feet as she stumbled behind the man. She kept her head down as she walked, concentrating on putting one foot in front of the other. The burn on her arm throbbed with a red hot fire as though he still held the heat of the ember to her skin. The shadows of other people passed by but Jaaniyah didn't look up. They wound their way past the roaring fire in the pit and entered yet another corridor within the maze of passageways when her captor paused to discuss something with another guard. Jaaniyah heard a rustling from a cell next to her. She didn't bother to look.

There was a startled gasp. "Nica." It was just a whisper.

Surprised, Jaaniyah turned her head to the side and looked down. A young man stared back with a horrified expression. Even in the dim light she could see the orange color of his hair and the freckles that riddled his face. She turned away. A prisoner—just like her. He would be no help.

The man holding the noose opened the door to her cell. As she entered he gave her a shove that sent her sprawling. Her aching head hit the stone floor with a jarring impact. Jaaniyah cried out in pain. The man's laughter echoed into the cell as he slammed the iron door shut with a resounding *clang*.

Jaaniyah didn't have the energy to stand up. Instead, she pulled her knees to her chest and cried.

"NICA."

It was another harsh whisper from across the hall. Jaaniyah ignored the voice. After an hour of repeatedly calling 'Nica', the voice had started to annoy her. Was the young man demented? Finally, she pushed herself into a sitting position and crawled to the front of the cell just so she could tell him to shut up.

"Who are you?"

His face lit up, then his look turned to one of confusion.

"Who am I?" he repeated. "What kind of question is that?'

"Just tell me who you are," Jaaniyah snapped. Blood had crusted around her nose and one side of her jaw and mouth were swollen.

There was a long moment of silence as the other prisoner contemplated her demand.

"I'm Toppen, of course. Toppen Bakerswith."

"Well, Toppen Bakerswith, I am not Nica."

Toppen's smile faded as he realized she wasn't smiling. "Of course, you're Nica. Madanica Santos. Who else could you be?"

Jaaniyah sighed. "How does Nica know you, Toppen?"

Another long silence stretched between them. "*You* know me because I delivered wine to the castle. Have you been struck on the head?" he asked.

"Yes, I've been struck on the head, more than once, burnt on the bare flesh of my arm, tied up, slapped so hard by bloody nose is probably broken and hauled across half the countryside trussed up like a pig for market. How could you tell?" Jaaniyah didn't try to stop the anger welling inside. It felt good to let it out. "Now I want out of this bloody place," she cried, "and I want Mosaba Santos HUNG FROM THE HIGHEST

YARDARM IN JARISA." Her words ended in a shout. It was only the abject fear she saw on Toppen's face that cooled her temper.

"Shhhh…Nica, please, stop, shhhh, stop it right now," Toppen pleaded with her. "By the Gods, you know what your father will do to you if he hears you talking like that. What in bloody hell is wrong with you? This is all because of that spy who tricked us. I knew I should have stopped him somehow…"

"I am *not* Nica," Jaaniyah ground out again. "I am Jaaniyah Jacoby and I have been kidnapped from my home and brought here against my will."

Toppen's mouth dropped open. "By the grace of Getheas," he whispered, "Nica, what have they done to you?"

Jaaniyah heaved a sigh at the uselessness of the conversation and thought about crawling to the back of the cell and hiding but she couldn't resist the opportunity to question this strange young man a little further. "How did you know Nica?"

"We were headed to Pont d'Suree to go to University." He craned his neck to look up and down the hallway. "We were escaping from Sartis," he said in a loud whisper. "We planned for months. Don't you remember?" The pleading look on his face convinced Jaaniyah of his sincerity.

"University? Nica was going to go the school? To do what?"

"*You* are very good with numbers and languages as well as the healing arts. Remember all those little animals you would nurse back to health? Especially that one black dog Mosaba tortured?"

Jaaniyah was silent. "Did Nica have any family?"

Toppen stared at her. "You don't remember anything about your own life?"

Jaaniyah sighed. "I'm not Nica. I'm her sister. Her twin."

His reaction vacillated between laughter and disbelief. Finally, Toppen shook his head with pity. "Oh, Nic, what have they done to you to push you this far over the edge?"

Exhausted, Jaaniyah turned and moved away from the door and lay down at the back of the room, cradling her head on her good arm. She wondered where Becknah was being held and if he was still alive. A new fear flickered inside her. What would Mosaba do when he realized she didn't know the location of the Getheas Stone?

The events of the last few days caught up with her. She couldn't think straight. How could she be locked in this filthy jail cell in some underground version of Lucede's lair? How could the man she loved be infatuated with a twin sister she hadn't even known existed? How could any of this be happening? She curled up in a ball on the floor and cried until there were no tears left.

FOOTSTEPS STOPPED BEFORE her cell. The metal door creaked as it swung open and she scrambled to the back of the dark room.

"Get up," a voice growled. "Mosaba wants to see you, now."

Toppen's worried face stared from the shadows of his cell across the hall as she was tugged into the hallway. This time she paid more attention to the route they took, looking for any possible exits or means of escape. But the hallways were dimmed and lined with shadows, making it hard to differentiate from one passageway to another. Carved from the porous stone that surrounded them, the hallways were hung with torches perched in metal brackets along the walls. Occasionally a torch had burnt out or blown out, leaving a patch of total darkness. Low moans and eerie disjointed wails drifted from the different cells she passed, making her skin crawl.

The guard pulled Jaaniyah along by a neck leash, but this one didn't seem to take pleasure in trying to choke her. He came to a stop in front of Mosaba's door and banged on the heavy portal.

"Enter," a voice called from inside.

The guard opened the door and pulled Jaaniyah into the room. The first thing she saw was Mosaba's big frame filling the large carved chair on one side of the room. Before him, a man sat slumped in a chair, his robe tattered and filthy. A surge of relief flooded her as she recognized Becknah's grey head. An empty chair sat next to the scholar. The guard pushed her forward toward Mosaba.

"Come in, come in, my little princess. We've been waiting for you," Mosaba said in a cheery voice that made Jaani wary. "Please, come sit." He nodded indicating the empty chair.

Jaaniyah drew close. Becknah's arms had been tied to the arms of the chair. His face appeared bruised and he looked frail, his entire body sagging with age and pain. The guard shoved her into the seat next to him.

"How are you?" Jaaniyah whispered. He gave her a feeble smile and nodded, though he looked awful to Jaaniyah. His cheekbones stuck out so prominently he reminded her of a cadaver. He started to ask her something when Mosaba cut him off.

"I've been informed by a reliable source that you two know where the Getheas Stone is located." He stared hard at both of them.

Jaaniyah didn't move, didn't make eye contact with Mosaba. It was as she feared. He wanted the impossible.

"You will tell me where the Stone is located." His tone was cordial, almost friendly, as if they were discussing the weather over a cup of tea.

Becknah cleared his throat and spoke in shaky Sartisian. "Your Grace, the location of the Getheas Stone is a legendary secret left by the Ancients, hundreds of years ago to be discovered when the stars aligned." He shook his head with regret. "I'm afraid we don't yet know the location of the Stone."

"Ah, but I think you do," Mosaba said. "Are you not a scholar? Can you not read the stars and divine these things?" His voice was calm, but Jaaniyah could see his fingers gripping the arms of his chair. "I've had word you are launching your own quest for the Stone." Though his voice remained low, Jaaniyah could hear the ragged undercurrent of madness.

Becknah started to shake his head but Mosaba interrupted.

"Here's how we're going to proceed. You will tell me where the Stone is located. I will send one of my soldiers to recover the Stone and bring it to me. Should my man fail to return with the true Getheas Stone then I will cut a finger from each of your hands and the head from his body." Mosaba threaded his fingers together and rested his hands in his lap. "Then we'll try again."

Chapter Twenty-Eight

ou know another way into the Ortawn?" Nica repeated in surprise. "How is that possible?"

"As you may recall, Sebande and I were on our own for a number of years. We did some exploring," Shanks said smoothly. Behind him Sebande gave a rueful half-laugh. "The Ortawn is carved from very porous limestone. At one time that area had great amounts of water running through it, which created the caverns underneath Sartis. The force of the water formed the rooms and chambers of the prison. There are several different ways in and out of the Ortawn, but this particular entrance is one we created ourselves, so I don't think anyone else knows of it."

"You created it? How?"

Shanks looked at Sebande. The dark haired soldier shook his head, his lip curled in disgust. "Why not?" he muttered. "She knows everything else."

Shanks cleared his throat. "Sebande and I—" there was a hiccup of hesitation, as though he still found it difficult to divulge their secrets— "we...uh...lived in the Ortawn for a while." He sat back. "We'll just leave it at that for now. Anyway, while we were there we dug an exit."

Nica had to bite her tongue not to pepper him with questions. There was probably nothing he could have said that she would have found more shocking. They'd *lived* in that ghastly hellhole? Had they been prisoners? Perhaps that was how Shanks had come to speak Sartish so fluently. She cleared her throat and tried to sound nonchalant at his startling disclosure. "And does this exit still exist?"

"No reason it shouldn't. It's a desert there. Nothing changes but the top layer of sand," Shanks replied. "But the problem is, all three of us can't go tramping into the Ortawn. It needs to just be one of us." He poked at the logs of the fire again. "And we can't leave you unguarded, so Sebande and I have discussed the situation and we're going to split up. He's going to go in after Jaaniyah and you and I are going to head back to Berjerac and look for that statue for the next clue."

That didn't sound good. "Why can't we wait for Sebande and Jaaniyah?" Nica asked.

"A horse travels slower with two people on it," Shanks explained. "Three horses traveling together are much easier to track then horses going in opposite directions."

Nica shook her head. "We can split up once we know they're safely out of the Ortawn." She crossed her arms. "And what about Versonga Blacksmeer? What if he's set a trap for when you return to the Ortawn for Jaaniyah? Doesn't he need to be found and dealt with?"

"Don't worry about Blacksmeer. Sebande and I will take care of him when the time comes."

"What if Sebande runs into trouble? What if he needs our help?" The more she thought about it, the less Nica was inclined to agree with them.

"Sebande will be fine," Shanks said, but his tone didn't sound convincing.

A long moment of silence stretched between them. The only sound was the twitter of birds high in the trees.

"No," Nica finally said.

"No?" Shanks repeated with raised eyebrows. He looked at Sebande to see if he'd heard correctly. His gaze shifted to Nica. "What do you mean, 'no'?"

Nica took a deep breath and raised her chin. "I mean *no*, I'm not leaving until Jaaniyah and Sebande are both safely out of the Ortawn." Nica dared Sebande with her eyes to challenge her decision. To her surprise, he dropped his head and looked away.

"Nica," Shanks said weakly, at a loss for words. "You've got to think this through. We can't risk you *and* Jaaniyah. You are both heirs to the throne of Jarisa. I can't knowingly risk your life to save hers."

"Well, that makes it simple enough. *You're* not risking my life," Nica said with a forced smile. "I'm choosing to risk my own life."

With a painful grimace, Shanks pushed himself up and walked away from the fire. Nica could tell by the way he held his shoulders he was angry. He stood at the edge of their small camp, his hands on his hips and stared out into the trees. She decided it was best to ignore him for now. After a while, he walked back toward her.

"We've been camped here too long. We need to move on. What's your plan?" His lips were unsmiling but his words were even.

He towered over her. Nica rubbed her palms down the front of her pants. "Well," she said slowly, "I have been thinking on it a bit." She heard Sebande cough. She turned to look at him but his arms were resting on his knees with his head bowed, hiding his face. Nica started again. "As I was saying, I was thinking maybe we should use one of Mosaba's tactics."

"Such as...." Shanks drew the word out.

"A diversion. I remember Mosaba explaining to me once about the vent holes in the Ortawn. He said they couldn't get plugged up or the smoke from the fire inside the Ortawn would force everyone out for fresh air. I asked why all the blowing sand above the Ortawn didn't fill up the holes and he told me they'd built metal shields, like little caps, over each hole. There was a piece of metal on the top that turned the cap with the wind so the sand was blocked from falling into the holes."

Out of the corner of her eye, she saw Sebande's head lift. "If we can block the holes, and then wait by the other entrance, maybe everyone will be worrying about the smoke instead of a few strange faces. We can go in, get Jaaniyah, and head north before anyone notices she's gone." Nica rubbed her hands up and down her thighs again. "That was what I was thinking, anyway."

"Shaun, it might work," Sebande said.

Shanks nodded. He stared off into the distance, thinking. "I remember those vent lids. They're visible and easy enough to get to. I wonder if they've thought to guard them?"

"Why?" Sebande snorted. "Who would dare take on Mosaba and the entire criminal population who hide in the Ortawn? Most want them to stay hidden down there forever." He shook his head as though trying to dislodge unpleasant memories. "The prisoners are usually as bad as the criminals who kidnapped them."

"It might just work." Shanks looked down at Nica. "Aren't you afraid of being captured by Mosaba again?"

"Yes," Nica nodded. "But I'm more afraid of you two going in there without me and not coming back out. Besides—" she shrugged as she got to her feet— "you and Sebande will take care of me."

THE SUN WAS high in the sky when they stopped again. To their left the Great Divide stretched, so vast in places the other side shimmered like a mirage. A group of huge boulders dotted the edge of the gorge, colored in the red and orange hues of the setting sun. They shot into the sky like giant markers thrust into the ground for a non-existent river to follow. Ahead of them a sea of sand stretched. Nica could hear the wind whistle as it soared over the unbroken terrain.

Shadows danced across the surface, making the sand appear to be undulating, like the moving back of a partially submerged creature.

"Why is it so windy?" Nica asked.

Shanks squinted against the brightness of the sun. "The wind comes from the Sea of Nephalon, up the Great Divide. There is nothing to stop it until it blows out over the desert of the Scablands or hits the trees on the other side of the Divide in northern part of Jarisa."

At the same time, Shanks and Sebande lifted their hands to shield their eyes from the sun and sand. Shanks pointed. "There she is. The third sister."

Sebande nodded in agreement.

"What are you talking about?" Nica asked. She took a step closer, leaning against the force of the wind. Shanks continued to scan the horizon as he spoke. "Most people don't realize the peaks of the Spires Mountains are visible across the desert. The mountains blend in with the rest of the shifting sand dunes, but their tips never move. We use them to gauge our direction."

"And who's the third sister?"

"There are a series of peaks within the Spires known as the Three Sisters. Sebande and I picked one to use as our marker to find our entrance and named her the third sister." Shanks wrapped his arm around Nica's shoulder. He put his head close to hers and pointed. "See, it's the one in the middle there, with the ridge like a fish hook?"

Nica nodded, enjoying his closeness. A twinge of regret tugged at her when he moved away to talk to Sebande. A short time later the horses were hidden among the trees, next to a huge boulder a short distance from the edge of the desert. As they stepped onto the sand the wind assaulted her, tearing at her hair and clothes. Every step was an effort. Shanks slid his arm through hers. "Keep your head down. Just follow my lead."

The whistling she'd heard earlier became a howling cry as they moved deeper into the sand-swept landscape. Even the deepening shadows shifted and moved, like dark clouds blowing through a winter sky.

Time became suspended as she planted one plodding foot in front of the other. Sand pricked her skin like a million tiny needles. Nica draped her cloak across her face so only her eyes were exposed. Then, out of nowhere, a wall of solid sand loomed up before them. With a sigh of relief she stepped behind the wind break.

"That was unpleasant," she said, as she shook the sand from her clothes. Their barrier was one of many little walls that had built up over the years from a combination of the natural limestone deposits and the blowing sand. Sebande dropped to his knees and began digging in one corner. It only took him a few minutes before he held up one end of a cable. Shanks squatted down beside him, and together they scraped away the sand. Because of the natural wind block, the sand had not accumulated in great amounts and it didn't take them long to expose a big chunk of rock.

Now that the wind was blocked the sharp odor of fire hung in the air. Shanks leaned down to help but Sebande shrugged him off.

"Don't rip your stitches yet," the dark haired young man said. "Wait until you need to do something really important, like save me."

Shanks laughed and backed off as Sebande tugged on the cable, pulling a section of the porous rock free. He tipped it to the side and together they peered into the darkness below.

"This entrance looks smaller now," Shanks commented.

Nica peeked over his shoulder. The smell of fire was much stronger, and her stomach clutched at the dark memories associated with the odor. "How long ago did you make this exit?"

Shanks rested one knee on the ground, and wiped his forehead with the back of his hand, leaving a streak of dirt. "About four years ago." He glanced at Sebande. "I guess we've grown a bit since then."

Nica was surprised to see Sebande actually laugh. "Thank the Gods. You were the scrawniest fourteen year-old I'd ever seen." Nica ran her eyes over Shanks' broad shoulders and long legs. Even though he was thin it was hard to imagine Shanks ever being scrawny. Sebande was even bigger than Shanks.

"Do you think we'll fit now?" Shanks asked.

"Only one way to find out," Sebande muttered.

"I wonder if we should make sure we can get in and out before we stop up the vents," Shanks said with a thoughtful look. "I don't want to force everyone out of the Ortawn if we can't get in."

Without another word, Sebande slid his feet into the hole and balanced himself with his hands. He lowered himself into the darkness until he got to his shoulders, then it appeared the hole was too small. In one fluid motion he lifted his hands above his head and dropped down into the darkness. Shanks leaned over and put his face low into the hole. Nica couldn't hear what they said. Suddenly, Shanks sat back and Sebande's fingers gripped the opening. He pulled himself up and struggled to position his broad shoulders so he could climb out without ripping his clothes and skin on the edge of the rocks. After a moment, he twisted, braced his hands on the rocks and pulled himself from the dark cavern.

"It'll work," Sebande said, huffing from the exertion. "The tunnel has remained hidden. It still feeds into the corridor by the cells." They spoke a bit more about the logistics of sneaking in while Nica waited. She had a million questions she wanted to ask about their time in the Ortawn but she bit her tongue. Shaun would tell her if he wanted her to know.

IT DIDN'T TAKE long to determine the vents were not being guarded. Shanks and Sebande used the weight of their booted feet to crush the metal into the holes, effectively blocking the outflow of air. With forty vents, it took less than an hour for the two of them to block the air going in and out of the underground chambers.

Nica waited behind the wind block, nervously checking their location every few minutes. It wasn't long before they both returned and hunkered down while they waited for their efforts to take effect.

After close to thirty minutes Shanks sat up. "Ready?"

Sebande went first.

The stone was rough on her hands as Nica balanced herself on the edge. She let herself slide through the hole and could feel Sebande's hands tighten around her waist and guide her to the ground. Shanks followed her into the Ortawn, careful to move slowly so as not to rip out his stitches.

They were crouched in almost total darkness in a narrow tunnel. One crooked shred of light pierced the darkness up ahead on the left. Nica drew her dagger and held it tightly in her right hand as they crept forward, fear making her stomach roil.

"We're going to enter an area where they keep the prisoners," Shanks whispered to Nica. "Just follow us and stay close. Keep your hood up and try to walk like a man."

Nica nodded then realized he couldn't see her. "All right," she whispered.

Eerie cries and moans echoed in the hallway as they walked down the dim corridor. Torches flickered along the stone walls. The smell of smoke hung heavy in the air and Nica fought the urge to cough. It was as she remembered—a place out of her worst nightmares.

Up ahead, two men turned onto the passageway toward them, deep in conversation. They paused when they saw their group.

"*Tye rank briuken?*" The taller of the two said, addressing Sebande. "*Sik miin utten?*"

Nica's heart skipped a beat. Sebande didn't speak the language. She opened her mouth to answer the question when Sebande replied.

Y're grantten srob. No puedikkin ware," he said in perfect Sartish.

The men continued on. Nica dropped her head as they passed. Her gaze landed on a face staring up at her from the shadowy depths of a cell. For a moment the world spun out of control. It was Toppen.

ica covered her mouth with her hand to stop from crying out. Shanks turned at the pressure of her fingers and peered back through the dim light.

"What is it?" She leaned close to his ear.

"Toppen," she whispered. "He's in the cell back there."

Shanks called to Sebande's receding back. "*Rorgen.*" Sebande glanced over his shoulder and stopped. Nica pulled Shanks back toward Toppen as Sebande retraced his steps.

"Nica." Toppen scrambled to his feet as she drew near, his face alight with excitement. "How did you get away from Mosaba's men? I've been so afraid of what he was doing to you. I almost didn't recognize you." Toppen's eager eyes went from Nica to the tall form who had moved in close behind her. His eyes widened. "*You,*" he whispered in shock. His gaze darted back to Nica in disbelief. "Why is *he* here, Nic?"

"Toppen." Nica ignored his question. "Have you seen someone who looks like me?" She clutched the bars of his cell, waiting for his answer.

Toppen's eyes traveled from Nica to Shanks to Sebande then back to Nica again. "*Exactly* like you?"

"Yes, yes, exactly, she's my sister, we're twins." She clutched the bars eagerly, sensing he had information.

Toppen leaned close to the bars and whispered to Nica. "Are they making you say this?"

Nica stared at Toppen for a second as his words sunk in. "Toppen," she snapped. "I'm not delirious. I have a twin sister. Jaaniyah Jacoby is my twin. Mosaba stole me as a baby."

The wine apprentice's expression went from confusion to concern to anger and he shifted his gaze to glare at Shanks. "Look what you've done to her. How can you stand there looking down at me like you think you're so much better when you've reduced Nica to some demented state where she doesn't even know who she is anymore? The Gods will strike you down for this."

Shanks' hand reached through the bars so fast Toppen didn't have time to move. He wrapped one big hand around Toppen's neck and squeezed until the boy's eyes bulged.

"Shut your mouth and listen to me," Shanks growled. "I don't give a rat's ass what you think is happening here. Have you seen a girl who looks like Nica or not?"

Toppen tried to nod his head.

"How long ago?"

"Ten minutes," he squawked.

"Where is her cell?"

Toppen pointed across the hallway.

"Where did they take her? To Mosaba?"

Toppen tried to nod again. Even in the dim light it was apparent his face was turning bright red and he started making a strange choking sound.

Shanks shoved Toppen back so hard the boy staggered backwards until he sagged against the wall. Shanks looked over at Sebande. "He must have her right now. Probably Becknah too."

Toppen bent over coughing. He rubbed his throat as he hurriedly stepped away from the door and out of Shanks' reach. "Lunatic," he muttered, gazing at Shanks with hate-filled eyes. His eyes shifted to Nica. "Are you all right, Nic? Have they hurt you?" He gave Shanks a wary glance then whispered, "Get me out of here. We can still get to Pont d'Suree."

"Oh, Toppen," Nica said in a low voice. "Everything has changed."

"What's changed?"

"Come on, we need to move." Shanks took Nica's arm and pulled her down the hallway in the opposite direction.

"Wait!" Toppen pleaded. "Let me out and I'll help you! Don't leave me."

"Toppen," Nica whispered, "We'll come back for you. I promise." Shanks pulled her far enough along the corridor she couldn't see his face any longer.

"Nica....Nic......"

The smoke became thicker as they moved through the hallways. Coughing could be heard and the babble of voices had increased in volume. Though one corridor looked the same as another, Shanks and Sebande wound their way through the stone tunnels as if they knew where they were going. Within minutes Nica was hopelessly turned around.

The people they passed were filthy, blending in with the darkness and rocks that surrounded them. The smell of rotten eggs and decay mingled with the smoke, making Nica want to gag. They reached the end of the hallway and looked down into a huge cavern. Far below, a fire burned, smoke billowing from the orange flames.

"What is that?" she whispered.

"The pit." Shanks pulled her to the left and the huge fiery cavern disappeared as they were swallowed by another dark hallway.

They passed a guard at a doorway, but neither Shanks nor Sebande paid any attention to the man. They went around another corner and Sebande stopped abruptly, leaning back against the rock wall.

"Sebande spoke in a low voice to Shanks. "Only one guard. No telling how many on the inside." He edged his back along the wall and peered around the corner. "No doubt Mosaba has an exit from inside the room." He pulled back and looked at Shanks. "How will we know if Jaaniyah and Becknah are in there?"

"We could take out the guard and see if we can hear anything," Shanks suggested, "but I doubt we'll be able to hear through that door."

A loud bang echoed against a wall.

"Why is it so smoky in here?" Mosaba's irritated voice echoed down the hall in their direction. The guard's mumbled reply was unintelligible.

Nica swayed. To have Mosaba so close again was terrifying. She put her hand out to brace herself against the wall and tightened the grip on her dagger. She would never be captured alive by him.

Shanks leaned close and wrapped an arm around her waist. "I'll take care of you," he whispered in her ear. He gave her waist a squeeze then turned back toward Sebande.

"Where's Thain?" Mosaba shouted. Nica could hear the stamp of his boots as he walked down the corridor.

"Which way?" Shanks whispered.

"East." Sebande leaned back to reply. He waited a few minutes. "He's gone. Let's go take a look."

"Wait here," Shanks said to Nica. He followed Sebande around the corner and Nica followed right behind, trying to step lightly so he wouldn't notice her.

Sebande walked straight up to the guard. "*Qarto Mosaba*?" he uttered in Sartish.

The guard started to answer, when he suddenly leaned forward with an odd groan. Nica wondered at the man's strange behavior when Shanks darted around Sebande and pushed open the door the man had guarded. It wasn't until Sebande grabbed the guard under the arms and pulled him into the room that she saw the hilt of his dagger protruding from his stomach.

Nica bit her lip as she hurried behind Sebande, trying not to look at the dead man on the floor. By the time she was inside, Shanks had already cut Jaaniyah free and she was in his arms.

Sebande dropped the dead guard and pulled his dagger free, casting a quick glance around the room for other guards. Expressionless, he leaned over to wipe the blood from the blade onto the man's shirt. With sure, swift movements, he cut through the ropes that held Becknah.

Jaaniyah turned from her embrace of Shanks. She ran to her sister and threw her arms around her.

Thank you, thank you, for saving me," she whispered. Nica took in Jaaniyah's bruised and swollen eye along with the traces of blood around her nose and mouth. She was surprised at the surge of emotion she felt at finding her sister alive.

"Can you walk?" Shanks asked, bending down to help Becknah stand.

"Yes, yes," the old man said. "We must go while we can."

"Sebande," Shanks called. *"Triste semparte les elas. Reela sa wizartio ley pondo brechna."*

Nica stared at Shanks. He was speaking in Corsosh. There was only one reason for that—he didn't want her to understand what he was saying.

"No," she said in a firm voice. "No—to whatever you're saying. We're staying together." She gave Shanks a steady look.

Shanks' look of surprise turned to one of exasperation. "Nic, we have to split up. Becknah needs help. We need to get both of you out of here while we have a chance." His voice was pleading.

"No," Nica repeated. "We go out together."

"Argue in the hallway," Sebande said. "And do it quietly," he muttered as he motioned for Jaaniyah to follow him. Jaaniyah cast a confused look between Nica and Shanks then hurried to stand behind Sebande. He pulled the door open and eased into the hallway, motioning for Jaaniyah to follow.

"At least pull your hood up," Shanks whispered to Nica, as he indicated with a jerk of his hand for her to follow Jaaniyah out the door. Becknah was hunched over and appeared to be in pain as he shuffled along with Shanks.

They eased out of the room and hurried down the corridor. Smoke was thicker now and the smell more acrid, causing her eyes to burn. Coughs could be heard coming from different areas, along with shouting down the corridors. They turned into one passageway filled with men running back and forth. Sebande abruptly steered them to another hallway that was less populated.

They passed the pit, smoky flames billowing forth, and moved into another dark passageway. Sebande turned another corner and suddenly Toppen's pale face was pressed against the bars staring at her.

"Nic. Help me."

Nica paused.

"Keep moving," Shanks said in a growl, his hands full helping Becknah.

Nica took another hesitant step down the corridor.

"Nic, get me out of here," Toppen cried. He gripped the bars so tight his knuckles were white. "Don't leave me. They'll kill me."

She stopped and looked at her friend.

"How can I get you out?" she asked. "Who has the keys?"

"Pick the lock," Toppen whispered. "Here." He shoved his wine corkscrew into her hands. "I'll tell you how."

Nica slid the dagger into her boot and took the corkscrew from Toppen. With trembling fingers she pulled the small blade out. At the end of the hall, Becknah's tattered robe disappeared as he followed Sebande and Shanks around the corner. She didn't dare yell. Nica wavered.

"Please Nic, please. Don't let me die in here. I'm begging you."

She looked back at Toppen.

"Yes, of course."

The door that stretched across the opening to the cell was mostly solid. The lock was located on the far side away from the bars through which Toppen was peering, making it impossible for a prisoner to reach the lock from inside the cell.

She hurried over to the lock. "All right, what do I do?"

"Slide the blade into the hole where the lock goes. Push it all the way to the back until you can feel pressure." Toppen hung onto the bars, twisting his head, trying to watch her. "Push until you hear the click. That's all it takes."

Nica fumbled with the small blade, trying to get it to feed into the hole. Finally she got the blade into the keyhole and shoved back as hard as could.

Nothing happened.

"I don't think it's long enough," she whispered. She looked down the hallway and wondered how far away Shanks and the others were now. Would she be able to find them again? Her heart pounded in her ears until she could hardly think. She jerked her head back down to the lock and pushed again, trying to twist the blade, hoping that it would hit the tumbler.

"Try again," Toppen commanded.

Nica angled the small blade and pushed hard, then pulled back and slammed it into the hole from a different direction. "I can't get it," she cried. She pushed again, as hard as she could. Just at the moment she was going to give up she felt the pressure release against the tip of the blade and a barely audible *click*.

"What do you think you're doing?" A deep voice asked from behind.

Nica dropped the corkscrew and turned with a start. One of Mosaba's guards from the palace stood before her. He wore a leather vest marked with the crest of Sartis over black breeches and boots. A curved sword swung low on one side. "Who are you?" he asked, reaching for her hood.

Nica jumped back and yanked her dagger from her boot.

"Don't touch me," she spat, holding the blade in front of her. All the hate she felt for Mosaba came boiling out of her at that moment. She would defend herself anyway she had to.

"A girl?" The man said in surprise. "Ho ho," he laughed, relaxing his stance, "you want to stab me, little girlie?" He chortled as he lunged for her arm. Nica whipped her knife to the right and stabbed forward with all her strength, aiming for a spot just above his oversized gut. At the same moment something swished by her ear and a thin sabre slid neatly into the center of the man's chest.

"No, but I want to." Nica barely recognized Shanks' voice, it carried such a deadly tone of malice.

The man's shocked eyes glazed over before he crumbled at their feet. Shanks pulled his sabre free as the man fell forward. The Sartisian's head flopped on the floor with a resounding thud. Shanks kicked him over and pulled Nica's dagger from the corpse.

"All right?" Shanks asked as he wiped off the blade and handed it to her.

Nica nodded. With a shudder she slid the dagger back into her boot.

Shanks gave Toppen a derisive sneer before he kicked the cell door open.

"You can come out now, you gutless coward," Shanks snarled. He pulled Nica away. "Come on."

An outraged bellow rent the hallways. Mosaba's furious roar echoed throughout the Ortawn.

"Run."

Nica followed Shanks down the hallway. She was right on his heels as he darted into the dark little tunnel where they had sneaked into the Ortawn. Sebande's worried face peered down from above.

"Step on my knee and I'll lift you," Shanks said in a rush as they skidded to a stop. Nica's sides were heaving and her breath came in short gasps. He dropped down and propped up his knee. Nica took a step back then ran up onto Shanks' knee and jumped for the opening. Sebande caught her arms and pulled her through in one smooth motion, setting her on the ground next to him. He thrust an arm down for Shanks and yanked him up through the opening too. With Shanks on safe ground, Sebande began to roll the stone back in place.

"Wait for me," a thin voice wavered from below.

Sebande shot a confused look at Shanks who frowned at Nica, then nodded. With a growl of disapproval Sebande dropped down and thrust a hand out for Toppen to hold, then pulled him free. With a grunt he pushed the rock back into place.

Shanks was already leading Jaaniyah and Becknah toward the forest, silhouettes mere shadows in the blowing sand. Sebande grabbed Nica's hand and pulled her along beside him as he ran to catch up with Shanks, leaving Toppen to fend for himself.

hey rode two to a horse; Sebande and Jaaniyah, Shanks and Nica, Toppen and Becknah. Sebande had given Jaaniyah his coat to cover her night dress, and some cloth torn from a shirt in which to wrap her feet.

"Pray that Heathron has control of the slivers," Shanks muttered as he urged the horse to go faster.

"How's your side?" Nica asked, fearful of the answer.

"It hurts like bloody hell, but I don't think it's bleeding," he said. "Thanks to my witch woman." He smiled over his shoulder at her. Nica returned his smile, relieved the stitches had held. She leaned her head against his back, trying not to grip his sides and exhaled deeply, relaxing into the rhythm of the horse.

It took several hours to reach the northern sliver. Nica could see no sign they were being followed. Mosaba and his men must have been sidetracked by the smoke in the Ortawn.

Sebande barely slowed as he directed his horse onto the narrow, winding land bridge. Nica sucked in her breath as Shanks followed close behind, trusting in the horse's ability to find footing on the sliver of land that projected out into thin air. Toppen stopped at the edge of the canyon before urging the horse forward at a walk.

On the far side of the canyon six Jarisan guards stood at attention, weapons poised, watching their passage. Shanks yelled as they neared the other side of the Great Divide. When they reached the other side Sebande urged his horse close to speak to soldiers with Jaaniyah clinging to his back. The guards stared at her, unsure whether to believe their eyes. Nica quickly pulled her hood over her head to avoid any questions that might delay them further and tucked her head against Shanks' back, content to remain invisible and listen.

It didn't take long to arrange a contingent of soldiers to escort them back to the palace. The soldiers split up, half riding before their group and the other half behind. Shanks sent Toppen to ride with the group of soldiers following behind.

"Pain in the arse, that one," Shanks muttered as he returned from depositing him with the captain of the guards.

It wasn't until they stopped for the night that any of them had a chance to talk. Becknah, appearing old and frail, immediately curled up by a small fire and went to sleep on the sparse scattering of blankets Shanks offered him.

"M'lady." Shanks looked at Jaaniyah as they sat huddled around a second, larger fire. "Your sister—"

"Jonn, stop calling me M'lady in front of other people," Jaaniyah snapped. "You never call me that when we're alone. It's fine to call me Jaani."

"Jaani, then." Shanks smiled. "Your sister believes we're on the path to locating the Getheas Stone."

Jaaniyah gave Nica a curious look. "You've deciphered one of the quatrains in the Avedla, then?"

"Two, actually, beyond the first one Becknah figured out," Nica replied. She sat on a rock next to Shanks and she leaned her shoulder against his and smiled. "But I did have a little help."

Next to her Sebande coughed and abruptly stood up, everyone's eyes following his movements. "I need to check on my horse," he mumbled. He looked pointedly at Shanks before he disappeared into the darkness.

"What have you found so far?" Jaani's voice sounded cold, her lips pressed in a straight line.

A confused frown etched across Nica's brow as she watched Sebande go. She briefly described the symbol of the crown and the eye, as well as the message from the 'T' quatrain to 'go through the veil of prisyms'.

"And what is a veil of prisyms?" her sister asked.

"We don't know that part," Nica said. "Yet."

A long silence stretched around the campfire. After a few moments Jaaniyah held her hands out to the warmth of the flames. "Based on my recent experience with that mad man, I can confirm Mosaba is obsessed with the Stone and thinks we know where it is. I do believe he'll do anything to obtain possession of its secrets." She spoke to Shanks as if the others weren't there. "Jonn, without question, it would be in our best interest to find the Getheas Stone before he does, if it truly exists. Upon my return to the palace I'll dispatch a group to continue the search."

"Where will you send them?" Nica questioned.

"There's a Valley of the Gods within The Spires Mountain range. A place on the Pian'glo Pass," Jaaniyah said thoughtfully. "It's supposed to be very ancient. My father was going to let Becknah start an archeological dig up there after the spring thaw." She lifted her head as though she'd made up her mind. "That's where I'll send the men first." She turned to Shanks. "Has there been any change in my father's condition?"

"No." Shanks shook his head. "Cottrai—" he nodded toward one of the guards— "is in Heathron's confidence. He knows your father's location. He told me the King is improving but not yet fit to travel."

"Then we must assume Tarantu remains at HighGarden?" Jaaniyah asked.

"When we return we'll put a twenty-four hour watch on him and find out how he's feeding information to Mosaba. In the meantime, Heathron is there, along with the other ministers," Shanks replied. "And Becknah will be back." He nodded in the direction of the bedroll where the old scholar slept near the fire.

Jaani's eyes flicked over to the old man, her expression grim. "Mosaba will be tracking us, no doubt?"

"No doubt," Shanks agreed.

NICA SAGGED WEARILY against Shank's back as they rode, leaning close to combine their warmth. They'd ridden for much of the day and the travel was much rougher sitting behind the saddle rather than in the leather seat. It was as if every bone in her body had been jostled over and over. Night was upon them again and the air had turned frosty. She could see the stars through the trees, sparkling above in a crystal clear sky while the crescent moon illuminated the forest with a wash of blue-grey light.

Sebande rode in the lead with Jaaniyah riding behind him. Occasionally, Nica peered over Shanks' shoulder to look at the pair riding ahead. It was an eerie sensation to see her sister on the back of Sebande's horse with her hair hanging free. It was as though she watched herself.

"Oh, thank the Gods," Nica whispered when Shanks reined his horse to a stop. Before he could move she pushed herself straight back over the rump of the horse and dropped to the ground. She gave the horse a pat on the flank, ignoring the dust that rose, and pushed herself away with a groan. Her legs were stiff, her back ached and she smelled like a horse.

Shanks climbed down with the same disjointed movements.

He looked over at her and straightened up with a pained expression. "It's painful to live around you, you know that?" he said. He raised his arm with a chuckle as she tried to swat at his head. Jaaniyah's cold voice made her stop.

"Jonn," Jaaniyah said. "Come here, I need to ask you something." Shanks walked over to Jaani, shrugging one shoulder as he tried to straighten the cramped muscles of his injured side.

A cool breeze brushed Nica's face like a warning. Once again, she wondered at the relationship between her sister and Shanks. She approached Sebande before the thought of Jaaniyah and Shanks together could grow any bigger in her mind.

"What can I do to help?" she asked.

Sebande straightened from where he was lining out the bedrolls and stared down at her. Nica waited, but instead of speaking, the muscles in his jaw clenched as though he held in his words.

"We need kindling," he finally muttered.

Nica nodded. He would tell her when he was ready. She went to collect the wood ignoring Jaaniyah and Shanks huddled together.

NICA WAS AWAKE before the dawn. Bird song chattered from the tree tops. The occasional scream of a monkey split the air. They'd slept around the fire, keeping the flames stoked throughout the night. For this one moment, a sense of peace engulfed her. Jaaniyah had been rescued. The King lived, as did Toppen and

Becknah. She thought of the Avedla verses and the ancient trail of which they spoke. Did the clues they'd deciphered so far lead to the Getheas Stone?

Her thoughts drifted to Shanks. She turned to gaze at the shadow that was his sleeping form. Shaun. His shaggy blond hair was visible beyond the edge of his blanket, his boots sticking out the other end. A depth of emotion she'd never imagined flooded through her. With a jolt, she realized she was in love with him. How had that happened? And did she even have a chance with someone like Shanks when a princess of the land he considered home loved him as well?

When Jaaniyah rose, she seemed to make a point of requiring Shanks' assistance for any number of tasks. Nica went to fetch more kindling for the fire, keeping her head down and trying to ignore her jealousy. Jaani had known Shanks longer than she had. It was to be expected their relationship would continue.

Nica was down near the creek when she spied a thatch of leaves woven together in an odd bundle and tucked between the roots of a giant Pandoxian tree. Curious, she reached for the oval shape and began to peel away the huge tropical leaves. When she'd peeled back the last leaf she sucked in a sigh of amazement at the contents. It was a wood carving of a woman with her hair piled high. A crown embedded with gems encircled her head. She had a broad nose and eyes that glittered with the icy fire of the rare shirpa stone. Nica pushed herself up and hurried back to camp.

"Look what I've found," she called to the others where they were gathered around the fire. As one they turned to look as she held up her find.

Jaaniyah stood up and gasped.

"Nica—" Shanks' voice was controlled. Too controlled. "Where did you find that?"

"Over by the river." She tilted her head. "I found it tucked among the roots of a huge tree."

Shanks let out a slow breath. "Nica..."

"Tell her," Jaaniyah said.

"What?" Nica looked from Jaaniyah to Shanks, irritated they both seemed to know something she didn't. "What's wrong?"

"Can you show me where you found it?" Shanks' tone was gentle as he got to his feet. "We need to put it back."

"What is it?" Nica's question died in her throat as Shanks froze. Silence descended over the forest like a blanket. Even the birds and wild monkeys ceased to twitter.

"Don't move," Shanks breathed. The tone of his voice was a clear warning of the seriousness of the situation.

With a sickening realization, the situation became apparent to Nica. They were surrounded. Faces stared at them from the shadows of the forest, blending so naturally with the surrounding foliage it took Nica several moments to realize exactly how many encircled them.

The people watching were a variety of heights, but none were taller than Nica. Their skin was as coarse as the trunk of a tree and covered with markings: dots, lines, swirls. Leaves were intertwined in their hair as though for decoration and their clothes were made from the fabric of the forest.

The Narsgededon forest people.

Her gaze traveled from one face to another, noting each person clutched a tall spear, cocked at an angle to fire on command. In a blink, the situation was clear. She'd found something that belonged to the tribe. Something important.

Shanks slowly held his hands up. *"Ranagstu' moab sinc ka'."* He stumbled over the unfamiliar words. A grumble went through the group like a ripple on a pond. One man raised his spear, his angry eyes locked on the carving Nica held. His gaze darted between Shanks and Nica as though debating who to attack first. As one, the entire tribe tensed and subtly shifted into a fighting stance.

Jaaniyah let out a whimper.

All the veiled references to the dangers within the Narsgededon came flooding back to Nica. Then Lady Angeline's voice echoed in her ear. *'Where ever did you learn the dicadian rhythms of the Narsgededon forest people? I don't believe I've heard five people in my lifetime be able to enunciate the ariatic structure of the harmonic contrast like that.'*

"In-gma a'ish tu li'e'," Nica said. Her voice was like a bell in the silence of the forest. "We wish you

peace," she added for the benefit of her travel companions. She sensed more than saw Shanks' startled reaction. "*Aman dia shung-sa, co dora' manag mi'i'i,*" she continued in a sing-song voice. "Please accept the safe return of your blessed gift."

"Nic, lay the flutar on the ground, slowly," Shanks said in a tone that offered no recourse. Nica bowed as she lowered the carving to the ground and gently released it.

"Back away. Don't look at them," Shanks instructed in a low voice.

"*Isla mong'tubo reegla ela bon day du'u,*" Nica spoke loudly so all could hear. "May the Mother forest bring you great bounty." She brought her hands together as though in prayer and dropped her eyes. Please let it work.

Silence stretched through the forest.

"*Ing shee'ma.*" An older man stepped forward and spoke in a guttural voice. His authority was undeniable. He pointed his spear at her.

All eyes shifted to Nica.

Nica nodded and moved toward the flutar.

Shanks swore under his breath. "What are you doing?"

"He wants me to hand it to him."

"No," Shanks said, then louder, looking directly at the older man, "No." His voice was firm.

A grumble went through the forest people again as they shuffled their positions, but Nica knew what she had to do. She reached for the wood piece and carefully picked up the sacred item. Cautiously she approached the leader. She balanced the wood carving on her open hands and held it out for the man to take. "*Sho shee'mo*."

His limpid eyes didn't blink, yet Nica didn't sense any animosity from the man. Merely curiosity. Her lips curved in a small smile. Though the man did not return the smile with his lips, she was sure she saw it in his eyes.

With his free hand he pulled at a piece of brown twine hanging around his neck. A small leather pouch was attached. He took one step forward and with a flick of his wrist flipped the twine necklace over Nica's head.

Behind her, Nica could feel Shanks ready to spring to protect her.

The elder's eyes lingered on her blond hair and she got the sense he was waging an internal battle with his curiosity. Finally, his eyes settled on hers again and he gave one slow nod of his head.

Without a further word the man reached with both hands, his spear now held loosely between his fingers, and took the gift Nica proffered.

"*Reega ma.*'" He said in his guttural voice as his eyes swept their group. His gaze stopped on Shanks. He nodded once at the younger man. "*Ranagstu' moab sinc ka*," he said, slowly repeating what Shanks had attempted to say earlier, as though for his benefit. A smile flitted across his face so fast Nica wondered if she'd actually seen it.

His eyes returned to Nica. He nodded once as he said in softer voice, "*Y'we'e mish a mu'u.*" He turned and without a sound they were gone.

"What did he say to you, Nica?" Jaaniyah asked in a trembling voice.

"He said she spoke like one of the people," Shanks answered. He moved closer to her and raised his eyebrows. "I'm impressed." His teasing smile back in place. "So many secrets you have, Lady Jacoby." Something deepened in his eyes and Nica's heart skipped a beat. "You intrigue me."

With a thump, Jaaniyah sank down to the ground. Her head slumped into her hands as sobs wracked her body. Shanks went to Jaaniyah and bent down to slide a protective arm around her shoulders.

Nica stared at the two of them, fighting her own emotions.

Sebande approached silently to stand next to Nica. "*Ela makata*, I'll help you gather wood for the fire."

Nica raised her head to force a smile for him. "And how do I say 'thank you' in Corsosh?"

"*Counte*," Sebande replied.

Nica nodded. "*Counte*, then."

NICA AND SEBANDE were warming some of the provisions gathered from the soldiers when Shanks joined them around the fire.

"That was amazing to listen to you speak to them, Nic," Shanks said. "I've struggled to learn this dialect for years. How is it you come to speak their language?"

Nica shrugged, still irritated at his constant solicitation of Jaaniyah. "Are they gone now, do you think?"

Shanks shook his head. "No, not all of them. There will be guards who stay. They won't allow us to see them but trust me—they're watching us. They know everything that goes on in this forest."

"Oh," Nica shivered. She looked around but all she could see were shadows among the surrounding trees. "Is that why Jaaniyah was so afraid? Did she think they were going to stab us with their spears?"

"Well, the Narsgededon poison the tips of their spears, so it's possible," Shanks said. "If the wound doesn't kill you, then the poison surely will. I suspect that's what's in the pouch he gave you." He nodded to the pouch that still hung around Nica's neck. "A significant offering of trust."

Alarmed, Nica looked down at the little leather pouch. Gingerly, she grabbed the twine from which the pouch was suspended and slid the little bag to the outside of her clothes. No sense taking any chances.

Shanks reached for a piece of meat that Sebande offered. "Also—" he added, almost as an afterthought— "the Narsgededon are said to be cannibals."

Nica jerked her eyes up to his.

Shanks gave her a crooked grin. "But that's not a proven fact—just a forest rumor." The corners of his blue eyes crinkled up as he laughed at her, his blond hair falling back. That was all it took. Suddenly her heart was singing and her chest felt so full she wanted to burst. She turned away before her eyes betrayed her emotions, frightened by how strongly he could affect her.

AFTER THEY HAD eaten they broke camp to continue on. Once again, Jaaniyah required Shanks full attention for some inconsequential task.

"Sebande," Nica put a hand on his arm. "Could you help me for a minute?"

Surprise flickered in his eyes but he nodded without asking. Yanking the string on the bedroll he was fastening to his saddle, he reached a hand and rocked the pack making sure it was secure before he followed her to the edge of camp. Nica reached down and slowly pulled her dagger from her boot. He blinked, but didn't move.

"Will you cut a strand of my hair?" She reached behind her head and lifted the top layer of hair. She circled her finger and thumb to show the thickness. "A long piece, from underneath?"

Sebande's face was a mask as he took the knife from her outstretched hand. With little effort he sliced her hair off.

"*Ela makata, histra mek'e*," he said, as he handed the knife and section of hair to her.

Nica smiled up at him. "Sebande, I'll look forward to learning Corsosh from you when we return to LaBricé." She narrowed her eyes at him. "And that way, we'll have no more secrets."

He leaned down so she would be sure to hear him. "Brave girl, kind heart," he said softly. Then he turned and strode away.

Nica watched his retreating back, surprised and pleased at his words.

"Are we ready?" Shanks called out.

Nica hurried toward the creek and the Pandoxian tree where she'd found the flutar. Breaking off a large leaf from a nearby shrub, she placed it carefully among the protected roots of the tree. She took the chunk of hair and laid the blonde strands across the green plant, wondering how long it would be before the forest people found her gift.

s Nica feared, Jaaniyah asked to ride with Shanks.

"Would you mind, Nic?" he asked.

Nica smiled and joined Sebande near his horse. After years of living around Mosaba, it was easy to mask her emotions. The tall young man leaned his arm down for her to grab and with one effortless tug, pulled her onto the horse behind him. Nica was pleased when he didn't wait for Shanks and Jaaniyah to mount their horse, but set off instead.

They rode through the day, pausing only to rest and water the horses. While they were dismounted Sebande pulled Shanks aside and had what appeared to be a heated conversation. Nica watched them covertly out of the corner of her eye, curious at what they discussed, for she'd never seen the two of them argue before.

Before they departed Jaaniyah came up to her. "Jonn and I have decided it would be best if you and Sebande delay your return until after we've had time to get back inside the palace walls. That way there's no chance anyone will see us together."

Nica took a deep breath, fighting the desire to say what she really thought.

"It would only be for an hour or two," Jaaniyah said. "Don't you agree that makes the most sense?"

Nica nodded, her mask in place. What she thought didn't matter to any of them anyway. "Perfect sense. Where shall I go when I return? Are there other rooms I could claim as my own this time?" She smiled sweetly at her sister. "So I don't disturb you, of course."

Jaaniyah nodded. "I'll arrange for a suite for an unnamed guest who wishes to retain their privacy."

Shanks joined them. "We should keep moving. We're within an hour of the palace now." He looked over at Nica. "Nic, we were thinking…"

"I've already told her, Jonn," Jaaniyah interrupted. "She agrees. Actually—" she gave Nica a conspiratorial grin— "she said she was pleased to have a little extra time with Sebande alone." Jaaniyah slid her arm through Shank's and pulled him in the direction of the horses. "Come along, Jonn."

Shanks' eyes narrowed. "You and Sebande are long lost friends now?"

Nica held up her hand to stop him. "Jaaniyah has done enough talking for all of us," she said in a cold voice. She turned on her heel and stalked over to Sebande. Something on her face must have indicated her mood because Sebande quickly vaulted onto his horse and reached down to pull Nica up behind him.

"You've heard we are to delay?" he asked.

"I've heard."

He kicked the horse into motion and pulled away from where Shanks was still helping Jaaniyah climb on their horse. "When we get closer, I'll veer off the path so they can continue on. There's a place not far from there we can go visit that has a nice view. I think you'll enjoy it."

Nica appreciated his kind intentions. It was clear he realized something was amiss between her and Shaun. Or perhaps, she thought, he'd known it would come to this all along. Because if she were honest with herself, why would Shanks have any interest in her? Especially when the future queen of Jarisa was in love with him.

She tightened her grip around Sebande's waist and laid her head on his broad shoulders. "Thank you, Sebande."

AFTER SHANKS AND Jaaniyah had ridden on to HighGarden, Sebande left the two guards at the trailhead and threaded his way through the trees and brush along a path that was practically non-existent. It took almost ten minutes before they broke free of the undergrowth and were able to walk their horse along a rocky shelf. Nica wondered how Sebande could even tell where he was going so rough was the terrain. He steered them down an uneven path which led to a cliff overlooking a lake.

Nica peered around his shoulders. "What's that?" she gasped. Below them steam rose from the water in small billowing clouds.

"It's a natural hot springs," Sebande said. He twisted around in the saddle and grinned at her. "Want a warm bath?"

Nica stared up at him in disbelief before she grinned and shouted, "Yes!"

He steered the horse down to the edge of the water and slid off. For the first time ever, he reached up to help Nica dismount. As Sebande set his horse to graze, Nica hurried down to the water's edge.

"*Asante*," she whispered in surprise. "It's almost hot."

Sebande chuckled. "You're sworn to secrecy though. Very few people know this place exists. I don't want to be taking my baths with a bunch of dirty soldiers."

Nica giggled. "I promise. But Sebande—" she gave him a teasing look— "where are you going to go while I take *my* bath?"

Sebande grinned, revealing white teeth. "I'll be guarding you, of course, M'lady."

Nica splashed the water at him. "Then turn around, sir."

Their close quarters over the last few weeks had reduced her inhibitions and she wasn't too concerned if Sebande saw her in her undergarments or not. Sebande turned on his heel and crossed his arms, his back straight as he perused the trees that surrounded the hot springs.

Nica sat down on a large rock and pulled her boots off, followed by her breeches and cloak, along with her jacket and sweater. She folded them neatly and left them on the rock. Clad in only her undershorts that reached halfway to her knees and her camice, which hung from straps over her shoulders, she waded into the warm water.

"Oh, it's so warm," she called. Once she got to knee level she sank into the water up to her shoulders and pushed off, floating. "This is heaven."

"I guess I should've asked if you could swim first," Sebande called, a hint of worry in his voice.

"Not to worry—I'll shout if I start drowning."

Nica lay back in the water and floated, kicking her feet as she luxuriated in the warmth. She flipped over and paddled forward, closing her eyes and submerging her head, kicking hard with her feet to glide underwater. She only came up for a breath of air before she plunged back under and soared through the water, weightless and free. When finally her lungs started to burn she kicked her way to the top, her outstretched arms breaking the surface of the water. Taking a big gasp of air, she flipped over on her back and glanced toward the shore. Sebande was bare-chested and poised ready to dive in, his eyes searching the water for her.

"I thought you were going to keep guard with your back to the water," she laughed.

His shoulders relaxed and he motioned her back towards the shore.

"I didn't know you could swim like a fish."

Nica swam back and reluctantly climbed from the water, shivering in the chill air. She tried not to stare at his chest. She'd never win in a fight against those muscles.

"I'll probably catch my death of cold now," she said as she tugged her dirty clothes back on, "but I'd do it again in a heartbeat. Thank you, Sebande."

"Stand by the fire while I take a dip," Sebande said. He stepped aside and revealed a small smokeless fire at his feet. Without glancing at her, he dove off the rocks, slicing neatly through the water.

Nica watched his dark shoulders move effortlessly through the water and wondered what his childhood had been like growing up in Corsock. He and Shanks both must have done a lot of swimming since they lived on an island.

It wasn't long before Sebande climbed from the water to shake all over like a dog after a bath.

"Argghhh!" he growled against the cold air. "That's refreshing."

He walked near her to pick up his clothes. Well-developed muscles rippled down his arms and chest. Sebande pulled his shirt back over his shoulders and squatted down next to where Nica sat by the fire. Her smile faltered when she saw the frown between his eyes.

"What's wrong?" she asked.

Sebande's dark eyes held hers. "I think it's only fair you should know something before we return to the palace."

Nica's sense of well-being immediately vanished and she waited with trepidation.

"Yes?"

He took a deep breath. "It has never been officially announced, but it's been Jaaniyah's—" he hesitated as if searching for the right word— "*desire* for some time now to become betrothed to Shaun."

Nica fought to keep her face emotionless. "And what is Shaun's desire?"

Sebande looked away. "I can't speak for Shaun. I don't think he felt there was any imminent need to make a commitment one way or the other, but I can't be sure what they've discussed." He shook his head. "He hasn't told me if he's intending to marry her."

A chill breeze blew over her and Nica clenched her teeth to keep them from chattering. "I'm not surprised."

Sebande nodded. "I thought you should be aware the princess thinks she has a previous claim on him." He stood up and pulled his boots on, making it clear the conversation was over. "We've been here long enough. We should go."

Nica busied herself with putting out the fire and spreading the half burnt logs as Sebande gathered the horse. She tried to convince herself she was grateful for Sebande's warning. Given the life of secrecy he and Shanks had led simply to stay alive, it must have taken a lot for him to reveal anything personal about Shaun to her at all.

When they were both seated and the horse was picking its way up the hill, Nica tightened her hands around Sebande's waist and said softly in his ear, "Thank you for telling me, Sebande. I needed to know."

He nodded his head. "Don't thank me too quickly," he said over his shoulder. "I still have to carry you into the palace over my shoulder like a sack of potatoes."

"WHO GOES THERE?" The guard belted out as they approached the gate.

"Sebande Vatier, on business for the king." Sebande nodded at the rotund gatekeeper as he passed through. "Bastille."

"Did ye hear the news, young Sebande?" Bastille chortled in his direction, not even paying attention to the limp person in the front of Sebande's saddle. "The princess is back." He clapped his hands in glee. "Jonn Shanks rescued her and brought her back home where she belongs. All in one piece, too." He practically skipped on his short bent legs as he closed the gate.

"I did hear something of it," Sebande said. "It is indeed fantastic news." He rode onto the stables, one hand steady on Nica's back. He pulled to a stop and slid from the horse, pulling Nica along with him, careful to keep the hood of her cloak over her head.

"Come along, friend. I'll see you to your rooms, yet again." He heaved Nica over his shoulder, more carefully than in the past, and yelled to one of the stable boys to brush his horse down. "Give him some extra oats. The beast has earned his keep lately."

Nica gritted her teeth as her stomach ground into Sebande's shoulder, swearing to herself she would never enter the palace of Jarisa in this fashion again. To Lucede's den with all of them.

"There you are." A familiar voice said as Sebande drew near. "Where in bloody hell have you been?" Shanks ground out from under his breath. "I was just about to come in search of the two of you."

"Nothing to fear," Sebande said. "We're here now." A door creaked open and Sebande stopped. "Would you like to take the package from here?"

Nica kicked her legs and jerked herself down. She'd had enough. "Just let me walk," she snapped. "Where am I going?"

"I'll show you," Shanks said. He reached for her arm but Nica jerked away. She grasped the edges of her hood to hold it in place as she tilted her head to look into Sebande's face. "Thank you."

His face didn't change expression but Nica thought she saw a glint of understanding in his eyes. Or was it laughter? Nica allowed herself to look at Shanks. His brow was scrunched in confusion as he took in her wet hair and damp clothes.

His gaze shifted to Sebande and his voice was incredulous as he asked, "Are you two *wet*?"

There was just a hint of a smile around the corners of Sebande's mouth as he replied with a shrug. "We did have an hour or two to kill." With a nod at Nica he walked away mumbling about tending to his horse.

Shanks turned to Nica as though to speak, but someone came around the corner of the corridor. Instead, he slid his arm under hers and guided her along the obscure passageways and back stairs up to her rooms.

"We've arranged for you to be down the hall from Jaaniyah. We're going to put some guards at the door and claim you're a visiting dignitary who has fallen ill. That should buy us a little bit of time until we come up with a better plan."

"Fine," Nica replied in a flat tone. "I'm not planning on leaving my room anyway." It was a lie, but she would be gone before Shanks realized the truth.

Shanks steered her along the hallway until they came to a set of doors where two guards stood at attention. He cracked the door open then put an arm out to stop her before she could enter. "Nic," he began, "can I come in? There's something I think we need to talk about."

Nica's heart fluttered. She wasn't ready to have him tell her about his relationship with Jaaniyah. Not yet. She hadn't had enough time for Sebande's warning to sink in. She held up her hand.

"I am really quite exhausted. Whatever it is, I'm sure it can wait until later." It took every inch of will to muster up a believable smile for him. Her heart hung like a chunk of ice suspended in her chest.

"But Nica…"

She cut him off. "I'm sure you've got more important things to do."

With a dark look, Shanks released her and took a step back, his face now a mask.

"I'll stop by and check on you later."

Nica nodded and pushed her way through the entrance, closing the portal firmly behind her. When the latch clicked into place, she sagged against the door, resting her forehead against the wood. Tears that had never fallen the many times Mosaba had hurt her now fell freely down her cheeks.

How could she think Shanks would care for her? She turned and stumbled to the bed and fell on the soft surface with a muffled cry. For once, she gave in to the pain inside and cried until she couldn't draw a deep breath. Everything she'd believed to be true about her life was a lie. She had nothing.

AFTER A LONG time the tears subsided and she lay on her side, like a body whose soul had moved on. She didn't belong in Jarisa. There was no place for her here. Jaaniyah would be Queen and would not welcome any threat to her authority from Nica. If Jaaniyah and Shaun married Nica wouldn't be able to stand the torture of living around the two of them. Toppen had been right. They needed to continue on with their original plan and head to Pont d'Suree. The sooner, the better.

Chapter Thirty-Two

ica bided her time, counting the days until she could make a clean escape. Shanks or Sebande came by daily to escort her from her room and walk around the palace with her. Like a little pet, she thought. There was a wall between her and Shaun now. Nica wasn't sure if it originated from her or him or both, perhaps. But it made her decision to leave that much easier.

Nica tried not to think of him, or of the time they'd shared together, but it was hard to push him from her mind when there was little else to occupy it except questions without answers. Sequestered in her rooms and with Jaaniyah in charge of the affairs of the palace, Nica rarely saw her sister.

Instead, Nica became a frequent visitor of Becknah, who had still not recovered his health from his ordeal in the Ortawn. He was more frail and his hands shook more than they had before. But he seemed glad for her company and freely shared his knowledge of the texts of the Avedla with her. She would sneak through the hallways and up to his tower and they would spend hours, hidden away, discussing the meanings of the verses and whether the clues she'd deciphered had really meant anything at all.

There were days when she daydreamed of continuing her quest for The Getheas Stone on her own, a sense of urgency still burning inside to find the Stone before Mosaba did. But it was impossible at this time, with Jarisa and Sartis at war.

SEVERAL WEEKS PASSED with no further news of Mosaba's location and no significant improvement in the King's health. Nica was debating how to broach the subject of Toppen with Sebande when the opportunity dropped in her lap. She'd asked Sebande to show her the stables so she could figure out the best way to steal a horse without being caught when he'd gotten sidetracked by a stable hand with a lame animal. Nica had wandered away from their conversation, eyeing the horses as she looked for a beast she could handle when a worker mucking out a stall backed into her.

She'd turned and gasped out loud when she'd recognized Toppen's orange hair.

"Nic," Toppen had cried out, but Nica had shushed him with a hand over his mouth. She'd glanced over her shoulder to make sure Sebande hadn't noticed them before she'd turned back and whispered urgently, "We have to leave. Can you get out at night?"

"Yes." Toppen had hissed.

"Meet me behind the stables at midnight tonight." At his nod she'd hurried back toward Sebande. When Nica had glanced over her shoulder Toppen had disappeared back into a stall.

TOPPEN'S FAMILIARITY WITH the stables and horses was a huge boon to their escape. Nica told him Bastille's name and Toppen boomed out his name as if he and the gatekeeper were old friends. Nica was dressed in her valote pants and cloak, her head covered by a scarf and hood. They slipped beyond the barricade and rode free into the forest.

They rode hard for an hour before they stopped and pulled up under several trees.

"Did you bring the map?" Toppen asked.

"Yes," Nica replied. She reached inside her cloak and pulled out the map she'd stolen from Mosaba. Toppen flicked a match and lit a small taper as she held it out for him to see.

"There's Pont d'Suree," Nica pointed. "Can you make it out?"

"Yes, I know where it is. It's just how to get there from here that we need to know." He grasped one corner of the map and held the flame up as he peered at the lines and pictures drawn on the page. "I think the best way to go is south toward Mar'ligaan and ride along the Cliffs of Seniesta then cut inland back toward Pont d'Suree."

"But that route takes us right along the Great Divide," Nica said. A worried frown creased her brow as she gazed into his face. "Don't you think Mosaba will have his men scattered along there? It's the border between the countries. The most likely spot for him to hide his armies waiting for an opportunity to pour over into Jarisa."

"The only other way is to go through the heart of the Narsgededon and up toward the Braaks'faa which is just as risky." Toppen held the light so he could see her face. "Besides, you know Mosaba doesn't have enough soldiers to have the whole border covered. At best, he's got men stationed here and there. If we keep our eyes open we should be able to sneak around them."

Undecided, Nica fingered the leather string that hung around her neck. At the last minute she'd tucked the small pouch the Narsgededon forest elder had given her inside her clothes.

"C'mon, Nica, it's quicker and easier just to ride south along the Divide." Toppen gave her a beseeching look. "That's the way we were going to go originally. We can pick up the old trail and pretend none of this ever happened."

Nica smothered an impulse to laugh hysterically at the idea of forgetting it all. If only that were possible. Though she could see his logic, she couldn't rid herself of the unsettled feeling gnawing at the pit of her stomach. But she didn't want to fight with Toppen so she nodded her head in assent.

A look of relief flooded Toppen's face and he sat back with a big smile.

"We've got to be very alert though," she warned. "Mosaba could have his men anywhere and I don't ever want to return to the Ortawn."

"We'll slip by so quietly they'll never even know we were there."

THEY RODE UNTIL dawn before they sought shelter near a lush growth of trees next to a stream. Already, Nica was sore from the saddle as though she'd been riding for days. She fought a groan as she climbed from the hard leather and put a hand on the small of her back as she worked out the kinks.

"How can soldiers ride all the time, day after day?" she asked with a grimace.

"You get used to it," Toppen replied. "I've heard your legs start bowing in the shape of a saddle if you ride enough years."

Nica set about gathering kindling and firewood for a small fire. The weather was a bit warmer as they went further south away from the mountains, but the bite of winter was still in the air and she quickly became cooled when she wasn't moving. She'd stored extra food from her meals since she'd returned to the palace, so if they rationed carefully they should have enough bread and cheese as well as a little meat to tide them over until they reached their destination in about a week's time.

It wasn't until they'd both settled into their bed rolls and Toppen had ceased his chattering that the magnitude of what she'd done struck her. She'd escaped. Again. Now there was no one to threaten Jaaniyah's crown or her planned betrothal with Shanks. Even Sebande might be glad to have her gone instead of always having to babysit her. A hot tear dripped out of the corner of one eye and she buried her head against her blanket to wipe it away. Perhaps Becknah would miss her.

"Six days to freedom," she whispered to herself. Six days to Pont d'Suree and a new life.

ON THE THIRD day they spotted several of Mosaba's men riding on the Jarisan side of the Great Divide. They were in an area where the canyon was exceptionally deep, with large shafts of rock poking up from a valley floor so far below it appeared to exist in miniature. Nica spied them first. There were three of them, making no attempt to stay hidden, by the looks of how casually they sat on their horses. Luckily, she'd caught Toppen's attention before he went barreling straight past them and instead they'd hidden in the trees.

"Which way should we go?" Toppen whispered

"Let's go directly away from them and cut back over to the road later," Nica said. Her pulse quickened at the sight of their familiar green uniforms. No doubt Mosaba had informed all of his guards to be on the lookout for someone fitting her description.

Toppen pulled out the map. "Look where we are." He pointed to the page. "Almost to the southern sliver. It's the last one before the coast. If we can get past these guards, I doubt Mosaba will have any other soldiers further south." He lifted his head and cast a worried gaze at the three men. "If we can just get past them, we'll be fine."

Nica eyed the forest around them. The further south they went the more tropical and dense the forests of Jarisa became. The thick undergrowth was threaded with vines which became a deadly trap for the horses.

"I don't want to push our luck, Toppen. Even if we lose half a day, it's worth it to not to give away our location." She pointed in the direction behind them. "Let's just backtrack and take the other trail." She glanced at the Sartisian guards. Though they were too deep in the forest to be seen, one of the men appeared to be looking in their direction.

"You're right," Toppen nodded. "That's the best plan." He folded the map and shoved it inside his jacket, jerking his horse's head close to Nica's mount. Her horse let out a loud whinny. Nica's eyes darted to the three men. Now all of three of them were looking in their direction.

"*Casanta mici*," she swore, tightening the reins in her hands.

"Follow me," Toppen said in a harsh whisper and kicked his horse into motion.

Nica yanked her horse's head around and followed him back into the forest, leaning low in the saddle. She gripped the animal tightly with her knees and glanced over her shoulder. The three Sartisian guards were headed their direction. Nica whipped back around and jerked her dagger from her boot. She would defend herself as long as she could. She was not going to go back to Mosaba alive.

issing?" Jaaniyah snapped. "What do you mean, *missing*?" She jerked around, her deep blue skirts swirling around her ankles, to stare at Jonn Shanks.

"She's not in her rooms, she's not with Becknah." His expression was tight, his eyes unreadable. "Toppen, her friend from Sartis, is gone also."

Jaaniyah's heart quickened. "Do you think she was taken?"

"No," he replied. His mouth was unsmiling. "I think she left on her own."

There was something about his reply that set her nerves on edge. Tension emanated from Shanks as he stood in the doorway, coiled like a carpidi ready to spring. All muscle and fury and passion.

"Why would she do something like that?" Jaaniyah asked.

Jonn took several rapid steps toward her, his agony suddenly evident. "Jaaniyah, if I've ever done anything to mislead you about my feelings, I apologize. I've always tried to be honest. Your father has treated me like a son and it's a debt I can never repay." He reached his hands out to her. "But I can't give you something I don't possess." His eyes pleaded for understanding.

She looked him up and down, taking in his long, trim legs and narrow hips that stretched into shoulders that seemed could bear the weight of the world. Part of her ached to hold him. His handsome face under his sun-streaked hair was so familiar, so much a part of her life that it was physically painful to think of him belonging to someone else. She'd loved him since she'd first laid eyes on the two wild boys her father had found in the forest and brought home three years ago. His beautiful blue eyes, his teasing smile, his air of danger; she'd never met anyone more perfect.

Even her father approved of him. She'd been trying to ensnare him ever since. To tame the wild boy, to make him see that he loved her—and if that failed, to make him realize he loved her kingdom enough to want her. But that was part of his appeal—he wasn't a young man to take orders from anyone. Even her.

A bitter smile twisted her lips. But for Jonn to fall in love with her identical twin—a girl she hadn't even known existed until a month ago—it was a bittersweet twist only the poets who sang in the town square could imagine. Her eyes stopped on his face. He looked so tormented she almost felt sorry for him.

"What exactly are you saying, Jonn?" She pinched her lips together to stop the tears that threatened to fall. She *needed* him to say it.

"I don't want to hurt you," he said.

"But?" She forced the word out of her mouth.

"I love her, Jaani." Shanks words were soft, his eyes tortured. "When I find her, I won't try to spare your feelings any longer or wait until the time is right. I'll declare my love for all to know." He dropped his hands. "It's only fair you know the truth. If you don't want me to return to Jarisa, I'll understand. But I've got to go after her."

Jaaniyah straightened her shoulders against the pain that wanted to knock her to her knees. Jealousy was a cat clawing at her insides and she threaded her fingers tightly together and held them in front of her to overcome her burning emotions.

"Of course you will come back." Jaaniyah frowned. "Where else would you go? She's my sister and belongs here in Jarisa. And you are my father's soldier. You saved his life. How would I explain your absence to him?"

Shanks' face lightened with a smile of relief. "Thank you, Jaani. It's right for both of us. You'll see with time."

A knock sounded on the door.

"We're loaded and ready," Sebande said from the doorway. He nodded at Jaaniyah. "M'lady."

Jaaniyah whirled to face Jonn. "Take whatever soldiers you need."

Shanks kissed her on one cheek, then the other. "Thank you, Jaani," he whispered before he disappeared out the doorway.

Jaaniyah stared at the empty doorway, frozen in place. How could he love someone who looked exactly like her but not love her? Her heart ached as though it had been broken in two.

"How would my father react?" she whispered as tears slid down her cheeks. "Like a king. And so then, shall I." Jaaniyah crossed her arms in front of her chest with a look of determination. "But we'll see who you love in the end, Jonn Shanks."

Chapter Thirty-Four

ica followed Toppen's zigzag path through the brush and wondered if he had any idea where he was going. Their horses were forced to jump through some parts of the trail, so thick were the vines and leaves that covered the path.

Toppen glanced over his shoulder and his face twisted with panic. Nica followed his gaze and to her horror, saw the soldiers were giving chase.

Toppen cut back through the trees and headed for open ground near the edge of the Great Divide. The hooves of the horses clattered on the rocks. Before they could cut back to the forest, two of the Sartisian soldiers, one of them armed with a bow, bolted from the forest and cut them off.

Nica jerked her horse to a stop next to Toppen's, the animal snorting in alarm at being forced to halt so abruptly.

"Hello—" Toppen called out in Sartish, holding his hands up— "we mean no harm."

The three soldiers pulled closer, their swords drawn.

"Declare yourself," said the middle rider. "How do you speak Sartish? What is your business?"

"I'm Toppen Bakerswith," Toppen began. "Wine apprentice traveling for Mosaba."

One of the soldiers peered over at Nica. He began to edge his horse in her direction and her heart danced in an unsteady rhythm. Without taking his eyes off her the guard called over his shoulder. "I think we've got something here."

Nica gripped her dagger tighter as the weight of the other two soldier's gaze settled upon her. She pointed the knife in their direction.

"Don't come one step closer," she said. For the love of the Ancients, why didn't she have a sword? She'd have to be right next to this one to stab him. "I will kill you if I have to."

His look of surprise shifted into a grin. "Ho, with what? Your words?" he chuckled. "I've been too long without a woman. I can see I'm going to enjoy you."

Nica clucked her horse into backing up a few steps, tapping the beast gently with her heels.

"What's your name, sweet?" The Sartish soldier urged his horse straight toward her. Before the animal had gone two strides a strange humming noise filled the air and a cross bow bolt landed in the center of the man's chest. His eyes went wide before blood spurted out of his mouth and he tumbled from his horse.

Horrified, Nica watched him fall, her mind trying to make sense of what her eyes were telling her. She jerked her head up as several more arrows whistled through the air into the group. The archer from Sartis only got one shot off before he was struck in the throat. The third soldier seemed to understand they were outnumbered and wheeled his horse around to race for the sliver.

Jarisan soldiers poured from the woods, their brown coats blending with the forest in the afternoon light. Before she even had time to react, Shanks was at her side, steering his horse around to grab the reins just under her horse's bit. He pulled her with him back into the forest away from the exposure along the rim of the Great Divide. Out of the corner of her eye she saw Sebande streak by, followed by several other Jarisan soldiers, their eyes focused on their prey.

"What are you doing here?" Nica cried.

"We've been following your trail for days." He indicated the Sartisian soldiers. "Are there more of them?"

"No," Nica said, "I only saw the three."

"All right, hold on." He gripped her reins as he led her horse down the trail, heading back the direction they'd just come. A scream of pure terror pierced the air, growing fainter until it faded into silence.

Nica shuddered. Someone had fallen off the sliver—but who?

A PAIR OF Jarisan soldiers fell in behind them, acting as guards, until they reached a small hut hidden among the trees. Once there, Shanks slid off his horse, dropping the reins to Nica's mount. The other soldiers busied themselves with their animals as Shanks walked back to Nica. He held his hand up to help her dismount.

His hand felt warm and rough against her skin as she gripped her fingers and stepped down from her horse.

For a long while he just looked at her. "Have I ever mentioned that you're a lot of trouble?" he finally said.

Nica returned his stare, though it was more in wonder that he stood before her. "I did tell you I could disappear right from under your nose."

He propped his hands on his hips, a smile playing at the corners of his mouth.

"And what was my response?"

She titled her chin up. "You threatened me."

"I *promised* to find you," he corrected her. "Hopefully this is the last time I will have to chase you down."

"You didn't have to come after me," Nica said in a low voice. "I understand your responsibility is to Jaaniyah."

"It's true—I do have a responsibility to Jaaniyah." Shanks cupped her face with both hands. "But I love you, Nica. More than I knew was possible." He didn't smile. He looked deep into her eyes until she feared she would melt from the inside out. "Where you go, I go." There was an honesty in his eyes and she knew his words didn't come lightly. "For now and forever." His voice softened and he rubbed his thumbs along her cheekbones. "Do you understand?"

"Yes." For once, she understood perfectly.

His lips were warm on hers and she returned his kiss with a hunger she didn't try to restrain. She inhaled his scent and buried her hands in his hair, pressing herself tightly against his hard chest. His lips slid from hers and traced a burning path along her jaw.

Nica's lips brushed his ear. "I love you too, Shaun," she whispered. He buried his face in her neck and held her close.

"Nica—" his breath was ragged— "don't ever leave me again."

SEBANDE RETURNED WITHIN half an hour, Toppen in tow. He reported that a Sartisian guard had fallen to his death off the sliver. Nica hoped to talk to her friend but Sebande sent Toppen with the other soldiers and didn't bring him anywhere near her and Shaun.

When he had finished with his other duties, Sebande sauntered over to where Nica and Shaun sat by the fire. He looked Nica up and down. "Still in one piece, I see."

"Yes, thank you for coming after me." Nica gave him a hesitant smile, not sure of his mood.

"Seems to be my new job," Sebande muttered. "At least you can cook." He cocked a dark eye at her. "Oh, that's right. You *can't* cook, can you? Why exactly did we risk our lives to save you, *again*?" But a smile tugged at the corners of his mouth as he walked off, still muttering under his breath.

LATER THAT AFTERNOON the Jarisan soldiers departed with Toppen, leaving Shanks, Sebande and

Nica alone in the hut. They sat in several rickety wooden chairs they had found, warming themselves before a small fire burning in the hearth.

"Why aren't we returning to the palace with the others?" Nica asked.

Shanks sat next to her, close enough to touch her, leaning back precariously on two legs of his chair. Sebande was on the other side of Shanks, quiet as usual, his elbows braced on his knees, staring into the flames.

"Because we're not going back to HighGarden," Shanks replied. "Remember Jaaniyah said she was going to send some troops up to the Pian'glo Pass in search of the Valley of the Gods because she thought there might be some connection to the Getheas Stone?"

Nica nodded.

"Well, she did and the troops were ambushed by Mosaba's men. Somehow he knew she'd sent a group there. Based on that and some other recent events we're convinced there's a spy in the palace. Someone in addition to Tarantu. Sebande and I—" he nodded at his friend— "are also convinced that we need to find the Getheas Stone before Mosaba does." Shanks put his hand on Nica's knee. "We think you're our best chance of finding the thing."

"Me?" Nica gasped. "Why not Becknah?"

Shanks shrugged. "You seem to have a special sense about these verses. I talked to Becknah at length and he told me you were quite brilliant in your understanding of the quatrains."

"Well, I..." Nica stuttered, "I don't know what would have made him think that. I enjoyed discussing the subject with him but...." Her words died off. "I wouldn't even know where to look without The Ages. That book is the key." She looked from one to the other. "But I didn't bring it with me."

Sebande pushed out of his chair and walked to his knapsack, leaning against one wall. He lifted the book out with an unemotional flourish.

"We brought it with us," Shanks smiled as Sebande handed the book to Nica.

She stroked the silver letters embossed upon the black leather cover, her finger tracing the odd symbol at the bottom of the book. She flipped the cover open and counted through the pages until she found the page she wanted. "Listen to this:"

"Above you'll find a glorified knight
Near year's end he returns to fight
His sword held high will be your guide
Follow to where power divides."

Nica lifted her head to find Shanks and Sebande watching her intently.

"I don't think Jaaniyah had read the quatrains before she decided to send the troops to the Valley of the Gods." Nica tapped the page with her finger. "This sounds like we need go to Berjerac—to that statue outside Ravensfell. Do you remember it?" She looked from one to the other. "It's the only thing I can think of that might fit this verse. What do you think?"

Shanks shrugged. "Sounds reasonable to me."

"Shaun," Nica began. She consciously chose to use his real name, here where it was safe without being overheard. She enjoyed the intimate connection it gave them. "What happened to the soldiers who went to the Pian'glo?"

"Slaughtered." His voice was flat, emotionless. "Mosaba's men apparently couldn't get the information they wanted so they killed all six of them." He heaved a sigh. "I suspect Mosaba is sinking deeper into his madness with each failure, while at the same time he becomes more desperate to succeed in this quest. It would be unthinkable if he were to find the Stone first."

THEY LEFT LATER that afternoon and headed north, following trails that looked like nothing more than animal tracks. Shanks and Sebande seemed to know the shortcuts like the lines on the palms of their hands. They traveled for almost two days striking through what looked like uncharted territory to Nica.

"Do you know where you're going?" she asked.

Shanks smiled and nodded. "We've made this journey too many times to count."

"But there's hardly even a trail."

"That's because we're headed to a sliver very few people know about." He gave her a sideways glance. "You're not afraid of heights, are you? Because this one's a little narrow."

Nica's stomach sank. "How narrow?"

Shanks gave her a teasing grin. "Well, it's wide enough for a horse's hoof, but not much more," he chuckled. "You might want to close your eyes and say a prayer when we go over."

Nica fell silent, unsure whether to believe him or not.

THE SUN EMERGED from behind the clouds at the end of the day, casting a golden glow over the umber colored stones through which they traveled. Once they moved away from the trees, the landscape was a wide open vista, stretching toward the gaping chasm that was the Great Divide.

The horses carefully picked their way across the rocky ground working toward the edge of the canyon. Nica's gaze swept the landscape, looking for the sliver they would cross. A few fingers of land stretched partially into the void but none appeared to reach completely across the great expanse. They pulled up their horses in front of a strangely angled sliver and stopped.

Suddenly suspicious, Nica traced the winding piece of land into the distance. Because of the odd twists and turns of the rocky path, it was difficult to determine how far the sliver stretched. She looked over at Shanks in alarm. They weren't going to risk their lives on this worm-trail of a cliff, were they?

"This isn't..."

"Yep."

"You can't be serious."

"Yep." On the far side of Shanks she could hear Sebande laughing under his breath. Nica considered the precipice before them. "I doubt the horses will even walk on that."

"They will," Shanks said confidently. "Do you want me to lead your horse?"

"No." But Nica wasn't sure she meant it.

"Listen to me, Nic," Shanks said, suddenly serious. "This is a bit dangerous. You have to give the horse his head. He'll know what to do. Don't try to steer him, don't squeeze his sides. Just relax and enjoy the ride, all right?"

Nica nodded, her palms sweating against the leather of the reins.

Sebande kicked his horse into the lead. Nica took a deep breath as she tentatively urged her horse to follow him. As the horse gingerly stepped onto the sliver, Nica's eyes were drawn to the breathtaking drop on each side, the vast open space all around her made it feel as though they were walking on air. Pebbles, jarred loose by the hooves of the animals, trickled off the edge of the rocky trail, rattling for a moment before dropping silently into the abyss.

Nica swayed in the saddle, suddenly dizzy at the open space plummeting away all around her. She gripped the saddle horn and squeezed her eyes shut.

"Are you all right?" Shanks called up to her.

She slowly nodded her head.

"It's shorter than it looks," Shanks said. "Enjoy it while you can because the view is spectacular."

Nica's eyes flew open. Was he serious? He sounded like he was enjoying this tightrope adventure. She cautiously turned her head and looked south down the canyon in the direction of the Sea of Nephalon. The view *was* breathtaking, in more ways than one, and for a second she realized how awe-inspiring the Great Divide actually was. And there, so far distant it appeared to be the horizon, she thought she saw the green-blue waters of the sea.

Her horse navigated around a wide turn and suddenly she was on the other side and surrounded by solid ground again. She released a sigh of relief and smiled at Sebande. "That was quick."

Shanks pulled up beside her and Sebande. "You can't tell from the other side, but this is one of the spots in the Divide where it's very narrow from one side of the canyon to the other."

"How did you ever find it?" Nica asked.

"Oh." Shanks shrugged. "We just happened to stumble across it one time."

Nica shook her head at his non-answer. Maybe it was better if she didn't know.

Shanks urged his horse into motion and Nica fell in behind him with Sebande riding behind her.

"Keep a sharp eye," Shanks said. "There are a lot of people looking for us here."

t was past midnight when they stopped to make camp in a cave tucked among a group of large boulders. The blackened walls of the stones silently spoke of the many campfires that had been lit in that location in the past.

Every bone ached as Nica slid from her horse and began to help gather kindling for a fire. She racked her brain for any other meaning to the Avedla verse as she bent down to pick up several branches beneath a large Junbutgen tree. The statue in front of Mosaba's castle was the only answer that seemed to fit the words of the poem.

THEY WAITED UNTIL late afternoon to start off on the final leg into Berjerac. They timed their arrival to be close to dusk, leaving enough daylight to inspect the inscription on the statue before it became too dark to read.

Nervous bubbles churned in Nica's stomach at being so close to her old home. There were people who might recognize her, even in her breeches and large cloak.

Before they left, Nica tied a black scarf over her hair. Without a valote hat or glasses to distort her features she felt terribly exposed, even with the dirt she had spread across her cheeks and under her eyes.

Shanks, however, was a master at disguise. She watched in amazement as he took the sap from an Olivante tree and rubbed it in his hair, turning his blond locks a startling shade of tobacco brown. He slicked his hair down and tied it behind his head, then motioned for her to come near and he did the same for her hair.

Next, he took a branch from a Tombango bush and stripped the bark, rubbing the sinewy strips over several off his teeth. The dark brown gummy material clung to his teeth, giving them the appearance of being quite rotten. Coupled with a crumpled hat he dug out of his saddlebag and the limping slouch he affected, he was hardly recognizable as the tall, blond, stalwart young mercenary of whom Mosaba had been so fond.

They had agreed that Sebande would remain behind at a distance; able to help if needed but not close enough to be associated with them. They secured the horses and slipped into town to mingle with the townspeople. It was a strange feeling to speak in her native tongue of Sartish and for a second, it was as if she'd gone back in time.

"There it is." She nodded toward the large statue centered in the roundabout in front of the castle. The large figure depicted a man mounted on a rearing horse, his sword raised above his head as though preparing to rush into battle. "Look at the way he's holding his sword," Nica whispered. "Does that look like he's pointing it towards something to you?"

Shanks strolled alongside her with his slouching, half-limping walk. "The only place that sword appears to be pointing is straight at Ravensfell," he said in a casual tone.

Nica nodded as her heart sunk. "That's what I thought too."

They came to a stop in front of the statue, and read the inscription praising the efforts of Hu'ugenok, a warrior who had defeated an invading army seven centuries earlier.

"Well, the quatrain says '*above you'll find a glorified knight'*, and he's a glorified knight." She peered closer at the plaque. "It says the fight occurred two days before the New Year so that would fit '*near year's end he returns to fight'*."

"Yes, but what about the '*returns*' part? He's not returning. He's carved in stone." Shanks said. "What's the next line?"

"'*His sword held high will be your guide'*.*" Nica looked up at the statue. "*Follow to where power divides*," she mused. "His sword points to the Ravensfell. Do you think it means the disruptive power of Mosaba? He has certainly divided Jarisa and Sartis. They used to be allies."

Shanks shook his head and cast an appraising glance at the huge castle before them. "I don't know. Could there be something *in* the castle?"

Nica looked over at the familiar building. She searched her memory, trying to think of anything that made sense with the quatrain.

"There you are."

Nica jumped as the sharp voice cut through the air. "I've been looking everywhere for you."

Panic lit through her veins like a wildfire and Nica clutched blindly at Shanks' arm as she jerked around. It was Lady Angeline. She would know that voice anywhere.

The large woman was crossing the circle like a ship cutting a wake through a harbor, all the smaller vessels scurrying to get out of her way. To Nica's immense relief Lady Angeline was focused on another girl who now wore an expression like a rabbit caught in a snare. Nica didn't wait to listen to the tirade she knew was sure to follow. She shoved Shanks and motioned for him to move. She wasn't going to take a chance that Lady Angeline might recognize her.

They slipped into the flow of people moving past the statue and drew nearer to the entrance to the castle. An idea was blossoming in her head.

"Should we go in?" she whispered to Shanks. "I know my way around well enough, we could probably cover a lot of the castle and remain unseen. Maybe we'll see something that makes sense."

He gave her a big smile, showing all of his rotten teeth. "If you weren't dressed as a boy, I'd kiss you right here," he whispered. He glanced over his shoulder and gave some sign with his hand, motioning toward Sebande who stood on the fringes of the circle, watching them.

"What did you tell him?" Nica asked curiously.

"That we were going in and to look for us within two hours."

"You said all that with one hand motion?"

Shanks grinned down at her. "We've had lots of practice sneaking into places we shouldn't be." Nica couldn't help but smile back, wondering at the stories that Shanks and Sebande could tell.

"We should cut around by the stables and go in through a back door near the kitchens," Nica said. "Nobody watches that entrance and we can take the back halls without drawing any attention."

They cut around past the grand entrance, careful not to draw any attention to themselves. The stables were busy with soldiers coming and going as darkness fell. Nica remembered seeing Jacoby here in this very spot, bloodied and shackled. She shuddered at the memory. What would she have done had she known the truth that day? What *could* she have done?

No one paid them any heed as they walked toward the castle and slipped in the back door. Nica heaved a sigh of relief when the door closed behind them and they were safely hidden in the dimness of the corridor.

"Where should we go?" she whispered.

"Mosaba's study seems the most likely spot," Shanks replied. "If there's anything of value, it would probably be there, don't you agree?"

Nica nodded. "Except I don't even know what we're looking for."

"Tell me the verse again."

"Above you'll find a glorified knight
Near year's end he returns to fight
His sword held high will be your guide
Follow to where power divides."

"So, we'll look for something where power divides." Shanks grinned at her. "Should be simple."

Nica rolled her eyes and started down the corridor. They wound through the familiar hallways, taking the servant's stairs up to the fifth floor where Mosaba's study was located. A well-lit corridor led to the room. Nica motioned for Shanks to stop as they neared and cautiously peered around the corner. Two soldiers stood talking at the far end of the passageway.

"The door is probably locked," Nica whispered to Shanks, who stood close behind, looking over her head.

"I can pick a lock—" he replied in a calculating voice— "if I have enough time."

"Should I try and distract the guards?" Nica asked.

"No, it's too dangerous. We need to try and stay out of sight if we can. Let's just wait a minute and see if they move on."

Nica drew her head back and leaned against the cool stone wall, rubbing the rough texture with her fingers. Was Mosaba still in the Ortawn? Or had he followed their trail to Jarisa?

"All right, they're gone," Shanks whispered after a few moments. "You wait here and I'll go pick the lock. If somebody comes I'll bluff my way out of it." He looked into her face. "You stay here. If it looks like it's going wrong, run as fast as you can out of here and get back to Sebande. Agreed?"

Nica hesitated then nodded her head. There was no sense arguing with him. If he got caught, she'd decide at that time whether to run or to stay and help. "Good luck," she whispered as he slipped around the corner and ran on tiptoes to the large set of double doors that led to Mosaba's office.

Shanks knelt before the big iron handles. It looked to Nica like he pulled something from behind his head as he worked on the lock. It took less than a minute before he reached up and opened the door. With a quick glance over his shoulder the other way, he motioned for Nica to join him.

She took a deep breath and darted around the corner, racing toward him. She slipped in through the barely open door. Shanks followed her and carefully pushed the door closed behind them, securing the latch again with a quiet click.

"All right, so far so good." He stood with his hands on his hips and looked around the room. "Where do we start?"

Several of the tables in the large room were covered with documents and maps, as though Mosaba had been considering every possible place something, or someone, could be hidden. Nica shivered from the cool air pouring in through the partially opened windows. They divided the room with Shanks starting on Mosaba's desk as Nica worked her way through the bookcases and cabinets.

The going was slow and they worked silently for more than an hour. Occasionally Nica heard Shanks mutter, "I didn't know Mosaba had a trading relationship with him." And then later, "Macaferson is employed by Mosaba?"

She found little in the bookcases that seemed of interest. The killing devices in the cabinets repelled her and she didn't spend much time looking at their grisly points and blades. Nica was beginning to feel discouraged. She moved over to the table where Mosaba kept his maps and thumbed through the stack.

The corner of an elaborate star chart caught her eye and on a whim she pulled it to the top. She loved tracking the movement of the stars and knew every constellation in the sky. She had secretly hoped to study with Becknah and learn to divine the secrets the celestial bodies held.

Nica ran her fingers over the parchment, tracing the familiar shapes. Her eyes stopped halfway across the page to stare in surprise at a figure shown there. She glanced at the edges of the map, looking for the name of the artist, for this map included Glandar, the missing thirteenth sign of the zodiac. Few history books or star charts ever acknowledged this constellation and it remained somewhat of a mystery.

She traced the thirteen stars that made up the shape of the knight who waited with sword in hand for the Fire Horse to appear on the horizon. Her fingertip traced the lines between the stars when she froze and leaned down to peer closer at the drawing.

Suddenly, the silence was broken by a mumble of voices nearby.

Someone was coming.

Nica's gaze shot past Shanks, who still stood at Mosaba's desk, to the private entrance that led to and from Mosaba's study through a back door.

"I don't care what his excuse is, I want to see him *now*," A nearby voice practically shouted.

Mosaba was here.

At the sound, Shanks jerked his head up, recognizing the peril they were in. He sprinted around the desk toward her. Nica took a deep breath and scanned the room. She was skilled at hiding from Mosaba on her own, but to hide two of them? It would be impossible in this room.

"And bring me more wine," Mosaba shouted. Footsteps sounded on the private entry stairs and Nica knew there were only seconds before the man would be in the room with them. Not enough time to get to the door. They had to get out of there.

Her eyes darted to the window. It was their only chance. She dropped the star map and flew towards the wall, pushing the leaded glass pane open further. Shanks was right on her heels.

She grasped the edge of the glass and jumped up on the sill, stepping hurriedly out onto the thin ledge. The height took her breath away and she raised her eyes, fixing her gaze on a point of light in the distance. She edged along the stone perch, trying to make room for Shanks. He inched onto the small stone shelf, his larger boots hanging over the edge, his back pressed to the wall.

"Hold on to me," he whispered, "and I'll hold onto the glass."

Nica nodded. With shaking fingers she bunched the side of his jacket and clutched the fabric. She just needed a minute to steady herself and she'd be fine. But they didn't have a minute.

"Rodjers, where is Shannan? I want his report," Mosaba yelled. The proximity of his voice made it clear he was now in the room.

Nica worked her way slowly along the ledge, moving away from the open window. Shanks moved with her, sliding his feet slowly along the stones. Far below, she could see traffic on the road headed to and from market. People shouting and carts trudged along, all oblivious to the two people on the ledge far above their heads.

"Keep going," Shanks said softly, "you're doing great."

"Why in the name of Lucede's is that window open?" Mosaba yelled. "It's freezing in here!"

 hey stood with their arms spread for balance, plastered against the wall, barely daring to breathe. She could not be captured. Nica glanced down at the walkway far below and for a moment thought the unthinkable. She would jump, just like Y'ong Toobu, to escape from Mosaba.

The window groaned as it was yanked closed. Nica released her breath and immediately felt her knees begin to shake. She was out of practice.

"All right?" Shanks whispered, looking over at her.

She nodded and gave him a shaky grin. With cautious steps she began to work her way over to the parapet. She slid her hands between the cutouts in the stone and pulled herself up and onto the balcony. Together they snuck through the shadows, avoiding the patrol on the upper walkway, and slipped into a shadowy corner between the walls of the castle.

"That was close," Nica whispered as she wrapped her arms around Shanks and held him tight, pressing her head against his chest.

"For a minute there I thought I was going to have to duel with Mosaba in his own castle." Shanks let out a relieved chuckle as he put his arm around Nica's back and held
her close. "Maybe we should try again later."

Nica lifted her head. "Do you have a death wish?"

"No. I just—"

She put her fingers against his lips. "It doesn't' matter. We don't have to come back."

"Why? Did you find something?"

Nica gave a quick excited nod. "We're in the wrong spot." At Shanks' frown she explained. "The poem isn't talking about the statue in front of Ravensfell. It's talking about Glandar, the golden knight—the thirteenth constellation." She pointed up to the sky. "You can only see Glandar in Sartis in December. Look where his sword is pointed."

Shanks turned his gaze upward. "Northwest."

"Yes." Nica nodded. "And what's to the northwest?"

"The Spires Mountains," Shanks replied.

"Exactly. And the beginning of the Great Divide."

THEIR ESCAPE FROM Sartis was without incident and after they crossed the sliver back into Jarisa they made good headway. As the three of them moved further north the peaks of The Spires surrounded them. The snow-capped tips reached higher and higher as they climbed. The rough-hewn craggy crests reminded her of a sleeping giant, poking crooked fingers into the gray sky.

As the path gained in elevation the heavy forest gave way to hillsides sparsely populated with craggy trees. The ground was peppered with rocky hills and cliffs that appeared to have been thrust toward the sky in a huge burst.

"We must be close to the start of the Great Divide," Shanks commented. "Did you know they say the Divide was created by a river? Legend says it was water that actually cut the canyon over the centuries."

"A river?" Nica said. "But Sartis is a desert. The canyon has been dry for centuries."

As they neared the highest part of the trail, beautiful white snowflakes began to drift down. Shanks gave Nica a grin that reminded her of a little boy receiving a favorite toy. She laughed at him, filled with an irrational happiness.

The snow continued to fall as they climbed and they soon found themselves in a magical, ethereal world. Each step of their horse's hooves caused the white powder to spray into the air in a cloud-like puff, their nostrils snorting out breaths of smoky air.

The trail through the snow-covered forest was breathtaking in its beauty, a dramatic change from the dense greenery and foliage of the jungles of southern Jarisa. Huge ice-covered cliffs of jagged rock rose abruptly on each side of the trail. Crooked rows of trees, dressed in sparkling white frosting, survived at impossible angles among the cracks and fissures of the huge rock slabs.

EIGHT DAYS HAD passed since their departure from Berjerac. Darkness was settling around them like a blanket as they walked their horses along a steep ridge above a winding gorge. The path took a hard turn through the trees then began to rapidly descend.

"Welcome to the Braaks'faa Valley," Shanks said. "Be on the lookout for ghosts."

"We can already see their bones." Sebande pointed to something ahead on the ground. Nica peered where he'd indicated and realized that what she thought were piles of rocks, were actually small piles of bones.

"Are those human?" she asked.

"Yes, and about the tenth pile I've seen so far," Sebande said.

Nica shuddered. She tried to recall what the verse from the Avedla had said about bones. Silently she recited the poem in her head.

> *Where tallest mountains and valleys collide*
> *The ghosts of scattered bones reside*
> *The tears of Gods this space created*
> *It is here the answer has so long waited*

Certainly part of the verse was fulfilled in this spot, Nica thought. But what were the tears of Gods? She eyed the frozen river but could make no connection between the two. She gave a mental shrug. Maybe it would become clear as they went further.

The piles of human bones, washed white with exposure to the elements, became more frequent the further they went. Nica searched the woods around them. So many dead. It was almost as if the air shivered with their ghosts.

When they emerged through the trees into a wide open area Shanks reined his horse in.

"Nic, look at that."

Nica urged her horse next to his. She caught her breath as she gazed where he was pointing. "It's breathtaking."

Towering above them was a magnificent frozen waterfall. Gigantic icicles had formed in the shape of huge teardrops, as though the melting water had frozen in the instant just before the drop fell, suspending it forever.

Sebande came up beside them and let out a low whistle. "Are those supposed to be tears of the Gods?"

Nica's mouth dropped open. The tears of Gods. She could think of nothing more appropriate than a waterfall. "Sebande," she cried. "That's it! This is where we're supposed to be."

THEY STOPPED FOR the night back among the trees, not far from the frozen riverbank. Nica started a small fire burning while Shanks set up camp and Sebande went in search of dinner. He returned with two rabbits which he quickly skinned and set to cook over the fire.

"So, what's the next letter of the quatrain we're looking for?" Shanks asked after they'd finished their meal. Nica had already looked it up earlier and memorized the lines.

"We're on the second 'E' of Getheas now." She recited from memory.

"What once had been exists no more
What is solid now was once a door
A veil of prisyms casts a brilliant light
But remains unseen in the dark of night."

"What's a veil of prisyms?" Sebande asked. "Isn't that what the row of letters from the clock tower in Berjerac spelled out?"

"Yes, exactly," Nica said. "But I have no idea what it means. It sounds like a piece of fabric to me."

"A glittery piece of fabric," Shanks mused. "I guess that might make sense."

"None of it makes sense to me," Sebande muttered.

Darkness settled quickly and Shanks and Sebande agreed on how they would split the watch during the night. They positioned themselves in a circle around the fire again, hoping to absorb the heat from the flames during the night. Exhausted from the many days of travel, Nica quickly fell asleep.

THE HOWL OF a carpidi woke her. Nica sat up and looked around. Shanks slept across the fire from her and Sebande stood with his back to them, on watch. He turned and added a chunk of wood to the fire, glancing at her through the sparks that flew up into the sky before turning around again to face the dark woods that surrounded them.

Nica shivered against the bite of the night air and pulled her blankets close as she settled on her back. She looked up into the sky and traced the patterns of several familiar constellations.

"Are you wishing?" A voice whispered low in her ear.

Nica turned with a start. She hadn't even heard him move. Shaun laid down on his side next to her and propped his head on his elbow to look at her. With his free hand he spread his blanket over both their bodies.

"I don't know what to wish for," she whispered back, pleased to have him so close and all to herself.

"Everybody wishes for something." Shanks reached out a finger to trace her eyebrow and the curve of her cheek.

"I wish for your side to stop hurting, then."

"Well, thank you very much." He leaned close. "But what do you wish for yourself?"

"*Counte,* you mean," Nica said with a sly grin. "Sebande taught me that that '*counte*' means thank you in Corsosh."

"Oh—" Shanks raised his eyebrows— "aren't you the clever one. Sebande's been giving away our secrets, has he?"

Nica stared up into the night sky. "Sebande and I have agreed to no more secrets."

Shanks lips twitched then he buried his head in her neck and laughed out loud, the sound muffled by her hair. Nica couldn't resist running her hand through his soft hair. He finally stopped and leaned back on his elbow again. "Perhaps *you've* agreed to no more secrets," Shanks said, still grinning, "but I suspect if

Sebande agreed to anything, it was to not *tell* his secrets."

Nica looked up at the stars and pretended to ignore him. "How many constellations can you find?" she asked. "I can see five."

Shanks reached over to tuck in the blankets on the far side of her and left his arm there, balanced on her stomach as he shifted so he could see the sky. The weight of his arm felt intimate and oddly comforting. "I can't see any—show me."

She tilted her head a little closer so she could feel the strands of his hair against her cheek as she pointed out the different constellations and told him their name and story.

"You're a very clever girl, Nica Jacoby," Shanks said in a low voice. Then his lips were on hers and she melted into him.

Chapter Thirty-Seven

hanks was gone when Nica woke. She lay back and thought of the last few days. They were the happiest of her life. She'd never had anyone love her before. It was a wondrous feeling. In her half-waking state she basked in the memory of Shaun, the feel of his lips on hers, the words he whispered to her.

"You look happy this morning."

Nica opened her eyes to find Shanks smiling at her.

"I am," she said as she threw back her covers and climbed to her feet.

"Now that you're finally awake, come with me." He grinned. "I've got a surprise for you."

Curious, Nica ran her fingers quickly through her hair and re-braided it, leaving the strands hanging long behind her back. Shanks led her toward the riverbank and around a point of land before he came to a stop.

"All right, close your eyes."

"What?" Nica started to protest, but she could see the determined look on his face. She snapped her eyes shut. "I have no idea what you're up to, but I …"

"Just hold my hand. It's only a short distance."

"But why can't I have my eyes…"

"Shhh," Shanks said. But Nica could hear the smile in his voice. She stumbled the first few steps, but

Shaun's grip held her steady. She relaxed as she allowed him to lead her.

"All right," he said, grabbing her shoulders and positioning her. "Open your eyes and behold the veil of prisyms."

Nica opened her eyes and gasped, her hands flying up to cover her mouth. Before them stretched the magnificent frozen waterfall. In a dazzling display, brilliant sunlight reflected off the ice in a rainbow of colors like the most fantastic diamond. What had been hidden by the darkness of night now sparkled in the light of day in a spectacular display of refracted light.

"That is the most beautiful thing I've ever seen," Nica whispered.

The waterfall appeared to have ceased in an instant, one minute pouring over the cliff above—the next, frozen solid. Jagged spears of ice vaulted off the cliff's edge, suspended in midair at such a dramatic angle it was easy to imagine the water thundering over the falls. The underlying ice held a hint of glacial blue that provided a cool accent to the ice crystals sparkling in the brilliant sunlight.

"Pretty spectacular, isn't it?' Shanks said as Sebande joined them.

"It's unbelievable," Nica whispered.

Sebande looked down at her. *"Cleur marisa,"* he said in Corsosh. "Breathtaking."

"Cleur marisa." Nica repeated with a nod, then looked back at the prisyms of light. "Wait a minute," she gasped. *"What once had been exists no more,"* she

said slowly. "The waterfall, or a *fall* of water, doesn't exist anymore. *"What is solid now was once a door."* She raised her eyes to the top of the frozen waterfall. "You couldn't get any more solid than that."

"What's the next part?" Shanks asked.

"A veil of prisyms casts a brilliant light—" Nica smiled up at him excitedly— *"but remains unseen in the dark of night."* She turned back to stare at the sight before them. "This is it. This is what the verse is talking about. It *has* to be."

"But didn't the clue on the clock tower in Berjerac say we were supposed to go *through* the thing?" Sebande asked.

Nica sobered. 'You're right. It did say to *'go through the veil of prisyms'*." She gazed at the waterfall perplexed.

"Let's take a closer look." Shanks walked along the bank above the river as Nica and Sebande followed. As they drew closer, it became clear the waterfall was frozen solid right up to the rock cliff from which it used to tumble.

"I don't see anything," Sebande said. "Not a hole, or a nook, or cave that will let us pass through a frozen solid waterfall."

Puzzled, Nica watched the fabulous movement of color play upon the shards of ice. She was sure they'd deciphered the cypher's box correctly. What else could the message possibly mean?

A slow-moving shadow passed over the group.

Nica looked up. Above them stretched the large black shape of a massive bird in flight. The animal had spotted them and was coming back for a second look. The skin on her arms began to crawl. She tugged hard on the sleeve of Shanks' jacket, her eyes turned skyward.

"Is that a...?"

Shanks tilted his head back to follow Nica's gaze.

"A harpy hawk."

As they watched, the lone hawk circled lazily around, his giant shadow brushing over them again. Nica had heard of the giant hawks. Mosaba had a stuffed harpy hawk hanging from one of the walls in Ravensfell, its giant wings outstretched. The birds were meat eaters and were said to be strong and vicious enough to attack and kill men.

"We've got to move," Shanks said. "He's seen us and they hunt in packs. It won't be long before there are others. We need to hide."

Shielding her eyes against the glare of the sun, Nica watched the giant hawk fly off over the trees. "But what about the clue?" she asked.

Shanks squinted up at the magnificent frozen waterfall. "All the signs suggest this is where we need to be. I'm just not sure if we can figure out how to get through the thing before the hawks are back." Frustration was etched on his face. "I don't know that we can take the chance."

"Shaun, we have to try," Nica replied. "If we can get through the veil, it might be the best way to hide from the hawks."

Sebande made a disgusted noise at the back of his throat. Shanks propped his hands on his hips. "Nic, you are too brave for your own good."

"I was thinking you and Sebande could look over here and I could go over to the other side and see if there's a way through the veil over there." Nica pointed to the far side of the river.

Shanks stared up at the frozen waterfall. "That won't work. You'd have to backtrack for hours to get over to that side."

"No it won't," Nica said. "I'm going to walk across."

Shanks eyed the treacherous expanse of slippery, uneven frozen riverbed. "Are you kidding? To climb down the bank is enough of a challenge. But walk across? If you crack through the ice and fall in—that would mean certain death."

"It's no different than climbing the turret ledge. You didn't seem too concerned then," she said.

"That was different."

"How?"

"The ice on the river may not support your weight. If it doesn't hold your weight, it certainly won't hold mine." He lifted an eyebrow at her. "And I'm not going to stand here and watch you drown. So think carefully before you offer up our lives."

Nica blinked to hide her surprise at his gallantry. Would he really risk his life to save hers?

"We've got to try. It's our best chance against those hawks. I've heard they hunt in the forest as well as in the open." She walked over to the edge of the riverbank and looked down the steep slope. She'd faced more difficult climbs within the castle in Berjerac.

"Nica, wait." Shanks followed her.

But Nica didn't stop. She clutched a nearby shrub and turned her back to the river, slowly inching her way down the steep, rocky bank.

"Focus," she whispered as she carefully picked her way down the rocky slope. At the bottom, the slope dropped away to the frozen riverbed. With great care, Nica set her feet on the frozen ice. Above, Shanks and Sebande watched.

Nica stepped on the frozen water, her arms spread wide to keep her balance. For a moment she thought of crawling, but one glance at the sharp edges of the frozen surface convinced her to stay on her feet. She half slid, half stepped further onto the river. The ice was much slicker than she'd anticipated and she curled her toes tightly in her boots, trying to grip the surface.

She took one small step after another, sliding her feet rather than lifting them up and down. So far there'd been no cracking noises that would suggest the ice was going to give way.

After what seemed like hours, she risked a glance up to see how far she was from the other side. It was with a jolt of relief she realized she was less than twenty feet from the far bank. Carefully counting the steps she made it to the other side. She placed her foot on the snow covered ground and scrambled up the rocky bank.

She shot a quick glance back over her shoulder. Shanks and Sebande stood watching her across the river. She hurried to the edge of the waterfall, searching for any possible way through the frozen wall from this side. After several minutes of scanning the brilliantly colored surface Nica's heart sank. Solid. Everywhere she looked, the wall in front of her was unyielding ice.

"There must be a way," she muttered. Desperation raged through her. The hawks could return at any moment. Every beat of her heart ticked away another chance to escape. The cypher's box had said to *go through the veil of prisyms*. But how?

"Nica," Shanks called.

Nica ignored him. She needed just a few moments more. She took a deep breath and closed her eyes, trying to center her thoughts. She relaxed her shoulders and exhaled slowly before opening her eyes to focus again. Her eyes scanned the sparkling cascade of ice, but there was nothing. No passageway. No clues to guide her. Her shoulders sagged, a sigh of defeat escaping her lips. She couldn't delay any longer. It was too dangerous. She looked over at the others and shrugged, holding her palms up.

Shanks waved her back.

Nica traversed the bank's edge, looking for an easier path down. She glanced up to check for any sign of the harpy hawks and a dark shadow within the brilliant spectrum of colors in the frozen ice caught her eye. Nica squinted, shading her eyes with her hand.

There was a sliver of an opening forty feet up the waterfall. Tucked behind one of the huge teardrops of frozen water, the opening could only be seen from a certain angle. But how could they possibly get up there? Her gaze traced the flow of frozen water down to the riverbed and realized there were steps of ice within the waterfall itself that could be used as stairs. Unless one was looking for a way to climb the frozen torrent, the steps would remain undetected.

It also became clear, however, they could only access the "door" through the veil of prisyms from the middle of the frozen river. They would have to climb up the center of the icy waterfall.

Nica waved to Shanks and Sebande. "I found it!" She pointed to the waterfall. "It's in the center, about forty feet up." Before she finished speaking Sebande had already reached the riverbed and Shanks was right behind him. A movement in the distance caught her eye and a chill ran down her arms. On the horizon she could see the faint shadow of giant, dark wings headed in their direction.

Moving as quickly as possible, she worked her way down the shorter bank and stepped onto the icy flow again. She took one small step after another, her arms spread wide, working her way toward the middle of the waterfall.

A loud *crack!* split the air.

"Sebande!" Shanks called. Nica looked up in alarm to see Sebande in the center of the river. As she watched, his arms started flailing as the ice beneath his feet splintered loudly and then gave way under his heavier weight. She watched helplessly as he descended through the ice into the frozen river.

Nica screamed as the dark haired young man began to disappear into the icy water. He clawed at the slippery, uneven frozen chunks of riverbed trying to stop his downward momentum. Nica thought he was going to disappear under the surface when at the last minute he caught hold of a chunk of ice and stopped himself. She could see the strain on his face and his muscles flex through his shirt as he fought to pull himself up. With an immense effort he got one knee up on the edge of the hole in the ice and inched his way onto the surface. Spread-eagled, he pulled with his hands and pushed with his waterlogged feet to move himself away onto thicker ice.

A large dark shadow swept over them. Nica looked up at the harpy hawk and shivered. The bird was low enough this time that she could see the white markings on its head feathers and the malevolent set to its beak. The hawk circled twice as though inspecting his prey before heading back the way it came. In the distance, other dark shadows were getting closer.

Sebande rolled on his side to look at the huge bird, then turned his head toward Nica. "Keep going," he called.

She continued to inch her way to where the frozen waterfall met the riverbed.

A few minutes later Sebande stood next to her, cold and shivering and Shanks began his trek across the icy riverbed taking a different route than Sebande had chosen. Nica turned back to eye the 'steps' she'd seen from a distance. Though not an easy passage, there were depressions within the jagged spears of frozen waterfall. They could balance on the modified steps to climb up to the opening.

"You go first," Sebande said.

Nica nodded. They didn't have any time to lose. She put her hand on his freezing, wet shoulder to steady herself, then placed her right foot up on the first depression in the wall. She pushed down to make sure it would support her weight then stood up and reached for the next step. It was a slow process as she tried to hold tight to the cold, slippery handholds. The cool air coming off the frozen ice chilled her. It wasn't long before she was shivering.

Nica inched herself up the waterfall, grateful for the many times she had climbed turret walls and trees at home. She knew the type of handholds and moves that would work most effectively to balance her weight. It wasn't long before she peeked above the final step and pulled herself into the opening she had seen from below.

"W..W..What do you s..s..see?" Sebande's teeth chatted with cold.

Nica stood in the opening and looked out, surprised at how high she'd climbed. She felt like some strange bird, perched in a frozen tree. She turned and peered into the tunnel behind her. Silver blue walls of luminescent ice wound away from her disappearing deeper into the waterfall.

"There's a tunnel that goes into the waterfall," she called. "It's all frozen." She came back out and peered over the edge at Sebande, working his way up the steps. Below him Shanks stood at the bottom. Sebande was only halfway up when Nica heard a piercing cry. Her breath caught in fear as she watched the fast approaching silhouettes of the giant hawks.

ere they come again," Nica called down. Now she could clearly see each individual bird. It was obvious the harpy hawks were coming with a purpose this time. She glanced down and could see that Sebande was shaking from the cold.

"Are you all right?" she called.

As though in answer, one of the hawks called too. A high, piercing cry. Startled, Nica looked up. The birds were gaining ground with each sweep of their gigantic wings.

Sebande grunted and focused on his ascent. Nica could tell his hands were so cold he was having a hard time gripping the icy steps. She debated whether to climb down and try to help him.

"Stay there," Shanks called from below, as if reading her mind. "Do not come down from that ledge," he commanded her in a rough tone. "I'll help him from this end."

Shanks started climbing and Nica was surprised at how quickly he moved up the frozen waterfall. He covered twice the distance in half the time.

Sebande's feet seemed to be numb. He was having trouble keep his boots on the steps. From below him Shanks began to hold his feet in place until he was ready to step up again.

Nica glanced from Sebande to the approaching birds. They seemed to be moving faster. Her knees began to shake.

"Hurry, hurry, hurry," she mumbled under her breath. She measured the distance and the speed at which the hawks approached. With a sinking feeling she realized that neither Sebande nor Shanks were going to be able to get to the top before the first hawk was within striking distance. She turned and scrambled around in the opening of the tunnel, seeking every piece of fallen ice that was big enough to throw.

Nica grabbed a chunk of ice with a practiced grip. She glanced down at Sebande and yelled, "Just keep climbing, I'll keep them away." Her first throw fell short of the approaching hawk. The bird cocked its large head to the side as it approached—as if to get a better view of Sebande's dark form against the ice. Spotting his prey, the giant hawk lowered his beak. The startling white plumage on the top of his head folded back as the bird plunged into a dive.

"*Mediche*," Nica whispered. She grabbed another piece of ice and took aim again, cocking her arm and waiting for exactly the right moment. *Now!* With all her strength she threw the ice at the hawk's head. The chunk of frozen water landed squarely between the bird's eyes, causing the hawk to veer off course. The bird's beak hit the wall next to Sebande with an explosion of ice chips.

Startled by the proximity of the attack, Sebande lost his grip and hung from the ice wall by one hand.

Below him, Shanks struggled to push his friend's foot back in place and maintain his own balance. With a piercing cry the hawk flew back toward the pack.

"Keep climbing," Nica called. She crouched at the ready, clutching two more chunks of ice, and watched the approach of the next hawk. Nica eyed the distance from the huge bird to Sebande. Could he possibly make it to the top before the next strike? Her instincts told her there was no possible way.

She stood up as the giant bird approached. The wash of air from the beat of the giant wings blew the hair back from her face. This hawk had learned a lesson from watching the first bird. He approached with talons outstretched, rather than his beak. It would be more difficult to hit a vulnerable spot on the hawk from this angle.

"Wait," Nica whispered to herself, 'wait... *now!*" She began to fire one chunk of ice after another at the hawk as hard as she could. Several pieces made contact, causing the hawk's wings to flutter in alarm. The hawk pulled up with a great thrust of its giant wings, then with a sharp cry turned and dove straight for Sebande.

Nica measured the distance in one glance and knew this time she wasn't going to be able to deflect the attack. Dropping to her knees she stretched a hand down as far as she could reach to Sebande.

"Jump!" she screamed. They were only going to get one chance.

Sebande looked up at Nica and bent his knees. With a mighty leap, he pushed off and stretched his arm up as high as he could reach. Nica grabbed his wrist and yanked him upward as hard as she could. Pure panic fueled her strength. They both fell backwards into the ice tunnel. Sebande landed just as the ice below his feet exploded with the force of the hawk's attack.

Nica scrambled back to the edge to look out from their perch. The hawks were lined up, one after the other to attack. Another bird was already preparing to dive. She jerked her head down to check on Shanks.

Fear consumed her.

Shanks had continued to climb while Nica helped Sebande to the top but he was still eight feet below the ledge, too far to jump. He seemed to realize this as well, for he had stopped climbing and had drawn his sabre, positioning himself for the next hawk's attack.

"Sebande, give me your blade." Nica commanded as she held her hand out.

Sebande didn't hesitate. He pulled his sabre from his side with a ringing sound and slapped the hilt into Nica's hand.

"Hold my feet," she commanded over her shoulder to Sebande. "I'll cover you from this side," Nica yelled down to Shanks. Nica dropped to her stomach and inched out over the ledge. Once she felt Sebande's hands around her ankles, she plunged out over the edge, hanging head first over the waterfall. She arched her back and raised her head to watch the approach of the oncoming bird. She could feel the strain in her stomach and back muscles as she waited, clutching the blade in her hand.

"Wait….. wait…" she whispered to herself, timing her attack.

The bird came at Shanks without flinching, as though testing his resolve. It wasn't until the last second that the animal sensed the potential threat of the two of them. Gripping the hilt with both hands and starting with the knife above her head, Nica swung her blade downward with a great stab into the bird's back. At the same time, Shanks sunk his sword up into the soft tissue under the bird's beak.

With a shattering cry, the bird twisted and screamed, pulling away from them to plummet to the ice below. Shanks hurriedly began climbing again as a fourth bird began to dive.

Sebande yanked Nica back and leaned over the ledge.

"Jump!" he roared to Shanks.

Shanks coiled his legs and sprang like a cat, catching Sebande's wrist. With a hard tug, the dark haired soldier pulled him up and over the ledge. Shanks had barely landed on the ice when they scrambled for cover as the giant bird struck the ice below the opening.

"Move," Shanks yelled to Nica. He grabbed Nica's wrist and pulled her away from the opening as another bird came close to the edge, flapping its wings in a great backwash of air, as if debating whether to land or not. They hurried further into the tunnel, out of sight of the Harpy Hawks. Outside they could hear the angry calls and cries of the birds still stalking them.

No one spoke for a moment as they gathered their breath.

"I'll take that." Sebande reached for the blade still clutched in Nica's hand.

With a start, she looked down at her fist and recoiled at the sight of the blood-stained metal. Shanks slid an arm around Nica's shoulders and kissed the side of her face.

"You all right?" he asked. She nodded as she relaxed against his hard chest. When Shanks released her, Nica could see the corners of Sebande's mouth were turning blue. A wave of concern washed through her.

"You've got to get out of those wet clothes," she said. Sebande's lips chattered uncontrollably as the cold air of the frozen waterfall chilled his soaked body. "I'm fine." He looked down the icy blue tunnel. "L..let's k...keep g...going." He looked at Nica. "*Counte, ela m..makata.*"

Nica smiled. She didn't need a translation this time.

Sunlight seeped through the frozen walls, illuminating the passageway with a brilliant blue light. Shanks led the way as they followed the winding path of the hallway until it ended in a circular chamber. Centered in the middle of the room was an icy pedestal with a thick, rectangular piece of emerald colored rock.

They approached slowly.

The stone was completely covered in writing and symbols. After a moment Nica realized the symbols were planets.

"Bless the Ancients, it's the Getheas Stone," she whispered.

Silence filled the room.

Nica tentatively ran her fingers over the intricate carvings embedded in the rock. Next to her Shanks slid his fingers under one corner and tried to pry it free from its stand.

"Frozen," he said.

Sebande attempted to move the stone too, without success. He slid his sabre from his belt and pointed his sword at the ice directly below the rock. With a sharp thrust he jammed the tip of the blade hard at the ice only to have it deflect off. Shanks pulled a dagger and gripped the handle so the blade pointed down. He jabbed at the ice several times trying to chip away at the frozen surface but to no avail.

"Wait," Nica cried, holding up her hand. "There's one more quatrain." She reached into the back of her cloak and pulled the thin book out of the pocket. "We never read the quatrain for 'S'. It's written in a language I didn't understand." She brushed the pages open and turned to the page for 'S'. With her finger running over the lines she sounded out the words:

> *Selo quatrand ser maba randatt mokata*
> *Histra e, ejob e, regatta e, murdaba*
> *Le cuiske fle monarche*

Garot de histra y'ar yian

"*Histra,*" she repeated in surprise. "I've heard that word before—it means heart." Her eyes flicked up to Sebande. "Isn't that what you said?"

"Yes." Sebande replied.

Nica caught her breath. "The final quatrain is written in Corsosh. It's as if Getheas knew we would be able to read it."

"Let me see." Shanks held his hand out for the book and translated out loud.

> *"The trinity will become the key*
> *The shape of a heart shall set me free*
> *Guard the secrets held within*
> *It's time to let a new day begin."*

He lowered the pages and looked at Nica. "What's the trinity?"

"It's three of something." She tapped a finger on her lip as she thought.

"I know that much," Shanks replied. "I meant what trinity is it referring to?"

"Doesn't the trinity have something to do with the church?" Sebande asked.

Nica's gaze locked on the tall dark-skinned young man. The church. The image of the carved doorway in the cathedral filled her mind. The Promise of the Ancients. She'd found the symbol of the crown there.

Then the clock in Berjerac had yielded the symbol of the eye.

"It's the symbols we've found with the quatrains," Nica cried. "The crown, the eye. There must be a heart somewhere." She looked up at Shanks in despair. "We must have missed one."

"What does it mean, the trinity is the key?" Shanks asked. "Do you think this stone is locked on here somehow?" He ran his fingers over the top of the stone and around the edges, feeling for anything that might be a latch or a lock. His hands froze and his brow scrunched down in concentration.

"What?" Nica asked.

He stepped back and leaned down, examining the front edge of the stone.

"It's a notch or something missing out of the stone."

Nica peered at where he was pointing. A small dark shape was etched out of the stone.

"That's the symbol we need." She snapped The Ages closed and stared at the front cover. "It's a heart," she breathed. "The third item is a heart." She held the front of the book up for them to see. "Look." She pointed to the design at the bottom of the cover. "I recognize it now. It's a crown, an eye and a heart layered on top of each other to form one sign." She pointed to the front edge of the stone. "It's the same shape here. The hole is where the heart belongs."

Shanks moved closer. "It's the book." His voice sounded unsteady.

"What?"

"The bindings on the corners." Shanks pointed to The Ages that Nica held in her hands. "If you put them together they form the shape of a heart."

Nica held the book out and stared at the metal clasps in each corner to secure the leather cover to the spine. The four corners each formed one fragment of a heart.

"You're right," she whispered.

She held the book out to Shanks. "Can you pry the metal pieces off with your knife?" He stared at the ancient manuscript for a moment, before he gently slid the tip of his blade under the corner of the first piece. He worked the blade under further and further until he flicked his wrist and the metal cap popped free.

One by one he released the bindings. Nica arranged them in her open palm, slowly putting the heart together like pieces of a puzzle. When she edged the last piece into position with the tip of her finger they all stared down at the small heart that rested in her hand.

"It's the right size," Nica said.

"See if it fits," Sebande said.

Nica placed the lower pieces into the hole first, to support the top two pieces as she slid them into place. Once all four pieces were lined up she pushed the heart firmly into place. There was a soft click and the stone tablet shifted ever so slightly.

Nica looked from Shanks to Sebande. With shaking fingers she lifted the rock tablet from the pedestal.

"The Getheas Stone has been set free," she whispered.

 can't believe it," Nica cried. "We found it! Becknah is going to be beside himself." She laughed gleefully. "He'll never come out of his study again." She gazed down at the tablet in her hands. "Do you think these words really hold the secret to the quatrains?"

"It does look like some kind of formula," Shanks agreed. He took the stone from her hands. "See how it's numbered?"

Nica peered closer at the etchings. "What language is that? I can make out some of the words but not all of them."

"Probably some archaic version of Jarisan. Or perhaps a combination of languages." Shanks shrugged. "Becknah will be able to tell us." A drop of water landed on Nica's cheek and she looked up in surprise. One by one drops were beginning to fall throughout the room.

Nica turned to Shanks and saw the look of concern that passed between him and Sebande. Her gaze swiveled around the room to see that the pedestal which the stone had been resting on was changing—thawing.

Shanks wiped several drops from his brow and looked around. "It's melting. We need to get out of here."

They ran back through the tunnel with Shanks carrying the stone tablet. Already water had pooled on the floor and they splashed through ice water instead of walking on solid ice. They reached the opening to the outside and looked out. The sun was a brilliant orb in the sky overhead, the harpy hawks gone. Rivulets of water were running down the face of the waterfall.

"Start climbing down," Shanks said. "Before the whole thing collapses. Nica, give me your cloak."

Nica unfastened the buttons and swung the garment in his direction. Shanks handed Sebande the stone and reached inside the cloak to feel the lining. He took the stone, slid it into the pocket within the lining and buttoned the cloak over his shoulders.

"The lining will hold the stone. I can get down without dropping it this way." He looked over the edge. The water was streaming past their feet as the walls and ceilings around them melted. "Let's move now. I'll go first and try to identify the handholds."

A terrible screech rent the air.

Nica covered her ears and looked at Shanks for an answer.

"It's the ice in the river—it's breaking up," Sebande said.

Shanks sat down on the edge with his feet hanging over. Bracing his hands on each side, he flipped around so he was facing the wall.

Sebande got down on one knee and held Shanks' wrist as he lowered himself down the face of the melting waterfall.

"All right," Shanks called as he found a foothold. Nica could see his fingers digging into the ice for purchase.

"Nica, you go next," Sebande said. "We don't have time to wait until he's off. Another few feet and you can go."

Nica sat down as she'd seen Shanks do and let her feet dangle over the edge. The icy water was bitter cold through her clothes and now she was without the added benefit of her cloak. She shivered uncontrollably as she checked on Shanks' progress.

Sebande gripped one of her wrists firmly. "All right, flip around and dig your toes in." Nica flipped over, comforted by the knowledge that Sebande could pull her back up if she slipped. She kicked a toe of her boot firmly into the ice and found it gave way enough she could get a grip. She slid her fingers along the face of the frozen waterfall, until she found a handhold with which to anchor herself. Moving carefully, she inched her way over the side and started her descent.

Shanks made steady progress below her and she tried to follow the path he was taking. Her fingers were numb from gripping the ice and water continued to flow off the face of the waterfall, splashing her over and over. Her entire body was shaking from the cold by the time she stepped onto the rough surface of the river near where Shanks stood waiting for her.

"Take the stone to shore," Shanks said. "I'll stay here and help Sebande." Before he could hand her the cloak another screech filled the air and the frozen riverbed underneath Nica's feet heaved like a bucking horse. She reached for Shanks to try and keep her balance.

"Hold on," Shanks yelled, gripping her wrist tightly so she couldn't pull away. As quickly as it started, the movement of the ice stopped. Parts of the riverbed were now vertical, where the river had heaved the layer of ice, while others sloped at a dangerous angle. It was almost impossible to keep their footing. "We've got to get you to shore."

They held onto each other, stretching their free arms out for balance as they skated and slipped their way to the river bank. More than once they both went down with a painful *thump,* landing hard on the ice.

When they reached the side of the river, Shanks immediately removed the cloak and handed it to her. "Climb up to the top of the bank," he said, then turned and began to work his way back to help Sebande.

Nica checked on Sebande's progress. Water was now pouring off the falls in small rivers. As she watched, Sebande pulled out a dagger and slammed it into the ice wall, using it like an ice pick, trying to anchor his weight as he descended.

Shanks was only halfway back to the waterfall when an explosion blew out of the center of the river. The rushing water underneath had finally forced free of the ice overhead which had been holding it captive. Chunks of frozen water flew in all directions and the white spray of water fanned over the suddenly moving river.

Without warning, a long spear of ice broke loose from the falls themselves, calving away and stabbing into the frozen riverbed with a thundering crash. The force of the impact knocked Shanks to his knees. The ice broke apart and another spray of water fanned the sky, soaking him.

A moment later, a shuddering vibration shook the remainder of the ice. The trembling caused Sebande to lose his footing and the dagger he had plunged into the ice slipped free. Nica watched in horror as his tall body swung wide to the right before he plunged in slow motion down the face of the waterfall. Nica screamed as he disappeared into the cold water, a splash marking his entry.

Nica could hear Shanks swear in Corsosh as he started picking his way across the rough ice again. "Watch for him!" he shouted to her. "If he gets sucked under the ice he's dead."

Nica held her breath, her eyes straining, her heart pounding, looking for any sign of Sebande. Suddenly a dark head appeared above the water.

"There he is," she cried and pointed. "I see him."

Shanks neared the edge of the broken ice and he threw himself onto his stomach. He began sliding in the direction Sebande was drifting. The two young men yelled back and forth but the roar of the river drowned out their words.

Shanks was getting close to his friend, when Sebande's dark head suddenly disappeared underwater again. Nica cried out in alarm, her hands clasped over her mouth.

As she watched, Shanks leaned over the edge and plunged his arms and head into the water.

Long seconds dragged by.

She could see Shanks' legs moving, trying to brace himself against the flow of the water.

Suddenly, with a burst of water, Shanks pulled his head out of the river, his arms gripping Sebande's body. Slowly, he inched his way backwards, straining to tug Sebande's big frame from the freezing water.

Nica scrambled up the bank and left the stone, still wrapped in the cloak, at the top. She whipped around and plummeted back down the steep slope to begin crossing what was left of the frozen river.

She could hear Shanks gasping with exertion as she neared, working to pull Sebande's dead weight onto the ice.

Ten feet from Shanks, Nica dropped down to her hands and knees and crawled the rest of the way to his side. She wrapped her hands around Sebande's arm.

"You take that side, I'll take this side," Nica cried. Shanks nodded a breathless assent. "On my count of three, one, two THREE." Together they lunged backwards, pulling Sebande onto the ice next to them. Even in the seconds they rested, Nica heard the ice crack beneath them.

"Is he alive?" she whispered.

"I don't know," Shanks gasped. He pushed himself to his knees. "We've got to get off this river."

Nica leaned forward and smoothed Sebande's black hair off of his frigid forehead revealing a bloody gash. "He hit his head," she said. Tears formed in her eyes and panic filled her voice as she wiggled his shoulder. "Sebande! Sebande, can you hear me?"

His eyes flicked open and gave her a baleful look. "What? No kiss for the dying man?"

Nica's jaw dropped then she laughed—a joyful sob. Tears ran down her face. "Only if you crawl off this river on your own."

IT FELT LIKE a year before they all stood on solid ground again. They'd just climbed to the top of the tall riverbank when a groaning screech ripped through the air, like some gigantic beast in a death throe. In one giant blast, the remainder of the ice shards that had formed the waterfall caved into the river. Thunder rent the air as the chunks hit the water, causing the ground to shake. The force of the water was more than the frozen riverbed could resist. Like a catapult, a torrent of water shot out from between the jagged cliffs far above and plummeted down into the river. With a painful screech the ice gave way in a final spectacular explosion and the water ran free down the center of the river.

Sebande ran a hand through his wet hair, smearing blood across his forehead, and grinned at Shanks. "Now *that's* a spring thaw."

"Not the best time to try and shoot the rapids," Shanks responded. The corners of his mouth turned up and suddenly they were both shouting with laughter.

Nica stared at them in amazement, her mouth half-open. "Only you two would find any part of that near-death experience entertaining," she said in disgust.

They were all shivering as they returned to their camp. Shanks built up the fire, and they changed into whatever dry garments were to be found. Nica opted to wear a pair of Shanks' pants, a rope holding the over-sized waist in place while her clothes dried. They huddled around the blazing fire trying to get warm.

When the feeling had returned to her fingers and her teeth had stopped chattering enough to hold the Stone without fear of dropping it, she placed the emerald plaque on her knees and ran her fingers over the lines carved there.

"What does it say?" Shanks asked. Sebande watched silently from across the fire.

Nica slowly sounded out the words inscribed at the very top:

Those who read these words be warned!
Within the quatrains of the Avedla lies Knowledge
Within Knowledge lies Paradise, Hell and
       Purgatory
Here inscribed is the key to the great Knowledge of
       Getheas

"What does that mean?" Sebande asked.

Nica looked up. "It means this stone holds the formula to know the future."

Chapter Forty

f the people of the Narsgededon Forest were aware of their passing, they didn't make themselves known. Shanks continued to carry the weight of the stone within the lining of Nica's cloak and wore it suspended around his shoulders. He traded his jacket with Nica so she could stay warm.

Nica enjoyed the feel of the soft buttery leather which carried Shanks' scent. She was filled with such a sense of contentment as they rode back toward HighGarden that for a moment she almost had a sense of coming home.

They arrived at the gate of the palace in early morning. This time she rode her own horse. At Shanks' instructions she had draped a dark cloth over her head and around her face, revealing only her eyes. Even with her garments, it was clear she was a young woman.

"Declare yourself!" Bastille called out, his oversized belly jiggling as he shouted.

"Sebande Vatier and Jonn Shanks. On business for the King," Sebande called out.

"Ho, Sebande," the gatekeeper called, a grin on his face. "Looks like you and the young Shanks have captured another wood wench. Why does she hide her pretty face? Is she cold? Or just shy?" He stepped close and patted Nica on the leg. "Come see Uncle Bastille, I'll warm you up, lass."

"Careful Bastille, she's a wild one," Shanks warned with a smile. "Her eyes might burn you." He looked down at the older man. "If she doesn't kick your teeth out first."

The man's eyes widened and he took a step back. Nica had to bite her lip not to giggle out loud as the guard's eyes traveled from Shanks to Sebande for an answer. The dark haired young man nodded.

"Vicious."

"Where's Heathron?" Shanks urged his horse through the gate. "Is he here?"

"In the barracks." Bastille threw a thumb over his shoulder as he walked the tall gate closed.

"And Becknah?"

Bastille nodded. "He's here, but the old man has looked pretty bad lately." The rotund gatekeeper looked them up and down with a hungry look. "Where've you boys been?"

"King's business." Shanks smiled as he urged his horse forward. "Bastille, you know I can't reveal our secrets."

"I was afraid of that," Bastille said with obvious disappointment. "Seems like you could share a little tale of adventure with a poor old soldier stuck on the gate day after day." His eyes followed their departing backs. "Adventure *and* a wild wood wench," he mumbled with a sigh, kicking a rock with the toe of his boot.

JAANIYAH MUST HAVE heard of their return for she was waiting on the steps above the courtyard as they walked from the stables. Nica saw her first, dressed in a glittering blue gown. Her long blond hair was pulled back into a tight chignon at the back of her head with a beaded ribbon wrapped around her forehead and woven into the strands. She looked every inch the royal princess. Nica dropped her head, conscious of her own filthy clothes and the ratty braids she'd tucked inside her jacket.

"Jonn." Jaaniyah called and gave a little wave as she watched them draw near.

Instead of responding, Shanks reached over and grabbed Nica's hand in his much larger one for all the world to see.

"Did I mention how appealing I find women dressed in men's clothing?" He gave her a wicked grin. "You remind me of a wood wench."

Nica giggled behind her shroud. "A *wild* wood wench, you mean."

Jaaniyah watched their exchange with narrowed eyes as the three of them stopped before her.

"Jonn." Jaaniyah leaned forward and kissed him on both cheeks then looked at Sebande. "Captain Vatier." She nodded at him in a prim fashion, for once seeming at a loss for words. She looked at Nica and forced a smile. "Welcome back."

AFTER THEY'D BATHED and eaten, Nica, Shanks and Sebande joined Jaaniyah in a private meeting room off Jacoby's library with Becknah and Heathron, who had only recently been informed there were two princesses to protect.

As they were being seated, Heathron stared in amazement from Jaaniyah to Nica.

"Bless the Ancients, there couldn't be two girls who look more alike than you do." His weathered face split into a wide grin. "It's like the Ancients gave us two gifts."

Shanks smiled and squeezed Nica's hand. "Tell us, Heathron—what is the news here?"

"Tarantu has been arrested and we've got his closest contacts under surveillance," Heathron reported. His voice dropped. "And you know about the attack at Pian'glo." The war minister shuffled in his seat. "Since then, Mosaba hasn't been seen. The last positive location we've had of him was in the Ortawn during the princess' and Becknah's captivity. Since then—no word, no confirmed sightings."

Shanks straightened. "Mosaba was in Berjerac just a few weeks ago."

Heathron looked at him in surprise. "You're sure of that?"

"Positive."

"Then he must have given up trying to follow the path to the Getheas Stone himself," Becknah interjected. The scholar looked as though he had aged twenty years since his capture at Mosaba's hands. The old man cast a worried glance at the group gathered. "He will put his efforts into acquiring the Stone through our knowledge."

"Which makes the timing of Jacoby's return critical," Shanks said. "If by some chance Mosaba knows the King is not in residence or that he'll be returning in a weakened state—that's when he'll pounce. We must be on our guard at all times."

"When are you him bringing home?" Nica asked.

"Any day," Heathron said. "Thistlewaite has given him approval to be moved." The Minister of War began a discussion about troop position as well as their plan to relocate Jacoby. When they finished their conversation Heathron pushed himself up from the table, then paused.

"Oh, I almost forgot to tell you. The most amazing thing has occurred. Becknah and I were just discussing it." He paused for a dramatic moment. "There's *water* in the Great Divide."

"Water?" Jaaniyah lifted her head in surprise. "What's the source?"

"We don't know. We sent some men up toward the Spires to see if they can find the headwaters. It's quite a mystery." Heathron shook his head. "Hasn't been any water in the Divide since the time of the Ancients."

Nica looked at Shanks to Sebande. Shanks nodded.

"Have you ever heard of a veil of prisyms?" Nica asked the group. At their blank looks she launched into their discovery of the frozen waterfall.

AS SHE CONCLUDED the story of the waterfall roaring back to life, Nica turned to Becknah.

"Becknah." Nica smiled at the old man. "How are you faring?"

He lifted a shaky hand from the table. "Fine, fine. Glad to be home." He smiled at her. "Your story is most fascinating, my dear. Most fascinating, indeed. I will have to revisit the books of the Avedla."

"We have something for you." Shanks reached under the table and picked up the cloak-wrapped stone. "Through sheer ingenuity, Nica followed a legendary trail. It is through her persistence and fortitude that we are able to offer this to you today." He set the stone in front of Becknah and pulled the cloth away.

Heathron peered down at the green stone. "What is it?"

Jaaniyah let out a gasp and jumped to her feet to see better. "Is that—"

Becknah adjusted his half-moon glasses as he peered at the large tablet of emerald green rock on the table before him. "Let me see what you've got here— what is that writing…. Looks to be a rather archaic version of—"

"But it can't be!" Jaaniyah whispered, staring slack-jawed at Shanks and then at Nica.

Becknah's crooked fingers lightly traced the etched lines. "Why, this is written in ancient Jarisan, and…other languages," he said slowly. "Some of these words aren't even used anymore." His brow wrinkled with a puzzled frown as he examined the stone further. "What have you brought me?" And what are these symbols? The planets? Why…"

"A war continues, destined to repeat," Nica said softly.
> *"Until two daughters, royal born do meet*
> *The time has come to heal the past*
> *Now what you seek can be found, at last."*

Becknah' face sagged in disbelief. "The Getheas Stone?" he whispered. He placed his shaking hands flat on the stone as though to absorb the very essence from the rock. "You've brought me the Getheas Stone?"

Nica reached over and slid her hand into Shanks with a tender smile.

"The legend exists?" Heathron sat back down in his chair with a thump, disbelief thick in his voice.

A single tear rolled out from under Becknah's glasses. "Bless the Ancients—it can't be true." He slid his hands over and around the rock. "The Getheas Stone?" A smile creased his face as tears rolled into his grey beard, then he covered his face with his hands and sobbed.

"Thank you," Becknah said with a sniffle, raising his head. "You have changed my life." He stood up and held out shaking hands to Nica. She slid her small hands into his wrinkled, crooked fingers. "This proves the texts of the Avedla are messages. Messages from the Gods." His lips curved in a shaky smile. "Thank you, my dear. Thank you from the bottom of my heart. You have fulfilled the purpose of my existence."

He released Nica and held his hands out to Shanks and Sebande. "I suspect you two had no little part in this." Becknah eyes sparkled with new life. "By the Gods, history is going to come alive before our very eyes. We'll know what the Gods knew." He raised his hands skyward and gave an exultant laugh.

IT WAS AN unusually warm winter day, several weeks after their return, that Shanks steered Nica to a stone bench on the far side of the walled part of the palace grounds. They sat underneath the bare branches of a brandyapple tree, looking out over the valley that ran down toward the Great Divide. Far distant on the horizon Nica could see the shimmering green of the Sea of Nephalon.

She'd taken to veiling her hair and her face under the guise of a traveling dignitary, whose religion required extreme modesty, thereby giving her total freedom throughout the palace. It was like being set free.

"Shaun," Nica said softly, leaning close to him, "I've been meaning to ask you something." When she was away from others she unpinned one side of her veil and let it hang loose.

"Uh oh," Shanks said.

Nica frowned. "What do you mean, 'uh oh'?"

"Well, if you start like that, it can't be good," he said.

She crossed her arms. "I don't know what you're talking about."

A call interrupted them.

"Mr. Shanks, M'lady. There you are." Becknah approached, huffing with his exertion. Since the receipt of the Getheas Stone Becknah had regained his former vitality and a new enthusiasm. "Young Shanks." Becknah nodded, then turned his attention to Nica. "M'lady."

"Good afternoon, Becknah," Shanks said. "Has the Stone revealed any secrets to you yet?" He smiled at the older man, putting his arm around Nica's waist and pulling her closer so there was room on the bench for Becknah to sit.

"Ah, yes, thank you," Becknah said with a sigh, as he pulled his crimson robe up and sat. "Don't mind if I do." He peered at them over his glasses. "I've found something interesting I think you should know."

Shanks raised an eyebrow, a grin teasing the corners of his mouth. "Have you been able to see the future?"

"Yes, I've made some headway with the Stone," Becknah replied in all seriousness. "The archaic terms have taken a while to decipher, but I believe I've come to understand their intent and I've applied the concept to a few quatrains with some success."

"What have you learned?" Nica asked.

"I have to tell you—it's disturbing." His lined face sagged into a worried frown. "Extremely disturbing."

Shanks and Nica exchanged a glance. "How's that?" Shanks asked.

Becknah leaned forward. "From what I've deciphered so far, the future looks grim—very grim, indeed."

"Why?" Nica gasped.

"Death…war…" Becknah's face twisted with a sorrowful expression. "Perhaps Getheas was right to withhold the knowledge of what is to come from us. It is a much too painful burden to bear."

"If what you're saying is true, Becknah, the best course of action might be to destroy the Stone," Shanks said. "Should access to the future fall in the wrong hands it could be catastrophic. Not everyone may care about the outcome of certain actions."

"That would be such a tragedy," the old man whispered, "but perhaps that's why the Stone has been hidden all these centuries. Getheas may have realized the price for knowledge was too great to pay."

"We can never let Mosaba get his hands on it," Nica said. She rested a slim hand on Becknah's arm. "He would not be dissuaded by the prospect of death or war. In fact, I think he enjoys them.

"You might be right, my dear," Becknah said. "There appear to be verses within the Avedla that speak of Mosaba."

A chill coursed through her. "*What?* Are you sure?"

"Even translated, the quatrains are still somewhat obscure, but they speak of the thief of Sartis, the stealer of children. They call him Sathos, which is the Jarisan name for Santos."

"And what do they say of him?" Shanks said with a guarded tone.

Becknah leaned close and whispered. "They speak of betrayal, of significant death, but they also say he is a descendant of Getheas."

Images and lost conversations danced in front of Nica's eyes. '*I am the true ruler of Jarisa. I am descended from Kings. It's my destiny to find the Getheas Stone.*" Mosaba had ranted and raved about many things, but those topics had repeated over and over. Ancient maps and books, to which she had paid little heed, now pricked at her memory. One conversation in particular came to mind. *There will come a time when you will help me in my quest, Madanica. It is your purpose for existing.*

A chill raced down Nica's arms. Was that why he'd stolen her? So he could control the timing of when she and Jaaniyah would reunite? Knowing that would put into motion the search for the Stone? Mosaba had claimed he owned some of the texts of the Avedla himself. Did he have access to some of this ancient knowledge?

"What are you suggesting?" Shanks asked. "That Mosaba might have some claim to the throne of Jarisa?" His words echoed his disbelief.

"I don't know for sure," Becknah said. "But there's something…I need to dig further." He straightened up. "I just thought you should know. If Mosaba believes the throne of Jarisa is his destiny then it might explain the exceptional risks he seems willing to take. My brief experience with the man suggests he has slipped into madness. Perhaps this belief is the prod that has pushed him over the edge." Becknah patted Nica's hand. "Whatever the truth, we must all be on guard constantly. Mosaba is a violent man with little mercy. We can't take any chances."

Nica shivered. Should Mosaba ever catch up with her again she was sure there would be no mercy.

Becknah departed and Nica looked down at her hands clutched together in her lap. The scholar's words had shattered her fragile bubble of peace.

Shanks slid his long fingers over hers. "This isn't the best time to tell you, but I have to leave for a few days."

Nica jerked her head up. "Now? Why? Are you bringing Jacoby back?"

He nodded. "Once he's here, things will be easier. We can announce your presence and all of the troops will be here to fortify the gates. Life can go on."

"It would almost be like waving a red flag at Mosaba though," she said.

"We'll track Mosaba down and deal with him," Shanks said with confidence. "I don't care who he thinks he is descended from," he muttered.

The clock tower tolled the hour and Shanks stood up, pulling Nica to her feet. "We'd better go," he said.

"How is Sebande?" Nica asked. "I haven't seen him since our return. Perhaps he can give me a few more language lessons while you're gone."

"I don't know," Shanks said in a strange tone. "He's been gone himself."

"Where?" Nica asked, sensing something.

Shanks shrugged. "He's been distant since we've returned. I've asked him if I've offended him and he says no. But, he keeps to himself." He shook his head. "Maybe it's the war." But his words weren't convincing.

Chapter Forty-One

everal days later the palace courtyard was buzzing with activity. Soldiers moved about in small groups, some practicing their sword play, others visiting the smithy, some standing guard at strategic points within the structure. The raucous barking from the hunting dogs, kenneled in their small shelters, echoed in the distance. Fragrant smells from the kitchens filled the air. Servants went from here to there and groups of men filled every corner, many she'd never seen before. Nica hurried down the courtyard steps to catch up to the tall figure striding away from her.

"Sebande," she called. "Sebande—wait!" The tall young soldier glanced over his shoulder at the sound of his name, then paused as she hurried toward him. "How are you?" Nica asked in a breathless voice as she came up beside him. "I miss seeing you glare at me all the time."

Sebande looked down at her with narrowed eyes and Nica laughed.

"Yes, exactly like that."

"Does Shanks know you're out here?"

Nica's eyes lit up. "Shanks? Is he back? Have you spoken to him? He's been so worried about you."

"You need to go back inside right now." He seemed very distracted and Nica wondered at the expression on his face.

"What's wrong? Are you unwell?" she asked, concern etching her brow. A sharp gust of wind blew across the courtyard causing the flag of Jarisa—a white crescent moon on a black background—to snap on its standard above the palace. Distracted by the flag's movement, Nica glanced up. A storm was blowing in.

At that same moment, the *bong!* of the clock tower resounded through the cool air. Drawn by the sound, Nica glanced at the clock. High noon. The astronomical sign for the lion was perfectly aligned with the number 12. As though a voice whispered in her ear, Nica heard the quatrain Becknah had asked her to read:

> *Between the cross and crescent moon*
> *When the lion stands at high noon*
> *A secret of blood, hidden by ancient lies*
> *At last revealed before one dies*

In what felt like slow motion, Nica turned and gazed at the spires of the cathedral in the distance behind her. A thin cross was mounted on the tallest peak. She looked the other way at the crescent moon emblazoned on the Jarisan flag. Her head swiveled to the clock tower and she stared at the symbol of the lion standing at high noon.

"Sebande...." she started to say, but the first volley of arrows sprayed the courtyard. Screams of pain and terror filled the air as people rushed this way and that to avoid being hit, creating a scene of absolute bedlam. Beside her, Sebande grunted in pain and Nica swallowed a scream when she saw an arrow embedded in his thigh.

"Oh blessed Gods," Nica cried. This was what Becknah had been trying to warn them about—Mosaba was attacking as the King returned. Her worst fears were realized as she spotted Mosaba's tall dark form standing on the steps which led toward the Great Hall. He held a shield in one hand and even from this distance she saw the familiar nine-headed whip tied at his belt.

Nica was jerked off her feet and slung over Sebande's back as he ran for cover. He dropped her between a tree and the wall.

"Crawl under the bench." He barked out commands in a low voice. "Don't move unless you have to. Keep your eye above us, make sure nobody comes over that wall." His fixed his gaze on her. "And find a way to cover your face." Then he looked down at the arrow protruding from his leg. Gritting his teeth, he broke the shaft off and tossed it aside, leaving only an inch of wood protruding and the arrow buried in his thigh. He drew his sword and held a dagger in his other hand and advanced into the melee.

Nica crawled under the bench and peered out at the madness before her. The guards who had been on the wall were firing down into the courtyard, while those on the ground were battling hand to hand. She slipped the dagger from her boot. She would do what had to be done if necessary.

In the courtyard, Sebande's tall silhouette battled against the men attacking and she watched in horror as soldiers and servants alike were slaughtered by Mosaba's soldiers. Where were all the Jarisan soldiers?

She lost sight of Sebande and with an uncomfortable pricking sensation, realized she was alone. The battles were becoming fewer and fewer, the moans from the wounded strewn across the courtyard becoming louder. Only a handful of men held out as most sank to their knees in defeat, their arms held high. Nica tried to scan the bodies lying on the ground but she couldn't see Sebande's large form.

Suddenly two pairs of boots came to stand near the bench under which she was huddled. The men were speaking in Sartish. As she listened, Nica realized they were Mosaba's soldiers. They were discussing the lure they'd used to trap the bulk of Jarisan soldiers and then locked them outside the palace walls.

Nica shifted her position, trying to move further under the bench when a pock-marked face suddenly appeared to stare at her.

"What've we got here?" A rough voice asked. "Come out, my little pretty," he said with a cruel laugh. He reached under the bench and grabbed hold of her arm. Nica tried to pull away but with a great heave he yanked her out of her hiding spot.

While his arm was raised to pull her to her feet she slammed her dagger into his side between his ribs as hard as she could.

Blood spurted out, covering the front of her coat. The man's look of shocked surprise quickly faded to a blank stare as his grip loosened and he slithered to the ground. As he fell, the man standing behind him was revealed. Nica stared up at the orange shock of hair.

"Toppen?"

"Nica?" Toppen's mouth opened in surprise. "What are you doing out here? I thought you were inside the palace."

"Why were you with that Sartisian man, Toppen?" A terrible suspicion suddenly filled her. She gripped her dagger and held it at her side, hidden in the folds of her cloak.

"What do you mean? What are you suggesting Nica?" He hedged, his face grim and unhappy.

Nica bit her bottom lip, fighting what her intuition was yelling at her. "Toppen," she finally blurted, "are you somehow involved in this?"

A multitude of emotions flitted across his face, before his lips twisted in a sneer. "And what if I am—" he whispered in a scathing tone— "you can't prove anything."

"Prove…" Nica gasped in utter shock. "Oh no, Toppen, you can't be. *Why?* Why would you let

Mosaba in? Look at the people dying here. For what? He's a madman!"

"And you'd rather live among your new family, wouldn't you?" He derided her. "You and your soldier friend, Shanks. Life in Pont d'Suree isn't good enough for you anymore now that you know you're a bloody Jacoby. You think you're a peg above the rest of us, don't you?"

Nica's jaw dropped. "What are you saying?" She stared at him in disbelief as her mind raced through memories of the time they'd spent together, searching for something—anything, that would explain his attitude. "Was this always your plan, Toppen? Did you leave Sartis with the intent of spying on Jarisa and finding a way to let Mosaba in?"

"So what if it was?" Toppen said in a mocking tone. "I'm going to be rich."

"Rich? And what about me?" Nica struggled to grasp his duplicity. "Was I part of the plan too? Did Mosaba know I would run?" She could barely force the words out of her mouth.

Toppen gave her a cruel laugh. "He was counting on it. With a little encouragement from me, of course."

Nica swayed. "He paid you, didn't he? To convince me to try and escape," she whispered with dawning awareness. "That's why Mosaba had you deliver wine so often. So he could bribe you into making sure I got back to Jarisa and learn I was Jaaniyah's sister. He wanted us to go after the Stone."

"Well, that part was mostly luck. Mosaba was going to have someone capture us after we got closer to Pont d'Suree and turn us over to the Jarisan soldiers. He figured your face would keep you out of the prison and that you'd keep me out of a jail cell." He puffed his chest out. "I had no idea that Shanks fellow would show up so conveniently, but that's fate, right? Things work out the way they're supposed to."

"So very true," a voice said from above.

Nica and Toppen both looked up in surprise. Shanks was crouched like a carpidi on the wall above them, a feral look in his eye. Toppen only had a split-second to react before Shanks sprang from the wall. Toppen turned to run but Nica kicked her foot out in front of his ankles, sending him sprawling. Like a cat, Shanks landed next to him. In one smooth move, he grabbed a handful of orange hair, yanked Toppen's head back and slit his throat.

"YOUR KING IS DEAD." Mosaba's nasal voice cut above the din as though magnified.

"Are you all right?" Shanks whispered to Nica. At her nod, he stepped close and crushed her mouth under his. "You need to get out of here," he said. "I'm going to lift you up so you can climb over the wall. There are Jarisan soldiers on the other side that will help you."

"I AM YOUR NEW KING—MOSABA SANTOS." The words reverberated across the courtyard.

Nica started to open her mouth, but Shanks put a finger to her lips. "No arguments this time." He slid his dagger into his belt and threaded his finger as a step for Nica. "I'm going to bounce you on my hands and on three, you jump, all right?"

Nica nodded and placed her foot in his hands, resting her hand on his shoulder for balance. "One, two, three." Shanks catapulted her into the air. She caught the top of the brick wall with her arms and walked her feet up the wall until she was crouched on top, hidden behind the branches of the tree.

"Good," Shanks called softly. "I'll find you. Be safe." For one long second his eyes held hers then he turned to face the courtyard, crouching down as Mosaba began to speak again.

"I, Mosaba Santos, am the true descendant of Getheas." He motioned toward Becknah, who stood nearby being held by a Sartish soldier. "Even your own scholar will testify this to be the truth. For that reason I will be taking up residence in the palace with my *daughters*."

A shocked murmur rippled through the crowd like a wave.

"Yes, daughters. Your princess is an identical twin." Mosaba motioned to someone in the shadows behind Becknah. A Sartish soldier pushed Jaaniyah out onto the step next to Mosaba. Nica's heart dropped into her stomach.

"One princess has been living with me in Sartis waiting for the time to reclaim her place in line for the throne. The other has been here in Jarisa with you. We have all been waiting for these two girls to reach the age when they could reclaim the legendary Getheas Stone. That time has come. And with it, change for the better." Mosaba reached over and casually rested his hand around Jaaniyah's neck where a thin rope rested.

Shocked cries could be heard. Those in hiding crept out, realizing a powerful shift was occurring.

"I will be taking up residence in the palace immediately and seeing to the affairs of state."

"Mosaba." Shanks' voice echoed in the stillness as he walked bravely toward the center of the courtyard. Nica gasped in alarm. She wanted to cry out for him to stop.

"You're a liar." Shanks held his sword and dagger at the ready as he stepped cautiously toward Mosaba. One brave soul lunged for him, but with two swipes of his blade Shanks dispatched the man to a bleeding heap. Another form rose and Sebande stood at Shanks' back. Several other Sartish men made a move as though they would approach but then thought better of it.

"Ah, Jonn Shanks," Mosaba said. "We meet again."

"You're a thief. A child-snatcher," Shanks called. "You *stole* Princess Jaaniyah's twin when she was a baby. Just for this purpose. You were willing to sacrifice her life for your gain." Shanks continued to move forward. "You were so desperate you plotted for seventeen years in the hope this day would come. But it's here and you still don't rule. Jacoby lives."

Shanks rested his boot on the bottom step leading to where Mosaba stood with Jaaniyah. He readjusted his grip on the dagger.

"SILENCE!" Mosaba screamed "JACOBY IS DEAD!"

"It was a corpse your men attempted to murder this afternoon," Shanks shouted. "The true King lives."

"I am the new ruler of Jarisa," Mosaba roared. "The Ancients decreed it centuries ago, and I have answered the call of destiny."

"NO!" a shaky voice called out. "I am Amistad Jacoby, King of Jarisa." A collective gasp rose as a grey haired man came around the far corner of the palace. A cheer went up as the King was recognized.

Sartish guards beat the supporters back into submission, their blows echoing in the afternoon air. While Mosaba was distracted by the arrival of Jacoby, Shanks quickly stepped up two more steps. Nica watched him from her aerial perch. Why was he getting closer to that mad man?

Mosaba's expression changed to one of sardonic amusement as he regarded the Jarisan King. "I was told you were dead, Jacoby." He carelessly waved a hand. "But it doesn't matter. Your reign ends today, regardless." Mosaba jerked the rope around Jaaniyah's neck and pulled her closer to him, using her body almost like a shield. "There's still time to make you dead."

"Release my daughter now and I'll let you live," Jacoby said in a steadier voice. "My soldiers are waiting for my command to destroy your meager troops. Let's not have any more bloodshed."

Nica watched Shanks. He was coiled like a spring, waiting—waiting for the perfect opportunity to save Jaaniyah and kill Mosaba. She would provide Shanks the distraction he needed. She crept along the top of the stone wall until she was clear of the tree branches and visible to all.

She slowly stood up.

"FATHER," Nica yelled. Mosaba and Jacoby both jerked their heads toward her. Even at this distance she could feel the obsessive weight of Mosaba's glare. "Mosaba, I don't speak to you. YOU ARE FATHER TO NO ONE BUT THE DEVIL!" The rage she'd held inside for so long came boiling out, amplifying her voice. "YOU WILL GET YOUR JUST DUE—" For that split-second she held Mosaba's full attention. Shanks' arm begin to move— "DEATH!"

There was a split-second delay as her words sank in, then Mosaba's eyes jerked back to Shanks. Jaaniyah yanked herself to the right and Shanks released the dagger with a flick of his wrist. The blade flew through the air to sink neatly into the middle of Mosaba's chest. A split-second later a second dagger, thrown by Sebande, landed in almost exactly the same spot.

Silence fell over the courtyard as Mosaba's expression twisted into a look of abject shock. He opened his mouth as if to speak but instead fell forward and landed face down on the steps at Shanks and Sebande's feet.

"LONG LIVE THE KING OF JARISA!" Shanks shouted as brown-coated Jarisan soldiers poured into the courtyard. He pumped his fist in the air then turned to face Nica, who stood on the wall and pumped his fist again. "LONG LIVE THE KING'S DAUGHTERS!"

Chapter Forty-Two

ica sat on the edge of the window seat and waited. She held up the looking glass one more time trying to see what her father would see.

There was a knock. Nica jumped to her feet and hurried through the antechamber to pull the door open. Shanks stood there, trim and strong, dressed in the finery of a Jarisan soldier. His dark brown coat embroidered with rich amber thread was in sharp contrast to the white of his breeches and the blackness of his tall boots. His razor thin sabre hung from his side. His blond hair was tied behind his head with a piece of leather, revealing the strong cut of his jaw line and the sculpted lines of his face. Nica appraised him with glowing eyes.

"You look beautiful." They spoke at the same time, then laughed together.

Nica covered her mouth as she giggled, feeling as light as a bubble floating on air. With Mosaba's death she was truly free for the first time in her life.

Shanks stepped forward and made a sweeping bow before her. "M'lady, you strike intelligent thoughts from my head with your amazing beauty." His eyes soaked in every detail of her appearance, from the tiny braids pulled away from her face to the curls cascading down her back. He reached out and ran a gentle finger along her cheekbone. "Nica, you take my breath away," he said softly. His eyes burned into hers with an intensity that he didn't try to hide.

Nica looked down and fingered a button on his jacket. "Take your breath away?" she said with a coy smile. "Sir, are you suggesting that I should bathe more often?"

"It would make no difference." He shook his head. "Your beauty shines from within." He leaned forward and kissed her with a passion that engulfed her. Nica melted against him but he pulled away.

"Shall we go meet your father?"

She bit her lower lip and nodded. Extending his arm, Shanks escorted her from the room. As they walked down the hallway he nodded to a well-dressed couple who in turn dropped into a bow and curtsy for Nica's benefit.

"I wonder if they think I'm Jaaniyah," she whispered, casting a quick glance over her shoulder.

"Possibly, but not for much longer. Soon you will be known to all of Jarisa as Juneedika." Shanks smiled and gently kissed her forehead. "You know, Jacoby told me about that day in Sartis when he saw you—he wasn't sure if he was seeing you in the afterlife or if you both lived. But he knew it was you. And he said he gave a prayer of thanks."

Nica's lips trembled as she gave him a wobbly smile. It was still a new sensation to have people care about her.

Shanks tilted his head to look into her face. "Do you know the meaning of the name Juneedika?"

Nica shook her head. "I know it's the name of a Jarisan deity, one of the Ancients."

"And so it is. Juneedika was the daughter of Saphren, the King of Kings. Her name means 'greatest gift'." He smiled at Nica. "Aptly named, I would say."

They stopped in front of a set of huge double doors. "I'll bring you in and introduce you, then wait out here for your return."

"I'm so nervous," Nica whispered, clutching his hands.

"The King is a kind and good man. He loves you, Nic. You'll be proud to have him as your father."

Shanks pulled the big door open. "After you, M'lady," he said with a bow.

Nica's knees trembled as she walked into the grand room. Huge windows stretched high making the room light and airy nurturing huge pots of tropical plants which flourished in the corners. A huge rounded vault in the ceiling was painted with intricate detail and crystal chandeliers hung from the ceiling, sparkling in the afternoon light like stars in the heavens.

At the far end of the room, sitting in a wash of light from the windows, sat a solitary figure. Nica clutched Shanks' arm as he walked steadily through the room to stop in front of the man. Shanks bowed low and Nica dropped into a curtsy. A grimace of pain shot across the older man's face as he pushed himself out of the chair. Shanks released Nica to reach forward and assist him.

Nica stared. This man looked nothing like the disheveled bloody wreck she'd seen fettered in Mosaba's castle yard outside the stables. When he stood to his full height he was nearly as tall as Shanks, with equally broad shoulders, thick arms and a commanding air. His grey hair swept back from his face in waves and his beard was neatly trimmed. She'd never seen a more regal man. But it was his eyes she noticed most. Almond-shaped with a kind twinkle, they were the exact shade of grey as hers.

"Juneedika." The King breathed her name and held his hands out to her.

Nica stepped forward, hoping he wouldn't be able to feel her trembling. His warm fingers enveloped hers and she realized for once, she wasn't afraid.

"My little girl," he whispered.

To Nica's surprise a tear ran down his face. He didn't wipe it away. Instead he swept her into his embrace, his breath warm against her hair. She could feel his body shake with emotion and tears welled up in her eyes. For once, her hope didn't frighten her. She was safe, secure.

"Jonn, stay." Jacoby's voice was firm, stopping Shanks' attempted departure from the room. The King released Nica from his embrace but held on to one of her hands as he sat back down. "Pull up chairs for both of you, would you lad, we have much to discuss."

IT WAS MANY hours later when Shanks escorted Nica away from the boisterous noise of the festivities that had introduced her as Jaaniyah's twin sister and Princess of Jarisa. They escaped from the Great Hall and went outside to take a moonlit stroll among the gardens. A contented sigh escaped her lips as they walked.

"Do you think Becknah will really destroy the Getheas Stone?" Nica asked.

Shanks laughed and shook his head. "Now that Mosaba is dead, I think Becknah feels he has a little more time to study the legend—like the rest of his life." Shanks pulled Nica's hand up to rest on the crook of his elbow. He gazed at her. "How are you feeling now that the world knows of you?"

"Overwhelmed and excited, and a little bit scared," Nica replied. "So many things I can't even begin to describe them all." She leaned her head against his shoulder and held his muscled arm as she smiled up at him. "But mostly happy."

"As you should be," he said gently. "You're home now."

"And what of you, Shaunte DeGran?" Nica whispered, "Are you home as well?"

"Whenever I'm with you I'm home," he said with a teasing smile.

"That's no answer." Nica frowned at him. "I've been meaning to ask you about your mother. You've never spoken of her."

He feigned a gasp. "You want to know *more* of my secrets?" He raised an eyebrow as his fingers swept a blond strand of hair behind her ear. "You are a nosy little thing, aren't you?" He kissed her on the cheekbone, his touch as fragile as a butterfly's wings as his lips moved down to the hollow below her ear. "Beautiful, but very nosy," he murmured.

"Shaun." Nica put her hands on his chest to push him away but found she didn't have the will. "It's not fair. You know more about me than I do and yet— you've told me next to nothing about yourself." She cupped his face with a gentle grip. "You've got to trust me with your secrets sometime."

He looked at her, his jaw set with a guarded expression, but Nica didn't get the sense he was angry. More that he was fighting himself to reveal personal information he'd kept hidden for too long. Fighting to trust her.

"You're sworn to secrecy?"

"I'll never tell," she promised. "Not even the day I die."

Shanks chuckled, his amused expression back in place. "I think that should be sufficient." He tucked her hand up under his arm and began to stroll again. "My mother was a pirate." There was a hint of bitterness in his words. "Just like my father."

"A pirate?" Nica repeated in disbelief. "You mother was a *pirate*?" She searched his face but his expression was blank, his secrets carefully guarded. "Tell me about her."

Shanks smiled as he bent his head to kiss her.
"No," he murmured. "That's a story for another day."

The End

www.ingramcontent.com/pod-product-compliance
Lightning Source LLC
Chambersburg PA
CBHW020500260626
47156CB00006B/1798